ht Vagabond Eight Vagabond Eig

THE SINS OF THE FATHER

THE
SINS
OF THE
FATHER

ALLAN
MASSIE

WITH AN INTRODUCTION BY
ALAN TAYLOR

Vagabond Voices
Glasgow

© Allan Massie 1991

This edition published 2012 by
Vagabond Voices Publishing Ltd.,
Glasgow,
Scotland

ISBN 978-1-908251-02-2

First published by Hutchinson in 1991

The author's right to be identified as author of this book under the Copyright, Designs and Patents Act 1988 has been asserted.

Printed and bound in Poland

Cover design by Mark Mechan

The publisher acknowledges subsidy towards
this publication from Creative Scotland

For further information on Vagabond Voices, see the website,
www.vagabondvoices.co.uk

First, as ever, for Alison
Then for Richard Cohen,
whose idea it was

Introduction

by Alan Taylor

The trial in Jerusalem in 1961 of Adolf Eichmann was what we have learned to call a media circus. Between 1941 and 1945 Eichmann was directly responsible for the transporting of over two million Jews to their deaths in Auschwitz-Birkenau and other death camps. By the late 1950s, however, he had sunk into semi-obscurity in Argentina, a favourite hiding place of fugitive Nazis. As his biographer, David Cesarani, acknowledged, he was "a colourless administrator of mass murder" and might well have remained so had the head of the Israeli Secret Service not received a tip off as to his whereabouts.

It was Hannah Arendt who first portrayed Eichmann as just another efficient cog in a wheel that was madly spinning. Far from being unusual or unique, Eichmann, at least to Arendt, was an ordinary man, easily replaceable, unimaginative, the embodiment of her resonant phrase, "the banality of evil". He had never himself physically murdered anyone. Rather he was the one who flourished his pen and signed the death warrants with no more thought than an author autographing books.

Thus, as Cesarani has acknowledged, "From the mid 1960s to the mid 1980s the mass murder of the Jews was seen as the zenith of modern bureaucracy, rather than as a throwback to barbarism. Nazi Germany was characterised as a super-centralised modern and hierarchical state in which power and authority flowed from the top downwards and officials decided the fate of millions. Mass murder was a 'medicalised' process or an economic rationalisation carried out by professional men, doctors and lawyers, in crisply pressed black uniforms, who consigned human beings to 'Fordist' death factories on the basis of quasi-rational decisions derived from racial eugenics and economic planning. Eichmann, the bureaucratic desk-killer par excellence, thus became a key to one of the most enduring approaches to the Nazi era and the 'Final Solution'."

Allan Massie was not the first Scottish novelist to recognise in the trials of Nazis which followed Germany's defeat a subject rich in fictional potential. Muriel Spark, of whom Massie wrote a formative study, attended the Eichmann trial for five days at the behest of the *Observer* and later drew on the experience for *The Mandelbaum Gate*, which appeared in 1965. For Spark, whose father was Jewish, the sight of Eichmann dissembling and deferring to the bench, as he had once deferred to Hitler and others in Nazi hierarchy, was sickening and disturbing. She had recently completed *The Prime of Miss Jean Brodie*, in which fascism is allowed insidiously to flourish in an Edinburgh school, and here she was looking into its face. Yet she could not side wholeheartedly with the Israelis in their re-established homeland. In particular, she found their attitude to the Arabs whom they had displaced deeply worrying. Out of all of this emerged in her novel in which the heroine, Barbara Vaughan, is made to think that, "Knots were not necessarily created to be untied. Questions were things that sufficed in their still beauty, answering themselves."

Whether Allan Massie would subscribe to such a philosophy is debatable. What one can safely say, however, is that such knots as he presents in *The Sins of the Father* are not easily unravelled. Throughout a prolific career as a novelist and journalist, Massie has been concerned with rejecting pat answers or solutions. Quick fixes are not his default. Simple solutions to complex problems are relatively rare. History is worth consulting for precedents and guidance. But the past was no more black and white than the present. The story of human beings is that of choices and circumstances and relationships. Why we act in one way rather than another is freighted with possibility and danger. Sentimentality is as pernicious as deceit. Good men are capable of doing bad things and vice versa, especially, but not exclusively, in a time of a war. That is a fact, the denial of which is a denial of the truth. In the Second World War, there were good Germans and bad Germans, as there were good Jews and bad Jews, even in the concentration camps. Ultimately, we are all Jock Tamson's Bairns.

In 1977, when he was 39 years old, Massie contributed an essay to a book of that title. In "Retrospective", he looked back and forward, noting as he did so that, "The past I write down today is then the past for today." He also decried "the beastliness of Predestination" while speaking up for Calvinism. "The image is the Kirk in the moorlands, man face to face with God: *reductio ad simplicitatem*. It is God felt as a pure Wind of Reason and also as something beyond reason." A couple of pages further on he recited Tancredo's conservative mantra from Lampedusa's novel, *The Leopard*, to which he has since returned often: "Things will have to change if we want them to remain the way they are." At the beginning and the end of the essay Massie describes how swans will drown ducks, for pleasure and because they want to.

All of the above sentiments have found their way into Massie's fiction and, in particular, *The Sins of the Father*. Interestingly, no overt mention is made in "Retrospective" of World War II. He was of course too young to have other than a bystander's view of it. What he knew of it and what the effect on him was he does not say. Born in Singapore and brought up in a farming community in Aberdeenshire, he would have been less aware of it than many boys of his age. His early novels, starting with *Change and Decay in All Around I See* in 1978, followed in quick succession by *The Last Peacock* (1980), *The Death of Men* (1981) and *One Night in Winter* (1984), had echoes, variously, of Evelyn Waugh, Anthony Powell, Graham Greene and even, in the case of the last mentioned, James Kennaway.

Of those, *The Death of Men* is perhaps the best indicator of how Massie's work was developing. Based loosely on the kidnapping of the Italian politician Aldo Moro in 1978, it combined elements of the thriller with a serious exploration of political and personal morality in the 1970s not only in Italy but across Western Europe, climaxing in "a grand orgy of hypocrisy". Massie's next novel in a similar vein was *A Question of Loyalties*, published in 1989, which can be viewed as a loose-fitting prequel to *The Sins of the Father*. Set during World War II in Vichy France, its central character is Lucien de Balafré, an idealist with a deep sense of duty, his aim during the war being to serve France. But that proves not to be as simple as it sounds and Massie uses Lucien to demonstrate that in a time of war individuals, whose view of the bigger picture is not as clear as it could be, can find themselves on the wrong side at the wrong time fighting the wrong enemy and supporting an ideology that their old pre-war selves would have found abhorrent.

By the time *The Sins of the Father* opens, however, the war is already slipping from view. The novel begins in the 1960s in Argentina which not only helped Nazis escape pursuit but, under the regime of Juan Perón, consciously offered them succour and protection. It is some two decades since Hitler's demise and in Buenos Aires it is as if the Holocaust had never happened. Franz and Becky are apparently in love and determined to be married. He is the son of a German engineer who is also a Nazi criminal; she is the daughter of a blind Jewish economist and a survivor of the concentration camps. When the two families are brought together by the impending nuptials, Eli, Becky's father, recognises – by his voice – Rudi, Franz's father, and sets in motion his apprehension and removal to Israel where he will be tried for war crimes, following in the footsteps of Eichmann who was found guilty and executed.

If that all seems too neat and symmetrical it is anything but. Nothing, save for Massie's style, is tidy in a plot that is as intricate as it is raw and discursive. As Rudi sits in the dock, Becky discusses with Luke, a young Israeli novelist, the comparative horrors of the Holocaust and Hiroshima. For Luke, the Holocaust wins hands down, which, he says, cannot be understood if "you don't realise that Hitler held out the offer not only of revenge."

"Revenge for what?" asks Becky.

"What you like," replies Luke. "Let us say for the humiliation of existence. Not only revenge, but hope. A clean sweep. A new purified beginning. You cannot understand it unless you are prepared to accept how attractive Nazism was in its early days... If I had been German, and not a Jew, I would, no, I might well have been a Nazi in 1928."

This, then, is the crux of Massie's intelligent, intellectually challenging and disturbing novel. It is meant, of course, to make us think as well as to entertain us. What happened in Germany from Hitler's rise to power until his craven suicide, we are led to believe, could have happened anywhere if the conditions had been similar. The exercise and acceptance of power was crucial to the reality of the Holocaust. Who did what to whom and when was, in a sense, as banal as producing motor cars. Moreover, Massie appreciates that the scale of the killing was so outrageous that it was almost beyond imagination and therefore capable of being dismissed from our minds. For who knows what six million people look like? How much space do they take up? Later in his peroration Luke tells Becky that large numbers became playthings. He is talking, initially, about the calamitous collapse of the German currency in the 1920s. Then he adds, "Besides, it is easier to kill a million men than ten. The ordinary person couldn't even bring himself to kill a single calf, but the slaughterhouse worker kills hundreds and goes home to a good supper."

It is hard to read this passage and not think of the then prevailing view of Eichmann, who for so long was deemed in the great scheme of things to be relatively insignificant. In that regard he is like Rudi, and much of what he – as a fictional character – tells us about himself is similar to much of the mythology that grew up around Eichmann. Like Eichmann, Rudi as a young man encountered Jews he hated. His life was going nowhere and he dreamt of killing himself. He had menial, dead-end jobs. Then, he tells Franz, he heard Hitler speak and it was as if he had been given a life-saving injection. "He spoke to me, directly to me, in an audience of thousands." The Bible contains similar descriptions of Christ's effect on those who saw him preach. "That was his genius," says Rudi of Hitler. "He spoke to those who had been isolated and who in their isolation had ceased to believe even in the possibility of their own existence. Unless you understand that, you understand nothing. I joined the party. Oh, moment of blessed release and fulfilment! I had become someone."

Rudi's conversion to National Socialism was religious in its intensity, as was Eichmann's. In Hitler, they both found their saviour, someone to lead them to the Promised Land, where there would be *Lebensraum* aplenty. But how men who had previously been nobodies could become mass killers is a mystery that has perplexed countless scholars and philosophers. What seems the most likely explanation is that somehow, without being specifically ordered to do so, they read his thoughts and gave him what he wanted. The sociologist Max Weber termed this "charismatic authority", which he described as "power legitimised on the basis of a leader's exceptional personal qualities or the demonstration of extraordinary insight and accomplishment, which inspire loyalty and obedience from followers." It is as if a whole population was not free to act individually and according to conscience. They were transfixed, mesmerised, automatised, brutalised, dehumanised. Their sin was made manifest in their inability to react, which makes *The Sins of the Father* a novel that continues to haunt our thoughts and force us to ask what would we do, what could we do, what must we do, if ever we are confronted with anything remotely similar.

THE
SINS
OF THE
FATHER

Lo pianto stesso lì pianger non lascia,
e'l duol che truova in sugli occhi rintroppo,
si volge in entro a far crescer l'ambascia…

The very weeping there forbids to weep,
And grief finding eyes blocked with tears
Turns inward to make agony greater…

Dante: *Inferno*, Canto XXXIII

PART ONE

Buenos Aires, Argentina

1964

One

If Franz was English, Nell thought, I would be charmed and reassured, even though he looks more like a best friend than a husband. Her own view of England was out-of-date: Brown's Hotel and Fortnum's; the minor public school where her father had been a housemaster for twenty years, and taught history for forty. She could picture Franz there, dewy in white flannels, a boy whom her father would undoubtedly have made a prefect. He was still today, in this city of shining skyscrapers and gaunt blocks of workers' apartments and the fringe shanty-towns, the sort of boy who would get to his feet when a lady entered a room, and hold the door open for her when she left, and write thank you letters. She was touched by his good and gentle manners.

They were eating chocolate nut sundaes in the Café Inglés, and Rebecca looked at her mother, and said, "Franz is playing rugby for the University tomorrow. Why don't you come and watch, Mummy?"

She spoke English as they had always done in the family. But Franz wasn't English, and his blondness was disturbing, not reassuring at all. Which was absurd.

Well, she thought, they are children. They look as if they haven't even touched each other, and Franz has still three years of his engineering course to go. But then she saw the look on Becky's face as she watched him, and thought, oh dear, I wasn't prepared for this, she can't take her eyes off the boy. And he was a nice boy, no doubt about it.

"Only the second team, I'm afraid," he said, "the second Fifteen. I would be awfully pleased if you did care to come. Mamma never has, but, you understand, she has a new family to care for…"

He spoke English, like most of them, with a touch of an American accent. How they deplore the Americans, and resent them, yet can't escape their influence, she thought. He does seem a nice boy. I hope Becky isn't in too much of a hurry.

*   *   *   *

She might have said, "Yes, she couldn't keep her eyes off him," but though she had long ago given up trying not to mention eyes and sight and seeing to Eli, all she said was what she had been repeating to herself since she knew she would have to speak to her husband about it: "We mustn't be prejudiced."

It was a weak, silly word and she knew he heard its ineptitude. Ineptitude: well, words weren't her line.

He continued to stroke Biba, their Siamese cat, but at the same time stretched out his left hand and lifted the arm of their old-fashioned manual gramophone, arresting Bruch's Violin Concerto in mid-phrase; the record continued to spin. She knew he would allow it to continue doing so, undisturbed by the faint whirring, and then, when they had finished their conversation, or as a sign that he thought it had gone far enough, he would replace the needle – acting by some sense which she had never been able to fathom – at almost the exact bar which he had interrupted.

"No," she said again, "we mustn't be prejudiced."

He smiled at her, making her still more nervous. He picked a cheroot from the open box on the little table and rolled it between his fingers, then lit it with an old petrol lighter. If the cat hadn't been on his lap, he would have used a match, which was the method preferred, but manipulating the box of matches required the use of both hands, and he kept one stroking Biba to keep the cat happy.

"He seems a nice boy," she said. "I don't think he's political."

He puffed out smoke.

"I've been worried," she said, "that she would choose someone who was. Rebecca feels things so deeply, she's got such a sense of injustice. But I want her to be safe."

"Ah yes," he said. "We would all like our loved ones to be safe. What does the boy's father do?"

"He's an engineer too. He's building a bridge up-country. They're divorced. The mother's married again. To a General, I understand, and they have a young family. I think the boy, Franz, feels a bit out of things."

"And is the mother German?"

"Oh yes, I think so. But I don't really know. I didn't ask. I just assumed."

He nodded.

"We'll have to see," he said, knowing she disliked hearing him use the word so naturally, and picked up the gramophone arm to let the music invade the room.

Nell drove her little Fiat with a zest that would have amazed her own mother. She could feel Becky tense in the passenger seat, but was happy to know that her driving wasn't the cause.

"Daddy really wants to see Franz? He's not angry?"

"You are silly, darling."

"You don't have to come. Or stay if you don't want to. We could easily come back to tea."

"No, I want to come, I've told you twenty times I'm looking forward to it. I was brought up on rugger, you know, being a schoolmaster's daughter. It'll be a treat, like old times."

They parked the car. She took her old Harris Tweed coat from the boot, and stomped across the field, a little flat-footed in English brogues. It was the first Saturday of autumn.

"I wish you had had some lunch though," she said. "It's not good for a girl of your age to miss meals."

Her own father had never been able to eat lunch on the day of a school match. He had had no sense of proportion, poor man.

They positioned themselves on the touchline. There were only a few spectators, mostly girlfriends. Becky knew them of course. Nell was glad to hear her laughing with them. She sounded happy, as a girl in love is supposed to be.

The game began. There was no doubt Franz was very graceful. Nell had had an old-fashioned Classical education and thought that with his long sunburned legs and his blond hair he had the look of Achilles; or perhaps Patroclus. Or the doomed Hector. She didn't know, but it was that kind of association, a Flaxman engraving. He played with dash and ran well and elegantly. Once he dropped a pass because he was looking at the player approaching to tackle him, and once he missed a tackle rather badly when a big forward ran straight at him. Towards the end of the game he broke through on the opponents' twenty-five and scored a try under the posts, touching the ball down with a flourish that called for admiration. Becky jumped up and down cheering. But his side lost all the same.

He approached them, his long legs glistening with sweat. He shook Nell's hand before he kissed Becky.

"It was so kind of you to come, Señora," be said. "I hope you enjoyed it. We're not very good, I'm afraid."

"Oh," she said, "I loved it."

Becky swung on the boy's arm. Her thin face, usually so white, was pink.

"Franz wants to take me dancing. Is that all right, Mummy?"

"As long as you're not late. You know how your father worries. And Franz, you must come to lunch with us. Perhaps next Sunday?"

"Why not tomorrow, Mummy?"

"Perhaps Franz already has an engagement tomorrow. Next Sunday?"

"That would be delightful, Señora. And you're right. I do have an engagement tomorrow. It's my father. He's in the city, only briefly, so of course I must see him."

"When can I meet him?" Becky said.

"Later."

"I wish it could be tomorrow, I'm longing for Daddy to meet you."

It was a lie, or a piece of self-deception. She was afraid of that meeting, because she cared for both of them too much; but she was anxious to get it over. In those days Becky ran towards danger naturally.

Nell returned home alone. She travelled slowly. She found an excuse to stop at two or three shops, and then she went to a café and had a pot of tea and a cream cake. She no longer denied to herself that she was putting off the moment of return. She was everything a good wife should be, considerate to her husband who had endured so many tribulations and bore them with courage and without overt repining. She would never leave him. But she took her time about returning to that four-roomed third-floor apartment filled with the stench of cheroots and the sound of music.

"Brahms," he used to say, "to understand the Germans you must listen to Brahms. People talk of Wagner as expressing the soul of Germany, but they are wrong. Brahms is the test. Behind the sound there is a vast and terrible emptiness which he yet regards with a primeval humour. Germans flock together for fear of the solitude that Brahms reveals as the natural and awful state of man..."

"Can't you forget Germany?" she once said.

"How could I? I am German. Germany made me what I am. Their greatest crime sprang from their greatest horror: the realisation that we were Germans also."

The street-lamps were lit when she emerged from the cake shop. In those days the public electricity supply rarely failed in the capital. "We

22

are Europeans, you see," the native-born Argentinians of good birth, her friends, would explain. "Things work in Argentina, despite everything."

"Everything" included inflation running at more than 25 per cent and a peso that had fallen from 8 to the dollar when they had arrived there in 1948 to 220. But they were right; it was still a country where Europeans felt at ease. Despite much, Eli had been comfortable until his sight went, and despite their galloping impoverishment, Nell still thought of the place as a southern hemisphere Surrey. And children were still taught manners; that mattered to both of them.

An army officer, wearing the uniform of a captain, and following with intent eyes and greedy open mouth the progress of a mulatto girl on the other side of the street, bumped into Nell. He recognised her as a lady, took off his cap, and apologised. Then, his boots glistening, he strode across the street, disdainful of the hooting and snarling cars, and took the girl by the elbow. Without pausing, he whisked her up a side-alley. She would obey him in whatever he wanted. Nell was sure of that.

But the city still neither frightened nor disgusted her. It was where she had made her life. Much had gone wrong, as lives do. Nell smiled it off. She was fortified by the great British delusion: that she had no illusions.

The front door of the apartment opened into a little hall, which then led into the kitchen, so that all their visitors – but there weren't many – had to pass through the kitchen first. This had come about when the original apartment, built in 1900 in the *Jugendstil* which had already been imported to smart, "European" Buenos Aires, had been divided by them towards the end of the Peron era. They let the two other apartments which they had formed by the division, and this supplied them, or had supplied them, with the greater part of their income. But now rents were (temporarily?) frozen, and rendered worthless by the inflation. So Eli's brother supported them, with an allowance from the United States. For a long time, Eli had refused offers of help from his brother – to make him fully experience the guilt of his own freedom from history, as he had put it once. Now, since blindness had overtaken her husband, Nell did not scruple to deceive him in this way. She had written to Solomon, explaining their position. She excused herself with the reflection that being allowed to help removed a weight from Solomon's mind – she was sure of this though she had never met her brother-in-law. If she had not been so sensitive about Eli's blindness she might have quoted the saw: "What the eye doesn't see, the heart doesn't grieve for"; but she couldn't bring herself to put her feelings in those precise words. But she approached them, and she had moments when she suspected that Eli knew what she felt, blamed her for it, but would not speak of it. Then she accused him of hypocrisy. And then she felt guilty and told herself that if anyone had a right to hide from the truth, it was Eli.

Because of the layout of the flat, it had become her custom to occupy herself in the kitchen before going through to see Eli. So now she made tea and, since she had been out so long, a sandwich for him of pumpernickel bread with pickled gherkins and sliced sausage bought from the German delicatessen on the corner of the block. Schumann's A minor Piano Concerto sounded from the sitting room, and she waited for the music to stop before carrying the tray through to Eli.

He didn't ask her about her day. He had abandoned that form of curiosity. Instead he said, "This marriage is a nonsense. Rebecca's far too young."

"It may be only a boy and girl romance. There's no need to worry. But he's a nice boy."

Franz feared disapproval. He reproached himself for cowardice, but couldn't eradicate his fear. He suspected that others saw him as confident, beyond the point of self-satisfaction. There were moments when he wished this was true. Many of his friends at the University envied him; he was what they would have liked to be. He stepped out of the shower and looked at himself in the long mirror of his mother's bathroom. He was just the right height, tall without being gawky, blond, smooth-skinned, free of body hair. Sometimes he was afraid he was merely pretty – his mouth too soft, too red-lipped, petulant in repose. To tease him, Luis had once said, "If you do your military service in the wrong regiment, my friend, they'll use you like a woman." The words – and the memory now – made him shudder. He ran his hands down his thighs and between his legs. Then, he threw himself on to the floor, and did a dozen press-ups. He took the shower attachment and squirted himself with cold water, all over, and wrapped a towel round his waist. He stood at the basin and began to shave. He had shaved the previous morning, and didn't really need to do so every day, but he was meeting his father for lunch, and wanted to be absolutely smooth-skinned. As he drew the razor down his face, stretching the skin on his cheek with the other hand, he thought of Becky pressing herself against him while they danced the foxtrot at the University Club (where rock-and-roll was still forbidden) and of how she had murmured her love for him. The towel slipped from his hips. He took another cold shower and, half-dressed, rubbed lotion over his cheeks, which were now free of down and quite smooth and soft.

Because he was meeting his father, he eschewed the jeans he would normally have worn on a Sunday, and instead put on grey flannels. He knotted a dark blue tie, and wore a pale blue blazer over his white shirt. He arrived at his father's club exactly one minute before the appointed hour.

Rudi was already there. Franz laid his cheek against his father's, which was rough and a little bristly, though he too had shaved as he did every day, even up at the works. He was shorter than Franz, dark-haired, thin and wiry, and when he had returned his son's embrace, he resumed the dark glasses which he had removed at his approach. It was dark and cool in the club, and he was drinking beer. He ordered a Stein for Franz, without consulting him.

For a little they talked about the boy's work. Rudi fired questions at him. They were pertinent and demanding. Sometimes Franz hesitated for an answer and then Rudi frowned. It was worse than the sort of oral examination the students were expected to undergo once a session. When he was satisfied, Rudi sat back, took a draught of beer and wiped his mouth with a handkerchief that he kept in his hip pocket solely, it seemed, for that purpose.

"You're not making a fool of yourself, at least," he said.

There was silence. Franz searched for a subject. He had promised Becky he would speak to his father about her, but it was too early. He had explained to her that he never found it easy to speak to his father. "It's not that I am afraid of him, or that he is particularly difficult. He's a wonderful father, really," he had said. "It's just that I never seem to know how to approach a subject with him, even when I know what I have to say, and it's important. Indeed the more important it is, the more difficult I find it."

"I know," she had replied, "it's like that with mine too." He took her hand in his, affirming their solidarity.

Then, to his surprise, Rudi started talking about his own work. They had been having difficulties at the bridge with the labourers and the local firm of sub-contractors. It was not an engineering problem. For technical problems there were always solutions.

"It's a problem," he said, "really of man-management, and human problems rarely lend themselves to neat solutions. That is one of the first things you must learn, son. Man-management is an art, not a science. It's something you can't be taught in school, but must acquire by experience. Fortunately I served my own apprenticeship in the art in demanding circumstances."

He paused.

"In the Wehrmacht?" Franz said, prompting him, without thinking. At once he regretted it. Mention of the war to his father led into a minefield. But this time Rudi smiled.

"In a special branch of the Wehrmacht," he said. "But that is forgotten. The war, and everything that happened then, now looks like a mistake. We have a new life, to make a success in."

And saying this, he got up and led his son to the dining-room.

It was called the Engineers' Club, and it was very European. They ate Wiener schnitzel with sauerkraut and potatoes roasted with onions, and drank Moselle. Rudi employed his knife and fork with brisk precision. When he laid them down, his plate was absolutely clean. Franz wondered how he could approach the subject that was on his mind. The dining-room was quiet, as usual on a Sunday. The only other diners were two very old men, who ate together every week, and had done so for half a century. They were thought to be pederasts, and Franz was always made uncomfortable by the rapid, and – it seemed to him – greedily assessing glances which they shot at him. His father did not speak while he ate. Franz seemed to himself to be holding the stem of his wine glass with an unnecessary and embarrassing delicacy. The waiter removed their plates, and almost at once placed a concoction of fruit, cream and pastry in front of them. It was the club speciality. Though Rudi claimed that he was ascetic by nature, capable of subsisting for days on dry bread and water, he had his spoon in his hand almost before the pudding plate touched the table. The sound of a military band came from a gramophone in the room beyond. The gramophone was being played by the two aged pederasts: "A little Sousa after luncheon?" one always asked the other, who nodded. It was a routine which was almost a ritual; they couldn't have digested their lunch without it. The music made the silence of the dining room all the heavier. It was dark and there was no sense of the city beyond. As they left the dining room and passed through the so-called library to the hall, Franz felt the pederasts follow him with their eager and hopeless gaze.

Was it because of them, and the discomfort they caused him, that he hadn't been able to bring himself to say anything to his father on the subject that was nearest his heart? Or was it because he was a coward? And were these things connected? Franz thought a lot, then and always, about cowardice.

His father seemed satisfied, though they had scarcely spoken after his initial inquisition. It was perhaps enough to have seen his son, to have gone through the paternal motions. Now they embraced. Rudi nodded, and Franz turned towards the door through which sunlight was streaming. They would not see each other for a month. He wondered how his father would pass the afternoon, until it was time to take the plane back to the north.

Franz loved the city. If you had asked him why, then, he couldn't have answered. Later, in exile, he would say, "Because it's only half made-up. It's a city of unfinished business which gives you the feeling, the conviction deep in your heart, that the business will never be finished. And that's what I prize. The sense of entropy. It's a city full of ambition that yet mocks ambition."

Now, that afternoon, he paused at a church, the Church of the Solitary Virgin, where a Mass was advertised to begin shortly, a special Mass, against the evil eye, *el mal de ojo*. "If you have been harmed, or think you have been harmed, don't fail to turn up." Luis would laugh at that; no question. "This is Argentina, brother," he would crow, "where we take no chances because we know that life is nothing but chance. So you don't believe in the old *mal de ojo*? All the more reason to take precautions. And you'll see – the types that turn up!"

And he was right of course: there, for instance, thrusting her silken leg out of her Mercedes and now advancing, was a lady in a pastel-shaded gown that had Paris, or school of Paris, written all over it, and swaying high heels to her strapless shoes, a Pekinese pressed to her bosom: you never knew, one of the servants, or her lover's wife, or her husband ... Franz pushed into the church behind her. There were stalls selling charms and reliquaries and crucifixes, and there were consulting booths, where the consolations of religion and medicine and magic were inextricably offered. It would have made Rudi furious, but would his fury have been also a sign of fear?

A little priest, a fleck of saliva at the corner of his mouth, accosted him. Franz hesitated, explained that he was only curious. Did all these people really believe in the operation of the evil eye?

"You must understand," the priest said, "we are all, each of us, individually, the source of power, and powerful emanations, even if unaware of it. We are all subject to mental waves which can occasion ill health or misery, and this is the visible sign of the evil spirit. Why should you suppose yourself unaffected?"

A fat man passed them, a white cockerel held under his arm.

"What will he do with that bird?"

"Who knows?" the priest said. "Depend upon it, it will fulfil a purpose. What would you like? This amulet to protect you?"

Franz turned and fled.

Later that evening, on the Florida, he encountered Luis. Luis was a little drunk, and was amusing himself by imitating the strut of a jack-booted soldier who paraded the street some twenty yards ahead, with an Alsatian dog on a chain leash. Luis laughed when he saw Franz, and hustled him into a café for a drink.

"So what did your father say?"

Franz screwed the whisky glass round in his fingers.

"Ah, your nerve failed?" Luis said. "So you are not yet an affianced man? All the better. Take Courage. Do you know, when I visited England as a boy – when my father was chargé d'affaires at the Embassy there, I was impressed to see advertising hoardings urging the people to Take Courage. I thought that very fine, that the Government should be so concerned for their moral welfare. Then I discovered Courage was a beer."

Franz leaned on the bar counter; examining his fractured face in the minor. Two businessmen with women, probably prostitutes, were drinking brandy at a corner table, and laughing. One of them had a look of Rudi, but it wasn't his father, who wouldn't anyway – Franz was sure – have consorted publicly with a woman like that.

Luis said, "I am going on to Rosita's. Coming?"

Franz shook his head. He was tempted, as always, by the city at night. The sense of danger thrilled and frightened him: he became a different person, one to whom anything might happen. Nevertheless he shook his head.

"There's a little girl with big juicy red lips made for my favourite diversion," Luis said. "She looks like the Sainted One herself."

"I thought you called yourself a Peronist?"

Luis lit an American cigarette – a Chesterfield.

"Indeed yes. Perón is the only solution left to us. Peronism is a great national movement."

"And yet you would let a girl who resembles the Sainted One do that to you, debase herself in that way?"

"You don't understand. It's precisely because she is like that that I need her to do that. She is everything at once, queen and victim, saint and debauchee. Why don't you join me?"

Franz shook his head.

"Sometimes," his friend said, "I wonder if you like women. They used to say at school that you were a queer. Is that what you really like? Don't be ashamed to admit it, dear boy."

"No," Franz said. "I'm in love with Becky."

"Oh, a romantic? In 1964. I congratulate you, and commiserate with you."

Franz felt himself flushing. But it was true. It was the truth he had to hold on to. What he wanted was to be with Becky. That way he would be free of himself. Marriage was a refuge.

Eventually friendships come to depend most on having experiences in common. It was like that with Eli and Kinsky. They met once a week to play chess, and though they rarely talked of the past, it was the past that held them together. "We are both refugees from reality," as Kinsky said, more than once, in the little antique shop-cum-gallery which he kept. The reality they had in common was too awful to be the subject for reminiscence. But it bound them together. No one who hadn't endured it could understand what it had meant. Both, in certain moods, despised everyone who had not lived in Hell. At other times, they simply despised each other. Eli was an intellectual, at once "arid and sentimental" in Kinsky's opinion; Kinsky was an aesthete, "with the brains of a chicken", according to Eli. Kinsky deplored Eli's taste in music, "typical of the worst sort of 1880s' *Gemütlichkeit*. Eli agreed with Adolf Hitler on one point – in finding the Expressionists to whose work Kinsky was devoted "deranged and decadent".

Kinsky was ten years younger, born 1910. He had got his looks back. Sometimes he said that losing them, feeling himself daily grow uglier, had been the worst of it. "The first time I saw myself in a mirror when they let us out, I wept," he would say, patting his hair into place. He was Viennese, and adored his city, but could never live there again. "I can't forget how the crowd cheered the *Anschluss*, and screamed with delight the day the Nazis marched in. Don't allow anyone to tell you that we Austrians were Hitler's first victims. Most of us were his most willing accomplices. And why not? Wasn't his mind formed in the slums of Vienna? Wasn't it there he learned to hate and fear the Jews?"

Kinsky wasn't a Jew himself. "Indeed," he had been known to say, "God forgive me, when I was young, I was anti-Semitic. It was the one point on which I agreed with Hitler. I still am, deep down. It's ineradicable, you know. I tell Eli that, and he agrees with me. Anti-Semitism is an inescapable feature of European culture. The thing to do is to recognise it, not to hide from the truth."

Eli agreed with him there. If you had asked him how he reconciled this agreement with his opinion, equally often expressed, that the attempt at the Final Solution was inspired by the horror of the realisation that people like himself were Germans too, he would have puffed the smoke from his cheroot in your face and answered that the test of a first-rate mind was the ability to hold incompatible opinions steady, and still continue to function.

"Well, my dear," Kinsky would say, "I've never boasted that my own little mind was first-rate, but I quite agree. After all, it was just the same with us, wasn't it? The whole appeal of the Nazi movement was camp as they come, and yet they killed six hundred thousand of us for being as we are."

Kinsky adored Franz. He met him first when Franz was fifteen, and Kinsky sold Franz's mother a painting by a young (and rather bad) neo-expressionist, whom he had taken up and was promoting. He delivered it himself to her apartment, because he had found that personal service of this kind was not only good business, but could lead to interesting social encounters. That was certainly so in this case. Franz admitted him to the apartment, and explained that his mother had telephoned to say she had been delayed, and she hoped Señor Kinsky would forgive her and await her arrival.

Kinsky giggled. "I'm sorry," he said, "it always seems so silly to me when we Germans call each other Señor and Señora."

Franz was embarrassed by the giggle and by the way Kinsky was looking at him.

He said, "I don't know why, sir, but I always feel uncomfortable when I have to speak German. Except with my father. You must think me very silly."

"Only in the nicest way," Kinsky said. "And don't call me 'sir', dear boy, it makes me feel antique, like something out of one of those dreadful novels by Thomas Mann."

"I haven't read any Thomas Mann."

"Why should you?"

"So what should I call you?"

"Call me Kinsky, just Kinsky. Everyone else does. And do you think I might have a glass of whisky?"

Franz flushed again.

"I'm sorry," he said, "I should have offered you…"

"Would you like to see the painting I've brought your mother?" He unwrapped it. Franz looked at it.

"I don't know," he said. "I don't think I understand this sort of art."

"Look," Kinsky said. He took Franz by the elbow. Franz was wearing a short-sleeved shirt and Kinsky held the cool flesh of his arm between thumb and forefinger. "Look," he said again, and with his other hand traced an imaginary line in the air, first one way, then the other. He released the boy's arm.

"I'll teach you about painting," he said. "To be honest, this one isn't terribly good. But I have others which are better. Come to my gallery some afternoon, and I'll give you a lesson in appreciation. Really, I mean it, it would give me pleasure. Shall we say Wednesday? Are you free on Wednesday? About four o'clock? Good. Here's my card."

He was on his most lively form when Ilse, Franz's mother, eventually appeared. He stayed an hour, and told them anecdotes of Vienna between the wars, leaving before they were tired of him.

"He's delightful, isn't he?" Ilse said. "So sophisticated and European."

Before he left, Kinsky had obtained the Señora's permission for Franz to visit his gallery "to learn something about art."

"Perhaps I'll form a little club," Kinsky said.

That was four years before Franz met Becky and fell in love with her. Meanwhile Kinsky had become Ilse's pet. She invited him to all her parties, and relied on him to smooth out her social arrangements. He was grateful. He often told her she was his dearest friend, and that she supplied the family he had lost.

"You remind me so much of my poor sister," he said. "We were very close."

When Franz fell in love with Becky, Kinsky was jealous. But he had known something of the sort would soon happen, and didn't make a scene. He had long ago learned to make do with less than everything he might want. Besides, he really preferred looking and imagining to physical encounters; he had countless photographs and a nude drawing which he had made himself and Franz still visited him and smiled at him and made him his confidant. It was as much as he could hope for; perhaps it was as much as he really wanted. He had learned to distrust the idea of possession.

So now, when Eli pushed the chessboard away, and lit a cheroot, and said, "You know the family, don't you?" Kinsky smiled and said, "Ilse is one of my dearest friends. She's charming. And Becky couldn't be more fortunate. Franz is a sweet boy."

"Hmph," Eli said, "I don't trust your judgement."

Nell looked up from her sewing.

"Don't be rude, Eli."

"It makes me uncomfortable," Eli said.

It was a hot evening and the windows were open. Swifts darted to and fro among the rooftops and television aerials. The music of a mandolin wafted a sentimental tune from a balcony across the street, mingling with American jazz from a neighbour's wireless. Kinsky sipped the red Chilean wine that Nell bought from the corner shop in three-litre flasks. He lit a Gauloise cigarette, holding the match in his fingers until it burned itself out, and curled round, black and tapering. Eli's face was troubled; hair sprouted white and wiry above the second button of his open-necked orange Aertex shirt; his fingernails, Kinsky noticed, were bitten short. It was curious that he had never observed this before. Did Eli sit by the open window, isolated by blindness in the midst of life, gnawing his nails?

"Uncomfortable?" Kinsky said. He repeated the word, first in English, and then in Spanish.

"Uncomfortable," Eli repeated, still in German. "It's the same feeling whichever language you use."

"I am not certain of that," Kinsky said. "Do you know, Franz and his mother prefer to talk Spanish when they are alone. Isn't that strange?"

"What's she like, Kinsky?" Nell said.

"Ilse? She's blonde. I suppose she looks a little like Ingrid Bergman. Yes, you could say she resembles Bergman. She has the same liquid eyes. And of course, you have met Franz, he takes after her."

He got to his feet. It was late, he must go home. He had enjoyed the game of chess, been able to tolerate – he smiled at this – the Brahms

Eli had insisted on playing, even though he knew his (Kinsky's) opinion of Brahms, which, not wishing to be offensive, he wouldn't repeat. He touched Eli on the shoulder, as near as he could ever go to expressing the affection which, despite everything, all their differences and their inherent opposition to each other, he supposed he felt. Eli grunted; Kinsky hadn't given him what he wanted.

And then Kinsky said, "Remember, old friend, I have nightmares too. Literally. I sometimes wake up shivering and wet with sweat."

("Kinsky was always dapper," Nell said once. "That was what makes me remember this confession.")

"I've let you down," Kinsky said.

"No."

"Yes, I have. I'm sorry. But I don't know the boy's father. I think however he is a good father. Stern, demanding, in the old style. Franz always speaks of him with respect. But I know why you are worrying. We are bound, aren't we, always to be suspicious of a German who has prospered here. Still, the suspicion isn't always justified. That's what I must point out. After all, I have flourished myself."

Nell accompanied him through the kitchen and out on to the landing beyond the door of the apartment. She shut both doors behind her.

"He can't sleep at night," she said. "Sometimes I think he chooses not to."

"Is he afraid?"

"Yes, that's what it is, he's afraid; it hadn't occurred to me."

"When is Franz coming here?"

"I can't answer that, he still refuses to let the boy come. And you're right, he's a nice boy, I've told him that. Sometimes, I tell myself that everything will be all right when he agrees to meet Franz, he'll be charmed. But I don't believe it. Oh, he is difficult now; you don't know how difficult he can be."

"He was always difficult, my dear. He survived by being difficult. Then he made his reputation – for the second time, don't forget – by being difficult."

"Oh Kinsky, I don't know what I would do without you."

"You must meet Ilse soon. That will help. Shall I arrange it for you – a tea party at my place?"

"Sweet of you, but I think I had better fix it myself. I'll telephone her tomorrow, I promise I will."

"Do remember, it's the children's lives…"

"I know."

"And they're good children."

"Of course they are."

Kinsky kissed her. She held him to her a moment, then listened to his steps dancing down the stone stairs and into the night, with a lonely and defiant gallantry that always pained her.

TWO

Nell and Eli went back further than they usually let on. There was guilt in their silence and some discomfort. It had been her grandfather, Marcus Sueffer, who had insisted that she spend some months in Germany in 1938. He was a music critic, and the author of a biography of Wagner whom he adored. It wasn't just the music that he loved; he was besotted by everything Wagnerian; he was perhaps the only person who had ever written enthusiastically about the maestro's sense of humour. He despised Nell's schoolmaster father, despised his daughter for having married him, but, for no reason Nell could account for, took a fancy to her. This expressed itself in his determination to see to it that she was liberated from the dismal Englishness of her father's house. Her father was himself doubtful.

"Of course I understand that Herr Hitler has done wonders for his people, and I admire him for that, but there's something about the man I can't like. He's a fanatic, you know, and it seems that some of the chaps around him are no better than thugs. They are bullies, and I have always detested bullying."

Nell disliked bullying too, but the prospect of a visit with her grandfather to Bayreuth (where they lunched with Cosima Wagner herself, and heard the grand old lady babble her adulation of "dearest Wolf", as she called the Fuehrer) and a subsequent six months in Berlin staying with her grandfather's old friend the Gräfin von Pfühlnitz, was sufficiently exciting to make her ignore her father's words, which didn't anyway carry much conviction. In fact, he pushed the subject aside, remarking that young Hutton had made another century, and was in his opinion promising to be the best batsman since Hammond had appeared on the scene. "Nothing flashy about him, that's what I like."

Nell liked the Gräfin from the start. She was an old lady who held herself very straight, partly perhaps to compensate for the perpetual tremor of her hand, and who looked down her nose at the world. She was a Prussian aristocrat, and sniffed at the mention of the Nazis. She made Nell welcome, and spoke so fondly of her grandfather that, years later, remembering this, Nell wondered if they mightn't have been lovers in the distant past. At the time it was impossible for her to imagine that the Gräfin could ever have performed the sexual act. Despite this difficulty, there were two children, both of course grown-up, to account for. Her son, Albrecht, was an official in the German Foreign Office, a mild-mannered man, forever flicking cigarette ash from his lapels; the daughter Magda, a beefy blonde, was married to a Saxon baron who had found it expedient to join the party almost as soon as it had come to power. "Saxons are idiots, my dear," the Gräfin said. "That's something you have to understand." All the same, the old girl wasn't above making use of this connection with the ruling party, and finding reassurance in the security it seemed to offer.

Nell found everything strange and enthralling. She liked the big ugly apartment with its heavy knobbly black furniture; the windows were never opened, and that seemed to emphasise the difference between here and home. She was just at the age to be seeking the experiment of living in a manner that was altogether foreign, and though the stuffy rooms gave her a headache towards four o'clock every afternoon, just before she generally went out for a walk, she yet relished the sense they imparted of there being another separate but parallel form of existence which was completely new to her. When she tried to explain this in letters to her cousin Sheila, her words made no sense at all, but the sensation was real enough.

She formed the habit of walking the Gräfin's Pomeranian in the late afternoon. She loved the streets, the bustle, the sharp Berliner humour, the variety of types; she would sit at a café on Unter den Linden and drink coffee and eat cream cakes; she always ordered too many and gave one to the little dog. What she liked most about these afternoons was the sensation of being solitary, incognito; she had lived all her life in the family atmosphere of schools where such a luxury was impossible.

Naturally she soon fell in love, a little. She was nineteen, and, though she didn't realise it, had come to Berlin in search of love. She fixed her attention on Albrecht; she and her girl-friends had long ago agreed that boys of their own age were callow. And Albrecht was a diplomat at a time when diplomats had a glamour for a whole generation of well brought-up girls. Moreover, he looked sorrowful; she was sure there was something sad in his past, which she would be able to cure.

Albrecht may have been somewhat embarrassed to find this pretty English child (as he thought her) in such unguarded pursuit. She wasn't his type of thing at all. But she was a nice child, and talking to her was in some degree at least a relief from the cares and perplexities which occupied him. Besides – and here he was callous – he soon realised it didn't do him any harm to be seen about with a blonde English girl. It distracted attention from his other interests, other activities, from the fact that, in more ways than one, Albrecht was an unsatisfactory subject of the Third Reich. He was careful to conceal this, but he lived with the fear of discovery. Nell represented relief from strain. For the truth was that, in almost every way, Albrecht was disaffected. He regarded the Nazis as scum, dangerous, disreputable, and wholly unattractive. His distaste was first aesthetic, secondly social.

On Sundays he would sometimes drive Nell out to an inn some thirty miles from the city, on the fringe of the forest. They ate sausages and fried potatoes and drank beer, and looked to the East: "Germany's unfinished business," Albrecht said.

"You don't believe that? That's what Hitler says, isn't it?"

"It's the one matter about which he is right. Our family estates are over there, you know, in what is now Poland."

On Thursday afternoons the Gräfin held a soirée, or *conversazione*. Nell soon realised that she was meeting a Germany of which most people at home were ignorant. Her grandfather of course was a devotee of German music, German philosophy, German civilisation, but he was known to be eccentric. It was the general consensus, she had found, that the Germans weren't civilised. "There's no such thing as a German gentleman, you know," her father would say. "The concept is foreign to the German nature." Well, the people whom she met at the Gräfin's would have proved him wrong. They seemed to her to leave the English suburbs and the Home Counties nowhere. The thing was: these people knew about life. They had suffered and survived; they had lost illusions. That's what she thought then.

Eli used to come to the Thursdays. He was probably the only Jew who did. But he was an old friend of Albrecht's, who introduced him to Nell as "the cleverest man I know. He's an economist. Schacht eats out of his hand."

Nell had learned enough of German politics to know who Schacht was, and to be puzzled.

"He exaggerates," Eli said,

When he smiled he looked ten years younger, and that first smile knocked Albrecht from his place in her heart. It was as simple as that.

"I don't understand," she said, meaning everything.

"You are amazed that I collaborate with the regime?"

"Yes," she said.

"But it's quite simple. You have an English saying – or is it American? – if you can't beat them, join them."

"I still don't understand."

"The only way to overcome the revolution is to lead it. Well, I don't claim to do that. But – you realise I am a Jew, don't you – the only way in my opinion to defeat the Nazis is to infiltrate their movement."

Did he, even then, believe that was possible? He was conceited enough, she told herself years later; no doubt about that.

But at the time she was impressed. And then Eli leaned over, and putting his body between her and the other people in the room, touched the corner of her mouth with his forefinger.

"You're in love with Albrecht, aren't you?"

She couldn't answer.

"He's my best and oldest friend. That's how I know," he said. "But it's impossible, I'm afraid."

"Why's that?"

"If you can't see, then I'm not the one, and this isn't the place, to begin your education."

She couldn't tell Eli that it didn't matter any more, not since he had first smiled at her.

Two days later, she lost her virginity. Eli dipped his finger in the blood and touched first his mouth, then hers, then licked his finger clean. She moaned. He smiled down at her. They were in his apartment. A lithograph of Kaiser Wilhelm II looked down on the bed. Schumann played on the wireless. In the sitting-room beyond, the Pomeranian, feeling neglected, began to yap.

"Albrecht could never give you that," Eli said. "You're a sweet child."

He lit a cigarette and put it in her mouth, then another for himself.

"It's so nice to be able to forget politics and everything," he said. "Eventually, there is nothing to equal the act of love with woman who really wants you."

He stretched out on the bed beside her, pale-skinned, wiry.

"You're very furry," she said.

"Virility."

Later he said he would take her out to dinner. "Ring the Gräfin."

"No," she said, "I can't do that. And what about the little dog?"

He tried to persuade her, but she was adamant.

"English principles," he said. She didn't know whether he was laughing at her or not.

That was how it began, and it went on like that for two or three months. There were many days when she could not see him, but when they did meet it was always good. The cold came to Berlin, a damp, penetrating cold that made her distrust the permanence of the city and conscious of the waste of plain, lakes, and leafless forest stretching away from the suburbs to unimaginable distances.

Towards Christmas, love made Nell afraid. She felt she had lost the privileges of the foreigner whom nothing can touch. She began to take a desperate interest in the politics she had been able to regard as a game for other people. She became aware of murmurings around her, of Eli and Albrecht breaking off conversations when she appeared. "You mustn't be involved," the lover said when she protested.

He couldn't see that loving him committed her to involvement. What happened in Germany happened to her, for that reason. When she tried to tell him this, he silenced her with a kiss.

"I'm not a child," she said.

"Believe me, I know that. I'm not a pervert."

"Oh you make a joke of everything, whenever I try to be serious."

"Not at all. There is nothing more serious than us. Believe me, everything will work out."

But, despite this, the future was a country neither chose, or dared, to explore. Sometimes she worried about that, being a conventional girl who had been brought up to expect that love led directly to marriage. It was indeed strange to think of herself as someone's mistress. Not that she was exactly what she understood by that; Eli hadn't after all established her in an apartment, which was what being a mistress meant to her, if it wasn't a matter of adultery.

One afternoon she was sitting with the Pom outside a café, when a thin young man in dark glasses approached her. She wasn't alarmed; love had given her the confidence necessary to brush anyone off. And she wasn't attracted; there was something reptilian about him. Anyway she distrusted men who wore sun-glasses in winter. But he addressed her by name, with a note of interrogation.

"Yes?" she said.

Something official about his manner prompted her to add, "If it a question of papers?"

"Why should you think that? I am sure your papers are in order. May I sit down?"

Without waiting for a reply, he pulled out a chair. The Pom sniffed at his ankles. He said nothing until the waiter had brought two more cups of coffee, and then: "Does your father know your lover is a Jew?"

"What makes you think you have the right to ask such a question? What the hell has it got to do with you?"

"Oh, I have the right. And I might ask also whether the Gräfin, whose guest you are, knows that the Jew is your lover?"

She felt herself flushing.

"Ach, I thought not."

"Who are you?"

"That is unimportant. However," he flashed a card at her. "I belong to a branch of the Reich Security Service which has the responsibility of investigating such matters."

"What matters? Love affairs?"

"No. Matters concerning Jews, and relations of Jews with Aryans."

"But I'm English," she said.

He permitted himself a smile. It was a very thin smile with no humour in it.

"Then you must know," she said, "that Dr Czinner is a distinguished economist and employed as a consultant by the Ministry of Finance and the Reichsbank."

"I know that that indulgence has been extended to him – and not yet withdrawn."

"I was frightened," she told Eli.

"That was doubtless the intention."

"He wanted me to spy on you. He made that very clear. I told him he was as absurd as he was offensive. But I don't like it. Eli, I've been long enough in Germany, darling, to know how things are. We don't have to stay here."

He put his arm round her shoulder, drew her to him, kissed her first hard, then very softly, on the lips.

"But I must," he said.

She allowed herself to be silenced for the moment. She felt fortified by love; like brandy on a cold day, it kept her warm and glowing. There were times when she seemed to have been interned in a madhouse: when she heard the Fuehrer on the wireless screaming against the Jews, or on that occasion in a restaurant in the Kleiststrasse when two bloated and rather drunk uniformed Nazis seized a middle-aged man by the collar and threw him against the wall and then kicked him eight times – she counted – and nobody dared to move. With a forkful of fish suspended in the air she watched the other diners lower eyes and pretend to be occupied with the food which, nevertheless, they could not bring themselves to lift to their mouths. Albrecht was with her that evening, and his hand, which was warm and a little damp, rested on her wrist; she knew he was imploring her to say nothing. Decent people, she realised, had become like the three monkeys: they spoke, heard, saw no evil, for fear they would bring evil upon themselves. The little man who had been beaten up was helped to his feet by an elderly waiter who escorted him to the lavatory, as soon as the two Nazis had made their happy departure.

"He's a lawyer," Albrecht said, "a distinguished one, who has had the misfortune to defend several enemies of the Reich."

"But how can you live here?" she said.

"We could talk of duty," Albrecht said.

When she told him about the man in dark glasses who had wanted her to report on Eli – she thought of it as sneaking – he only said, "Now you see what we're up against."

She was impressed by his confidence; of course she wanted to be deceived, to be told that her fears were no worse than nightmares, and that everything would come out all right. She had been brought up to believe this, in the right class of the right nation, to which nothing worse than accidental and personal tragedy could happen; terrible in itself of course, but involving the victim in no generic cataclysm.

As if divining her thoughts, Albrecht touched her cheek with the back of his hand, and said, "They too are dreamers who won't, or dare not, confront reality. They set up an ideal Germany which is unrealisable, and so, in order to realise it, as they think, they must destroy. They refuse to see things as they are, to see, in short, that Jewish culture, Jewish science, have been the most vital forces in German history throughout the last century. But because their view of life is not founded in reality, it cannot prevail. It is a form of perverted Platonism they offer, and I say with Nietzsche that the cure lies in Thucydides. In the end, Nietzsche says, it is courage in the face of reality that distinguishes a man like Thucydides from Plato. Or, I might add, a man like Eli from Hitler. Plato, Nietzsche says, is a coward before reality, consequently he flees into the ideal. So is Hitler, that's how he acts therefore. Thucydides has control of himself; so has Eli. Consequently he also maintains control of things. So does Eli."

"That's all very well," Nell said, "and I admit this is all miles above my head, but how can you say Eli maintains control of things, when nasty little men are able to spy on him and ask me to do so?"

Albrecht said, "Believe me, Eli knows what he is doing, while they move like sleepwalkers."

It was through Albrecht that she met Kinsky, and through Kinsky that she came to understand Albrecht. Then she saw all three of them – her lover and her two friends, for Kinsky was so funny and charming that he at once became a friend – as men who were performing an intricate dance on a high wire stretched across an abyss, without a safety net.

"Why don't you run away?" she asked Kinsky.

"I am always about to do so," he said, "next week. But then something, or someone, happens to prevent it. And I ask myself: where would I find life as interesting as that which is forced on me here?"

"Oh," she said, "you are all three so stupid, so pleased with yourselves."

Like little boys, she thought, not daring to refuse a dare.

For a few weeks she was angry with Eli, and refused to see him. Not seeing him made her miserable. Not seeing him meant that she did not even have the reassurance that he was all right, hadn't been damaged, beaten up or arrested. That was absurd, for he relayed messages to her through Albrecht and Kinsky and telephoned the Gräfin, who passed on the message that Nell wouldn't see him. Nevertheless she woke, frightened, in the night, hearing a dog bark from the next street, listening to the murmurs which so easily translated themselves into the sound of boots ascending the staircase of the block of flats where he lived.

In the spring, Hitler marched into Czechoslovakia smiling at the promises he had given Chamberlain and Daladier at Munich. Nell went to the cinema and saw the tanks rumble like dull fate through the streets of Prague. The audience applauded, and she left the cinema and telephoned her lover.

"I've been wrong," she said, "I must see you at once."

She was certain he would now himself admit that he too had been mistaken, that he had failed to read reality correctly. When he said, "Yes, come to my apartment, I've missed you so much," she took heart, not only because of the love and desire she heard in his voice, but, as importantly, because the suggestion of his apartment rather than a bar or restaurant seemed to her to indicate that he might at least be nervous of appearing in public as the Jew with the blonde English lover.

But, after they had made love, as she was dying to do, he suggested that they go out to a restaurant for supper. Then she exploded, called him selfish, arrogant, pig-headed; he didn't care for her happiness; he was infatuated with this image of himself as someone who couldn't be wounded, couldn't be frightened, was indifferent to events, superior to fate.

"You're a Nazi yourself at heart," she screamed. "You too think you are a superman."

He put his arms round her. The room was quite dark and filled with the scent of roses. They were still naked. He stroked her thighs, kissed her breasts, worked long hard fingers against her buttocks, urging her to surrender everything – will, judgement, fears, trinities of heart, mind, body, past, present and future – to him once again, now and forever, amen. She pulled herself away.

"No," she said, pulling on stockings, doing up her suspender belt. "No, I can't. You're all blind," she said, "to the reality which you boast of fighting. Kinsky at least" – she stepped into her knickers and heaved them up – "has some excuse. He's in love with a love that keeps him here. He's mad, but ... you don't even have that excuse." She buttoned her blouse. Eli sat back, still naked, in a chair and watched her shadowy movements. For the first time he seemed to find nothing to say. She put on her skirt, hooked the eyes. "If you loved me..." she said, and stopped on the old line, feeling it worthless.

"Ah yes," he rose, and slipped into a silk dressing-gown. "That word."

"I thought it meant something to you."

"Something, yes, but not everything."

She held a shoe in her hand. For a moment it seemed to her that she was about to hurl it at his head.

"You think the worst can't happen to you, that you're somehow protected."

"No," he said, "I don't think that."

The moment passed. The shoe was now on her silk-stockinged foot.

"You're going back to England," he said, "and that's the best thing. I love you. I don't know if I will always love you, because in my opinion it is foolish to make such a boast, but I love you now, and I know it is best that you return home. There's no future for you here."

"For me?" she said. "What about us?"

He took a rose from the bowl, and then, lighting the lamp, carefully removed its thorns with a pair of nail scissors. He slipped it through the lapel button of her jacket and fastened it there with a pin. He held the jacket out for her to put on.

"It will wither," he said, "before you are home. Nevertheless…"

She collapsed on the bed, weeping.

"A cut rose, an English rose. Is that how you think of me?"

"No, my dear. But you can't stay here."

"And you can? Couldn't there be a future for us together, in England perhaps?"

"Oh yes," he said, "if I married you, would that get me an English passport, as Erika Mann got one by marrying that English poet? No, I think not, I am sure that only applies to wives, not to husbands. Besides it would make me look foolish. No, I'm joking. I'm joking because it hurts me too, but I have to say it. If I came to England with you, you would not be marrying the man you have loved here in Berlin. And I would miss him too. I would be ashamed to have run away, and our marriage would be curdled by the resentment I would feel. I have work to do here. Later, perhaps…"

The words hung in the air, then slipped away, like the sun disappearing behind an evening hill.

"There will be no later," she said.

Of course her heart was broken; she let her friends (like Sheila, to whom she confided everything) know this. And when war broke out her apprehension was extreme. At least, until then, there had been letters, however carefully worded. And she knew from a friend of Albrecht's, in the Embassy in London, who once – at Albrecht's suggestion, she was sure – took her dancing at the Café de Paris, and then did so several times, presumably now for her own sake – that all three of her friends were still safe, however little that might mean. But then came the war, which for her meant, first of all, silence. And then anger with Eli festered. She told herself it was irrational, and then she argued that if he had loved her, he would have preferred her to whatever he thought he might achieve in Germany: "Which is nothing, nothing," she told Sheila again and again.

Nell did war-work, first in the Ministry of Information, and then at the BBC. Speaking German was an advantage at least. Her grandfather died, and there was no one to whom she could speak sympathetically of Germany. In 1942 she married one of her colleagues, Ivan Murison. The marriage was a mistake from the start; they had both got the other wrong. In the spring of 1946 she left the BBC, and went to Germany to work for UNRRA. Ivan had helped there at least; he had many contacts as a result of the reputation he had begun to gain in the last year of the war. It was his reports from the stricken and demoralised Germany of the first months of the Occupation which, as he wrote in his autobiography, "set me on the path to fame".

Nell was horrified by what she discovered in Germany. During the war she had schooled herself to hate the enemy. Now she was dismayed to see how they had fallen. When a fellow-worker said, "They asked for it," she snapped back at her, "You never knew them, did you?" Of course her colleague was right: they had asked for it. But so did Lear; so, even more so, did Macbeth. That didn't mean that you crowed to see them brought down.

What distressed her most was to see the way in which so many of the former Master Race fawned on their conquerors, quick to assure anyone who might even possibly listen that they had never believed in Hitler. The fact that this was true of her own German friends didn't stop her from finding these protestations pitiable. It was a terrible thing to have to apologise for what you had believed or, even worse, to lie about it.

She had known from the start that her principal motive in taking this job was less the desire to be of help than the hope that she might find out what had happened to Albrecht and Kinsky and of course Eli. She had not realised how hard it would be to seek information in the midst of chaos. She got nowhere. They were, it seemed, among the millions who had simply been erased. But she couldn't think of them as three among millions; she refused to accept that her friends could be reduced to statistics.

The further she pushed her enquiries, the more difficult it became. She realised that people just didn't want to know: her friends were the wrong sort of German. They had been neither outright Nazis to be punished, denazified, redeemed; nor the open enemies or victims of the regime. Even Eli's Jewishness was of no help; he was seen as a sort of

Jewish Quisling by those few who had heard of him. She had thought that perhaps Albrecht might have been one of the heroes of the July '44 plot against Hitler; but that didn't seem to be the case. His name didn't appear in the lists of victims of Hitler's panicky and infuriated revenge. Had he, she wondered, perhaps compromised with the regime, his nerve failing, and gone under with it, or slunk off, disguised by a new identity?

As for the Gräfin, who might have helped, she was surely dead. The quarter where she had lived had been right in the line of the Russian tanks.

That winter Europe froze hard. The mud stood up in great ridges resembling a lunar landscape in miniature. Crows fell dead from the trees. Fuel was short. When people returned exhausted from the work of reconstruction, they crawled into bed, and huddled under the blankets. It was worse than the war, they said; the electricity supply failed so often, they might as well have had the black-out again. There were no bombs, but it seemed that the world was held in suspended animation, awaiting the bomb to end bombs. Then it snowed. In the little town in Bavaria where Nell was stationed it snowed for four days without stopping. Nothing could move anywhere. The scene resembled an idealised nineteenth-century illustration, except that there was no joy in the cold. The weather and the world were joined in hostility to man.

When movement at last became possible, a new truckload of refugees arrived, displaced Germans driven in terror from an East eager to be rid of them, stripped of their possessions, stripped, for the moment, of their conviction of their own virtue. Nell moved among them and was aware yet again of the difference of her feeling. Whatever they had done wrong, whatever evil individuals among them had committed, they had now been reduced to mere humanity. They were abased.

One day, Glenys Middleton, one of the few colleagues for whom she felt any warmth, said to her, "One of the mutts has been asking questions about you."

"About me?"

"It was your voice, he said."

"Where is he?"

"Moved on, I think. Pity you weren't here. Or perhaps not."

"But who was he? What was he like?"

"Like them all. A skeleton."

It could have been any of them, removed from this chance of a chance encounter by the action of someone passing a piece of paper from one office to the next. But equally it might have been someone compromised by his experiences, whom she had met briefly, but who recognised her, and who feared that she might identify him, ripping away the facade of a new personality which he had constructed. Such a one couldn't know that her integrity was corroded, even corrupted, by pity: that she would have let him pass, leaving punishment to God or conscience. It might even, she thought – "Don't be absurd," she told herself – have been that spy in dark glasses. But she could not anyway have identified him, had never known his name, retained no memory of his personality except for the sense of menace that she had felt behind the dark glasses, and the taste for conventional rectitude, for doing things by the book of rules, which she remembered from the thin mouth. Of course, he wasn't to know that she could never think to know him, and it would be natural for him to remember the English blonde he had questioned and feel uneasily certain in his narrow self-limited world that she could never forget him. How could she, he would think, do so, when he was his own entire world?

These were fantasies, mad thoughts that came to her in long hours of sleeplessness. She had grown accustomed to waking after three or four hours' sleep, and lying restless, anticipating the dawn that brought with it the resumption of her chilling and miserable task, which she felt was nothing more, when you came down to it, than the cataloguing of a Hell in which no one had believed. For Nell, who had been brought up to say the General Confession and who had chanted the Magnificat at Evensong Sunday after Sunday, concluded in these months that Nietzsche, whom Albrecht had so fervently expounded to her, was right, whatever anyone said to the contrary: God was Dead. We lived with the consequences of his demise, and the first manifestations had been grotesque parodies: Communism and Nazism.

Her response to insomnia was correctly English. She began to take long walks every afternoon. There was a touch of spring; crocuses were in flower. She would have liked a dog at her heels. But there were few dogs in Germany then. Who could feed one?

She returned from one of these walks to find Eli sitting on the hard chair in the corridor outside her office, emaciated but unmistakable. He smiled to see her. She all but fainted. How had he got there?

"I walked."

"Yes," he said, in response to the question she hadn't yet dared to ask. "I was in a camp. Yes, Auschwitz. And then in Russian Poland. And then I walked. But let's not discuss it. Tell me about yourself."

Grotesque, again. Your lover reappears from Hell, and is smoking an English Goldflake cigarette which he has cadged from an orderly, and which he holds in precisely the old manner in the right corner of his mouth while he talks from the other side; and it is all the same, all at once, though he has no teeth. Almost seven years have passed, and he has indeed crossed from the other side. Without trumpets.

"Now we can get married," he said.

"But I am married."

"That doesn't interest me."

"No," she said, "it doesn't interest me either."

THREE

Nell said to Eli, "Don't you think they might have just the same sort of certainty that we had?"

"That is stupid. How could they? A little boy and a little girl."

"I was a little girl in Berlin in 1939, and I was quite certain then. So were you, even though you tried to deny it."

"I never denied it. I merely couldn't give it precedence."

That was of course what she had never been able to forgive him, even though in the first years of their marriage she had pretended otherwise. Curiously, it wasn't until after Kinsky had followed them to Argentina – not that he knew he was doing so – and they had met him again and resumed their conversations, that she was able to confess her resentment. For Nell, Kinsky came to take the place of a priest.

So, now, she called on him at his gallery. He was busy setting up a new exhibition.

"You don't like it?" he said.

"Not much."

"Well, it's new. So you wouldn't, my dear."

"Is it really new, Kinsky?"

"Of course not." He made her a cup of coffee from the espresso machine which he had installed at the end of a corridor between the two rooms of the gallery. "There's nothing new and there's nothing true, and it don't signify. Who said that?"

"Tell me."

"Your English novelist Thackeray. See how well read I am. Do you think it's true?"

"I don't know."

"Well, it can't be, can it, if it is. What's wrong, my dear?"

"Eli."

"Oh," Kinsky said, and sat down, balancing his coffee-cup at a precarious and awkward angle, as if it had nothing to do with him.

"He still refuses to see Franz. Becky's miserable, and he doesn't care. I think he's jealous."

Kinsky smiled.

"It's not that he has a phobia about the Germans," she said. "I could understand it if he had. But you know he hasn't. He still thinks of himself as German as well as Jewish. He still thinks – oh I don't know what he thinks. Will you talk to him, Kinsky?"

"My dear Nell, I have been talking to Eli for thirty years, and never once in that time has he taken my advice. Have you thought of turning round and opposing the match?"

"Of course, but he would know what I was doing."

Kinsky was the only person who guessed how deeply and frequently she now disliked Eli, how she was repelled by his certainty of virtue.

He said, "I have something to tell you."

He had had a visitor the previous day. An American in a seersucker suit, who had pretended to be interested in painting, but was utterly ignorant. "He said that picture over there reminded him of Klee. Well, it couldn't be less like a Klee, could it?" No, Kinsky had at once read him for what he must be: CIA. The man had been curious about Kinsky's history, and then had mentioned Eli. "He was well informed, acquainted with what must, I suppose, be a fullish dossier, even if it evidently stops short of absolute knowledge at important points. But he knew that Eli had worked with Schacht, and of what had happened to him in the war, and after, and then he asked, why didn't he go to Israel?"

"And what did you say?"

"I told him what Eli always says: that there are too many bloody Jews there. He didn't laugh, but he made a note."

"I can't think why the CIA should be interested in him. Not now."

"It's their job to be interested in people."

"But Eli?"

"Yes, even our blind economist. All the same, I can think of an immediate reason. There is after all only one."

"Oh yes," Nell said, understanding.

"After all, Franz's father is German, and any German in South America has secrets, and fears, and friends on whom he relies and has relied?

"Do you, Kinsky?"

"Of course. An old queer needs all the friends he can muster, especially in a police state."

Nell knew Kinsky was right. "Has Franz spoken to his father yet?" she asked Becky that evening.

Her daughter sat at the little table in her bedroom with a textbook open before her. She didn't lift her head when Nell spoke, and her long dangling hair hid her face.

"Not exactly. But his mother has written to him. Maybe Franz too. I'm not sure. Anyway, I can't see that it matters. It's our life."

Nell sat down on the bed and leaned on one elbow. She thought of saying, "We only want you to be happy," but didn't. Becky turned round, lit a Kent, blew out smoke.

She's writing to you, asking us both to tea."

"Do you like her?"

"Mm. She's all right."

"Kinsky's fond of her, I think."

"Can't Kinsky talk to Daddy?"

"I think maybe he will."

The invitation came. Nell dressed herself in a tweed skirt and twinset bought at the Scotch Shop; she wore a string of pearls. "You can't go in jeans, darling."

"Why not? I feel … oh," seeing her mother's face, "all right, I won't argue, this time."

"What time will you be back?" Eli said.

"About six, I suppose."

"Very well."

They left the apartment to the sound of Brahms.

"Does he know where we are going?"

"He pretends not to."

Franz's stepfather, being a General, had an apartment in a big block behind the Plaza de Mayo. Something about the blank-faced building, its determined and unconvincing grandeur, reminded Nell of pre-war Berlin. They ascended in a lift, made in Birmingham in 1924. The lift shaft was enclosed in a metal grille, so that, as you mounted, you might see people from the lower apartments waiting to descend. But this afternoon, they passed nobody. Even the house plants in tubs outside the apartment doors had a dusty air, as if they had been there a long time, untended and forgotten, house plants of a dreaming city.

A stocky Indian maid, wearing a black dress and a plain white apron, opened the door. The lobby of the apartment was very dark, the air close and heavy. Nell anticipated the aroma of boiled cabbage which she had known in Berlin, but the smell was cloying and spicy; like a convent, she thought. It was a place where reality was kept at a distance.

The drawing room was large, running the width of the apartment and opening on to a terrace where sad oleanders were speckled with the dust that pervaded the city centre in dry weather. The maid, clicking annoyance, closed a French window that opened on the terrace, cutting off the sound of traffic in the street below. She told them to sit down. Becky took a tissue from her bag and wiped her hands. Nell peeled off her gloves and laid them on the arm of the chair. The maid went out. They didn't speak.

The mood lightened with Franz's entry. He shook Nell's hand, kissed Becky, who had leaped to her feet.

"My mother won't be a moment. She apologises. Someone has just telephoned."

He was restless, talked about trivia – the weather, rumours at the University, the American Presidential election. An elaborate French rococo clock – imitation French rococo, Nell thought – chimed four.

"It's always going fast," he said. "I'm sure it's not more than quarter to."

The wind rose outside, throwing black shapes of birds across the winter sky.

Ilse entered, stout, apologetic, in a yellow frock.

"This Argentina, always confusion…"

She paused.

"Shall we speak English?" she said. "It gives me pleasure to speak English."

"Or German?" Nell said. "Would we be more comfortable?" she asked in that language.

"Does Rebecca speak German? I hadn't realised."

"Oh yes, often, with Daddy…"

"That is nice."

The maid wheeled in a trolley, poured tea. Franz handed round a plate of egg sandwiches, made in the English style, with crusts removed. The maid returned with a cake stand, in silver Art-Nouveau elaboration, like something from a Viennese coffee house, 1910. There were petits fours, a fruit cake and a magnificent *Sachertorte*.

"Franz's favourite, he adores chocolate. So do I," Ilse giggled.

"I haven't had a tea like this in years," Nell said.

"Oh, I adore tea, my favourite meal, Earl Grey from Jacksons of Piccadilly. I hope that is all right. We have friends in the Embassy in London who supply us."

"It couldn't be better."

Ilse beamed her pleasure.

"This is nice. Of course Kinsky has told me so much about you. He adores you."

Nell felt an alliance forming. Kinsky was right. Ilse was nice. She pressed food on them. Nell found herself eating with pleasure. Franz urged Becky to try the *Sachertorte*. She blushed, then had a second slice.

"Gosh, it's good," she said.

The teapot was refilled, the maid being summoned by a tinkling handbell. Ashtrays were indicated.

"Franz, take Rebecca and show her the apartment. Play her some of your barbaric music. Jazz," she said to Nell. "Actually, to let you into a secret, I adore it myself."

"Oh, so do I," Nell said. "After all it's our generation. Bix Beiderbecke, Joe Venuti, the Hot Five... She invoked the names tenderly, summoning up afternoons of dancing to windup gramophones.

"Red Nicholls and the Five Pennies, Benny Goodman..." Ilse giggled. "They condemned it as barbaric music. My brother and I had to hide our records and could only play them when we were alone in the apartment, with the windows shuttered."

Nell thought of an afternoon in a punt, drifting down the Cam, her own brother working the pole, while Bix's trumpet soared into "Goose Pimples" and "Since My Best Gal Turned Me Down".

"Eli, my husband, hates jazz. He plays Brahms and Schumann."

"Oh," Ilse said, "that's something he has in common then with Franz's father. He adores Brahms. Aimez-vous Brahms?" she giggled again.

"Not much," Nell said.

They paused, silent, at the brink.

"You know Eli's a Jew," Nell said. "Franz has told you that, hasn't he?"

"Oh, I think that's all terribly *vieux jeu*. It was all such a mistake, don't you think?"

"It's a matter one is bound to bring up when speaking to Germans. In circumstances like this, I mean. Of course, Eli still thinks of himself as a German too. He likes me to read German poetry to him, Hofmannsthal and of course Goethe. Then he criticises my accent. He's blind, you know."

Ilse poured Nell another cup of tea, freshened the pot, poured one for herself.

"Such a tragedy," she said, "and a brilliant man too, Kinsky tells me. Franz is afraid of his father. It's sad. Of course he doesn't know him very well..."

"I realised," Nell said, "that he was finding it difficult to tell him about Becky. I'm sorry it makes things so difficult, but I'm glad to find this is the reason, I had thought there might be something more to it..."

"Oh no, I am sure not," Ilse said.

Nell wondered whether Ilse still saw her first husband, what terms they were on, why the marriage had broken up, but didn't care to disturb the mood by asking any of these questions.

For some years now, since he had finally gone blind, Eli had ceased to be troubled by nightmares. Nell found this strange, for in sleep time does not pass, but all moments are as one, and it was hard to understand why one period of a life, so long dominantly oppressive, should all at once be eliminated from the imagination that works in the darkness. While Kinsky was still fearful to sleep without drugging himself heavily, Eli, who for years had woken up screaming and had had to change out of pyjamas soaked with the sweat of his terror, now drifted through the night like a boat on calm water. Nell was distressed to find that she found this distressing. It seemed his new tranquillity diminished both him and what she felt for him. Comforting his nightmares had given her a deep pleasure; now she was denied the certainty that in his worst moments he needed her most. His blindness was no substitute; it irritated her as his nightmares never had.

In the first years of their marriage, when they lived in London, in a flat on the east side of Charlotte Street, his daytime confidence had irritated many, especially Gentiles, who saw him as a cocky pushing Jew, and who could not forgive him for not showing the marks of his suffering. Some of his Jewish friends were equally displeased by his determination to live in the present, to make something of himself. They were almost all in fact doing the same thing, but they had moments when they felt paralysed by guilt simply because they were alive, and their families and communities were dead. Eli seemed to brush this guilt off. "I am not responsible for the crimes of others, or the misfortunes of others. I have nothing with which to reproach myself, neither my attempts to avert calamity, nor the failure of my efforts, nor what happened to me subsequently, nor my survival. Indeed I glory in my survival." That was the message conveyed by every inflection of his voice, by the brisk social manner, by the thickset shoulder-swaying walk. Everything seemed calculated to deny his knowledge that there were Jews who distrusted him, who could not accept that his sojourn in Hell cancelled out the ambiguity of his earlier record, his time as Schacht's adviser, his contribution to Germany's economic recovery under Hitler.

He had friends in London, economists and men in government service, who he expected would be ready to help him. But somehow – Nell never understood just why – the offers of help never materialised. He was received well, it seemed, returned from meetings with reports of enthusiastic responses, keen discussions, fruitful consultations. Academic posts hovered on the horizon, then dipped behind the clouds. He contributed a few pieces to *The Economist*, wrote an article for *The Times* on "Problems of Liquidity in Reconstructional Conditions", which attracted favourable attention, even though its Keynesianism was dismissed as being of an immature variety by those more aware than Eli could be of the last developments of the Master's theories. Nevertheless, even this article didn't lead to the sort of regular commissions which he had anticipated when it was accepted. He did not repine; he set himself to write a book, justifying his own history. It was never completed.

Nell found the balance shifting between them. Eli needed her, something she hadn't expected. At first she was gratified. Only she knew at what a cost his public optimism was maintained. He could not bring himself to describe the nightmares, but he didn't need to. She had seen the photographs, as everyone had, of the piles of corpses discovered at Belsen and Buchenwald; she had worked with refugees. There was nothing she didn't know, she sometimes thought, about the camps, except what mattered: what it felt like actually to have been there.

She knew something else, she alone. She knew why Eli refused to follow what seemed to many people his obvious course, and settle in Israel. She got tired of hearing him say, "Too many bloody Jews", even though she knew that in one sense he spoke the truth. He really did think that. But, more important, he was afraid. In Israel he would have been confronted by the reality of his failure, of his terrible misjudgement, of his arrogance. She remembered how, in the Berlin days, he had combined his contempt for the Nazis with his happy confidence that he could influence them, even lead them by the nose, save himself and his people by making himself useful. She didn't know what the Jewish term for an "Uncle Tom" was, but there must be one; and she knew Eli was afraid and ashamed. She had read an entry in his journal: "If I made a mistake, and it seems I did, then it was because I acted by reason; that I had lost my sureness of instinct. And yet at the time it felt as if I was acting instinctively; if I was, then I made no mistake. Now, reason tells me to go to Israel; instinct says no. 'All that is good is instinct – and hence easy, necessary, free.' So: I act thus."

To the surprise of everyone except Nell, he accepted an invitation, secured for him by an admirer, to lecture in economics at the University of Buenos Aires. "Why not?" he said, "I understand that the Argentine is a country where we Germans feel at home."

He said this often: many who heard it shivered at the irony, little understanding that, like all who are ironists by instinct, Eli found both sides of the coin equally true. "I act; therefore it is," he said with a smile that frightened.

Nell reproached herself when she found her love transmuted to dislike. Her reproach was the keener because she found nothing for which to reproach Eli. He was a model husband, faithful, honourable, in his manner loving. That side of things was all right. He was a doting father when Becky was little; nevertheless one who was firm when firmness was needed. All that was fine. She could see too that he was admirable. He worked hard, provided for them.

She went over these things in her head again and again. When they made love, it was still all right, and almost what it had been. And yet of course she reproached him, if only to justify the dislike she was forming, experiencing indeed, the way you experience the beauty of a view or the cold of a winter morning. She told herself: it was his cynicism. He would talk of "the morality of sympathy as the symptom of a weak age". Then the rebellious thought struck her: he is spouting the poison with which they tried to kill him. When he said, "It is absurd to suppose that reconciliation is possible between Jew and Arab," she wondered at his indifference. For really he didn't seem to care. "I observe things, that's all," he boasted, "and state what I see. It's not a matter of drawing conclusions."

Nell experienced the cynicism as aridity, and found wastes of sand extending in every direction from the point where she had made her life. Kinsky was her only confidant; even to him, she did not dare confess the profundity of Eli's cynicism. After all, Kinsky in a lighter manner was a cynic himself. What shocked her was that Eli seemed every day to confront the question "Why go on?" and then shrug it off.

"You don't need to worry," Kinsky said, "he has got beyond suicide. So have we all, unless we are corrupted by guilt and pity."

What she couldn't say was that the thought of Eli's suicide drifted into her mind as a means of escape for her.

But now at last she was angry. His refusal to meet Franz was wounding Becky. She told him he was a coward, that he was afraid of the memories which meeting Franz would stir. Then she accused him of jealousy. He smiled, and admitted it.

"And I don't see the point of it," she said, "since they are in love, and will certainly marry."

She was sure of that herself now, since her tea with Ilse. Indeed, though Ilse was a silly woman, they were on the way to being friends. Her kindness was irresistible. She even suggested that her husband, the General, could put himself about to improve Eli's pension position: it was wrong that such a distinguished man should suffer even genteel poverty. And she looked at Nell as though she thought she could do with a new pair of shoes.

"But I understand," Eli said, "that the young man hasn't yet spoken to his own father."

"I'm sure he has."

"No, my dear, you know he hasn't. I have asked Becky. When he does, then things will be on a different footing."

"Very well," Nell said, "Becky will see to it."

"So what?" Luis said. "Everyone's afraid of his father. That's life. Father is like God."

"Oh you make a joke of everything," Franz said.

They were in the little bar on the Florida again. Luis ordered more beer.

"So I make a joke of everything?" he said. "What else can you do here in Argentina, in the year of our Lord 1964?"

"Even Perón?"

Luis drank some beer, licking the foam from his lips. "Especially Perón. Perón is one big joke. That is why I believe in him, in his neces-sary return. He is the prince of jokes."

"Was Kennedy a joke?"

"Of course. *Ich bin ein Berliner* – in a Boston accent. Didn't you tell me a Berliner is a kind of bread roll? Let's go to Rosita's…"

"No, but wait. I can't see my father as a joke. You don't know him. He has never even raised his voice to me…"

"That girl who looks like the Sainted One, I tell you, *mon vieux*, she is one hot cookie, as they say in Boston. A veritable Berliner. So what? So he doesn't raise his voice. Does that make him less of a joke? I bet he wears dark glasses inside. He does? Right, you can stand me the girl like the Sainted One. Or we could have her together. How would that be? I get a stand thinking of it. Look."

He swung back on the chair to make the truth of his words visible. Franz shook his head.

"No," he said, "I have promised Becky."

"What? That you won't come to Rosita's with me? Really, old chap, you shouldn't talk of such things with your fiancée, it isn't nice."

"No, not that, fool." Franz smiled at his friend. "I don't know what I would do without you, Luis. No, I'm going to tell my father tomorrow. And that will be hard enough, without a night in your company at Rosita's."

"Pity," Luis said. "I liked the idea. But have it your own way. So why should your father object?"

"I've told you a thousand times."

"And I still can't believe you. Tell me again."

Franz paused. He looked across the room, soft red mouth a little open. Luis, catching that profile, felt the urge to hurt. Franz had that effect on him, often. He was a victim, Luis thought, but a victim who should be in uniform, and on his knees, crying for mercy.

"Tell me again…"

"Because her father is a Jew. It sounds silly, now, doesn't it?"

"No," Luis said, "it's only a sick joke: that a German should still dare to object to a Jew. Come to Rosita's. I'll even pay for you."

"Oh very well, but I'll pay for myself."

"Well, we'll have her together. Have you ever done that?"

"No," Franz blushed.

"Of course, I was forgetting. You're in love with Becky, and true to her, despite being a queer at heart." He put his arm round Franz's shoulder and hugged him. "I adore you. You know that. Now let's go get our balls swallowed. We'll make a man of you yet."

"Of course I know of the girl's father," Rudi said. "He's a distinguished man, even if he has been unfortunate. I am only disappointed you didn't speak to me sooner. You have obviously been wondering about the matter. Remember, son, all I am interested in is your happiness. It has not been easy being a good father, in the circumstances…"

He took off his dark glasses and rubbed his knuckles into his eyes. He rubbed hard, and when he took his hands away, Franz saw that the eyes were a little bloodshot.

"Everything I've done has been done for you," Rudi said.

He beckoned the waiter, asked him to bring them a bottle of champagne.

"I'm a man with few friends," he said. "I live for my work and my family, which is indeed reduced to you, Franz. Now you are going to add to it. Of course I am pleased."

Franz was suffused with guilt, love and pity: inextricable emotions. He had been wrong to doubt his father, right to love him. What he had thought of as a frightening self-sufficiency was revealed as loneliness. Rudi lifted his glass: "Your health, and the young lady's." The wrong picture flashed before Franz's eyes: the young girl, with the puffy lips, Isabellita, lowering her mouth towards him ... he felt himself blush.

"Ah, I can see that you are in love," Rudi said, and drank his champagne. "There's a lot I could tell you about marriage, but as for now, all that is necessary is to express my happiness and wish you well..."

If Luis had been there, he would no doubt have found his father's formal archaic manner of speaking yet another joke. But Franz was overcome with relief. I need Becky, he told himself, trying to slide her image on to the screen. But it was still the wrong face that he saw.

"And you know her father's Jewish?"

"Are you apologising for that? You must not do so. They are a remarkable race. Consider what they have achieved in Israel."

It was the moment to ask what he had always desired, and feared, to know. The sensation of intimacy was such as to suggest that Rudi might answer. Yet he dared not risk shattering it. He picked up his glass.

"I'm so grateful," he said.

"And your mother approves?"

"Oh yes, she has quite taken to Becky. I'm sure you will too."

"I'm sure I shall. But up country, of course, it's a different type of girl that I am accustomed to."

Franz telephoned Becky as soon as he had said goodbye to his father.

"It's fine. He approves. It's amazing. He's going to get in touch with your father himself. I can't believe it was so easy. I can't think what we have been worrying about. I love you."

"I love you too. Oh, what a relief."

"Isn't life marvellous?"

Nell read the letter from Franz's father to Eli. He listened without interrupting. She sipped her tea, which was almost cold. Eli took his napkin and wiped egg from his face. He had become a messy eater, something which displeased her because he had once been fastidious.

"It's a good letter," she said. "He writes well."

"A bureaucrat's style, and he misused the subjunctive in the third sentence."

"I don't suppose he writes many letters," she said, "except business ones. Anyway, the main point is that he says the right things."

"Oh yes, he says the right things."

"And we shall of course accept his invitation."

Rudi had invited them to lunch with him, en famille as he put it, at the Engineers' Club the following Sunday; he would fly down specially for the occasion, though it wasn't, as he remarked, a weekend when he would customarily find himself in the city; nevertheless he was eager to enjoy the pleasure of meeting the parents of the girl his dear Franz so wished to marry.

"Wouldn't it be better if he came here?" Eli said.

They were sitting at the table where they took all their meals, except for the more and more numerous ones which Eli preferred to have served on a tray, which was then fixed on to the armrest of the high-backed wooden chair where he passed most of his days. Nell's eye took in the faded cushions, the stains on the carpet, especially in the vicinity of Eli's chair. It was raining that morning, slanting on a brisk south-easterly, and the windows of the apartment were closed, as Eli anyway preferred that they should be. The light was murky in their living-room, and the air rank with the smell of Eli's cigars and the myriad unpleasant odours of a room that is almost permanently inhabited.

"No," she said, "he has invited us. It would be rude to suggest that he change his plans to fit us."

Besides, she thought, if that is what you preferred, you shouldn't have been so reluctant to make the first move.

A little later, Nell left to do the shopping. She was glad to be out in the streets. The rain had stopped, but most of the women were dressed in raincoats, or carried umbrellas. She supposed they had domestic problems of their own, but there was something reassuring in their manner of going about their business. There was an air of subdued opulence to this part of the city. People grumbled about the inflation, but half the women she saw were carrying plastic bags which proclaimed that they had made purchases at the sort of stores which Nell scarcely ever entered now. She wondered if she should buy a new dress for Sunday, decided her grey with the white collar would have to do. There would be enough – too much – more than they could afford – to be spent on the wedding.

She telephoned Ilse from a coffee shop, to tell her about the letter.

"Are you to be there?"

"No," Ilse said, "at least I haven't been asked, and wouldn't expect to be."

"Oh, I had hoped you might lend me moral support."

"Darling, you won't need it. Rudi can be difficult and unpredictable, but he's not an ogre. Besides, from what Franz says, he's determined to do everything correctly. He'll be the soul of politeness."

Eli had grumbled at being forced into a suit, made to wear a tie. Now that he could no longer see how others were dressed, he had grown contemptuous of the whole business. It was as if he wished to force notice of his disability and his poverty on everyone, as if he took pleasure in making others uncomfortable. No, there was no "as if" about it; he definitely did. But Becky had coaxed him into acquiescence. He complained that the trousers were too tight – he hadn't worn them for a year; and Nell was surprised to find that she hadn't noticed he had put on weight.

Franz and his father were waiting for them in an anteroom, a dingy place with heavy black furniture and bad, dark, late nineteenth-century oils depicting mythological scenes in a self-indulgent manner. There was a "Judgement of Paris", remarkable only for the manner in which the light fell on Paris, to whose charms the eye was therefore directed to the exclusion of those of the three goddesses, doubtless an unintentional manifestation of the painter's own interests. Paris looked rather like Franz actually, as Becky later pointed out, to his embarrassment.

Nell's first thought was that Franz's father was quite unremarkable. From Becky's account of the guarded, even fearful, respect with which Franz viewed him, and also from what Ilse had said, she had built up the image of someone who would be formidable from the start. Instead she saw a small man, a slight man, with thin, black, receding hair, high cheekbones and a prim mouth; he wore dark glasses even in the gloom of that dismal chamber, and, though he had first wiped his hand on the back of his trousers, the palm that enclosed hers felt damp.

There was, again, a hesitation as to what language should be spoken. Franz and Becky habitually conversed in English; so of course did Becky and her mother. Nell and Eli nowadays usually spoke English too, so that was really the language of their household. On the other hand, Franz spoke German with his father, and chiefly Spanish with his mother. Spanish would have been the neutral language, and was indeed that in which Franz's father greeted them, apologising to Nell for the poor quality of his English.

"I learned it at school," he said, "and then had little cause to use it for a long time, and now, when I am compelled to speak it, I do so, I think, with an American accent which you might dislike."

"Oh no," she said in German, "Franz has a slight American accent, which I find very pleasing. "

They went through to the dining room. There were the two old pederasts, picking over their Wiener schnitzel in preparation for their Sousa, and, as before, darting timid glances at Franz, who was, again, uneasily conscious of their direction and import. And there was also this week a family party, celebrating, it seemed, a birthday, for, very soon after Franz's father had ushered his guests to the corner table he had reserved, a large cake was brought to the other party and greeted with loud hand-clapping and cheers.

Franz's father had ordered champagne, which was already on ice. Eli alone declined it, expressing a preference for a still wine, which was immediately ordered.

"I very rarely drink champagne myself," Franz's father said, "certainly not French champagne, which I cannot often afford, but I thought it appropriate to the occasion. But we have a very nice hock here, on which we pride ourselves, and between you and me, Doctor, it is a better wine than this fizzy stuff."

They occupied themselves with the menu, which was short.

"We eat so many steaks at the site," Franz's father said, "that I am always eager to eat something different on my rare visits to the city. I can recommend the goulash, it's always well spiced."

Nell and Becky obediently followed his advice. Eli ordered a steak, which Nell would have to cut up for him. Franz had a steak too. They talked for a little about the wedding. They were agreed that it was desirable that Franz and Becky both finish their course at the University.

"Nevertheless," Rudi said, "there is no absolute reason why they should not be married while still students. I'm told it is quite common now. One doesn't wish to be old-fashioned. What do you think, Doctor? You know more about university matters than I. Is it your opinion that early marriage disturbs study?"

"I know no more than the next man about these matters."

"Besides," Nell said, "it's impossible to generalise."

She couldn't understand why she had felt uneasy. Franz's father was an ordinary little man, nice, eager to please, rather dull she thought. Well, that mightn't be fair. This wasn't the sort of encounter at which you were expected to scintillate. She asked him about his work.

"Building a bridge," he said, "well, it's always an interesting challenge. One feels one is doing something worthwhile, at least. Of course, in this country, the quality of labour is the problem. The inflation, also, it adds unpredictably to the cost of the project. It's impossible to remain within the original estimate. Of course, that is allowed for in the contract."

The strains of Sousa came from the next room: "The Stars and Stripes Forever". Eli wrinkled his nose.

"I'm quite of your opinion," Rudi said, "empty tedious stuff."

"I suppose it's harmless. I don't care for military music. And as you say it's tedious."

"I've always-liked a brass band," Nell said, "and it's cheerful." She waggled her fork in time to the music.

"Well," Rudi said, "I suppose it is pleasant trivia, but we men look for the sublime in music, don't we, Doctor?"

"They tell me you are an enthusiast for Brahms."

"Now that is music."

"Unfortunately one can't tell a man's character from the music he likes. I love Brahms myself." Eli took a piece of bread from the basket and mopped up the gravy on his plate. Rudi did the same.

"I've been told," he said, "that to eat in this manner, as we are both doing, is a sign that you have been really hungry. So we are alike there too, Doctor."

"You can't be surprised that I have known extreme hunger," Eli said. "How long have you lived in Argentina?"

"Seventeen years, no eighteen … a long time. With all its faults I have come to think of it as my country. Germany seems a long way distant. To tell the truth I sometimes catch myself thinking in Spanish now. But my Spanish is very poor – I mean grammatically. It is the vulgar Spanish of work camps and illiterate labourers."

"Quite so," Eli pushed his plate aside. "And why did you decide to come here?"

"Oh, I made a mistake. I thought Germany was finished. I looked round after the war at the piles of rubble and the people's faces, and I said to myself, 'That's it, *kaputt*, there's no future here. It's no place to bring up my family' – which, as events have shown, 'the German miracle' as they call it, was wrong. Nevertheless, since young Franz has turned out here as he has, I can't regret it. Do you ever think," he turned to Nell, "do you ever think of the strange workings of Fate? Consider: the diversity of background, the concatenation of circumstances, the sheer, as we interpret it, series of accidents, that have been necessary to bring these two young people together, and now we look at them" – he raised his glass to each, to Becky, who was smiling with the happiness of her certainty that this meeting to which she had looked forward with such apprehension was rolling along with the ease and comfort of a luxurious motor-car, to Franz, who leaned over to place his hand on Becky's and give it a little squeeze – "yes, we look at these dear children," Rudi resumed, "well, not exactly children, we don't wish to insult you by calling you children – nevertheless that is how we must think of you – and what are the words that come irresistibly into our mouths? That they are made for each other. Yes? Isn't it so? Isn't it extraordinary to think of all that has been necessary, sometimes painfully necessary, let's not forget that, and yet the culmination, the end result, as they say, of it all is something so sublimely right? Isn't it, Doctor, like the working out of the great themes of a symphony?"

Eli sniffed. "Chance," he said, "nothing but chance. Life is a series of random happenings. Isn't that what the physicists tell us now?"

"Ah, but man is a pattern-making animal. From these apparently random happenings, it is our instinct to create significant shapes. Isn't that so? Again, I return to the image of a symphony."

"Which comes to a resolution of its themes? Very well, but this is imposed on events by the intelligence."

"Or extracted from them?"

"And, tell me, I am interested," Eli said, "do you find such a pattern in your own personal history?"

"In my intellectual development, certainly. But this is conversation for another occasion, too serious perhaps for our present celebrations."

He turned to Becky. "I am very anxious to get to know my new, or rather prospective, daughter-in-law. What are your principal interests, my dear?"

"Oh, nothing much, the usual things."

"Come," he said, "you are a modern girl, even in Argentina, which is not a modern country. You have your ambitions, you don't see yourself as a hausfrau, I think?"

"Well, not exactly, and Franz doesn't see me like that either."

"Good. Excellent," Rudi smiled. It was a thin smile, a smile with a nervous authority behind it. He was in charge of the situation. He teased her, complimented Nell, made a little unmemorable joke. He was like a conductor; they all followed his lead. The waiter brought them pudding, the Club speciality again, that concoction of fruit, pastry and cream. Rudi said, "I judge a girl by her ability to eat at least two helpings of this. I'm sure you won't let me down."

Over coffee, Eli asked him what part of Germany he came from.

"Oh, I am a Saxon. Yes," he smiled, "I know what they say, a stupid Saxon. My father was an official in the postal service, but he had the good fortune to marry a girl from the Rhineland, so that I perhaps escaped something of the dull muddiness of the Saxons. But of course I have inherited some valuable qualities from my Saxon forefathers: persistence, I think, a refusal to give up."

Franz and Becky made their excuses. There was a concert they had tickets for. They left with good wishes and smiles and the feeling that the lunch had been more of a success than they dared hope. When they got into Franz's little car, they kissed, in relief and self-congratulation.

Rudi lit a thin black cheroot. He remarked that details of the wedding would, he supposed, be for Nell and Ilse to arrange. "Always remember only that you may rely on my co-operation. I am sure it is all going to be a splendid success." He began to talk of Argentina's problems, speculating, as everyone did, on the prospects of stemming the inflation; then apologised for his presumption in doing so in the presence of "a real economist, even an expert, if I may say so, in such matters."

Eli lifted his head, directed his blind gaze at him.

"It doesn't trouble you," he said, "that I am a Jew?"

Rudi waved his cigar.

"I find that all out of date," he said. "Yes, I confess to having once had a prejudice in that direction, as was common, but, now, let us say, I have learned better."

"That is kind of you," Eli said.

Nell held her breath, tried to think of a means of redirecting the conversation, failed, as Rudi said, "Come, let us be honest with each other, Herr Professor. I know what you want to know. Was I a Nazi?" He smiled, as if calling Nell to admire his boldness. "But of course I was. There. You would not believe me if I said otherwise." He sat back, like a child pleased to have given the correct answer to a catch question, or like an alcoholic who has refused a drink.

"Yes," he said, "I don't mind admitting that I saw Hitler as our Man of Destiny. But you yourself, I think, worked with Schacht in the Reichsbank, and the success of your work there contributed, did it not, to the high regard in which the Fuehrer was increasingly held?"

"God forgive me, yes."

"Precisely. God forgive you. All of us Germans who survived have need of forgiveness. We went astray, horribly astray, and we did so, did we not, on account of our idealism?"

FOUR

Kinsky once suggested that Eli's blindness was psychosomatic. That was too simple, even naive, an explanation, life, apart from other considerations, rarely working out so neatly. Yet there was of course an uncanny neatness to it – as he understood himself. He had been wilfully blind in the Thirties, and the pressure of denying his blindness had contributed to that isolation which his physical blindness at last confirmed. He had for a quarter of a century or more resisted the temptation of introspection, resisted that other temptation of indulging his guilt, had maintained, if ever the matter was raised, that he had been right to work with Schacht for Germany's economic recovery – even at the price of bolstering Hitler. Without prosperity," he would say, "there is no possibility of civilised politics." His had been indeed a form of idealism, and in conversation, in the middle Thirties, at least as late as 1937, he had even been prepared to grant to individual Nazis credit for being imbued with the same sort of idealism themselves – as Rudi still claimed. They had formed their opinions, Eli would say, in reaction to the moral disintegration of Weimar, which itself expressed its nature in the disintegration of the currency. Nell had heard these arguments too often. Now, when they no longer spoke of serious matters, scarcely could be said to converse at all in this bleak winter of their marriage, she wondered if he still rehearsed them over and over again in frozen solitude. Was his addiction to Brahms in some curious way an attempt to claim that everything he had thought and done could be reconciled, as indeed Rudi had asserted, into a satisfying symphonic pattern, that mystery could be accommodated, inconsistencies reconciled?

Kinsky came to see them that evening. He was eager to hear how the lunch had gone. Nell was pleased to see him. His arrival would break the enveloping silence. "I think it went all right," she whispered to him in the kitchen before admitting him to the living room where Eli sat smoking, sliding his hand along the cat's back, listening to sounds from the street, listening harder, she feared, to voices from the past. She made coffee, brought in a cake: Kinsky had always had a sweet tooth.

"Well," Eli said, "a father's consent is, I understand, out of date."

"Darling, it was in our time too," Nell said, exasperated. He paid her no attention.

"It's odd," he said to Kinsky, "how relieved I was to hear him confess to having been a Nazi. I wouldn't have believed him if he had denied it. Well, I said to myself, at least I understand you. That's a basis."

"But you are troubled, old friend," Kinsky said.

"Why should I be? In this new life in the New World, isn't it natural that my daughter should choose without reference to the past? A past which survives only in one's own head?"

"Of course," Kinsky said, "nobody now believes that the sins of the fathers should be visited on the children."

He took a forkful of coffee cake, sipped coffee. There came to Nell an incongruous picture: Kinsky with his head shaved, his shoddy prison suit emblazoned with the pink triangle, slurping thin vegetable soup, hot water through which vegetables had been strained: the same man, the same life.

"What does the man do at his bridge?" Eli said.

"Oh, he's an engineer, I gather. Not the top man. A functionary, doubtless efficient."

"And protected?"

"If he needs protection still, undoubtedly yes."

It was growing dark. They had none of them thought to switch on the electric light. Eli puffed at his cigar, withdrawing into contemplation. The telephone rang. Nell answered it. It was Ilse, also anxious to learn how the meeting had gone. Nell spoke in a light, cheerful manner. Ilse was relieved. Nell understood how her happiness too was bound up in the happiness of her son and their daughter. Ilse laughed: "Oh it is so good to hear you speak like this, my dear. We must have lunch together, to make plans. Tomorrow? Why not? Excellent. Will you come here? I am so happy."

"That was Ilse. She had been worrying. You know, I think she has become really fond of Becky, for the child's own sake as well as on account of Franz's happiness."

"Of course she is," Kinsky said. "How could she fail to? Becky is such a sweet child, always has been. And so intelligent. Ilse's not intelligent herself, of course, but Becky is sufficiently intelligent not to make her uncomfortable. She has tact. This is an excellent cake, as always, my dear. May I have another slice, please?"

Eli said, "All the same, there's something wrong."

"What?"

But at that moment the door opened and Franz and Becky entered. The atmosphere changed: they glowed with youth and love. They carried hope in their eyes and their every movement. Even Eli sensed it. Becky kissed him, and he smiled. They had gone, after the concert, to the cinema at the University Film Club: a revival of *Sunset Boulevard*. "You never saw anything like it," she said, "like Scott Fitzgerald gone crazy."

During that night, Nell felt Eli turn over, heard him mutter, "I won't believe it."

When she taxed him with it in the morning, he said he didn't know what she was talking about.

"I must have been speaking in my sleep."

"Are you sure," she said, "there's nothing you want to tell me?"

He paused: "Nothing."

As soon as Nell had gone for lunch with Ilse, Eli made some telephone calls. At last he obtained the number he wanted and dialled it. He was asked to hold, then Franz's father came on to the telephone.

"This is a pleasant surprise."

"I wanted to thank you first for the lunch yesterday."

"Not at all. It was a pleasure to meet you and your gracious lady. Not to speak of your charming daughter. I quite understand my son's feeling for her."

"There is something else," Eli said. "It may not seem important to you, but it is something you said. You remarked that you had inherited a quality from your Saxon forefathers. Now I have forgotten what it was, and I have reached a stage in life when little things, like such acts of forgetfulness, irritate me, perhaps unreasonably. Would you mind repeating it?"

"My dear chap, what could I have said? Let me think. Ah yes, persistence, a refusal to give up. We Saxons, you know, are like old dogs that have got hold of a bone, and won't let it go, however mangy."

"Thank you," Eli said. "You will, I am afraid, find all this very stupid. But you can't imagine, until it happens, how painful the process of ageing can be. And how humiliating."

"Not at all. I'm delighted to have been able to put your mind so easily to rest. And, if I may say so, I observed no sign of any diminution of your faculties."

"How could you tell?"

"Oh, I have long known your reputation, and admired your work, in so far, that is, as a poor engineer can understand its more rarefied flights."

"I see," Eli said. "I had wondered – I tend to an uncertainty about such matters, owing to my blindness – I had wondered if we had met before."

He held his breath, imagined, in the pause that followed, a pause as long perhaps as it might take a man to draw on a cigarette and expel the smoke, that he felt a similar intake of breath shudder along the telephone wires from the works hut far to the north where Rudi sat sweating in a work-shirt, the telephone damp in his hand; he imagined calculation.

Rudi said, "You must develop a sensitivity to voices, but it is inconceivable that you could have remembered mine. I once addressed a question to you, after a lecture, at the University. You couldn't possibly have remembered that."

"Of course not," Eli said. "What I heard, doubtless, was the echo of another time."

"Just that," Rudi said. "We are rich in memories, or cursed by them. But now, with the prospect of this marriage between these two dear children, we are about to construct happier ones, the final allegro of the symphony."

He paused again. Eli heard talk in the background. Rudi's voice returned.

"I am so sorry, I am required urgently. I was so pleased to meet you yesterday and your gracious wife, and of course charming daughter. To our next meeting…"

Eli restored the telephone to its rest, lit a cheroot. His hands were trembling. He called out to the cat, which, with a loud miaow, leaped on to his knees. He sat there, stroking, puffing, perplexed.

He hesitated. Everything told him he should consult Nell, but he could not bring himself to do so. It had always been his habit to take decisions without advice. He disdained reliance on another's judgement – it didn't accord with the picture he held of his own being that he should act other than by himself. "I act, therefore it is." That was it; he had always held to that view of reality. A man's first duty is to his own nerve, and nerve, in this sense, implied first of all the act of judgement. Very well, that was clear. It was the only way he had ever been able to continue to be himself.

"All good things," he said to himself, "approach their goal crookedly. Like cats" – he stroked Biba – "they arch their backs, they purr inwardly over their approaching happiness; all good things laugh."

He had no evidence. But he had always proceeded without evidence. It was what had marked out his genius from those of his colleagues who had pursued a more careful path. He had struck out, blindly – and been proved right. Yes, right, he said to himself, even when the world judged me wrong. And by the standards of a certain world, he would be wrong again now. The more wrong, the more right. "Cast out false gods," he said to Biba. He had always loved cats. They lived for themselves, taking what they needed, and, because they acted in accord with their natures, what they needed was good and did not disgust them. He too knew what he needed now. It was not revenge. It might not even be justice, for he distrusted justice as practised. What then? He laughed again. The words had been supplied for him: the working-out of the symphony, the right shape, something beyond and above justice. He picked up the telephone again.

His second call got him the name and number he required. He placed a call to Tel Aviv, made his contact, spoke for ten minutes, was redirected to Vienna. "There is no proof," he said, "only my own certainty. No doubt you receive many such calls. The world is full of aggrieved lunatics. I understand that. I merely give you my information, throw a stone into the pond. Over to you."

Where, he thought, will the ripples end? These idiot Nazis worshipped Nietzsche, whom they could not read. Didn't they know the last meaningful words he wrote before the cloud of madness enveloped him? They were in a letter "to friend Overbeck and his wife": "Although you have so far demonstrated little faith in my ability to pay, I yet hope that I am somebody who pays his debts – for example, to you. I am just having all the anti-Semites shot." He signed it, "Dionysus", that figure who stands for "the older, still rich and even overflowing Hellenic instinct, the will to life..."

Yes, he thought, even a blind unsexed economist can retain that, whereas those who so misread the only philosopher who understood the interplay of emotion and reality, substituted for it the will to death. And there is no contradiction, despite appearances, when I say triumphantly, "I am having all the anti-Semites shot…" The will to life accepts the need, the probability of death.

He laughed again: "Biba," he said, "cats are the only true Nietzscheans. Perhaps I too am a cat, or an honorary one."

Franz and Becky were playing tennis, a doubles match on a covered court at the Polo Club against Luis and his fiancée Gabriella, a dark beauty of seventeen who regarded Becky with a mixture of admiration, envy and disapproval: she herself refused to allow Luis to kiss her, except in greeting, and then only in company. She was almost silent in his presence, but chattered like a sparrow when alone with Becky, who in turn liked her without understanding her, and admired the languorous grace of her tennis. The two pairings were well matched: Franz was steady, Becky adroit at the net, Luis capable of spurts of inexplicable brilliance, Gabriella rich in dreamy passing shots. They had taken to playing once a week, before lunch, when they would drink beer or Coca-Cola and eat hot cheese sandwiches. Becky was the only one of the four whose parents were not members of the Polo Club. She had felt shy there at first, self-conscious before the older members, one of whom she had heard ask what that little Jew girl was doing here. On being told that she was engaged to the son of Señora Rubin de Cevellos, the General's wife, the questioner had laughed and asked what the world was coming to. "We'll be having niggers here next," she added. "I'm surprised we don't," her friend said, "considering the American influence and the sort of people admitted now. I always say, 'Where the Jews lead, the niggers follow.' "

Becky saw Franz flush, and laid her hand on his arm.

"It wasn't worth it," she said as soon as they were out of hearing, "never worth making a scene about such things."

He allowed himself to be persuaded, but felt ashamed a week later when Luis overheard a much milder anti-Semitic remark – one that might almost have been no more than a joke – and demanded – and got – an apology.

"You can't let them get away with it," Luis explained. "I've no love for Jews in general myself – making exception of course for friends like Becky, who, as you know, is far too good for you, old chap. But that's not the point. It's a matter of honour. Nobody can insult anyone with whom I choose to associate. That's all there is to it. You lack a proper pride, old boy. I suppose it comes from being German and accustomed to defeat.

Remember old Prince Bolkonski in *War and Peace* deriding Napoleon and asking whom he had ever beaten?"

"Yes, Luis, you've told me often. Only Germans. Everyone ..."

Luis joined in the chorus, "Everyone has always beaten the Germans."

"Anyway," Franz said, "I think I am an Argentinian. I carry an Argentinian passport."

They came off the court now, Franz and Becky having taken the third set 8–6. The boys were sweating like colts after a gallop, Becky was flushed, laughing, panting, red-faced indeed, hanging on to Franz's arm despite disapproving stares. Only Gabriella, showing no more than a touch of dewiness, seemed unaffected by the match.

"What a game," Franz laughed.

"Yes," Gabriella said, "I enjoyed it."

"So, you see," Franz laughed again, "you see, Luis, this time Prince Bolkonski was wrong."

"Not at all, you carry an Argentinian passport, don't you, and besides, Becky is half-English, only half-German, and that half" – he raised his voice – "Jewish, and no doubt that made all the difference, for you must anyway admit, *mon vieux*, that it was her interceptions of my returns of your not very formidable service which really settled things. And now, my friends, the human frame – this one anyway – calls out for beer."

The boys were drinking their second bottles and they were all (except Gabriella who managed things more dextrously) licking the hot cheese which had escaped the sandwiches, from their fingers, when the steward approached to tell Franz there was a telephone call for him from his mother. He rose, languid as any athlete after effort, and lounged across the room, his sweater thrown around his shoulders, the sleeves dangling free. Becky couldn't but be aware how many other eyes followed his progress, and hugged the thought. Luis ordered more beer for himself and Franz, and a second bottle for Becky. Gabriella made a little moue.

"If you get fat, I will not marry you."

"Then there will be a scandal, such a scandal."

"You would be absolutely right, Gaby," Becky said. "A fat Luis would be disgusting."

"Let me tell you, young lady, that there is no prospect of that, none at all. Gabriella here will be fat before me, which will not of course alter my undying love, we men being more constant, you see."

Franz returned, sat down, picked up his beer.

"Is something wrong?" Becky said.

For a moment he didn't answer. She wondered if he hadn't heard or was pretending not to.

"No," he said, lighting a cigarette. "No. I don't think so. Mamma wanted to know if I could tell her where my father is. Apparently she couldn't find him at the site number."

"For me," Gabriella said, "it is very strange that people should think it right to divorce, and even stranger that divorced couples should think to communicate directly with each other."

"For you, my angel," Luis said, "most things in the modern world are strange. That is why I am marrying you: to learn more about the habits of thought inculcated in an eighteenth-century convent."

"You are a liar. You are marrying me because I am beautiful and my family is rich and well connected and your mother approves of the match."

"He seems not to have left a number where he can be reached. That is unusual."

"Are you sure your mother has got it right?" Becky said.

"Well, she is sure. She is puzzled."

"You have told me yourself that she sometimes gets muddled up on the telephone. That's all."

"Still," Gabriella said, "I find it strange. If a marriage has gone wrong, then it seems to me the civilised thing is ..."

"Angel, they have unfinished business – Franz here – of course they have to communicate."

"All the same," Franz said, "I don't understand your attitude."

"I just don't want you to be worried," Becky said, "when there may be nothing to worry about. That's all."

They went and showered, changed out of their tennis things, returned in cashmere sweaters (Becky's a present from Franz) to play bridge, for which Luis had a passion. The afternoon drifted away. They sat in the bay window that overlooked the polo lawns. It was the off season, but some stable-boys were exercising the ponies. Two or three times Becky lifted her eyes from the green baize and looked out across the grass to the scrubland beyond and saw horsemen emerge along the winding tracks that led through the heather, broom and birch, planted there long ago by the Englishmen who had founded the Polo Club, and who perhaps shared Nell's desire to think of the place as a South Atlantic Surrey. The riders would be city people – lawyers, businessmen, even perhaps teachers at the University or some of the private schools – who kept their horses at livery at the Polo Club stables, and rode regularly for exercise or recreation, or to remind themselves of their youth on family estancias, perhaps to pretend to themselves or others that they had had such a youth. But the riders completed for Becky the picture already formed by the dim comfort of the leather-chaired club room, the riffling of cards being shuffled over the green baize, the afternoon tea with Dundee cake which they would order between the first and second rubbers; it was a well-ordered picture composed in accordance with established principles, one that excluded the poverty of the shanty-towns and the uncertainties that simmered under the surface of the country's life and occasionally erupted into violence that had no aim beyond the satisfaction of some obscure impulse.

Becky was dummy and crossed over to the window. The declining sun touched the birches with rose. Over to her left the lights of the city were coming on. A boy and a girl rode out of the woods, holding each the other's hand as the ponies picked their way along the track. Then the path divided round a statue – the life-sized figure of some Hero of the Liberation – and the girl's hand fell away from the boy's, their ponies slanted either side of the statue, and then both were lost to her sight beyond the range of the window.

She turned round. The sunlight lay butter-golden on her lover's cheek. Then the steward, with a word of apology, pulled a string and the curtains drew together, closing them into the intimacy of the card room, and the world out.

"I'm sorry," Franz said, "the contract depended on a finesse…"

"Your bidding was wrong," Luis said. "Bridge is a matter of fitting your actions to the information available. Of course it requires flair too, but fundamentally it's a science."

"All the same," Becky said, "we went down because of Gaby's inspired bid, and you can't say that was scientific, Luis."

"I do not like counting," Gabriella said.

"Absolutely," Luis said, "Gabriella has flair, I possess the science. That's why we make an unbeatable team."

"Well," Becky said, "we're pretty good ourselves."

"I don't know about that," Franz said. "We went three down. Of course, if the finesse had come off…"

The next morning, Franz telephoned Becky before she was up.

"He sounds agitated," Nell told her.

"Oh dear." She perched in her white towelling dressing-gown on the arm of a chair, nestling the telephone between her cheek and a raised left shoulder. She answered in monosyllables, as Nell occupied herself in making coffee and bringing a cup for Becky. Then she went back to the kitchen. Eli was still in bed. She heard Becky say, "I'm sure you are making a fuss over nothing ... all right, not nothing ... but you said yourself how your mamma gets the wind up ... there is probably ... no, I'm not taking it lightly, I hate hearing you sound so worried ... but just think how it will annoy him if you barge in and there's nothing wrong ... all right then ... no, of course I'm not angry, I understand your concern, I just hate to hear you so worked up, when it may not be necessary ... yes, of course, I love you ... me too ..."

There was silence. Nell came through from the kitchen. Becky was still cradling the telephone. She held it out towards her mother before replacing it on its rest. Nell waited. Becky looked away.

"It's strange," she said. "Franz and his mother think his father has disappeared. I don't know anything about it. But it seems no one else does either. Franz is going to fly up there this afternoon."

Without waiting for a comment from her mother, she fled to her bedroom. There was no need, Nell thought, to mention this to Eli. They had maintained a silence about Rudi since the evening of their lunch together. Since then, however, Nell had found herself thinking of him as Rudi rather than as Franz's father. There had been something appealing about him, something lost and lonely; she saw his confidence as a shell, his authority as an act of assumption, precariously maintained. He was such an ordinary little man, with such an ordinary insignificant name, Rudi Schmidt, which must belong to thousands of others too, and she had pictured him in his evenings after work sitting in a room without character, or stretched out on his bed, in his work-clothes with only his shoes removed, waiting for night and the next morning when he would have a function again. He had the loneliness of a spoiled priest, she thought, and now, if he had really vanished, there would be no gap, no hole in experience, where he had been. It might be as if he had never lived.

But Franz was worried, and perhaps pained, and Becky too. With some reason, no doubt. You couldn't be absolutely indifferent if a German of Rudi's generation did a midnight flit. They all lived under a perpetual suspicion. The past of the whole people was disturbed by spectres. She picked up the telephone.

"Ilse," she said, "it's Nell.'

"Oh darling, I don't know what to say. It's all so strange…"

"But it may be nothing."

"That's true. Only…"

"He may have a girl somewhere."

"Oh, I don't think so."

"Or have had an accident."

"Yes, that is possible… Nell, we mustn't let this, whatever it is, affect the children. They love each other, we must bear that in mind."

"She was afraid. I don't know of what. But she was afraid."

Kinsky handed her a cup of coffee, lit a cigarette.

"Well," he said, "I expect you are right. You couldn't be wrong about recognising that, could you? Any more than I could. But, Nell, it may be nothing."

"Well, yes, that's true. Only I don't believe it. You don't either, do you?"

"Have you spoken to Eli of this?"

"No, not yet. I don't know why."

"You were afraid he would be pleased."

"Why should he be? The lunch went off all right. I think he doesn't dislike Franz, and, whatever else, he adores Becky. He wouldn't want her to be hurt. Why should I be afraid? But you're right, Kinsky, all the same. I don't know why."

Franz had a seat just in front of the wing. He looked down at the sea of grass, at the emptiness of this half-made land. Whenever he ventured from the city, even for visits to the estancia owned for a hundred and fifty years by Luis's family, he experienced a sense of insufficiency. There was a proverb Luis liked to quote: *Dios arregla de noche la macana que los Argentinos hacen de dia:* "God puts right at night the mess the Argentines make by day." He quoted it with a laugh, which frightened Franz. Mightn't it be, he sometimes thought, that God had in reality created Argentina as the ultimate ironic comment on the futility of his creation?

The pampas rolled below him. A line of Borges came into his head: *Sólo faltó una cosa: la vereda de entrente:* "Only one thing was lacking: the other side of the street." What an image of more than Argentinian existence! He ran his finger round inside his collar; the shirt stuck to his back. His mouth felt dry; for a moment he thought he was going to be sick, as the plane lurched in an air pocket. The hills came into view. Becky was to be the other side of his street, but would it be built?

The manager of the site had sent a car for him, an old Chevrolet. The driver chewed an unlit cigar. Franz hesitated whether to get into the front beside him, or to travel in the back like someone superior. He wondered which his father would have chosen. The driver made no move to help him decide, and when Franz opened the front door and settled himself beside him, neither removed the cigar nor made any remark. The radio whined love-songs. The man drove fast, not well, with much crashing of the gear box and sliding at corners. The car's tyres were lacking in tread.

Dr Santander, the site manager, received him in his office. There was coffee waiting, also *anis*. Dr Santander sipped at a sticky glass, and gave off a smell of unwashed flesh and unwashed clothes. He wore a short-sleeved flowered shirt, and sighed heavily.

"It is most inconvenient," he said. "You speak Spanish?"

"Yes, of course."

"It is most inconvenient," Dr Santander said again. He pushed a stubby glass across the desk towards Franz, swatted at a fly with an American girly magazine, missed.

"Three days ago," he said, "he didn't report for work. Perhaps he is ill, I thought. But no, his room is unoccupied. It is most inconvenient."

"And there was no message?"

Dr Santander sipped his *anis*.

"You don't drink," he said. "Why not?"

"Sorry." Franz picked up his glass, and sipped.

"We are busy here, very occupied. There is a penalty if the bridge is not completed on time, and now my second-in-command … evaporates …"

"Did he take luggage with him?"

Dr Santander sighed. He turned down the corners of his mouth, and picked up his magazine again, holding it aloft as if daring the fly to settle.

"It is possible," he said. "On the other hand it is possible not."

"Do you mind if I have a look at his house? It is a company house?"

"Perhaps."

"Have you reported his disappearance to the police?"

"Three days is inconvenient for me, but for the police, not so much. Maybe he has a girl…"

The blonde on his magazine cover was arched backwards over a low bench in what must have been, even for a gymnast, an uncomfortable position.

"Yes," Dr Santander said, "that is possible." The fly settled on his blotter. He struck, missed again, then, laying the magazine down, traced the line of the model's curves.

"Or perhaps something has happened to him. Perhaps he has been kidnapped. Isn't there perhaps some political group that doesn't want your bridge to be finished?"

"No," Dr Santander said, "everybody wants our bridge. It is a noble work. I am sorry there is nothing I can tell you. By all means, go and examine your father's house. By all means. I am happy to offer you my co-operation. Perhaps you will find evidence of a girl."

"And the police? Do you object if I consult the police?"

Dr Santander poured himself another *anis*, and sighed again.

"Up here, my young friend, people do not consult the police. The police consult them. Ask my secretary to direct you to your father's dwelling."

Dr Santander's secretary was a plump woman in her early thirties, who quickly told Franz that she was not Argentinian, despite her name, but French, and that she preferred to be addressed as Yvette rather than as Señora Jimenez.

"I don't choose to remember my husband too much," she said, "but it's better, I find, to be a married woman up here. Of course your father was always a gentleman."

"Dr Santander thinks he may have gone off with a girl. Does that seem likely?"

"It seems likely that Dr Santander would think so."

She escorted him to a concrete bungalow with an unfinished look, standing in a shabby street on the fringes of the little town. It was about two miles from the construction site.

"His car is here, you see," she said, pointing to a dark green Volkswagen, about five years old. "Nobody told me his car was still here. Of course he sometimes rode into the site on his bicycle. For exercise, he said."

She produced a key.

"Pedro – that's one of the office clerks – who went to look for him, found the door open, but locked it and brought the key to the office. It seemed the best thing to do."

There were two rooms in the bungalow, a narrow bedroom with a camp bed, a chest of drawers and a rail on which three suits were hanging, and a slightly larger living room with two wickerwork chairs, a television set, a row of bookshelves, and a table, with a single wooden chair thrust back from it. A recess contained a sink, a refrigerator, and a cooker. The plaster in both rooms was cracked, and a long wavy line ran across the ceiling of the living room. Bluebottles buzzed round a plate which lay on the table; there were scraps of potato, already acquiring a sheen of mould. A half-empty beer bottle and a smeared glass stood beside it. The single chair suggested that no one was ever invited to eat there. Apart from the evidence of the meal, the room was very neat. There was a pile of carefully folded newspapers beside one of the wicker chairs. The walls were bare of pictures, but there were two photographs on the top shelf above the books. Both were of Franz, one as a small boy kneeling beside a spaniel; the other, taken when he was about six-teen, show him in the cadet's uniform of his school. Franz picked up the one with the dog; the spaniel, Mutzi, had been the principal casualty of his parents' divorce. Ilse had insisted on keeping him, but the dog had pined for Rudi and died within the year.

"A house is a machine for living in," Yvette quoted, "if you call it living."

"I feel ashamed," Franz said. "It never occurred to me that he was so lonely."

He picked a record off the turntable – Schubert's *Winterreise* – dusted it, and restored it to its sleeve. Then he noticed that the control knob was still in the "on" position. He turned it off. He pulled open a drawer at the other end of the table from where his father ate. It contained some papers. There was a batch of his own letters, tied up in red ribbon, a bank book, bank statements and papers relating to tax. The drawer was very neat. There was space between the different bundles; pens, pencils and a rubber were precisely aligned.

The sound of cars driven fast, then stopping outside, disturbed them. Doors slammed, footsteps approached the house. The door was thrown open and a police lieutenant marched in followed by two other uni-formed officers. All were armed, and one of them had his pistol out of the holster. The lieutenant paused, smiled, inclined his head.

"It was reported to me that you had arrived."

He picked up the photograph of Franz as a cadet.

"Yes," he said, "I should have recognised you in any case. I am Lieutenant Vilar. Jorge Vilar. I think we must talk. I think we should talk alone. Forgive me, Señora Jimenez, my men will take you home."

"I have my car here, Lieutenant."

"In that case, they will follow you and see that you arrive safely. As I have remarked before, it is not wise for a lady to travel by herself after dark."

When they were alone, he took two bottles of beer from the refrigerator, and knocked the caps off. He handed one to Franz and waved him towards a chair. He himself stood in the middle of the room sucking at the neck of the bottle. His boots gleamed.

"So," he said, "this is a bad business."

"I understood from Dr Santander that he had not reported my father's ... disappearance. He believes there may be a girl in the case."

"It was not necessary for him to report it. I already knew. What I didn't know, and don't know, is why, and being ignorant of that I have not known whether I should report it elsewhere."

"I'm sorry, I don't understand you."

Lieutenant Vilar perched on the corner of the table. He drank from his bottle, dangled one long shiny boot, which held Franz's gaze.

"It is possible," he said, "that I know your father better than you know him yourself. You see, he has been in a sense my responsibility."

"I'm sorry," Franz said again, "I'm afraid you have lost me. Why should he be your responsibility?"

"At the same time, because of that, I have spent many evenings here, in conversation. He had much to teach me."

"But why was he your responsibility? Is it usual for police officers to be assigned responsibility for individual citizens?"

The lieutenant waved the idea away with his beer bottle. For a few minutes he did not speak. Instead he gazed at Franz. It was a sort of scrutiny, like the preliminary to investigation. Franz dropped his eyes.

"I flew up here, because we were worried. My mother had tried to telephone my father."

"On account of your forthcoming marriage?"

"Yes. How did you know of that?"

"It doesn't matter how I knew," he said. "Go on."

"No, I suppose not. Well, anyway, she was worried, and it seems rightly. I don't think he left of his own accord,"

"No?"

"This meal, not cleared away, that's not like him. And you say there is no girl."

"No, I didn't say that, but there isn't."

"Well then..."

Franz was at a loss. He had flown up not knowing what to expect, and everything since his arrival had confirmed his feeling of insignificance. He had led a sheltered life, he was accustomed to things happening as he wanted them to. He had rarely had to ask hard questions of himself; life fitted him like a well-made suit. It came to him that his lack of curiosity about his father had been total, reprehensible also. It had never occurred to him to wonder what his father was like when he himself wasn't there; it was as if his father had existed only for him. Of course, he had his excuses; he had always known that his father's past covered tracts of forbidden territory. But he had been happy never to seek to withdraw the blanket. Now he was the one who felt naked.

The lieutenant eyed him. Franz shifted in his chair.

"Your father has needed friends. I have been their representative. People only need friends when they already possess enemies. Hadn't you thought of that?"

He got off the table, flicked a speck of dust from his boot. "We will go and eat," he said. "Then I will tell you what you need to know."

They drove into the little town, and through it, to where a suburb straggled along the riverbank, and stopped at a tavern on the outskirts. The lights of the car showed up the rippling water, and the lieutenant said, "There used to be a dock here. Gone now. Finished." The tavern was a single long room with a line of tables against the wall. The lieutenant led Franz to the far end, and they settled themselves. There were only half a dozen other diners and the lieutenant had put a lot of space between them and the other occupied tables. He produced a long thin cigar, bit the end off and offered it to Franz. Then he lit one for himself and sat back against the whitewashed, but now grubby and smoke-stained wall. When a waitress approached he ordered steaks and a bottle of wine without consulting Franz.

"It is all they know how to cook," he said. "That and eggs. But I think you need a steak. When I have come here with your father, he always orders eggs but they are cooked in poor quality oil, I am afraid."

The waitress was a big girl, a *mestiza*, with wide hips and a sullen expression. The lieutenant scarcely looked at her, but Franz watched her progress up the room. She wore sandals which flapped as she walked. A man at another table stretched out his hand and pinched her bottom as she passed, but she paid no attention.

"Your father made love to her once a fortnight," the lieutenant said. "I don't think he even knows her name. She doesn't cost much."

Franz blushed.

"I wasn't thinking of her like that," he said.

"No?"

The lieutenant drew on his cigar.

"Is it possible," Franz said, "that my father has been kidnapped? By guerrillas?"

"We have no guerrillas in this district."

"It was only an idea I had. You said you were assigned to keep an eye on my father. Why was that? He's not a criminal."

The lieutenant laughed. It was a soft laugh, an expression less of amusement than of his sense of superiority.

"I am a philosopher," he said. "Perhaps you have studied philosophy at the University? I never had that opportunity, but nevertheless that is what I am. An existentialist. You know what that means? It means that reality is now. That is the only reality we have. Memories are real because they belong to now, but the past is not real, it is dead. So? You wonder why I tell you this. Well, for me, you see, your father is the man I have known, honourable, unambitious, thoughtful, yes perhaps a little dull, but nevertheless one with whom it is possible to converse. A luxury that, in a place like this! Very well, so I say to myself, perhaps he was not always that, but he is now. It is what he has made himself, what he has become. Life is a perpetual journey of becoming. Do you agree?"

Franz said, "I don't know, I've never really thought about it. I suppose I would say we are what we are rather than what we seem to be."

And then he thought of Luis standing naked over the girl who, he insisted, resembled the Sainted One, in the tawdry gold and purple of Rosita's establishment, and of Luis escorting Gabriella, and...

"So I am not interested," the lieutenant said, "except in my professional capacity in what a man may have done. What he is doing now is the expression of what he is, for we all possess the capability of performing the extremes of what is commonly called virtue and vice. We are all capable of anything, it seems to me."

"Are you saying there is no difference between a good man and a bad man?"

"The concepts are meaningless. There are only acts."

"But what has this to do with my father, or his disappearance?"

The waitress brought them their food and the wine. The lieutenant introduced Franz to her as Dr Schmidt's son. She made no response. Perhaps she was afraid of the police officer. As she passed the farther table, the same diner again pinched her bottom, and again she proceeded as if nothing had happened. And it might be that it was nothing. The lieutenant ate very quickly, but without giving the impression that food was important to him. When he laid down his knife and fork, he slipped his hand into the inside pocket of his tunic, and took out an envelope. He removed a photograph from it, and laid it face down on the table.

"There are people who would pay tens of thousands of dollars for this photograph. Or would have done so."

He pushed it towards Franz.

There was writing on the back: "For Jorge in settlement."

"Pick it up. Take a good look. Examine it carefully."

It showed a young officer, in jackboots, with swastikas on his epaulettes. He wore the Iron Cross, and stood before a gate, with the legend *Arbeit Machts Frei* in the sky above him. Barbed wire rolled over the walls to his right and left.

"So?" Franz said. "I have always known my father was in the Wehrmacht." He turned the snap over. "You are Jorge? In settlement for what?"

"A debt. It is unimportant."

"I don't understand. You make it sound as if you were, I don't know what – blackmailing him?"

"No," the lieutenant said, "we were friends. But that is the uniform of the SS." He put his hand on Franz's arm. "This doesn't matter to me. It was a long time ago. But it explains why it was my duty to, shall we say, keep an eye on your father. He had friends sufficiently powerful to arrange that."

"It seems you failed in your duty."

"Yes." The lieutenant took out a nail file and tapped the table. "Your prospective father-in-law is a Jew." He began to file his nails. "Why don't you ask him where your father is?"

"But that's ridiculous," Franz said, "Dr Czinner is blind. Didn't you know?"

"I know that your father was very nervous before meeting him."

"Besides, he regards anti-Semitism as out of date."

"I'm sure he does." The lieutenant bit off the end of another cigar, and lit it. "The question is whether Jews share his opinion. He would not have agreed to meet Dr Czinner – surely it should be Professor? – but for you. But for his love for you. At any rate, you have a coincidence here, that is something at least. So I repeat: ask Dr Czinner."

Franz knew he couldn't: either Becky's father would laugh in his incredulity, or he might confirm the lieutenant's suspicions; and that would be worse.

"Come, I shall take you to the hotel."

"I left my bag there. But first I would like to spend some more time in my father's house."

"In the morning. You will have time in the morning before your plane."

Franz acquiesced. It seemed he had been doing nothing else since the lieutenant had broken in on them. And he still couldn't understand his interest. He attempted a direct question. The lieutenant smiled; he had told him all he thought it prudent to say.

"But you think he is in some danger."

"That depends on what you mean by danger. His life is not immediately threatened. That is not the way these people work."

"Which people?"

"You do not really need to ask that, Franz. But if you do, I repeat that you should enquire of Dr Czinner."

"And what should I tell my mother when I call her?"

"That he has indeed disappeared. That is all you know. And that you will be on the midday plane. If you still wish to see your father's house again, call this number and I will have you fetched. But you will learn nothing. If he kept a diary for instance, that too is gone. But what could he have put in it?"

He led him to the car. When they stopped outside the hotel, he turned himself round and looked Franz in the eye, while the feeble street lamp threw his own face into shadow.

"You're a nice boy," he said, "as your father spoke of you. But you don't know yourself very well, do you? I am afraid you are going to find out a lot, about yourself and others. And then you may no longer seem such a nice boy."

FIVE

There was a fortnight of nothing. Franz met Becky the day after his return from the North, and for the first time quarrelled with her. He accused her of resenting his anxiety. She told him that was silly; of course she understood it, and felt for him. She wanted to be of some use, but – she said – he was shutting her out. Was it going to be like that in their marriage?

He looked at her as if he didn't understand what she was talking about. Then he said, "If we are ever married. I don't see how we can be."

"What do you mean?"

But he turned away and wouldn't answer. She started to cry, and he made no move to comfort her. She picked up her satchel and ran. That evening he telephoned to apologise. He didn't know what had come over him.

He tried to force his mother to the point they had always avoided. He told her of the photograph the lieutenant had shown him.

"I realise I've been a coward," he said. "But so have you."

"What do you mean?"

"The war. Why have you never spoken to me about the war?"

"We agreed we wouldn't. Your father and I agreed that. It is not a subject either of us has enjoyed discussing. And it couldn't affect you, *Schatz*."

"It couldn't?"

She pulled at a handkerchief.

"It's caught up now, hasn't it?" he said.

"We don't know, we must wait, wait and pray. Perhaps there is some simple straightforward explanation. I hate to say it, but perhaps he has met with some accident."

"In the middle of his supper?"

"Yes, that would be best."

"Leaving a bottle of beer half-drunk?"

Self-pity is the most corrosive of emotions, and is abrupt in its ability to take over the unwary. Franz knew that his reaction to whatever was happening was adolescent. His anxiety was justified; the response, "Why should this happen to me?", was not. And yet what other response could he make? He was a child of the sun who now found his thoughts tending towards that "virgin for those who have nobody with". Which was absurd: he was rich in friends.

"I'm contemptible," he told Kinsky. "What I had never realised was that my father lived for me."

"You will always find people ready to think they are doing that, my dear boy. Only, in truth, nobody ever does live for another person. That is a comforting delusion, what Shakespeare called 'a flattering unction to lay to your soul'."

"You should get drunk," Luis said. "Come with me to Rosita's. Or just get yourself laid."

"A gentleman called you," his mother's maid told him. "Will call again."

He was surprised to discover that it was Lieutenant Vilar. "Have you any news?"

"No, I'm afraid not."

"Then why are you calling?"

"I was worried about you."

"About me?"

"Because you understand so little. About yourself, about everything. That made me worried. Tell me I am stupid."

"No," Franz said. "I am grateful. I am worried myself. But about my father. What can have happened?"

"Be patient. These people will not, as I assure you, kill him."

"You speak as if you know who they are."

"Oh, I think we both know who they must be. Have you spoken to Dr Czinner?"

"No."

"Are you afraid to do so?"

Franz laid down the receiver. He looked at his face in the glass. "I've got a weak mouth," he thought. He went through to the bathroom and showered. Naked, he felt both guilty and vulnerable. Lieutenant Vilar understood him too well: he had always known he was a coward. A couple of years before he had been involved in a certain incident at the

Military Academy where he was studying. A boy in their class, a few months younger than himself, Bastini, had complained to the authorities that Luis's cousin, José-Maria, had stolen his essay, copied it out and presented it as his own, while he, Bastini, had had no work to hand in, for which omission he had been punished before lodging this complaint. The matter was investigated and Bastini was proved right. The proof wasn't difficult. Bastini was a clever boy, while José-Maria was a dolt. He was such an idiot that he hadn't realised that Bastini's work was far better than anything he could have done, or that at least was what Franz believed. Anyway, José-Maria was reproved, though not punished because his father was an under secretary at the Ministry of Defence. Even the reproof infuriated him, and he determined to have his revenge on Bastini. Luis smiled and agreed with him that Bastini was "a little cad". Franz nodded, not caring to advance a contrary opinion, though he had always rather liked Bastini, who was amusing and pretty as well as intelligent and quick-witted.

Anyway, he was committed to help, if only because he was afraid of what Luis and José-Maria might think if he refused. So the three of them ambushed Bastini after Chapel that evening and hustled him off to a gardener's shed in a corner of the grounds. José-Maria had bribed the gardener to let him have the key, allowing him to believe it was a question of a girl.

"What are you going to do with me?" Bastini said, when he saw José-Maria lock the door of the shed.

"We're going to punish you. Take off your clothes."

Bastini had soft curly hair and very long lashes over big brown eyes which now filled with tears. Nevertheless he obeyed, whimpering, perhaps because he was afraid things might be worse if he didn't.

José-Maria picked up the cherry-coloured trousers the boy had discarded, and sniffed inside them.

"He's not fit to wear a uniform," he said, and passed them to Luis. "He really is a disgusting beast. Say, 'I'm a disgusting little Italian.' Go on. Say it."

He picked up a cane which he had concealed in the shed earlier in the afternoon.

"Bastini, say it."

The boy, who was now naked and whose skin had a curious translucent quality – later Franz wondered if this was how terror manifested itself – was shaking with fear or revulsion and threw a look of anguish at

Franz, who didn't know how to reply to it and averted his eyes. Then he heard Bastini mutter the words.

José-Maria commanded the boy to bend over a bench. He obeyed. The cane swished and cut into the buttocks which, Franz noticed, were rather plump and quivering. This happened three times. The first time, Bastini uttered a yelp. Then he screamed. José-Maria tossed the cane aside.

"This is too easy. The little brute's such a coward, it's no fun. So we're going to bugger you, Bastini."

The boy squirmed, and again uttered that beastly little yelp. José-Maria undid the belt of his trousers, and Luis held Bastini's shoulders. Afterwards, José-Maria and Luis changed places.

"Your turn, Franz."

"No," Franz said. "I don't want to. I couldn't bring myself to."

"Well, I see your point," José-Maria said. "He is such a little beast. Very well."

He threw Bastini on to a pile of dirty garden sacks where he lay sobbing. Then he tossed the key on top of him.

"See that you give this to Pedro," he said. "You'll be in worse trouble if you don't."

He took Franz's arm as they left.

"That was clever, Schmidt," he said. "I could see you wanted to, but it was you he really wanted to do it to him. So your contempt hurt him more than anything Luis and I could do."

Franz shuddered. For the truth was, he had indeed felt an enormous desire to do just as José-Maria asked, and if he had been alone... But what puzzled and disturbed him more was that throughout the whole episode he had felt himself to be one with Bastini, he had been both torturer and tortured, and he knew that in some recess of his being Bastini had really welcomed his degradation.

"Do you know why Bastini sneaked on my cousin?" Luis asked when José-Maria had swaggered off. "It's because he was jealous. He used to be José-María's bitch, and then my cousin threw him over for young Ovaldes."

"No," Franz said, "I didn't know that." He longed to ask Luis what he had felt, but did not dare to do so.

That wasn't quite the end of it, for a couple of nights later Franz was awakened to find Bastini sitting on his bed. Without saying anything Franz put his hand on his thigh. Bastini fell over him kissing him on the lips, then crawled into his bed. They were lovers for two months, until Bastini disappeared without warning at the end of that term. Later Franz got a postcard from him, sent from Rome; it came in an envelope and showed the statue of the boy with the thorn in the Capitoline Museum. Bastini said his family had come back to Italy and that Franz was the only person he missed. "Otherwise I hate Argentina." He gave an address, but Franz never replied. There was nothing to say, and everything that Bastini had taught him about himself had frightened him. They had never talked about the episode in the shed.

But now that he was frightened again himself, he stood towelling his body and thought of Bastini. What had happened to him? What could have happened to someone so lustful and so cowardly who in the end scarcely seemed to exist for Franz outside what they had done together? But when Bastini, in his jealousy, had told tales on José-Maria, hadn't he known what he was inviting? And hadn't he, therefore, wanted it? He put his hand on the basin to steady himself: trying to picture Bastini now, he had transposed Becky's face over the boy's naked body.

He got into his two-seater – an English car, a Triumph TR3 and drove round to the Czinner apartment. He drove fast, either to give himself the chance of an accident which would avert his visit, or to prevent himself from changing his mind. Even so, he hesitated before getting out of the car; there was still a chance of putting it off. But then he heard his name called, and, looking up, saw Nell waving to him from the balcony.

The evening sun slanted into the apartment, falling on the aquatint reproduction of Turner's painting of "The Golden Bough", which Nell had inherited from her grandfather, and giving it a ruby richness that, while not bringing its resemblance to the original exactly closer, nevertheless imparted to it a strength and profundity it usually lacked but which did indeed belong to the painting itself. "It used to terrify me when I was small," Becky had once told Franz, "and truth to tell, the story still does. It's a horrible story."

"I don't know it," he had said.

"Well, the man in the picture is a priest. He is also a runaway slave and he guards the Golden Bough which is sacred to Diana, and he has won the post by killing the previous priest, and all the time he is on the look-out for the new contender who will kill him."

"I remember," he said. "Isn't there something also about him guarding the entrance to the Underworld?"

"I don't know," she said. "Isn't that a different story?"

"Maybe it is, but they're both about power, and how you can't enjoy it because you are always alert to whoever is going to try to deprive you of it. It's all very like Argentina, it seems to me."

But this evening wasn't somehow at all like Argentina. It wasn't only that everyone there – Franz and Becky included – had loyalties that bound them to older countries, with longer and still more twisted histories, which had also some sort of moral and cultural integrity that no one could find in the land where they had all arrived; where they had arrived too, Franz thought, not in hope, as immigrants should travel, but rather in what amounted to abdication from hope, effort and responsibility. Yet, for this moment, as Nell passed him a coffee cup and a slice of cake, and Becky opened another bottle of a fruity and aromatic pink wine that Kinsky had brought, the hopelessness which was the pervasive mood of the country, breeding resentment and apathy, shot through by spurts of random violence, was dissipated. Franz sat deep in his chair and watched the sunlight play on Becky's cheek and turn loose strands of hair the colour of harvest. He couldn't think why he had been loath to come. He was at peace here. It was home, and love.

"We were talking," Kinsky said, "of whom we would like to bring back from the grave. Myself, I can't decide between Socrates and Oscar Wilde."

"Socrates would make us think," Eli said. "Too dangerous. Besides, there was something decadent about Socrates."

"When I was a girl," Nell said, "I was in love with all sorts of dead people: Disraeli and Lord Rosebery. Leonardo, and Cesare Borgia, and the Viper of Milan."

"Who was the Viper of Milan?"

"I can't remember. He was the Duke in a story, and a terrible villain, but so attractive, a sort of Renaissance Heathcliff with polish."

"That doesn't help, Mummy. We don't know who he was either. No," Becky screwed up her face, wrinkling her nose. Her eyes sparkled. "I would bring back George Orwell, to let him see how wrong he got everything."

"Everything?" Eli said. "It's an interesting idea. But no. I used to meet him in London and found him tiresome."

"Would you bring back Brahms?" Franz asked.

Eli laughed.

"Oh no, his music I already have, and Brahms himself wasn't interesting. He had the same woman once a week in a brothel for more than twenty years, and when she died he transferred to her daughter. No, it has to be Goethe, the only man who ever indicated to the Germans what a good life could be like."

"Ah," Kinsky said, "how occupied we all still are with the idea of 'good Germans'."

"It's natural, isn't it," Franz said. "After all, everyone here is or has been involved in – what would you call it, sir?" – he inclined towards Eli, forgetting that he could not see his gesture – "the melodrama, perhaps of Germany. And we are all, whatever passports we hold, to some degree Germans, except ..." he paused; he had not yet found a satisfactory means of either addressing or referring to Becky's mother.

"Except me, you mean. But my grandfather, whom I adored, brought me up to love Germany. He was himself obsessed by things German. So I have never been able to escape it either."

There was a silence as if everyone was brooding on Nell's use of the verb "escape".

"Twenty past, angels passing," Becky said. She put her hand on Franz's. "I'm so glad you've come," she whispered while Nell rose to make another pot of coffee.

"All the same," Eli said, "the two great Germans – I speak of teachers, not musicians – must be Goethe and Nietzsche, and of the two, I think ... I think, for an evening like this, Goethe. Both understood, you could say incarnated, that essentially Nordic passion for the ancient world, which curiously you find so much more strongly expressed in the Anglo-Saxon races than among the Latins who inhabit the lands of Antiquity. Sun, sea and the clear light that dispels illusions. Whatever is best in the German character tends towards Italy."

"Italy," Nell said, pouring coffee, "what wouldn't I give to see Italy again, to be in Rome or Florence or one of those little towns of the Castelli, or on the Bay of Naples and the Sorrentine peninsula. You can't imagine the beauty, children."

"Yes," Eli said, "it's the primal source of life. Whatever the archaeologists say, we are bound to believe that life as we know it originated in Greece and Italy."

"How can you, a Jew, speak like that?" Kinsky said.

"Oh, I do not underrate what we have given the world, but nevertheless it appears to me that all this monotheism was a mistake, one that has led the world into a blind alley." He laughed. "How much more sensible, how much closer to one's experience of what is real, to divide one's worship between Apollo, Dionysus and the Great Mother. How much more sense Adonis makes than Christ! How much more sense even that descent into the depths, which I assume still hangs on the wall there – I refer to the rendering of 'The Golden Bough' – fanciful though it is – than our stern and life-denying moralities!"

To Franz it seemed at first as if Eli was talking merely for rhetoric's sake. Perhaps it appeared that way to Nell also, for she smiled and said, "That's all very well, my dear, but to me Italy means first of all *spaghetti al pescatore* under a vinewreathed arbour overlooking the *campagna*. Do you remember that restaurant at Ariccia called Il Paradiso?"

Becky said, "Well, I shouldn't mind living in Italy myself."

"There's no reason why we shouldn't," Franz said. "We're not bound in any way to Argentina."

"An apartment in Rome," Becky said.

"Within five minutes of Piazza Navona," Kinsky said. "There's no doubt I should come to stay with you. Do you remember, Nell, that fountain with the boys and the tortoises?"

And he proceeded to tell of how a certain Count, or possibly Prince, Mattei had had the fountain built as a present for his wife, and transported to the little piazza outside the family house, between the old ghetto and Largo Argentina – "yes, indeed". The job had been done at night, and in the morning the Count opened the shutters of their bedroom, called his wife to the window, and there it was – "the most beautiful little fountain in the world".

"Do you hear that, Franz? I'll expect no less."

"Alas, there's no such workmanship now," Kinsky said. "In our century we have preferred to direct our superior talents to destruction."

"Poor Italy!" Eli said. "Raped a thousand times by Nordic invaders, and yet still our inspiration."

Franz thought of Bastini who had wanted life to be sweet and comfortable, and had obeyed the laws of his own nature, and lived in fear as a result. He pressed Becky's hand.

"I must go," he said. "Shall we have lunch tomorrow?"

As they passed through the kitchen, Nell laid her hand on the boy's shoulder.

93

"You are being very brave. I haven't asked you about your father, because you would have told us if you had any news. But we feel for you, and remember, we are on your side, and Becky needs you – yes, you do, darling. I wouldn't normally say it, but Franz isn't living through a normal time."

They sat in the park after lunch and listened to the band. It was just warm enough to be pleasant sitting out of doors. The band played Viennese waltzes, and after their bottle of wine over lunch they responded to the mood of the music: light, sensuous, exhilarating. Over lunch they had talked of the "situation". They had talked it out and arrived nowhere. But the talk had done them good. They had not quarrelled, which both had been afraid of doing, and they were united against whatever was going to happen. Yet Becky had not been able to bring herself to ask anything specific about Franz's father; that barrier remained solid between them, even though for the moment both pretended that they could not see it.

The band played the waltz from *Der Rosenkavalier*, the music surged over them, drowning the laughter of children playing on a nearby roundabout; there, swans, prancing horses, even (a touch of local colour) llamas, rose and swooped. Becky watched her lover in profile. She said, "We must go somewhere. I can't wait."

He turned towards her. She looked up at him, her thin face touched with pink, her lips parted.

"I mean it," she said again.

Two policemen swaggered past. Snatches of their conversation, which was about football, were carried to them. Franz took her hands.

"Are you sure?"

She nodded, saw the surprise in his face.

"We must," she said. "Look."

She took her hand out of her pocket and held it open, palm uppermost, to display a key.

"A girl I know gave it to me. She shares an apartment with two other American girls, secretaries at the Embassy, I think. They'll be at work."

"What girl?"

"A friend of mine called Alexis. Come on."

She put the key back in her pocket. They got up. Franz laid his arm across her shoulders. They hurried, awkward as the participants in a three-legged race, towards the park gates. They passed the bandstand where the military band, in its cherry-coloured uniforms, broke into a selection from Italian opera. As they turned out of the park and climbed into the little sports car, the "Grand March" from *Aida* boomed them towards happiness. Becky pressed Franz's thigh.

Two hours later, they heard the door of the apartment open. For a moment they lay very still, like criminals. Franz rested his left arm round Becky. Her hair tickled his cheek. He was free of doubt, caught up in eternity, in goodness. She turned round, kissed his lips, pushed her hand between his legs.

"I love you," she whispered. "Again…"

Later, he dozed. Then he sensed that he was alone. He heard voices; the swish of water, felt stupid with happiness. Becky placed a cup of coffee on the table by the bed, sat down, and stroked his cheek. She was dressed now, but he slipped his hand up her cotton skirt, and she let it rest there. A fragment of Latin verse came into his head: *Neque enim malignior fortuna! Eripiet nobis, quod prima hora dedit* – "A more malignant fortune can never take away from us what this first hour has given." But he didn't speak it. It wasn't a time for other men's words. Petronius had killed himself at Nero's command, with mockery on his lips.

Becky said, "Come and speak to Alexis, she's dying to meet you; have a shower first, there's a towel over there."

Alexis was a long-legged, California-beach blonde wearing only knickers and a bra. She sat on a stool, painting her toenails, and looked over her shoulder at Franz, through a forest of hair worn in the manner of Brigitte Bardot.

"Hi," she said.

The tip of her tongue stuck out as she concentrated on her task.

"Don't mind me," she said, "I'm going to be late as usual."

"It's good of you to let us… I'm very grateful."

"What are friends for? I don't like this colour, honey, I don't think it's me. Still, it does him good to be kept waiting. These guys think they're the tops. If this is New Spain, then God save me from Old Spain is all I say."

"I thought New Spain was Mexico."

His smile robbed the correction of offence, or so it seemed, for she laughed and rose from her contorted position in one easy movement – Venus from the sea perhaps – and smiled back.

"Boy, am I glad to meet you at last. Am I tired of hearing Becky on the subject, or am I?"

Becky came through from the little kitchen. She held out a flowered dress which she had been ironing.

"Like I say," Alexis said, holding out her hand and laughing, "what are friends for?"

She slipped the dress on.

"Aren't you going to wear tights?" Becky said.

Alexis looked down at her toes.

"Hell, no, why spoil the effect. He says he is some kind of liberal. He can take bare legs. Test his principles. 'Bye, darlings, must fly."

"She didn't even remind us to lock up," Franz said.

"No, she's crazy; I adore her. She does just what she likes and loves it. And she's clever, you know. Works for some international agency, I don't know which, UNESCO maybe." She came and sat on the arm of his chair and wove her fingers through his hair, then she slid over on to his lap and kissed him.

"You don't mind that it wasn't the first time for me?"

He shook his head.

"Really?"

"Really."

"Really and truly?"

He kissed her lips.

"He was an American boy, called Joe. Last summer. He was a friend of Alexis's brother and they were both staying here."

"It doesn't matter."

"He was sweet. But he wasn't like you."

When he stopped the car outside the block of her parents' apartment, and said, no, he wouldn't come in, she said, "It's not because of Joe?"

"Don't be silly."

"Because really he wasn't that important."

"You're crazy," he said. "Did you know that? But you're also perfect. So was this afternoon. That's why I won't come in now. Because it was perfect. OK?"

"OK. Do you love me?"

"For ever and ever, amen."

"Me too," she giggled. "I mean I love you too, not myself."

SIX

Franz didn't notice the Studebaker parked behind his car in the University car park, and he wasn't aware of it following him out of the University grounds, along the boulevard and then through the narrower streets of his route. Most days he might have observed it and wondered about it, but today he was too happy. He had spent the night in deep, yet dreamy, sleep, and woken relaxed, blissful and triumphant, and the mood had stayed with him throughout his classes. It wasn't until they were caught at a traffic-light, which had in fact turned green, though movement was impossible, the crossing ahead being jammed, that the Studebaker eased itself alongside him, and the driver rolled down the window and said, "We need to talk. You need to talk to me."

He spoke in English, and Franz examined him. He had a lean head with very fair hair cut very neatly, and he wore a blue-and-white checked seersucker suit and a navy blue white-spotted bow tie. He had a gold ring on the little finger of his left hand, and the hand holding the steering wheel was covered with little golden hairs that shone in the sunlight. The hands themselves were very pale in colour and manicured, and he wore a Rolex wristwatch.

Franz took all this in while he wondered at the approach and couldn't think of a suitable reply.

"Pull in by that big bar on the left once we get across the Avenida."

He had an American accent, and he spoke with the authority of a movie hero.

The Studebaker was slow away when it was at last possible to move – it was probably an automatic – and Franz had put enough distance between them to get away if he chose. But curiosity won. He eased the Triumph towards the pavement, and was out and waiting before the other car was parked. The man in the seersucker suit detached himself. He was shorter than he had looked sitting down; a movie star who would have to be stood on a fruit box to make love to a girl with legs as long as Alexis. He held out his hand to Franz, and then pushed ahead of him into the bar where he ordered two large Manhattans. He watched their concoction, giving directions, and then took both glasses and led the way to a table in the corner, though there was supposed to be waiter service only in that part of the café. But no one came to reprove them. Perhaps he was known there. He pulled out his wallet, extracted a card and handed it to Franz. It gave his name, Calthorpe Binns, and that of a newspaper in Indianapolis, and his address – Buenos Aires.

"I usually get called Cal," he said. "I've been anticipating our meeting with pleasure, Franz."

"I shouldn't have thought Argentinian affairs were so interesting to readers in Indianapolis," Franz said, "for a paper to afford a correspondent here. Which state is it anyway? Minnesota?"

"No, Indiana. Well, you are right, they're not. But it gives me status, and then when I file a story, it gets syndication."

"Look," Franz said, "I think I can guess what you want to talk about. But there's nothing I can say, nothing I can tell you."

"You're not drinking. Don't you like Manhattans? Hell, when I think of the trouble I have gone to teach them to mix one right! 'Look,' I said, 'Scotch is Scotch and I have nothing against it, it's a great drink, but it doesn't belong in a Manhattan.' You're mistaken, son, you don't know what I want from you." He picked up his drink and emptied the glass. " 'Rye,' I told them, 'you can't make a Manhattan without a good rye whiskey.' "

A tall man wearing a straw hat and a biscuit-coloured suit – clothes too summery for the crisp morning with a touch of frost – sat down two tables away. He took a cigarette from a case, and fitted it into a long amber holder. A waiter flickered towards him, and he ordered coffee and an *anis*.

Calthorpe Binns took a coin from his pocket.

"There's a juke-box over there," he said. "Go and put something on. Choose three records. I don't mind a bit of noise."

Franz selected two Elvis records, and then, in deference to Cal's age, a Sinatra one.

"That's better, you can't hear yourself think now. What does the name Kestner mean to you?"

"Nothing that I know of."

"Rudolf Kestner. Rudi Kestner. *Standartenfuehrer* Kestner?"

"Look, what is this?"

"And you of course are Franz Kestner." He waved to summon the waiter. "If you don't like Manhattans, would you rather have a beer? Or perhaps an ice cream?"

He lit a Camel cigarette.

"Beer, is it?" he said, and gave the order to the waiter. "And now the *Standartenfuehrer* has disappeared, and nobody knows where he is. You must be worried."

"Of course I'm worried, if you are talking about my father."

"Who else? And the disappearance took place a few days after he met a certain German-Jewish doctor, who had the misfortune – we needn't put it stronger than that – to have done time in a concentration camp, perhaps even consigned to it by the *Standartenfuehrer* himself. What do you make of that, Franz?"

Franz looked at the table.

"I don't make anything of it," he said. "Dr Czinner's blind, didn't you know?"

"And deaf and dumb? I hadn't heard that. And you are still seeing his daughter? In fact, I have reason to suppose that you made love to her yesterday in a flat that is the property of the US Government."

"Is that an offence?"

"Couldn't rightly say. In certain circumstances, it might be made to seem one."

Go climb your thumb, Franz thought, but instead said merely, "What the hell is this? Are you going to explain?"

"Patience, sonny."

Cal Binns sat back, nursing his new Manhattan. The gentleman two tables away looked at Franz. Cal Binns intercepted the glance.

"We'd better take a ride," he said. "You can leave your car here. I'll tell Ramón to keep an eye on it."

He drove the Studebaker in a newly casual manner, with only one hand on the wheel. He chain-smoked, screwing up his eyes. It seemed to Franz that he watched the rear-view mirror more closely than the road ahead. They left the part of the city with which Franz was acquainted and drove towards the harbour. The car bounced along a cobbled road between warehouses; a line of rails for a tram ran down the middle of the street. There were weeds growing between the rails.

"You're not a journalist," Franz said. "You're something else. Is it CIA?"

"Sure I'm a journalist. Been with the good old *Monitor* twenty years. Maybe I dabble a bit elsewhere, but so what? You want to see my Press card, my accreditation?"

"All right," Franz said. The car had stopped in front of a boarded-up warehouse. "But you won't get a story from me."

"Sonny, I'm the one that is telling you a story. Hell, I'm showing you the story. We get out here. There are some friends want to meet you."

"Wait a minute. Whose side are you on?"

"I'm just looking after the interests of certain friends, that's all. The sixty-four-thousand dollar question is, whose side are you on, buddy?"

He led the way down an alley that ran between two warehouses and towards the waterfront. It was overgrown with tall pink-flowering weeds; life had moved a long time ago from this part of the docks. They crossed a footbridge over a little channel, or canal; empty beer-cans floated on the water, hardly moving. A rat plopped from the bank.

"Just speak the truth," Cal Binns said. "That's all that's required of you, it's all that's required of any of us."

He knocked on a door in the side of the building. The top half opened a crack. Then Franz heard bolts being slid open, and Cal led him into the building. He marched straight across a yawning deserted hall. The man who had opened the door for them followed Franz. He wore carpet-slippers and his step was a soft-shoe shuffle. Cal Binns knew his way. He went through a doorway on the other side of the hall, along a narrow passage off which opened doors leading into what had once presumably been offices. He knocked at the third or fourth of them.

They were admitted to a small room where four men sat playing cards at a Formica-topped table. The room was lit by a single naked bulb and the air was heavy with tobacco smoke. All the men were middle-aged to elderly and all wore open-necked shirts. A fifth man, who had opened the door, slipped out of the room. The oldest of the party, a thickset balding fellow, who wore a flowered short-sleeved shirt and had a cigar stuck in the right corner of his mouth, raised a hand, palm foremost, to Cal Binns. Then he swept the cards towards himself, made them into a pack, shuffled it twice, and planted it on the table. He got to his feet. Without removing the cigar, he hugged Cal Binns, and then turned to face Franz. His scrutiny was intense. Then he threw up his arm in a salute.

"Heil Hitler."

When Franz made no response, he lowered his arm, smiled, and clapped him on the back.

"I have never agreed with your father about your upbringing," he said. "Consequently, you don't even know who I am, do you?"

Franz shook his head.

"There, you see." He inclined towards the other three card-players, who had all slewed round in their seats to watch. "It's ironic, isn't it? I'm in effect, young man, what I daresay you would call your godfather, and you don't know me."

"I didn't even know I had a godfather."

"Well, I say only 'in effect', since I do not believe in any Christian God. No more than your father does. You look like your mother when she was young. A pity. A boy should resemble his father. I shan't tell you my name, since it would mean nothing, nor that of my comrades here. For that's what we are: comrades and friends, and comrades and friends of your father too. Come, sit and let us drink to him. You can call me Klaus, that's sufficient."

A bottle of local brandy, a soda siphon and some stubby glasses were placed on the table. Klaus settled himself, raised his glass.

"Our comrade in distress."

Then he began to talk. He expatiated at length, with many subordinate clauses, criticising his "dear Kestner" for thinking it possible to detach himself even in some degree from his past.

It wasn't, he assured Franz, that his father was ashamed of it, rather that he urged them all to consider the past as something irrelevant, "mere history", separate from a new existence. "Which isn't, I assure you, dear boy, possible, if only because our enemies refuse to let the past die. Therefore we too, in self-protection as well as on account of our own self-esteem, must struggle to keep it alive, save it from the dead hand of history." He smiled: there was something wonderfully inviting about his smile, like a promise of initiation into the arcane springs of being. At the same time, it was a greedy smile, ready to swallow you up. Franz sipped his brandy and waited.

So, Klaus resumed, their dear comrade had made mistakes, and now he was suffering for them. His refusal to defy history meant that Franz himself had grown up in ignorance. And what was the result of this ignorance? Catastrophic! He proposed to marry a Jewish girl.

He paused, lit a fresh cigar, blew out smoke, waved his hand, palm downwards, over the table.

"Filth."

The speaker was a lean man with a twitch in his right cheek.

Klaus smiled again. "Well, we would have thought so, would we not? But one has to admit now that the Jews have surprised us. Yes, indeed! One has to admire what they have achieved in Israel."

"Thanks to us," said the youngest-looking of the group, a battered blond with a duelling scar. We have made that possible. We taught them that struggle is the motive force in history."

"Indeed," Klaus said, "the Israelis are well on the way to being our best pupils."

It wasn't enough, however, for Franz to have proposed to marry a Jewess, Klaus went on. He had to choose Dr Czinner's daughter. Klaus shook his head. Dr Czinner was the worst sort of Jew, one who had pretended to co-operate with the Reich in order to work the more effectively for its destruction. It had been a mistake to send him to a camp; he should have been shot out of hand, or hanged. But that had been Kestner's decision. And now: it was Czinner who had betrayed him; there was no question of that.

"So you see, Franz, you are caught up in an authentic tragedy."

He pushed the brandy bottle towards him and licked his lips. A drop of spittle escaped the corner of his mouth; it was stained brown by tobacco juice.

"Your father made the mistake of trying to live independently of the group, of believing that he could in this way escape the past. But the past has caught up with him and arrested him."

"How can you know all this?"

"My dear boy, we have our friends." He gestured towards Calthorpe Binns. "The company he works for plays both sides of the street."

"*The Indianapolis Monitor?*"

"If you like, sonny."

"And it is thanks to Mr Binns that we know there has been a hitch in their plans, that your father is still in Argentina. Unfortunately we do not know exactly where, but we are certain he has not yet left the country. Which, dear boy, is where you come in. You have an affection for your father?"

Franz blushed: "Of course."

"There's no 'of course' about it," said the man with the duelling scar. "We got rid of that ridiculous bourgeois nonsense. Family affection! An idea for Jews and the sort of idiots who read novels by Thomas Mann!"

"It survives," said the fourth card-player, a thin, wizened man with a yellow complexion. "It is that which has destroyed poor Kestner after all."

"Precisely," Klaus said. "It is, as you say, bourgeois, Jewish, liberal, everything we rightly despise and detest. We shall turn the enemy's weapon on the enemy. The situation is not yet altogether lost, as long as Kestner remains in Argentina. Do you know, young man, what they will do with him if they can?"

Franz looked away. Then he lowered his eyes and fixed them on the table. The Formica was peeling away at the corner where he sat, and he got his thumb under it and worked it. If they were right, if what they said was true. He remembered pictures of Eichmann in his bullet-proof glass cage, defending what could not be defended, except on terms which were no longer admissible. He had no idea what his father would be charged with, but that was what would happen. He would be put on display. Come and view the Monster, but with none of the bitter humour of a Freak Show. And Ilse too would be confronted with brutal facts which in her own heart she would always deny – since such denial was necessary to the way she lived her life – but which her friends would believe. And she would know they did. And as for him – he couldn't bring himself to think of how his friends would feel, or Becky. He pulled at the Formica. The whole family, all of them, would be like Bastini, reduced to objects of contempt, thrown down on dirty sacks. He remembered how José-María had tossed the key of the torture-chamber on to the boy's gleaming and trembling body, saying "Lock up behind you and return the key to its keeper."

"Yes," he said. "I know what will be done to him."

Klaus smiled. "It can be prevented," he said, "as long as he is held in Argentina."

"Do you mean you plan to rescue him?"

"That would be a possibility – if we knew where he was. But there is no need for heroics. There are other methods."

"Dr Czinner has a daughter." Klaus smiled. It was a silly schoolmaster's smile, intended to convey effortless superiority, and it irritated Franz; yet he also felt the first rustle of fear. He had thought that these old Nazis, ham actors though they seemed to be, were at least on his side.

"That's absurd," he said. "I understand the implications of what you say, but you can't do that, you can't threaten her."

"Can't?" The man with the duelling scar laughed. "He says 'can't' to us, the child."

"My father," Franz said, "my father would never allow... he would never let you use Becky in any way... as a counter in a bargain, it's obscene."

"Our experience," Klaus said, "is that people make all sorts of bargains when they consider their interests at stake. Ask Dr Czinner. He knows."

And as he spoke, Franz recalled that only the other evening Becky's father had murmured, "I too have played Faust in my time." He had disliked the remark, which showed in his view an unbecoming vanity.

"So you will speak to Dr Czinner. The bargain is simple. Your fiancée for your father. She will be released when he is."

Franz felt a glass being thrust into his hand. For a moment he held it there, as horrified by its suggestion of conviviality, conspiracy, concern for his condition, as by the words he had heard, words the significance of which he was unable immediately to grasp. It is not true that bad news hits you like a blow; it forces itself on you like the suspicion turning to certainty of cancer. The mind struggles against acceptance. With a short arm jerk Franz threw the brandy at the face that loomed over him. But the head turned away. Some liquor splashed on Klaus's shoulder, the rest fell short even of the wall behind.

"She is quite safe. No harm will come to her. You will tell Dr Czinner that."

"You can trust him, sonny," the American voice intervened. "Believe me, I possess a comprehensive experience and I would be reluctant to so asseverate without evidence that would stand up."

"Mr Binns's company is our guarantor," Klaus said. "Come, Franz, you must be ready to help us. It is the only way to save your father."

Franz felt a hand fall on his shoulder. He looked up. His gaze was filled with the man's smiling face.

"No," he said, "no."

"You are naturally disturbed. You have never encountered reality before. Believe me, you will come to value it. To escape from a dream world, that is the important thing."

The hand squeezed his shoulder.

Calthorpe Binns drove him back into the city. They did not speak. Binns drove with one hand on the wheel. When he finished a cigarette, he took another from the packet in the breast pocket of his shirt and lit it from the stub of the first. For a moment he had both cigarettes, butt and replacement, in his mouth at the same time. Then he threw the first one out of the window without extinguishing it. Occasionally he hummed: "It happened in Monterey ... in Old Mexico-o ..."

He eased the car into the kerb.

"You should go to Czinner straightaway," he said. "Your car's fine, you owe Ramón a tip. Just remember. It's a simple operation. A means of exchange. Czinner's an economist, he understands the market."

"I don't understand."

"Oh yes, you do, sonny."

"What's your role in this?"

"I'm a middleman. I keep an eye on things. See the boat doesn't ship too much water. Don't waste time. It's got a limit."

But the meaning was there. It's always been there. Iphigenia knew that. Sacrifice either of oneself or of others is a temptation. Eli would offer himself in place of his daughter. They wouldn't be interested. And Franz saw Becky's face set white and frightened against a future she had not made; and then his father ... his father's face would reveal nothing, neither fear nor hope nor anger. He would read the situation differently. Life which he had both made and known had caught up with him. But Becky... Franz did not dare to drive his car. He stood on the sidewalk isolated from the crowd that thronged round him, by what he had learned of man's capacity. Anyone seeing him would have observed only a handsome boy who looked as if he might have forgotten something, or have lost his way.

The cat purred, and thrust its head into Eli's face, rubbing his chin, rasping with pleasure, clawing at his chest. His hand moved over its back in gentle strokes. He had not spoken since Franz without apology or introduction, making no effort to break the news gently, had told him what had happened. He had spoken in German, in a few frank brutal sentences.

Eli put his hand under the cat and turned her round and she settled herself along the line of his thigh, facing away. He lit a cheroot, using the old petrol lighter.

"You blame me," he said.

Franz didn't reply.

"Of course you do," Eli said. "Furthermore you must think me treacherous. I suppose you are right."

"None of that matters," Franz said. He got up and went to the window.

It was now late afternoon and the street was deserted, except for three or four children dancing their way home from school. "It's Becky that matters."

"She left for the University as usual this morning."

"Where is Frau Czinner?"

Eli knew that she had asked the boy to call her Nell, but he respected his formality now. What had happened had made them irretrievably enemies, whatever eventually worked out for Becky and the boy.

He said, "It's important that you understand, Franz."

"Nothing is important except Becky, just at this moment."

"She will be all right. Nothing will happen to her."

That wasn't of course true, or rather any truth it might have depended on his grammatical expression, that use of the future tense. Things had happened to her already. In the moment of arrest – which was the word he used to himself – she would all at once have grown up. She would have learned what had previously only been words to her; just as he had himself, and her Aunt Miriam and her Aunt Sarah and her Uncle Mark, and her grandfather and those cousins whose names he couldn't even recall: that the world cannot be controlled. But still he repeated: "Nothing will happen to her."

He sensed Franz turn, approach him, standing over him. "What do you mean? That my father will be set free? That you will arrange for the exchange to take place?"

"No," he said. "I don't mean that."

"But you must. Becky is all that matters."

"She will be all right. As for your father, I must tell you that I had word he left Argentina this morning. He will be in Israel tomorrow. It will be in all the papers, on the wireless and the television. So now do you understand? He cannot be set free."

There was silence. Then the sound of sobbing. Eli smoked and caressed the cat. He said, "Talk to your American friend. You'll see, he won't allow them to go too far. And they depend on him. These clowns depend on the CIA as much as on the Argentinian police. Kidnapping, holding to ransom, that's one thing … beyond that, no. Becky will be all right."

Franz said, "And if she isn't, will it have been worth it?"

Eli drew on his cheroot. The boy's question led into a desert where he no longer wished to travel. Once he had thought of himself as an explorer, prepared to endure hardship, the heat of the day, the night cold that entered the bones, and to think himself rewarded not, as easier spirits were, by the occasional moments at an oasis, but simply by the experience itself, and the knowledge, the consciousness, of that experience. To be able to say, "I have been there and lived." That was the significant thing in existence. Without that, all was merely palliative, like that soft green English countryside without horizons, which he had learned to loathe. It was in the wilderness that you found yourself. But in recent years, in his blindness which might – he would smile – be thought wilderness enough, he had been content to retreat, to dismiss the idea of value from his mind, relapse into mere existence, getting through the day, living as almost everybody did. But the past wouldn't release him: it had forced him into the desert again, and now the boy's question danced before him like a will-o'-the-wisp.

"Will it have been worth it?" Franz said again.

Getting no answer, he continued – and this time his voice, though challenging, seemed to come to Eli from a long way distant: "How could you do this to us?"

The easy answer was denial: "I have done nothing to you. What people do they do to themselves."

But he couldn't make it. There was casuistry there, for it was a perversion of the truth to pretend that he hadn't known, when he made those calls to Tel Aviv and Vienna, that his words would explode in his daughter's life. Wasn't that after all why he hadn't mentioned it to Nell?

So he said, "There are imperatives. Your own father would tell you that. It is how he has acted himself."

"I don't understand. Is it revenge? Do you hate me too?"

"Revenge is an imperative. The English philosopher Bacon called it 'a sort of wild justice'."

"But why?"

"Why do you love my daughter?"

"Because … because … you can't answer that question."

"But you have. Motivation is beyond comprehension. That is the answer."

"But if that is true…"

The boy paused.

"This is crazy, this sort of talk."

With a cry that contained a sob, he fled from the room. Eli listened to his footsteps descend, faster and faster at the turning of the stair, until they died away.

SEVEN

Franz was in a bar where he had never been before. He had ordered whisky and a handful of tokens for the telephone. The late afternoon sun slanted in at the doorway, and there were still prettily dressed girls with men in business suits sitting at the tables on the pavement. He could hear laughter and happiness. He took out the card Calthorpe Binns had given him, and called the first of the two numbers listed, which was that of his office. He listened to the ringing in a room that he knew from the first ring was empty. Then he tried the other number; there was no reply there either. And when he replaced the receiver, he wondered whether he would have dared to tell the American that his father had already been spirited from Argentina. He couldn't share Dr Czinner's confidence that Becky's captors would throw in their hand at that point. Why wouldn't they seek to put pressure on Tel Aviv?

He knew that he should call his mother. But it was impossible. He ordered another whisky.

Then he searched in his address book, found the number of the flat where he and Becky had made love, and, when a crisp voice answered, asked if he might speak to Alexis. He told her he must see her. Would she agree to meet? Of course, she said, as if this was the most natural request in the world.

"Yeah, I know where you are. I'll be right over."

It was as if she had some idea of what had happened.

But when he saw her enter, the swing of her blonde hair and the relaxed confident stride causing male heads to turn, and provoking a wolf whistle from a gang of youths who hung around the news-stand, he knew that this was nonsense. Nobody burdened by knowledge could move that easily.

He told her the story from the beginning.

"That's rough," she said. "I appreciate your confidence."

"The curious thing is that I am not horrified to find out what my father was. I suppose I have always had a suspicion. Do you know this Calthorpe Binns?"

"Everyone knows Cal. He's a standing joke."

"He didn't seem like a joke to me."

"No, but he's a prick."

"Is he CIA?"

"I guess he might be."

"That business of knowing that Becky and I had … in your fiat. How could he know that? And is it US government property?"

"They pay the rent. 'Cos of Katie, one of my flatmates."

"Is she CIA too?"

"Lord, no, she works at the Embassy… But look, what are we going to do?"

She put her hand on his knee.

"I'm with you," she said, "body and soul. Poor Becky."

"Her father thinks they'll release her when they find out there's no chance of a bargain. Or that's what he says. I wish I could believe him. I hoped you might be able to help me locate Calthorpe Binns. He's my only link, but he's not at either of the numbers on the card he gave me. I was desperate. So I called you. I hope you don't mind being involved."

"Let's go look," she said. "We could try the Press Club."

But he wasn't there. Alexis cashed a cheque at the bar.

"We may need a lot of money," she said.

They took a taxi and headed on a tour of the bars, and then later of the nightspots. Alexis seemed to be known in most of them. She was greeted with a smile and a "Hi Alexis," or "Hi honey" by doormen, waiters, army officers, the stout Negress who kept a bar favoured by transvestites, two policemen, and a crippled seller of lottery tickets.

"Do you know everyone in this city?"

"I don't know that man with no nose over there, I'm relieved to state."

Her energy and exuberance were remarkable. He almost resented the enthusiasm with which she threw herself into their quest. It was as if she had forgotten the reason behind it. But he knew she hadn't. "I can't bear to think of Becky frightened," she said. "And it's no good hoping she may not be frightened. Anybody would be in her shoes. It's the not knowing that does it."

Calthorpe Binns had been seen early that evening in two or three of the bars. Then the trail seemed to run cold. Alexis asked Franz if he thought he could find his way again to the warehouse where he had met the Nazis. "She might be there, you know," she said.

"You mean she might have been there all the time, while I was there?"

"Seems likely."

He shook his head.

"I don't believe I could."

And he burst into tears, his whole body trembling. He felt her arm around him, her hair brushing against his cheek.

"You must think me an idiot."

"No, why should I?"

"It's all so hopeless."

"Look, Franz," she said, holding him close to her and speaking low, "you've got it in your head that you must find Cal Binns, but it's going to come to the same thing whether you find him or not. They're going to know their plan has bellyflopped when they hear the news bulletin. You've got another priority, it seems to me, to break the news to your mother. You can't let her find out from the news bulletins."

He didn't have to urge Alexis hard to get her to accompany him to his mother's apartment. She seemed to have constituted herself his guardian angel for the night. In his agitated state, he was overwhelmed by her goodness. It was in such contrast to everything else that he had learned that day. He couldn't imagine why she should be ready to put herself to such trouble.

"Because I like you and I adore Becky, dumbo."

As the lift mounted, she put her arms round him and kissed him on the mouth. He held her tight. He was grateful to her for not offering words of reassurance which they would both recognise as lying. There could never again be any absolute certainty for any of them that things would turn out fine. In a few hours they had been severed from the optimism proper to their age. Maybe Alexis had previously learned that the world was different from the way it had been sold to their generation, but for him the realisation had come unheralded. All the propositions on which he had based his life had come unstuck; it was like stumbling through a dark night, and the moon all at once revealing an open grave. How could he have been so blind? Hadn't the wretched Bastini's experience already warned him?

Voices came from the drawing room as they let themselves into the apartment. Franz hesitated. Alexis squeezed his arm.

His mother met them at the door.

"There's a gentleman who needs to see you urgently. We didn't know where you were."

She smiled at Alexis.

"I'm a friend of Becky's," Alexis said, and gave her name. Ilse stepped aside. Franz saw that his visitor was Calthorpe Binns.

"Hi, Cal," Alexis said. "Snap. We've been hunting you all over town."

"Hi, Alexis." Binns did not rise from the armchair in which he sat clutching a square tumbler of whisky. "Hi, Franz."

Franz's stepfather, the General, elegant in a grey suit, said, "Señor Binns and I have been enjoying an interesting conversation, but it might be helpful if someone would let me know what the hell is happening. I detect undercurrents, which make me uneasy. Franz?"

The name was a command. Franz hesitated. He walked to the window and looked out on the city lights. Somewhere – out of the light, or perhaps with a single naked bulb directed at her face, was Becky. He turned round. Binns smiled at him. "Did you talk to Czinner?"

Alexis said, "You've made a balls-up, Cal."

Binns sucked at his whisky.

"We've had our obligations to fulfil," he said.

"Franz," the General said, "when you went north to look for your father – and I wish your mother had told me in advance of your investigation, which it would have been wiser to leave in my hands – did you encounter a certain Lieutenant Vilar?"

"Yes," Franz said. "He looked after me. Why do you ask?"

"He won't do so again. He's been murdered. Rather horribly. I have photographs, but I won't show them to you. I wanted to speak to you about your conversation with him. However, Señor Binns's arrival persuades me that the poor lieutenant is only one small part of a more intricate puzzle."

The General sat on the arm of the sofa, above his wife who had subsided there. He swung a long leg, gazing, as if in admiration, at the knife-edge crease of his trousers or the high polish of his black English-made shoe. He placed light fingers on Ilse's bare shoulder.

"My dear," he said, "this is all going to be unpleasant, I fear. You will have to be brave. Or would you rather leave us, and let me handle it?"

Ilse returned the squeeze of his hand.

"I will stay," she said. "I think perhaps I have let too many other people handle too many things."

"As you like, my dear, but it is going to be unpleasant. I wished only to spare you as much as possible. Franz."

So, for the second time that evening, Franz told the story as he had encountered it. When he had finished it was as if Becky's fear was in the room with them.

Franz said, "Why did you hide it from me, Mother? You must always have known what my father did. What he was."

The General's fingers tightened on Ilse's shoulder. She looked up, thrusting out her chin, and, for a moment, for the first time ever for Franz, she looked ugly.

"You talk of such things," she said. "It is easy to talk. What was I to do? He was my husband. He was the father of my son. He is your father. What would you have had me do? Denounce him to the Jews or the Russians or the Americans, who were anyway – as you can see" – she gestured with a terrified vague push of the hand towards Calthorpe Binns – "ready to overlook whatever he had done, in return for what he could do for them. And what in the end had he done? Only what he was commanded to do. But, eventually it was impossible for me also. That is why we separated."

"My darling," the General said. "You have nothing with which to re-proach yourself. Franz, you will not speak in that manner to your moth-er. You will apologise, now, please... Franz."

Franz felt the touch of Alexis's hand.

"Whatever I have done, I have done for love of you, Franz," Ilse said.

"I'm sorry, Mother. But Becky... I'm almost out of my mind..."

"Oh, that poor girl... Carlos, my dear, what can be done for her?"

"That is the next matter," the General said.

The telephone rang.

For a moment it seemed as if nobody would take the responsibility of answering it. All feared the news it might bring. Even the General hesitated.

"It's for you, Franz."

"Luis? ... No of course she isn't. What? It can't be... Oh, Christ... Look, Luis, where are you? Right, stay there. I'll ring back."

He replaced the receiver, turned to face them like an actor confident of holding his well-drilled colleagues. But there was a tremble in his voice.

"That was Luis. He wanted to know if Gabriella was here. Apparently she was going to spend the day with Becky. She was going to call him, and hasn't done so…"

The General lit a cigarette. Franz saw the tension leave his body. He smiled. It was a smile of which his subordinates would be wary, but at least it was a smile.

"Mr Binns," he said. "It seems to me that your associates, or rather your clients, are fools. They must know that it is one thing to take someone like Miss Czinner, quite another to seize a girl with the connections of Señorita Carmona. And then there is Lieutenant Vilar. Have they gone mad? Franz, I think we may stop worrying. Mr Binns will make it clear to his clients that they must release the girls."

"He can also tell them that they are too late," Franz said. "By now my father is in Israel."

It was that night Franz learned that people really did have separate lives, which were not merely extensions of his own. Of course he had always known this intellectually, as we all do, but he had never felt it before. He had had warnings: the Bastini affair was one such, and he had sometimes tried to imagine how Bastini managed to live with his shame and his self-knowledge. But even this he imagined only in the way you might speculate about a character in a novel, someone who couldn't really be said to exist except in the lines given him. Now, as he sat in Alexis's apartment, waiting for Luis whom they had bidden there, after they had crept from the intolerable confinement of his own home, he struggled to come to terms with the otherness of life.

That his father, as an officer in the SS, had been responsible – though in what precise capacity he didn't know – for some share in the Final Solution of European Jewry; and that this was the same man who looked on him with a tender if remote affection, and ate the club pudding of pastry, fruit and cream, with such enjoyment. How did you connect these two pictures, and, more important, what went on in such a mind? And what was going on now in the aeroplane that was delivering him to Israel?

That Becky was a prisoner somewhere, afraid, with Gabriella who would be weeping, because nothing in her life could have prepared her to feel powerless.

That Becky's father had betrayed his father, that he had found his love for his daughter inadequate, when set in the scales against … what? He had denied that it was a passion for revenge.

"Drink this coffee. You've had enough whisky."

But that wasn't true. It was the whisky which granted him the capacity to endure what he now understood. He thrust his glass at the girl, who sighed, refilled it and said only, "You must be sober…"

"Isn't there a news bulletin on the BBC World Service?"

"In a quarter of an hour."

"Oh Alexis, I don't know what I would do without you."

He clutched her to him.

"Luis will be here soon," she said.

"It's going to be all right," she said; but he heard the lie in her voice. They both knew that whatever happened, it would never be all right again.

"It's not like her to be late," Nell said, "without letting us know. I've told her often, as long as we know…"

Eli did not reply. His silence took on a new irritation for her. He played Schubert songs, and his eyes filled with tears.

"I'm going to telephone Ilse to see if she's there."

"No," he said, "don't do that."

To her surprise, Eli, who no longer took an interest in public affairs, who described world politics as "an inferior version of the *commedia dell'arte*", asked her to tune in to the BBC World Service. She half-listened to the news bulletin as she toasted cheese in the kitchen. There was nothing in its catalogue of human folly and ill-will that could interest him.

"She must be with Franz. It's too bad of her not to have let us know. But something may have happened to her."

"What?"

"Anything."

The doorbell rang.

Franz turned off the radio. "I thought there might be something by now," he said.

"I'm sure there won't be till morning. They will want to announce it with all the stops out."

"Oh God."

"Look…"

"I can't bear to…"

Even the intimacy that they both felt frightened him. He was so conscious of the lines of her body as she sat on the arm of his chair with her hand stroking his cheek. He knew, and knew she knew he knew, that in other circumstances they would abandon words, go to bed, make love; and that what restrained them now was not so much Becky, or decency, as the superstitious thought that their betrayal might bring her bad luck; and perhaps that Luis would soon be with them. Even so he slipped his arm round Alexis, pulled her on top of him, and kissed her on the mouth.

"No," she said, but didn't move.

Then she said, "Your stepfather frightened Cal Binns. Did you get that? He left him scared as all hell. He's quite a man, the General."

He kissed her again.

"I adore Becky too," she said. "She's like a flower."

It was Kinsky. He was out of breath and his eyes, his whole face, looked wild. He looked strangely younger. He said, straight out, panting, "Ilse telephoned me, I can't believe it."

"Who's there," Eli called, above the wireless which was now playing a snatch of opera.

"It's Kinsky."

The music stopped.

"Kinsky? What are you doing at this time of night?"

"Ilse telephoned me," he said again, "I still can't grasp it."

Nell followed him through into the living room. Eli sat in his chair with his hand on the knob of the wireless. It was the volume control he had turned down, but not off, and she was aware of a murmur in the background.

"Would somebody tell me what this is all about? You obviously know," she said to Eli.

"Ilse's in the most terrible state. It's as if her whole world was crumbling. And she has constructed it with such care."

"We interrupt the programme with a newsflash." Eli turned up the sound. "It is reported from Tel Aviv that the Nazi war criminal Rudi Kestner, the right-hand man of the SS chief Reinhardt Heydrich, and the chief accomplice of Adolf Eichmann in the Holocaust, has been captured by Israeli agents and will land at Tel Aviv airport later this morning. This report is as yet unconfirmed. We hope to bring you fuller information in our regular bulletin at six o'clock, Greenwich Mean Time."

*   *   *   *

Alexis slipped off Franz's lap. She moved as if she was floating and she stood with her back to him and smoothed her bottom; he watched the fingers extended against the blue denim.

"That's it. That's Part I, I guess, and this" – as the doorbell rang – "sounds like your friend Luis."

"Alexis…" but she had gone through the apartment in answer to the door, and Franz was left alone. He poured himself another whisky, and drank it quickly, then another which he stood holding in both hands as Luis entered the room.

"So, boy, what gives, what is this?"

"Tell him the whole story, honey."

"I don't know the whole story… I don't even know what I know…"

"But who is Rudi Kestner?" Nell said. She took off her spectacles and held them, like counsel making a point to the jury, in one hand. "I don't mean that. I mean – what is the significance? Of course I know who Kestner was, is, I should say…"

"Nell," Kinsky said, "Kestner is Franz's father."

"Do you remember," he went on, "in Berlin in 1939 or late '38, you told me of how a man approached you in Unter den Linden and warned you about your relationship with Eli? That was Kestner."

She sat down, plomp.

"No, that's impossible… I would have known. I would have recognised him when…" But it wasn't impossible. She had liked that man even while he frightened and disgusted her, and she had liked Franz's father with reservations which were certainly different, and yet…

"Oh my God. Does Becky know?"

"Where can I find this Binns?" Luis said. "Just tell me, and I shall strangle him. First though I shall pull out his teeth one by one till he confesses where they are."

"It's not like that," Alexis said. "Cal Binns is only a middleman, a go-between. And they'll be all right."

"Becky will be all right," Eli said. "There is no reason why she shouldn't be now."

*   *   *   *

"It's a mess, Luis, it's an inferno, and don't think I am not in the deepest pit of Hell."

"What makes you think I give a damn where you are, my friend? What I fucking want to know is why you are sitting here on your backside?"

"My God." Nell looked at her husband. "This is your doing. And don't you see, you blind fool, Becky is harmed, ruined, whatever happens to her now?"

EIGHT

Franz watched the screen, a little breeze from the open window playing on the back of his neck. Four Israeli soldiers ran towards the plane. The steps were lowered, and they trotted up them. Then a man in an open-necked white shirt appeared in the doorway and waved them back. They obeyed, confused. One of them was a girl with a shock of heavy swinging dark hair; she looked a little like Gabriella. The man in the white shirt signalled a greeting to the world's press. There were photographers everywhere: the television camera cut to the ranks of kneeling men, others pushing and jostling behind them. The man in the white shirt withdrew again into the plane. There was a pause. It seemed to last the length of a commercial as the camera held the shot of the empty doorway. The man in the white shirt returned, at the head of a small group. They descended the steps. There were five or six of them. The open-necked white shirt looked like a sort of uniform. But there in the middle, distinguished only by the cuffs on his wrist (the hands crossed in front of his body), was Franz's father. He still wore his dark glasses, but two others were wearing dark glasses also, and it was only the manacles that made him any different from the crowd that surrounded him. He looked calm, blank-faced. Maybe he had used up expressions in the days since he had been snatched from his bungalow.

The press surged forward but were restrained. There were now more policemen and more soldiers on the tarmac. Some of them were shouting and gesticulating, and you could hear yells coming also from the crowd that was held back even behind the press. Then a jeep came up very fast, followed by a small black van. Rudi was hustled into the back of the van. Three or four of the white-shirted figures clambered in after him. The two vehicles drove off, followed by motorcyclists.

The cameras cut to an interview room. The man who had come out of the plane first described the circumstances of what he called the arrest. He didn't mention Dr Czinner. He said only "Acting on information received…" He said that Kestner had tried at first to dispute the iden-tification, "but we weren't having that, and he desisted." Of course he had been well treated. This was a serious business: An act of justice, not revenge, and so naturally the accused will be given every facility to conduct his defence, and will be treated in the manner enjoined by the Israeli penal code. No, Kestner would not be permitted to give an interview. No, the press would not be permitted to question him. That was a matter for the court.

A journalist said, "Is it true that two girls are being held hostage in Argentina, and that there are proposals for ransom?"

"I have no information on that subject, but the Israeli Government will never consider any such proposition. Kestner will stand trial for his crimes against humanity."

The General rose and switched off the television. "I'm amazed they asked that question about the girls."

Franz looked away: "Where are they? What's happening? You were so sure they would be released."

"We must keep the newspapers from your mother. This is terrible for her."

"Did you know about my father, Papa?"

"Yes, of course I did, Franz. There were arrangements, you see, to which it was necessary that I be privy. They … broke down … As for the girls, the matter is more complicated than I thought. Your father's friends have made fools of themselves. The murder of Lieutenant Vilar was, as the saying goes, worse than a crime. You know the rest."

Vilar's body had been found on a rubbish dump on the fringes of the capital. It had been mutilated.

"At first," the General said, "it wasn't certain that your father's friends were responsible. Vilar was last seen in a brothel, a male brothel… That, we thought, accounted perhaps for the form of mutilation … though it wasn't clear, nothing was clear … then …"

"But why should they want to kill him?"

"It was Vilar's job to protect your father. He failed. Perhaps they murdered him to encourage the others. Perhaps it was an interrogation which went wrong. That is my opinion… Then they mutilated him, to disguise the circumstances, as a blind …"

Franz thought of Vilar offering him a woman, then of the manner in which the policeman had rested his hand on his shoulder as they said goodbye.

"In any case the murder has alarmed them. That means, I am afraid, that the girls are in greater danger than I thought."

"You mean, for fear they can identify their captors?"

"That's possible."

"But that's mad. After all, I can identify the men I spoke to. I would know the man Klaus again anywhere."

"You don't understand. It wouldn't occur to them that you might not be on their side. They are acting after all to save your father."

"By imprisoning and terrifying the girl I'm going to marry?"

"Yes, they are fools… perhaps different people are following different courses."

The telephone rang.

"Splendid," the General said, "bring him up, will you, please."

The lift took a long time to mount. They were in the General's office on the top floor of the tall building that houses the Ministry of Defence (Special Services Section). Franz had never been there before. The General preferred to keep work and family absolutely separate. It was a large square room, furnished in spartan style; there were four abstract paintings, one in the centre of each wall. You could look down to the ocean from the windows. The General's big colonial desk was uncluttered.

There was a knock at the door. A soldier ushered their visitor in. He was a balding, middle-aged man, with rimless spectacles and a puffy unused face. His complexion was pale, with a touch of grey in it, and when he offered his hand, the palm was a little damp.

"This is Mr Dukes, from Washington," the General said. "He has flown down at my request."

Mr Dukes took a little pill from a small leather box and popped it in his mouth.

"Elevators," he said, "agitate my cardiac organ. You will pardon me if I rest up a moment before we converse."

They waited. Franz was impressed by the General's tranquillity, and by the indifference to their reaction which the American displayed.

"We have a certain awkwardness," the General said. "Your Mr Binns seems to have been careless and a touch over-zealous."

Mr Dukes licked his lips, then patted at his cheek with a tissue.

"Cal Binns is a good operative, but we never put him on contract."

Franz realised that contract would never come. Perhaps Binns had sought it for years. He had hung on in Argentina, no more than a stringer, picking up a scrap of information here, doing the odd dirty jobs there, a useful man who could be easily denied. Now he had – it was clear as Mr Dukes expatiated – gone too far, acting on his own initiative, misinterpreted the situation, gone out on a limb.

"Sure," Mr Dukes said, "some of those involved have had a very genuine utility. We owe them something. But we don't owe them all that much, and we don't owe them what they owe us. There is, that is to say, an imbalance in the indebtedness. I guess Cal Binns has outstayed his welcome."

The General smiled. "Mr Binns is an honoured guest. We wouldn't wish to disturb him. But, you must understand, his activities have disturbed his position. It will not be possible to renew his permission to remain in the country unless he is of real assistance to us now. Let me be frank with you, Mr Dukes."

He got up and went to the mahogany-veneered cabinet in the corner of his room, took from it a Thermos flask and three glasses. Then he poured three Martinis; they were still cloudy with cold. He dropped an olive in each glass.

"I am what passes for a liberal in this country..."

The words flickered across Franz's mind, like a torchlight dancing in the night searching the explanation of some mystery, hunting the interloper in the garden. Labels: Liberal, Commie, Jew, Nazi, Peronist – it was for labels that men killed, that his father had – there could be no doubt – committed atrocities, and was now on the brink of suffering or whatever. Beyond the brink in fact. Bastini had been labelled, Kinsky too. But the label had infected his life and Becky's and Ilse's and Nell's. Was it because only Alexis at this moment seemed to be free of a label that she seemed the most desirable, as well as most enviable, of people?

Mr Dukes was speaking of political implications, damage limitation, creative tensions. Sentences rolled their abstract nouns like clouds across the sky. Yesterday, because they couldn't any longer sit around waiting for the telephone to ring, Franz had driven Alexis to the beach. He found himself seeking the right adjective in any language to describe the colour of her thigh sparkling with salt water, but he didn't need a word; he could see the thing. That surely was reality. He put his finger on her thigh; it came off damp and he licked it, tasting Alexis, sun and sea in one instant. He would have liked to lie there and run his tongue along its line, but something restrained him. But he still felt the weight of her wet arms around his neck and the yielding and thrusting of desire and the brushing contact of mouths, and saw her huge cornflower eyes open close to his, and heard her whisper "How can we?" and knew the answer to it all was "How can we not?" How can we not be traitors? But also, in what sense is truth treachery?

But that too was the question. It was the central question. It was the question of his father's life.

"Unfortunately Cal had been imbibing and it was difficult to extract sense from his account of the kidnap situation."

"Perhaps you could sober him up, Mr Dukes."

"His doctor prescribes hospitalisation."

"Very well. We shall be the better able to keep him under observation."

"He recommends despatch to the USA."

"I fear we should object to that."

"You misunderstand me, General. The cause of Cal's condition would appear to be his apprehension as to his own security."

"His apprehension is well-founded if anything happens to these girls. You can tell him that from me."

"Negotiations in my view should be based on the assumption of a degree of amnesty…"

"No," Alexis said, "no, darling, not now, not yet, not while…"

"But after…"

"Maybe not after…"

She ran out into the sea with long strides shortening as the water chopped at her legs.

"Are you sure," she left him pondering her question, "that you are not using me to punish Becky for what her father has done?"

He was sure of nothing but what he wanted then. Becky might be dead.

"… a degree of amnesty."

Franz's attention had wandered. He had lost the thread of the conversation. His stepfather, the General, flicked a minute particle of ash from his cuff. He sipped his Martini and watched the American.

"We have no responsibility for Cal's friends," Mr Dukes said.

"I don't charge you with that."

Alexis lay on her back, with her knees drawn up. Her belly was flat and brown. The skin wrinkled as she eased herself into another position, digging her shoulder blades deeper into the white sand. He couldn't tell whether her eyes were closed behind the dark glasses. He turned over on his front, his face on the sand, but still allowing him to look at her profile. He let his right hand fall gently on her body, and she allowed it to rest there.

"General, this position is, let's not deny it, embarrassing for both our Governments. You appreciate of course the nature of our relationship with Israel. So let's level up."

Mr Dukes popped a violet-coloured pastille into his mouth.

"It's been a great pleasure to meet your stepson, but it appears to me that we might more conveniently hope to arrive at a negotiable position, if we were able to talk in seclusion and privacy."

"Very well. Franz, you will wait, please, next door."

"No," Alexis kissed him, "no… if we do what you want now…"

"You want it too…"

He drew her to him and kissed her again, this time on the lips. He forced his tongue into her mouth.

At last, she said again, "No", and pushed his arms aside and freed herself.

"It's because you're disturbed. You'll hate me later if we do."

"No," he said, but the battle was lost, he knew that. He read reproach and self-reproach in her eyes, which filled with tears. "Maybe if things had been different."

"But they're not, they're the way they are."

He stood in the outer office, looking out over the city. The sky was grey, with heavy clouds rolling in from the sea. "The other side of the street had not been built." That was true of more than Argentina. Luis's anger had evaporated, or rather its expression had done so. He had made his dramatic point; that satisfied his need for action. Now he waited, like the rest of them. Franz sighed. It distressed him that he couldn't imagine what Becky would be feeling. He couldn't put himself in her place.

A secretary came in with a cup of coffee. He drank it, forgetting the Martini he had just had. Half-way through the cup, he remembered it, and said to himself: this is me, I accept whatever comes my way.

Alexis had said, "Don't come up to my apartment, please. You mustn't. I don't trust us if you come up to my apartment."

He stood, listening to the lift carry her away.

"So," the General said, "Mr Dukes has gone and matters will arrange themselves. We have come to an understanding. The girls will be released, probably by tonight. You can rely on that. I told you things would arrange themselves…"

He picked a cigar from its box and rustled it between his fingers. He pushed the box towards Franz, and clipped the end off his cigar and held a match to it. He looked at Franz through the flame.

"But I do not think your marriage can go ahead," he said. "I don't think it is seemly. Your mother, I am afraid, does not agree. She has a tender heart, as you know. But that is how it seems to me. And also, I think it will be better if you leave Argentina for some while. I don't conceal, Franz, that this business embarrasses me. There could be consequences, but they will be more manageable if you are not here. So perhaps London. Perhaps you could transfer your studies to Oxford? That might be a good idea."

"You want rid of me," Franz said.

The General puffed smoke from his cigar.

"You're not a fool, Franz," he said. "I've never thought you a fool. Naive, sentimental, but not a fool. Not like your friend Luis."

"You've been very kind to me since you married my mother, but you want rid of me."

"Shall we say your continued presence causes difficulties?"

"Very well. One question. Is this part of the bargain you made with Mr Dukes?"

The General smiled, "Why should you think that, dear boy?"

Franz said, "There's one thing I must tell you. I am going to have to go to Israel. You must understand that."

"I understand it. I regret it also. You can do no good there, not in any way."

"All the same, I must go. And another thing, I am still going to marry Becky. All this has nothing to do with us. When it's over, that will be the end of the chapter, which will not concern us any longer."

"You would do better to forget about her." The General smiled. "Your mother will be distressed to hear of your plans, I fear, but we cannot arrange our lives to satisfy our womenfolk."

PART TWO
ISRAEL
1965

ONE

It was extraordinary to be felt over by a girl in uniform and army boots, and to realise that she experienced no embarrassment. Then he was out of the customs shed, and standing in the air-conditioned hall, which was like everywhere and nowhere. Even the people surging around him reinforced his apprehension: there was no common physical type, but they cohered.

He didn't have to wait long. A large black-bearded man waved a sheaf of papers from the far side of the hall, bustled over and seized his hand.

"I told you I'd be here," he said. "Bloody traffic. I'm Saul Birnbaum. No difficulty picking you out. You're like your photo."

He picked up Franz's luggage and hurried him towards the car park. He threw the bag into the back of a battered Volkswagen, and squeezed himself behind the wheel.

"No prejudice, you see. German car. The best. Do you know something: it was an uncle of mine drew up the first blueprint. Fact."

There were streaks of grey in his beard, and his white shirt, open at the collar and worn without a jacket, was stained with sweat. He drove very fast, with much hooting, to the hotel where he had reserved accommodation for Franz. They went up to his room and ordered beer. When it arrived, Dr Birnbaum sat down and waved the beer bottle in Franz's direction, indicating that he should seat himself also.

Franz said, "I ought to thank you."

"Say no more."

"For the arrangements, of course. More particularly for accepting the case."

"I'm a lawyer. An officer of the Court. Say no more. Besides, kid, you've said it. In your letters. Much appreciated."

"Dr Birnbaum…"

"Call me Saul. This is Israel, kid. We have abolished formality, don't you know? All men are equal, hierarchy is out, judges have cousins who work as plumbers and Cabinet Ministers help harvest oranges."

He sucked at his beer bottle.

"Saul, then, will I be allowed to see him?"

"Sure. Not today though. I didn't fix for today in case you were de-layed. Today you relax."

The noise from the street prevented silence from being silent. Franz was disconcerted by the lawyer's goodwill. He didn't know how to reply. He couldn't pick a question from the number that teemed and tumbled in his mind, and it was impossible to offer any remark that wasn't a question.

"You've won me a bet," Saul Birnbaum said.

"How?"

"My colleagues said you wouldn't come."

"What made you think I would?"

"What your father said."

Franz blushed. "I don't know that I can do any good," he said, "but …"

But − but do you view my father with horror? − that was what he ought to ask.

Saul Birnbaum heaved himself up.

"I must work," he said. "I'm overwhelmed. You take it easy, kid. If you want lunch, ring room service. That'll be best today. There may be reporters about. I'll send my secretary to show you round this afternoon. Fine? About four. Anna she's called. OK. She'll bring you a message about seeing your dad."

Franz lay down on the bed. Heat swelled in the street below, but the air conditioning worked. The hotel room was without character, the fur-niture neither pleasing nor ugly. Jet lag, or perhaps the beer, made him sleepy. He took off his shoes, socks and trousers, lowered the Venetian blind, and got between the sheets. He fell asleep and didn't dream. It was the first dreamless sleep he had known since he had been forced to know what he now knew. He rubbed sleep from his eyes, and was hun-gry. Room service would send him coffee and eggs in fifteen minutes. He had time for a shower.

The girl who arrived while he was drinking his second cup of coffee was neither beautiful nor ugly. That was a relief, either would have been distracting. (And yet wasn't distraction just what he needed?) She was stocky, very healthy, and had a fine shadow of moustache.

"I've come to show you the city," she said.

"Can't we just go to the beach?"

"The beach? You're not on holiday."

"Very well. But I must dress."

"Don't mind me."

But of course he did. He took his clothes through to the bathroom.

"It's very good of you," he said, as they settled into her car, a red Fiat 500.

"I'm an employee."

There was, in truth, he thought, little worth seeing. Tel Aviv gave the impression of having been built in a hurry. The blocks of apartments and offices fulfilled their function, and that was all there was to it. He was bored. Nothing appealed to his imagination. She hadn't even shown him the prison where his father was being kept. She bombarded him with information, statistics to which he found it impossible to pay any attention. She was playing the guide in a very professional manner, and she disliked him, which was uncomfortable.

"Look," he said, "this isn't necessary. It must be time for you to go home. I mean, it must now be past your working hours. You're not obliged."

She swung the car off the highway, down a bumpy lane, and halted in front of a café-restaurant with metal tables in a scruffy garden.

"We will have some beer," she said. "So you are not impressed with our city."

"I don't know what makes you think that."

"I can tell. I have heard about your fiancée. Saul has told me. Has she recovered?"

"I think so. Yes. Thank you."

"And you have left her in Argentina? Notwithstanding everything that has happened. I confess I don't understand that. For me, personal relations come before everything."

"Even Israel?" he said.

"I don't make a distinction," she said, "between Israel and personal relations."

A breeze stirred from the sea. The bray of a donkey came from an olive grove. They were on the fringe of the town. Franz could see orchards of orange trees, olive groves, and then, there was emptiness, the desert.

"So you think it strange that I have come?" he said. She licked a foam of beer off her upper lip.

"I don't know," she said. "Yes, strange. It's a question of morality.

There are actions that cancel out bonds, yes? But not for you? That I find strange."

"There are moments," he said, and paused.

She cut into the silence. "You don't dare to ask, but I will answer: my father, four grandparents, two brothers and my sister. My mother died giving birth to me. A friend, the wife of a Protestant pastor, took care of me. I'm twenty-one."

"I understand," he said, "you must find my behaviour inexplicable."

"Not that, no, strange."

He wrote an account of this meeting and conversation in the journal he had determined to keep:

> She said she didn't want vengeance, only justice. I wish I understood what people mean by the word. Then she asked me to a party: "Why not? Nobody blames you." I said my presence might make others uncomfortable, as well as myself.

Saul Birnbaum collected him the next morning. Franz had hesitated over what to wear: settling first on dark blue linen trousers, brown slip-on shoes, and a blazer. But it was too hot for the blazer; he exchanged it for a cotton combat jacket, disliked the connotations, finally met Saul in a white cotton cardigan worn loose. It was 8.30; the lawyer was half way through a thick cigar. He said, "We have to get your dad some cigarettes, he's started smoking again."

They stopped at a bar, which was also a tobacconist's, for coffee. Saul laid aside his cigar and crammed a doughnut into his mouth.

"I aim to eat nothing before lunch." He patted his belly. "It never works."

He bought a ten-pack carton of Chesterfield.

"Shouldn't I pay for these?"

"Not to worry."

Franz didn't know who was meeting Saul's fees. That was a point he must bring up.

"Have the journalists got at you?"

"No."

"They will. Like I said, refer them to me. But there's one chap you should meet. He's a novelist who has a column in one of our dailies. Very young. Maybe twenty-five. He's called Luke, he'll get in touch."

In the months Franz hadn't seen his father, the two photographs used by the Press – of the dapper officer in SS uniform and the weary hangdog figure in handcuffs, the one fusing with the other as a type of sado-masochistic fantasy – had made it increasingly difficult for him to recall the father he thought he had actually known. And this father was not restored by the man who sat waiting for them behind a large bare table, and who rose, a little stiffly, to his feet as they entered.

Rudi had put on weight. There was a suggestion, never previously present, of a double chin. And he hesitated a moment before advancing to embrace Franz, as if he feared that his son might refuse that sort of recognition. But Franz laid his cheek against his father's and felt him tremble.

"I was sorry," Rudi said, "for what those fools did to your fiancée. Sorry, angry and ashamed."

They sat down. Saul pushed the cigarettes over to his client, who however took one from a pack already open in his breast pocket, and lit it from the book of matches which was the only object on the table.

"I haven't brought you anything, just myself, I'm afraid," Franz said. "I thought I would wait and see what you needed."

"There's a good library here," Rudi said.

Franz had a photograph for him, the one of himself as a boy with the spaniel Mutzi, but he didn't know how to give it to him.

"How's your mother?" Rudi said.

"She's all right. She's distressed, but she's all right "

"All this must be a check to her social ambitions. I'm sorry." He seemed to speak without irony. "And perhaps to your marriage, but I hope not."

"It was Becky's father who recognised you."

He hadn't meant to say that.

"So I understand. Well, you're a different generation."

Saul Birnbaum took a maroon leather case from his bag and extracted a cigar. He cut the end off, and removed the band. It lay on the table: Franz picked it up: H. Upmann. Saul held a match to it in mid-air, and put the cigar in his mouth and lit it. He blew out a cloud of smoke.

"I tell you again, you ought to smoke these, Rudi. They do you so much less harm than cigarettes."

"Cigarettes are better suited to my nervous condition."

"They exacerbate it."

It was, Franz saw, already a ritual between them.

"Besides, I don't know that I am in a position to worry about the long-term effects of cigarette smoking."

Saul laughed, "You see, Franz, your father is in excellent spirits, as I told you. Now I must go. I must work. I have arranged for a taxi to collect you in half an hour, which is all that is permitted, and take you back to your hotel. I will tell Luke to ring you there. OK?"

Dearest Mamma,
I saw Father this morning. He appears well, both physically and mentally. His first question was how you were.

I went to the prison with his lawyer, who is very genial. He seems confident. I hope he is as able as he evidently thinks he is. I don't think we need doubt his commitment, even though I confess I don't understand it. But then I understand so little. Least of all why he has received me as a friend, as has his assistant or secretary, a girl called Anna, despite the fact that her own family ... but you don't want to hear about horrors.

I haven't yet had an opportunity to discuss the line of defence with Dr Birnbaum (that's the lawyer – Saul). But I can't see that it can be other than that Father was a mere functionary; and that line didn't save Eichmann, nor did it work for others.

We must therefore nerve ourselves for the worst. The question is not the verdict but the sentence. There I think Saul may be effective. He acts as if he has a card up his sleeve...

Franz laid down his pen. Saul wore short-sleeved shirts. Well, it was only an expression. He added some enquiries about his mother's health and his stepfather's. Sent love, and signed off. It wasn't a good letter.

He picked up his journal:

How to understand Father's equanimity? It is as if he has been preparing himself for this moment since he accepted that the war was lost. He asked me if I believed in God. I said no; then I remembered that before leaving Buenos Aires I went to the Church of the Solitary Virgin and lit a candle for him, and admitted this. "Oh," he replied, "that's just like turning the money over in your pocket when you see the new moon, I've always done that. Now I've no money to turn and I can't

see the moon from my cell, which has no windows, anyway."
He knew I wanted to talk about the war, which we have never of course done. "I never had any doubts, you know," he said. "That's what they'll get me for, that I never had any doubts ... I don't see myself as a monster. Is that a failure of my imagination?"

"The fact that you can ask me such a question proves that your imagination is active."

"I'm not sure," he said, "that that reply isn't merely clever. Don't be merely clever, Franz."

My impression: that the balance between us has shifted, and that, as a result, we are for the first time growing close. What does that say about me?

The telephone rang. It was the journalist Luke. Franz didn't catch his surname. He would pick him up for lunch.

Darling Becky,
It's hell without you, but would it be anything other than a different kind of hell if you were actually here? That's what I ask myself. By accident, I have put such a load on you that I don't see how we can ever get rid of it, or how we can live under it. This is not a rejection, but it's how I see things. For the rest of our life together, I am going to have to be making amends, to be careful. I'm not sure even now that it's possible. That's why I slept with Alexis if you want to know. It wasn't simply physical attraction, though that was there. It was the fact that I didn't owe her anything.

This is a lie. I never slept with Alexis. She wouldn't let me. But you were right: I wanted to. I still do. Sex free from obligations and values. You can't imagine what that would mean to me.

My father knows it was your father who informed on him. I almost wrote "betrayed".

If I had written "betrayed" it would have proved we have no possible future.

And yet if I can't imagine a future with you, I can't tolerate the prospect of one without you.

Sartre was a fool when he said Hell was other people. Hell is oneself.

Father as Faust??

The letter had drifted into his journal. That was where it belonged. He took the sheet and placed it between the pages of the book, and started again.

Darling Becky,

I'm no good at letters, but I miss you awfully.

I could write about my feelings, and we are going to have to try to come to terms with the mesh of obligation, recrimination, guilt, fear, tenderness and love, some day, some day.

I went to see him this morning. He is very calm, and he is still himself as I knew him. Does that make it worse or better?

When I look at the people in the streets or the waiters and barmen and chambermaids in the hotel, I see orphans my father made. Do you understand how terrible that is?

He knows it was your father who… I don't know the word to use, but perhaps I don't need one. He was horrified by what happened to you. I think he was sincere. You may say, to hell with his sincerity, and I will understand that, but I thought I would tell you.

Please write to me. I love you.

He put the letter in an envelope before he could change his mind, and took the two down to reception and got stamps and posted them. Then he stood in the doorway of the hotel looking out on the street. A mother passed with four curly-headed children in tow; they all wore shorts and the sun shone on them. The children were eating ice cream or sucking lollipops. Across the road a group of young people hung around a café. They were passing a bottle of Coca-Cola from hand to hand. He looked at his watch. It was half an hour until Luke was due. He crossed the street and sat at one of the tables and ordered coffee. Nobody paid him any attention. He wished he could understand what these boys and girls were saying. He didn't even know what language they were speaking. They might be Arabs.

He bought a postcard to send to Alexis. But what could he say, except, "Wish you were here, to make things less complicated"? Which could anyway only be true in one sense.

The young man greeted him in the hotel lobby. He wore jeans and a pink shirt, and his handshake was warm. He was short, three or four inches shorter than Franz, and stocky. He wore a cigarette in the corner of his mouth like Humphrey Bogart.

"Luke," he said, and clapped Franz on the back. "We'll go for lunch."

He took him to a restaurant, where he ordered lamb kebabs and rice, and a bottle of local wine. The kebabs were spicy and came with yellow and red peppers. Luke tore at the bread and smiled at Franz. It was a good smile, friendly and without calculation. They could have been old friends.

"I'm not giving you an interview," Franz said. "I'm not ready for interviews. I don't know if I ever will be."

"Sure."

"Saul told me you were a novelist as well as a journalist. Why has he taken my father's case?"

"You'd have to ask him that. No, I just wanted to meet you. Call it curiosity. We've a lot in common."

"Nice of you to say so, but I don't see it."

"Sure, we're both Eichmann's children… know what I mean?"

The phrase was absurd. Franz accepted that heredity for himself; it seemed he had no choice, but for a Jew to claim it? He looked at the nose which had been broken (playing football, Luke said, touching it) and the brown eyes that flickered with humour, and the strong brown hand that tore at the bread and poured the wine, and he was puzzled.

"German, Jew, Gentile, Israeli, everything we do, all the attitudes we adopt, are the expression of that inheritance. Do you see? Besides, we've got our Jews here, only we call them Arabs. There are Zionists whose idea of dealing with the Palestinian problem is a sort of Final Solution."

"You're not one of them, I take it?"

"No, I'm not. What are your impressions of Israel, Franz?"

"I'm impressed, and disappointed. Impressed by the energy and the friendliness, disappointed by what you've made of it. *Sólo faltó una cosa: la vereda de enfrente*."

"What does that mean?"

"It's a line of Borges: 'Only one thing was lacking: the other side of the street.' "

Luke laid his hand on Franz's.

"You feel that too. Maybe we can build it."

For a moment the hands rested together, the warm brown on the white.

In the afternoon Luke drove him out of the city and across the country towards the Jordan. They passed a town on a hill.

From the road the apartment blocks looked mean and jerry-built.

"Bet Shemesh," Luke said. "Maybe you should see it. It's not nice."

Franz was surprised.

"I thought you would want to show me the best of Israel."

"Everyone else'll do that. Not me."

The apartments were set with distances between them, empty lots either awaiting new buildings or perhaps intended to be covered with vegetable gardens, miniature orchards or chicken runs. Some of the buildings were constructed on top of concrete pillars, and stood disconsolate like stranded storks. Weeds grew in abundance and from the clotheslines, stretched above the dusty ground, hung shabby garments which no washing could, it seemed, render clean. There was a square on the top of the hill, a square open at one side, and in fact shaped like a horseshoe.

Luke stopped the car there. It was late afternoon now and most of those in the square were in work-clothes, blue cotton overalls, the uniform of the Mediterranean.

"It's not what I expected," Franz said.

Luke smiled, lit a cigarette, gestured towards a group of middle-aged men, mostly unshaven, who were standing smoking outside a café.

"What was your Borges line?" he said.

Franz repeated it. "Are these Arabs?" he asked.

"No, they hate the Arabs. These are what we call Oriental Jews, from Iraq maybe, or North Africa. They hate me too, or they would. As a kibbutznik, you see, or as a cit from Tel Aviv. Doesn't matter. I'm an Ashkenazi, a European Jew, a socialist. But you can't tell them from the Arabs, can you, just as my grandfather who was a doctor of medicine was indistinguishable from his colleagues in Danzig. Let's go have a beer."

Franz laid his hand on Luke's arm, arresting him.

"You won't let on who I am?"

Luke smiled: "Who do you think I am, baby?"

"But what are you trying to prove?"

"Nothing. Do you know what my party says? – it says we must change these people immediately, refashion them in our image."

"But I know them," Franz said, "they're what we call in Argentina the shirtless ones, or just *el pueblo*, the people. In Argentina, they look to Perón. He wrote a book called *La Fuerza es el Derecho de las Bestias*, Force is the Right of Animals, or perhaps, the Law of the Jungle."

"Oh," Luke said, "we have our Perón, a Perón in waiting. I'm very much afraid his time will come."

"So will Peron's: again. I see why you brought me here: to make me talk about Hitler."

"We'll do that, but later. Now let's have that beer."

It was night and they were in Luke's apartment in the city. The ashtrays were full. They had finished eating, stew of kid with dumplings, followed by fruit. Luke opened another bottle of wine. His wife, Rachel, removed her shoes and stretched out on the rug. A violinist played Hungarian gypsy music on the gramophone.

Rachel said, "Between the three of us we're not seventy."

"If you mean," Luke said, "that we are too young to take the weight of the world on our shoulders, then I can't agree with you."

She lifted her hand. Their fingers intertwined.

"Your fiancée's Jewish, isn't she, Franz?" She looked up at him and smiled.

"Yes," he said.

"You don't know what you have let yourself in for."

"Her father was in Auschwitz. Before that he worked for the Reichsbank. He's a famous economist. He collaborated with Schacht. It was he who recognised my father ... and made arrangements for his capture."

He spoke the words as if they had nothing to do with him, as if he were recounting a history lesson: "In 1870 Bismarck, realising the opportunity afforded him by the French insistence that the Hohenzollern candidate for the Spanish throne should renounce his claim permanently and irrevocably, suppressed the conciliatory telegram which the Kaiser wished to send, and thus precipitated the war by which the German Empire was created..."

It meant nothing, put like that. "Luke hates this trial," she said.

"Let's change the music," Luke said. He put on a record of Edith Piaf. "Have you been to Paris, Franz?"

Franz shook his head. Rachel and Luke were no longer holding hands, but the bitter-sweet music that filled the air bound them together; yes, and Franz with them. Smoke pricked his eyes.

"I'm sorry for you, Franz," she said, "but it seems necessary to me."

"A moment ago you wanted to quit yourself of responsibility. You did, darling. I don't hate it, I fear it. There are two kinds of nostalgia; there is the kind in which we are indulging now, with Piaf and the gypsies, which does no harm because it's no more than relaxation, and there's the other kind. We Jews are nostalgic for suffering, we can never have enough of it."

"Do you mean that for Jews my father's trial is a sort of self-indulgence?" Luke jumped to his feet. He crossed the room and opened the window. "Come here, Franz."

A scent of lemons and oranges hung on the night air. The lights of the city extended far away, but beyond the lights, the moon rose behind a black density of mountains. Luke waved towards them.

"Beyond that, the desert. But we can't even smell it."

He was perhaps a little drunk. Later, they drank more, and Franz slept there on a couch.

Franz puzzled over Rachel's claim that Luke hated his father's trial. It didn't make sense to him. He could not see that Luke felt the past as his own personal albatross, a curse hung round the neck of Israel. The Holocaust might in his view quite properly disturb their sleep, that was to put it with absurd mildness, for nightmare was inescapably the inheritance of his generation, yet he had formed the opinion that it should be kept as something private. Otherwise nothing could stop the Jews from perpetually presenting themselves as a special case, deserving of special treatment, demanding it indeed as a right; and as long as that was so, they would never be admitted as an equal partner to the family of nations.

Franz, however, had more immediate worries. There was first his father and his father's state of mind. He was disturbed by the humour Rudi brought to the whole business of his defence. "Of course," he said, "when it comes to the trial itself, I shall fight my corner. Like a mad dog, if that's the way they want it. But you must see, son, that it's a charade. All the essential decisions were taken, the judgements made, the verdicts delivered and even the sentences determined, almost twenty years ago. You can't therefore expect me to take this farrago of legality seriously. I know what will happen to me, and, believe me, I am quite prepared. My only regret is the embarrassment it will cause you."

His choice of the word "embarrassment" was cruel. Rudi was no longer like himself. He was a fool of an actor, a comedian, whose performance threatened to be celluloid-perfect, smooth as Warner Brothers might have made it.

Franz sighed. He moved about his room, which was itself a species of cell. There was nothing for him to do. He was superfluous. There was scarcely even a walk-on part for him. He had imagined that he would offer aid and comfort to his father. There had been something heroic in the part he had assigned to himself. Without in any way condoning the monstrous crimes of the regime, without compromising his own integrity, he would nevertheless uphold the sacred obligations of family, and, in doing so, reinforce indeed that same integrity. And, instead, he wasn't needed. The play would proceed without him. If he had a privileged seat in the orchestra stalls, that wasn't at all what he had wanted. Quite the reverse: to be that sort of spectator was worse than not being there at all.

Yet he couldn't leave, even though Rudi had suggested that he should. "There's nothing for you here except what you don't need," he said. "I gambled on being able to construct some sort of meaningful family life for us, and it has failed. You should go back to Argentina." The terrible thing was that he couldn't be sure that Rudi didn't mean it.

He confessed to Rachel that he had shrunk all his life from the responsibility of being German.

"I don't understand what you mean," Rachel poured him coffee from an Italian machine.

"I have never faced up to what the Germans did."

She smiled.

"Well, perhaps if you are only beginning to think about it, it's natural that you should feel as you do. I wish Luke was here. He puts things so much better than I can. My grandfather, I must tell you, was the *Oberjude* of a town in Poland. Do you understand what that means?"

"Of course."

"Of course," she mimicked him. "Of course... how easily you say that. He was a physician, with honorary degrees from half a dozen universities, including Leipzig. As the *Oberjude* he was head of the council responsible for the administration of the ghetto. The principle on which they worked was one of co-operation with the Nazis. My grandfather was much exercised with the problem of how to make the ghetto work-shops function efficiently. If they did so, you see, they were of value to the German war effort and so the worst would be postponed, though of course if the Germans won the war, it would nevertheless happen. But the thing was to keep the future away, at a distance. Then his brother, also a physician, was shot one day in 1941, on a street in the ghetto. His offence was failure to remove his hat in the presence of a policeman, as required in the orders which the Jewish Council had ratified. But even after this, my grandfather continued to work to make everything func-tion smoothly. He resisted the idea of resistance. He was not religious, and I do not think he had faith in anything but science. He even de-spised socialism. Before the war he greatly admired Germany. He said he felt at home there. I am told he once said, 'Whether the German people become drunk on victory or are overcome by the agony of defeat, I, with my mark of Cain, will be the first to face danger and suffer punishment.' He was murdered of course. He didn't even reach Auschwitz."

She leaned forward. Her long hair, black with a sheen of blue, hung loose.

"Why did you bring flowers?"

There was a wave, natural as the line of the hills, in her hair, which brushed against the dense mass of dark red carnations.

"Are you the sort of boy who was brought up to bring flowers? Or was it spontaneous? Tell me about your mother."

"No," he said, "tell me about yours."

"Oh, my mother, she was all right. She married my father before the war, and he had a cousin in New York, and they got a visa, and did well, he's a doctor of medicine too, and they agitated for 'Second Front Now', and then after the war did less well, because of their political affiliations, and then they came to Israel in '49. It's a success story. He was a member of the Knesset, till he got cancer."

"You don't like them."

"I never said that… Besides in Israel, everyone adores their parents, they're so lucky to have them, didn't you know?"

It was late afternoon. Franz had come back to say thank you. If there had been a concierge, he would have left the flowers and a note with her. But Rachel had insisted he come in, have some coffee.

"Have you seen your father today?"

"Yes. For half an hour."

The terrible thing was that he hadn't been able to find anything to say. He had been more conscious of a bluebottle buzzing than of the remarks that had dropped from his father's lips.

"It must be difficult for you. Have you been besieged by the press?"

"Not yet."

"I'm surprised. You will be."

"Do you know Saul Birnbaum?"

"Only by reputation and what Luke says."

"Is he good?"

"He's Israel's most flamboyant lawyer. You didn't tell me about your mother."

"Mamma? She's married to an Argentinian General. Mamma's like a cat. She seeks out comfort."

"Do you think she knew?"

"Knew what?"

"About your father?"

"My stepfather could be head of Internal Security, and Mamma would still shop at Harrods – that's the big department store in Buenos Aires, named after the one in London – and give dinner parties."

"You sound bitter."

"Bitter? No, I think she's very sensible."

She lit another cigarette.

"I must go," he said.

"No, don't. There's no need to." She looked round the sitting room which hadn't been tidied from the night before: the cushions were crushed, the ashtrays unemptied, flies buzzed in the dregs of wine, records lay out of their sleeves, and the couch on which Franz had slept still bore the signs of his occupancy, though he had rolled up the sleeping bag and folded the blanket.

She said, "You could come to the market with me if you like, and stay to supper. Luke would be pleased. Come on," she tossed her hair back and smiled at him, "you can't have anything to do."

"All right," he said, "thank you. You're being very kind. I don't understand it."

"Like Luke says, we're all Eichmann's children. Think of me as a sister."

"It doesn't make sense, but I will. Do you mind if we go by my hotel to pick up any mail?"

The envelope with the Argentinian stamp contained four closely typed sheets on copy paper, and a single page in Becky's round and open script, which would have led a graphologist, he had sometimes thought, to attribute a greater degree of assurance to her than she possessed. It was partly her lack of assurance that he loved, or rather her brave assumption of an assurance that she did not own. But perhaps a graphologist would be more subtle. He pressed the sheet of writing paper to his cheek.

Dear Franz,
I know that's not how a love letter is supposed to begin, but endearments embarrass me, you know that. Got your letter from London and don't know what to say. Can't write to you directly about things. Things are pretty bloody here, Mummy not speaking to Daddy. Kinsky is my only support, but there's something creepy about him now. Went to see your mother yesterday and it seemed to me she was pretending all the time that nothing had happened. Anyway, since I can't write directly to you about what I feel, I'm sending you a copy of something I wrote for myself. Alexis sends love, she's a support too of course.
Love, Becky.

He turned to the enclosed typescript pages.

My first thought was, this can't be happening to me. Maybe that's what everyone thinks when things happen to them. For two days I watched a spider make a web. It fascinated me, and then Gaby screamed at me and tore the web away. "Do you think they're going to rape us?" she kept saying.

But when we were set free – and I still don't know how that happened – one day the door was just left open and we ran out into a yard full of moulting hens – and I learned what had been happening and who F's father was, it was then that I felt really as if I had been raped. Gaby – I don't know what she felt – but she behaved as if it had all been nothing more than a terrible liberty. But I knew differently.

So I got home and I couldn't bear to see Franz, not after I knew. It was Alexis who got me to change my mind. And that was strange, because she let me see that F had wanted to sleep with her (stupid euphemism) and I realised that this had been an escape from complication for him. Well, I can understand that. Alexis is very sexy, and I love her, she's my best friend, maybe, but you can't take her seriously. I think it's because she's American. But when Franz and I did meet, we couldn't speak. When he touched me, I shivered. That's Jewish flesh you're touching, I said, but not aloud. Up till now I've never bothered about the Jewish side of me. There was the odd incident at the Country Club and at school, but I'm C. of E., Mummy saw to that.

Mummy? Why did she marry Daddy? Kinsky says they adored each other. Kinsky says, you can't imagine what energy, what style, what panache he had when he was young. He was glamorous, Kinsky says.

But they don't get on now. I knew that, even before this.

I didn't mean to write in this silly schoolgirlish way. I meant this to be a sort of Credo, an attempt to sort things out. Instead it's more like automatic writing. I imagine myself on a psychiatrist's couch and just spouting.

So: let's start again. I have been badly brought up, and that's Mummy's fault. She's tried to make me into a safe English girl, in Argentina of all places, where you are surrounded by men who despise women. (I don't think Daddy despises women, but I'm not sure. If I had been a boy, I bet he would have talked to me about the past. Now I realise he has never ever done that.)

It was the nice English girl who met Franz and fell in love with him. Hopelessly, I thought at first, especially when kind friends told me he was queer. (If you ever read this, Franz, you don't need to worry. I've put that suspicion away long ago. Well, I would have had to, wouldn't I?) But I'm not going to write about you, Franz, here. Not yet. Do we have a life together? I don't know.

Franz's hand jerked, knocking the glass to the pavement where it shattered. He got down on his knees, collecting the larger pieces. Then a sheet of paper floated off the table. He seized it in mid-air; "But I'm not going to write about you, Franz, here. Not yet." Her hair tickled his cheek, he thrust his hand up the cotton skirt, her tongue slid into his mouth. The waiter bustled towards him with a dustpan and brush. Franz ordered another beer. The waiter hesitated before complying, perhaps wondering if he was drunk, after the broken glass. Rudi told him he occupied himself with chess problems, "and playing the games of the Masters".

The trouble is, I realise, that I don't know anything. My up-bringing has been too successful. So I've been reading, in an attempt to catch up. It's absurd that I should have to catch up. I've seen the photographs of Belsen and the other camps, well everybody has. And all I said was: Horrible. But I haven't been reading history: I know the facts, or enough of them. Did you know that Hitler said, "The masses need something that will give them a thrill of horror." Well, they got it. The really horrible thing is that he may be right. Won't the trial of Franz's father give everybody a thrill of horror all over again?

Or take this: Jung treated three young girls, for hysteria, I think. They confessed that when they were approaching pu-berty they had had revolting dreams about their mother. They dreamt of her as a witch and also as a wild beast. It didn't make sense to them: she was beautiful and kind and a won-derful mother. Years later she went mad, and then moved on all fours barking like a dog or growling.

I don't know why that sticks in my mind. I don't know why anything sticks in my mind.

I read over all this and said to myself, you must stop being a coward. Daddy is always quoting Nietzsche: "Since God is dead, all is permitted." I have never known whether he does so ironically, or whether he really believes it. So I went to him and asked him.

At first I thought he wasn't going to answer. Then he said, "There's no irony. And Nietzsche wasn't advocating a pro-gramme. He was merely recording what he observed. When people no longer believe in God, they don't believe in noth-ing, they believe in anything. That's a fact. Even nihilism is a something, not nothing."

"Mummy says you informed on Franz's father."

He stretched out his blind hand and sought me. The nails bit into my shoulder.

"It has required courage to ask that. The answer is, I was compelled to. By something which the Nazis set out to kill. Conscience. You could say I gave Franz's father the opportunity to rediscover conscience."

When I charged him with caring nothing for my happiness, he withdrew his hand.

"You're too old to play Juliet," he said.

I had lunch with Gaby and Luis yesterday. We went to the Polo Club as usual. How can I write "as usual", when nothing was as it used to be? But that's not true. Everything was the same, only different. Luis has changed. He no longer teases Gaby, and, not being teased, she behaves, suddenly, like the middle-aged woman she will be within a few years of their marriage. I can already see her worrying about the servant problem, and eating too many sweet cakes and talking about going on a diet. As for Luis, he was so polite to me that conversation froze. "Who would have thought," he said, "that Franz had such a heredity?" I could see him wondering about me. Was he really wise to associate with someone of my background? Hadn't the whole friendship been a mistake? I made an excuse and left early.

I couldn't bear to go home, to enter that silence. And I found I was frightened in the streets. It seemed that every man who looked at me knew what had happened to Gaby and me, or thought he did, and so I was soiled. I wondered if Gaby felt like that. Even when we were in the loo at the Club she only made conversation about her latest make-up. A young Army officer stopped me, and began to speak. It was as if my Spanish had deserted me, I couldn't understand what he was saying. He ordered me to undress, or that's what I thought, but I knew it couldn't be true, even while I was horrified and believed it with one half of my mind. And then I realised it was Ramón with whom I used to go dancing and that he was making a joke about his being in military dress. "Are you sure you're all right?" he said, and I understood that, and he took my arm and led me into a café, and bought me a brandy. "It's terrible what has happened to you, Rebecca," he said. "Believe me, I feel for you," and then I dissolved into floods.

"I'm so confused," I said, and he was so nice, he didn't even seem embarrassed. All the same, after he had escorted me to Kinsky's gallery, he was relieved to be able to get rid of me. That's the effect I have on people now.

Kinsky fusses over me like an old woman. I think he thinks of himself as my aunt. He is so different from Daddy that it's hard to believe they can be friends. He kept telling me not to do anything rash, that I needed time to come to terms with him. That's when I said, "Perhaps I should go to Israel."

I hadn't thought of it before. As soon as I spoke, it seemed the natural unavoidable thing to do. Kinsky stroked my arm. There was a photograph of Franz on his desk. I picked it up. He had been taken unawares. His mouth was a little open – perhaps he was speaking – and he had that vulnerable little boy look that sometimes excites me and at other times makes me want to kick him. Or maybe both at the same time. "You're in love with him too," I said to Kinsky.

This wasn't a discovery. But I wouldn't have been bold enough to say it before all this.

"Oh, that's all over," Kinsky said. "I gave up crying for the moon a long time ago."

We spoke about Mummy and Daddy. He said that Daddy had always been afflicted by self-righteousness. It had caused all the trouble in his life. As for Mummy, "You remind me of the way she was in Berlin, my dear."

"Do I? How?"

"Vénus toute entière à sa proie attachée…"

"That's nasty."

"Believe me, I don't mean it that way. I think it's beautiful."

When I got home, Mummy and Daddy were eating toasted cheese. They weren't speaking. Then Daddy stretched out to put a record on the gramophone.

Mummy said, "If that's your bloody Brahms, I'm off to bed." But she would be able to hear it from their room.

At the bottom of the last typewritten sheet, Becky had scribbled:

> I shouldn't send you this, there's too much about you, and much too much about how I feel. But maybe if we are to have a chance, it's necessary. I'm going to talk to Mummy about a flight to Israel in the morning.

He passed the sheets to Rachel, and smoked a cigarette while she read Becky's words.

"You're lucky," she said. "I hope for your sake she comes."

TWO

In the next week Franz spent most of his time with Luke and Rachel. He visited his father every day, and found that the distance between them grew. When he mentioned this to Rachel, she said, "Maybe that's kindness on his part. Maybe he thinks it best for you to disengage."

He made more than a couple of attempts to see Saul Birnbaum, for a consultation which would help fix his own mind on his father's defence; but each time he was put off with a plea of urgent business. So he was thrown back on Luke and Rachel, and was grateful to them, though it puzzled him that they were so friendly. He even suspected Luke of using him for future copy.

Yet it was Rachel with whom he was mostly alone, for Luke went to his newspaper every day, and also spent two hours shut in their bedroom writing at the desk there. Franz was surprised that Rachel didn't work – wasn't that expected of every young Israeli woman, even mothers? And why wasn't she a mother?

"I'm fighting hard against being a good Israeli wife," she said. "I keep trying to maintain my American identity."

"Do you still have an American passport?"

"Sure, and aim to keep it."

She had the frankness he associated with Americans. She explained that, though her parents had come to Israel in '49, she had remained in Brooklyn with her aunt (her mother's sister) and her husband. She had just entered High School – Franz was surprised to learn that she was half-a-dozen years older than himself – and not knowing how the emigration to Israel – "the return home, I mean" – would work out, they had persuaded themselves, that was how she put it, that it wasn't a good idea to interrupt her education. Maybe they were sincere, she didn't know. So she hadn't come to Israel except for holidays until she was grown-up, not indeed until she had met Luke, who was then on a scholarship at Columbia.

"I don't speak Hebrew, maybe you've noticed?"

"Shouldn't you learn it?"

"Between you and me, Franz, I think the whole concept stinks."

They were on the beach, eating kebabs and falafels bought from a stall. Sunlight sparkled on her salty legs. Her thighs were short and thick; they didn't seem to belong to the same girl as her sharp-featured, distinguished face. He thought of Alexis striding into the waves, rising out of them with the water falling away from her legs, and of Becky walking naked with the proud self-conscious step of a girl happy in love, from the bed in Alexis's apartment to the bathroom. There was something to be said for Rachel's stumpy legs; life was already sufficiently complicated.

"The first evening we met, you said that you thought my father's trial was necessary. I'm puzzled you should think so. It doesn't seem to fit with your general view of things. I mean, you seem less than enchanted about Israel."

"Sure. I didn't mean it was necessary for me. Quite the reverse, if it pleases you. Only that they couldn't do without it."

"Who are they?"

"They're all around us." She waved her hand along the beach which was filling up as people, on their way back from their offices, stopped off for a swim. "Don't you understand? The same way Hitler needed the Jews, so the Israelis need the Nazis. They're our justification. They're the justification of all this. So, any time the national spirit seems to be flagging, it's useful to turn up someone like your father."

"I see what you mean. But the Nazis' crimes were real. That's what's so horrible."

She stretched out a towel, crawled on top of it, and lay face down, letting the sun get at her back. She turned her head towards him, keeping one cheek on the towel.

"Sure," she said, "and if the Nazis had won, he'd be a hero, like the Jews who blew up the King David Hotel."

"But that was different," he said.

"Yeah, that was different."

Luke was always edgy at the start of the evening. This took the form of sniping at Rachel. Most of the time she paid no attention. She told Franz that Luke was stuck on his novel, or rather that it wasn't going well. His first book, published four years ago, when he was only twenty-two, had been hugely admired, caused him to be recognised as the voice of Young Israel. That made him uncomfortable. It had been a patriotic story; its hero was a young French Jew, whose father had been a Communist zealot murdered by Stalin in the Great Purge. The hero had spent his boyhood hidden in an attic in Paris throughout the Occupation. The combination of these experiences had destroyed the two faiths in which he had been reared. The State of Israel promised to restore him. Then he was wounded, and his wife killed, by an Arab bomb. The explosion cost him his sight. The story was contained in his mind as he struggled behind the bandages to come to terms with these catastrophes.

"Don't read it. It stinks," Luke said now. "I blush to think of it, and as for the praise it received…," he made a vulgar gesture of contempt.

He was proud of the second book, a young woman's account of her unhappy marriage to a soldier. It had been attacked by the religious press. But the new novel wasn't moving. So, in the evening, he criticised Rachel's appearance, cooking, household arrangements, and accused her of frittering her life away.

"I didn't marry a squaw," he said. "You won't believe it, but she has real talent as a painter. Only she won't work at it. And she was a promising actress, she used to be in the theatre. But now, oh no…"

Rachel laughed, "I was a lousy actress. You've said often enough, *Schatz*, that when you want to damn anyone you call them promising."

Franz was surprised and moved to hear the German endearment, which, when he was a child, his mother used to employ in addressing him. But the realisation that Luke was having these difficulties made him all the more suspicious of his motives in befriending him, especially when, pouring brandy after supper, he said, "But you must have been curious about your father when you were growing up. Didn't you ever ask him what he did in the war…?"

"No," Franz said. "My mother told me not to."

"And you didn't ask her?"

"You don't know my mother."

"And what did you think when she told you to steer clear of the subject?"

"I believed her. She said it was a painful subject, which would only distress him."

"I guess it would and all," Rachel said. "Honey, Franz isn't in the dock."

"You have a lovely choice of phrase, my darling," Luke smiled, and reached for the brandy bottle.

"Well, we didn't make the world," he said, "but we sure did inherit it."

*   *   *   *

The next morning Saul telephoned Franz while he was still in bed.

"I'm coming over right away," he said. "Wait for me. Don't go out. Don't answer the telephone."

Franz washed, shaved and dressed in a hurry. Then he called Room Service and asked them to send up a pot of coffee with two cups. Saul's urgency made him anxious, but maybe it was not as important as it seemed. Maybe Saul was the sort of man who postponed things and then insisted they were done in a rush. After all, he had been trying to get hold of him for days and had been stalled time and again. But what could have happened? Could his father have killed himself? How would he feel if he had done so? Or – he remembered the ageing and stupid Nazis in Argentina – there might even have been an attempt at a rescue. After all, everyone knew that the Nazis had friends in Arab countries; and not only friends.

"No," Saul said, as, without thinking, he met him with a barrage of such questions, "no, it's not as bad as that. Or as good. I tell you, this case has me in such a spin that I don't know what's good and what's bad."

This made no sense. Franz wondered if the lawyer was drunk.

"No, it's you I'm worried about. I feel responsible for you. There's no reason why I should, you're a Gentile and the son of a man whom for my sins I am obliged to defend, which I shall do, I assure you, with all the professional competence at my command, but whom in other circumstances I would have been happy to slay with one blow of my fist, as Samson slew the Philistines. Do you understand that?"

"Yes," Franz said, "and thank you for being honest. I'm quite happy to know that that's the basis on which you are ready to defend my father. It makes it less of a farce."

He pushed a cup of coffee towards the lawyer.

"So what is it?"

"I've let you down, that's what it is. I promised to try to keep you incognito, and I betrayed that to Luke – you can't keep any secrets in Israel."

"But Luke's, well, I've come to think of him as a friend."

"Sure, and it's been noticed."

He slapped a newspaper on the table.

"You won't be able to read this. It's in Hebrew. This," he tapped the paper with the corner of his folded spectacles, "is a popular paper, owned by one of the smaller extremist parties. When we say extremist in Israel, we mean right-wing. Maybe you know that."

He opened the paper, and pushed it towards Franz. "Look at this."

The photograph showed him with Luke and Rachel sitting at a café table.

"The caption reads, 'A Friendship of Equals: Luke Abramowitz with Kestner's Son.' The piece is really an attack on Luke, but it also blows your anonymity."

"Well," Franz said, "that had to happen some time. But what does it say about Luke?"

His first thought was the fear that this would cost him their friendship, and that the caption was accurate: he had felt it to be a friendship of equals.

"Oh, it's salacious and scurrilous, but it's just politics. Luke's accustomed to this sort of thing. The implication is that he doesn't give a damn for what the Jewish people have suffered, because he is a rootless cosmopolitan with an American wife and now with Nazi friends. It stinks."

"It makes no difference to your defence though?"

"No, I suppose not. But I've thought it a good idea to fix a press conference, and produce you at it."

"What good will that do?"

"It will save you from being besieged by journalists seeking exclusives."

"But I've nothing to say."

"I've arranged for it to take place in my office. That way we can control numbers and keep a grip on things."

There were some thirty journalists and a dozen photographers. Saul had provided a large room which, he explained to Franz, they kept for use by their company clients for annual general meetings and suchlike occasions. Franz wore a dark suit and a subdued tie. Most of the journalists were in shirt sleeves. So was Saul. They sat at a table at the end of the room with a carafe of water and two glasses in front of them. The girl, Anna, who would act as interpreter if necessary, settled herself at the corner of the table, at an angle to Franz, who tried to catch her eye, and extract a smile. The room, despite the air-conditioning, was hot. Some of the journalists were sweating, and Franz rubbed his brow with a handkerchief. But when he touched his cheek with the back of his hand, the sensation was icy. He sat with his hands below the level of the table, holding them together, the nails of one digging into the fingers of the other, behind the knuckles. Saul explained that Mr Schmidt would answer any questions in English or German directly, but that others would have to be translated. There was an immediate request that his answers should be translated also.

"If he answers, as he promises, in English, I don't think that will be necessary," Saul said.

"Why do you call yourself Schmidt? Your name's Kestner, isn't it?"

"I have been Schmidt since I remember. It's the name on my passport."

"Are you denying that your father is Rudi Kestner?" Franz glanced at Saul, who nodded.

"That's something that, I understand, has to be established."

"Do you mean that part of his defence is going to be denial that he is Kestner?"

"That's a question for Mr Birnbaum, not me."

"But you're not denying that the man held under the name of Kestner is your father?"

"Oh no."

"You've nothing clever to say about that?"

"I've nothing clever to say."

"Are you a Nazi?"

"No."

"A Nazi sympathiser?"

"No, I'm not that either." He hesitated, took a sip of water. "I don't see how anybody could be that, now."

"So you don't deny that the Nazis murdered six million Jews?"

The questioner was one of the two women among the journalists – a thin, black-haired girl with a red, full-lipped mouth, who spoke with an American accent. Saul Birnbaum slipped a sheet of paper towards him: he looked down. "Careful. Minty Hubchik, Yank, v clever."

"You're not sure," she said.

"That's the generally accepted figure, isn't it?" Franz said. "I don't know any reason to argue with it."

An Israeli journalist: "But it doesn't horrify you?"

"I haven't said that."

"You're getting a little wide of any mark, friends," Saul Birnbaum said. "Mr Schmidt isn't on trial, you know."

That wasn't how it struck Franz. Without having done anything wrong, his validity was in question. He was like Isaac, his eyes seeking the alternative ram in a thicket, meanwhile in danger of being sacrificed to the original jealous God. But which God was that?

"What do you think of Israel, Mr Schmidt?"

He stopped before the apparent innocence of the question, gazed at the little old man with round spectacles who had asked it, in a voice so low that it had been necessary to have him repeat his words.

"I'm impressed … by the energy and commitment to a cause …"

The little man scribbled his reply. What could it matter to anyone? Franz looked over their heads at the clock on the wall. The thing had lasted less than five minutes.

"I believe that your stepfather is a General and a minister in the Argentinian government? Won't your association with this case damage him?"

"He's a General, yes. I don't think he's a minister. Not currently. And I can't speculate, I don't know enough about…"

His voice died away. About anything, was what he had really wanted to protest.

"What is your connection with Luke Abramowitz? Is it true that he has signed a contract to write your father's biography?"

"I haven't heard so."

"So what's your connection?"

"He came to see me. We got talking. That's all. You'll have to ask him."

"Good boy," Saul muttered. Had the microphone picked that up?

It was the full-lipped girl, Minty Hubchik again, with her hand up.

"Two questions. They're connected. Am I right in asseverating that it was Professor Eli Czinner gave the tip-off that led to your father's arrest? And are you still engaged to his daughter?"

Again Saul cut in, "Come, come, lady, you can't expect the boy to answer that."

But the intervention was too late to stifle a buzz of excitement, then a babble of conversation, which drowned his words. He leaned over to Franz and whispered that he didn't need to respond. "Dumb chick, I don't know why she is letting go of that information."

There was a silence. Franz looked back at her. She held the tip of her pencil poised against her lips. She knew she was right, and she knew he was uncertain about the second part.

"No," he said, "I'll answer. As to the first part of your question, yes,

I believe you are right. I understand Professor Czinner's motives." He paused, wanting to add, "So does my father", but he didn't know whether Saul would approve, or would feel hampered by the admission. "As to the second part, the answer is yes. Simply yes."

"How will you feel" – the questioner was a large, red-faced man, in a white linen suit, and he spoke English in a rich and superior voice which Franz recognised from the movies as belonging to a certain type of English actor – "how will you feel about this marriage if your father is sentenced to death, as I assume he may very well be?"

"Come, come, Mr Murison," Saul said. "You're infringing forbidden territory in that assumption."

"No assumption, dear boy, merely a hypothetical question…"

"Then I would guess that Mr Schmidt can't tell you how he would feel in a hypothetical situation."

But of course he could. It was not after all merely a hypothesis; it was a question he had been living with for months now. And the answer was blunt: "I'm responsible for my own life, I'm not going to be constrained by what an older generation did or chooses to do. And that goes, must go, for Becky also." So he said it, and blushed. He had given them a headline, a ridiculously Hollywood story.

"It was good, your press conference." Saul clapped him on the shoulder. "You carried it off, boy."

But what was the point of it? He couldn't see that anything had been gained or averted. He couldn't escape the feeling that, in talking with all the honesty he could muster, he had made a fool of himself. And he still wasn't sure that Luke and Rachel would want to go on seeing him, and that prospect dismayed him.

"Luke is furious. He says we have to go south to recover. We'll pick you up at the hotel. OK. What time are you back from seeing your father? Eleven? Fine. He's so furious he's going to take the day off work. See you – We'll go to Ashkelon. You ought to see Ashkelon. Down the coast. OK."

"Coming to terms, that's the thing," Rudi stretched himself. Sunlight glanced through the narrow grille, and lay on the table like melted butter. "I detached myself from those who had been my colleagues, the clowns or zealots, who in a fit of barely comprehensible folly, abducted your girl, Franz. They wanted to go back, to pretend, you know, that certain things had not happened. Madness. Refusal to contemplate reality. Inexcusable. Now," he laughed, "I've been brought back, but in a different fashion and one which I would have avoided. Yet now that it's happened, well, it's happened. That's all. Do you think this world is a training-ground for spirits?"

The question was inconceivable. That is, it was the sort of question that only students pose to each other. Franz was amazed to hear it coming from the lips of this father, whom he had accustomed himself to think a dull man, mechanical and punctilious in duty, even while he admired and feared him.

"We've never talked about the war, Father," he said.

Rudi lit another cigarette, pushed the pack towards him. The two soldiers, sitting on chairs at either end of the table – so that to a casual observer the four of them might have been engaged in a game of bridge, played at a table awkwardly shaped for the purpose – fixed their eyes on the transaction. Then one of them produced a lighter and lit Franz's cigarette. Rudi urged the pack in the soldier's direction, and the offer was accepted.

"The war? We're going to go over my war in too exhaustive detail. I'm not ashamed of my war. Whatever people say, war is beyond good and evil. Katyn and Dresden and Hiroshima prove it. It's proved every day in war, only less dramatically."

"So what do you accuse yourself of?"

"Credulity. When I was working on these remote sites, with so little in the way of congenial company, I used to read every evening. Have you read Jung, Franz? No? Do so. He wrote an essay called 'Hitler and the Germans'. I think that was the title. It was certainly the substance. I wish I'd read it in 1933 – but it wasn't written then."

He laughed again, and smiled.

"It makes everything so clear. I learned one passage by heart. 'He' – that is, Hitler, Franz – 'represented the shadow, the inferior part of everybody's personality, in an overwhelming degree, and this was another reason why they fell for him. But what could they have done? In Hitler, every German should have seen his own shadow, his own worst danger. It is everybody's allotted fate to become conscious of and learn to deal with this shadow. But how could the Germans understand this, when no one else in the world can understand such a simple truth?' "

He looked at Franz as if to say: there, everything is now understood, and therefore to be forgiven; what a clever boy I am to have seen this.

Rachel sang as they drove down the coast to Ashkelon. She sat in the back seat of the Citroen 2CV and sang the blues. They crossed over a stone bridge, and Luke told Franz that the Egyptians had been defeated there in the War of Liberation.

"This was the limit of their advance, and so the bridge is called 'Ad Halom: Till Here'. It was, we said, as Isaiah says, 'in that day shall Egypt be like unto women; and it shall tremble and fear because of the shaking of the hand of the Lord of Hosts, and the land of Judah shall become a terror unto Egypt…' "

"Typical misogynist brute," Rachel said, " 'Egypt shall be like unto women.' " She switched registers: " 'Go see what the boys in the back room will 'ave,/ and tell them I'm 'aving the same.' "

The road dipped towards the sea and was fringed with flowering shrub roses. Sycamores and cypresses grew abundantly. To their right sprawled the ruins of Ashdod, the Philistine city of Dagon, the fish-headed god. Then they turned off the coast road.

"There is something I want you to see," Luke said, and the car climbed, past a reservoir, to a high point from where they had a view of the coastal plain and the sea on one side and the mountains of Judah rolling and heaving to the east. The road wound between hills and then emerged on a plateau covered with fields of maize and wheat and orange groves. He stopped by a water-tower.

"A land flowing with milk and honey," Franz said.

"This is Negba," Luke said. "It means 'To the South'. The kibbutz here was established in 1939. It was wiped out in the War of Liberation. Then it was rebuilt. Only this water-tower, which was used as a lookout point, survives from the original settlement."

They got out of the car. Luke led them to the military cemetery and stopped before the War Memorial. It showed three huge figures, two men and a girl. They were holding hands and their chins were tilted upwards in heroic style. Its simplicity was impressive, but it also reminded Franz of posters he had seen celebrating the heroes of the Soviet Union. He was about to remark on this, then saw there were tears in Luke's eyes as he gazed at it. Luke turned away, entered the cemetery. It was very neat and very still, and the stones were white. Only the sound of a tractor disturbed the silence. He stood before a grave, his head bowed.

He had a rose in his hand. Franz hadn't seen him take it from the car. He bent down and laid it on the grave.

"Thank you, Michael," he said.

Then he turned away, and took Franz by the arm.

"You don't mind that I brought you here," he said. "I wanted to, to help you understand. Michael was my brother. He was half grown up when I was born. He was killed in the first hour of the war, defending this kibbutz where he had been accepted only six months before. His faith in Israel's destiny was complete. This kibbutz looks to the south and God promised Jacob, 'Thy seed shall be as the dust of the earth, and thou shalt spread abroad to the west and to the east, and to the north and to the south, and in thee and in thy seed shall all the families of the earth be blessed.' Michael never doubted that: all the families of the earth, it's significant, isn't it?"

They lunched at a little restaurant in the old town of Ashkelon. It was cavernous, with an arched roof that dated back to the Middle Ages at least.

"Perhaps your Crusaders, perhaps the Moslems, who knows? It was a great trading city. Twenty years before your First Crusade Rabbi Benjamin of Tudela reported that there were two hundred Jews here, and that merchants came from all quarters of the world."

"Though possibly not Germany," Franz said.

They ordered red mullet, which tasted fresh, of the sea, and pigeon, because, Luke said, they used to worship the dove in Ashkelon, and Roman coins from the city depicted the bird.

"Herod the Great was born here. According to Josephus, he built baths and fountains, costly fountains, that were admirable for size and workmanship."

"A jerk," Rachel said. "You could say as much of Albert Speer. As for the Massacre of the Innocents, doesn't that make him a prototype Hitler?"

"There's some dispute as to whether it actually took place."

Franz took a piece of Arab bread and mopped up the gravy on his plate. He remembered his father and Dr Czinner both doing that at the Engineers' Club, on an afternoon when life stretched before him, green and level as a polo field. But the pang of memory was momentary. He was caught up for the first time in the romance of Israel, in the sense that what was happening here now represented a new stage in a journey that had extended from the beginning of time, that the Jews had been offered what was denied to others, a second entry to their Promised Land. Wasn't it in fact a third chance? There had been the return from the Babylonian captivity, though he was hazy about that.

"I wish I knew the Bible better," he said. "I feel I'm missing so much."

He was envious of Luke. Rachel shared something of this envy; that was why she was showing herself so crabby. And this, he realised, had been conceived by Luke as a day of reparation. He had been wounded by that newspaper caption, even though as a novelist he should have been accustomed to criticism, and as a journalist have known its worthlessness. But it had flicked an open wound. He was permitted to criticise Israel, but resented criticism of his criticism, for that suggested that he was some sort of enemy, whereas he knew he criticised as a lover, in the same way as he got at Rachel for making less of herself than she could.

Luke ordered a second bottle of wine. It was pale yellow in colour, with a taste of almonds and came from vineyards near the border with Lebanon.

"Was Goliath from Ashkelon?" Franz asked.

"No, Gath, a few miles away. Kiryat-Gat, it's called now. Gath means a winepress cut in the rock. They are excavating the mound of old Gath now. Some people think it is not Gath itself since the findings so far offer evidence of a Jewish settlement, rather than a Philistine one. But they'll come to that, I'm sure."

"Does it matter?" Rachel said. "I don't see that it matters."

"Of course it matters."

"Why? You don't wear a skullcap, you're not religious. You're a modern man, what does it matter to you?"

"The Bible matters because it is the history of our people. It is important that it be justified."

"Can't you be honest, Luke? What you really want is evidence of the Covenant, anything that will let you believe that the Jews have a God-given right to this land, even though you don't believe in God, as far as I can see. It makes me sick."

She threw down her napkin and ran out of the restaurant. She stumbled on the top step and her sunglasses fell to the ground, but she kept on running. Franz rose, picked them up, and looked out: she had disappeared round the corner. He returned to the table to find Luke pouring more wine.

"Rachel's afraid of Israel," Luke said. "She hopes I may become such an international success that I am offered a Chair at an American university. A visiting professorship anyway."

"And would you take it?"

"It would be desertion."

Becky's father could have got out of Germany long before the war. He was already sufficiently distinguished, sufficiently competent and experienced in any case, to have got a good job in England or the United States. What had made him stay on? Obstinacy? The feeling that that too would be desertion? And if he had not remained, perhaps none of this would have happened – but that none would have included his own meeting with Becky.

"Do you believe in Fate?"

"In what sense?"

"The obvious one, I suppose. That things are bound to happen."

"Oh no. We are each masters of our fate, responsible for our actions."

"And yet you believe, deep down, that God gave this land to Israel?"

Luke smiled. He shook his head, took a sip of wine, and, not looking at Franz, said, "Nothing makes sense, does it? Nothing coheres. And yet we are obliged to behave as if that wasn't so."

"My father has been reading Jung. Does that surprise you?"

"No. It's natural, if he is a man of any worth, that he should be seeking explanations."

"Is Rachel all right? Should we go after her?"

"No. Leave her alone. She'll come back when she's ready." He twiddled his wine glass. "Have you ever read *The Bacchae?*"

"No. What is it?"

"A Greek play. Euripides. Don't look so surprised. Why shouldn't a Jew read Greek?"

It was, he said, a play for the twentieth century. Franz would understand why when he read it.

"But what happens?"

"Pentheus, King of Thebes, and his mother Agave, deny the divinity of Dionysus, the god of darkness and passion, and instead insist on the supremacy of reason, order and light. But it is too much of a strain, this denial. Agave becomes a secret devotee of the god she has tried to deny, and Pentheus is tempted to spy on his mother and the other worshippers in their secret rites. Inflamed by the god, they seize the king and tear him into pieces."

"Yes?"

"You have to effect a synthesis, I suppose. You can't become whole if you deny truths merely because they are uncomfortable."

"Are you suggesting that I am like Pentheus?"

"God help us, we all have our moments when we resemble him. It's one of the greatest temptations there is."

They did not notice Rachel return, until she laid a camellia in front of each of them.

"I'm sorry. I don't know what got into me."

"You dropped your sunglasses. Here you are."

There was no singing as they drove back to Tel Aviv. At the hotel Franz found a telegram from Becky, saying her flight arrived the following evening.

He stood at the desk, imbibing the telegram, and was turning away to mount the stairs to his room when a voice called him from the bar.

"Mr Schmidt."

"Yes?"

He didn't move. It was dark in the bar and the voice came from a corner.

"I've been waiting for you. Won't you join me?"

It was the English journalist in the crumpled linen suit, whom, that morning, Saul had treated with a wary respect. Franz sat down.

"You made quite a hit at our little press conference, dear boy. Have some brandy."

The Englishman snapped his fingers to attract the barman's attention. There was nobody else in the bar.

"We are not quite strangers," he said, "though that may surprise you."

He was sweating despite the air conditioning, a big man, with thin sandy fair worn long at the back, bloodshot eyes, a fleshy nose and a small pursed mouth which gripped a little cigar that he didn't trouble to remove as he spoke. He put his hand on Franz's leg just above the knee and squeezed it. It was a light squeeze and he had removed the hand before Franz had time to protest.

"Charlie has told me so much about you, and now I find you are engaged to marry Nell's daughter. Amazing."

"I'm sorry, I don't understand."

The waiter brought brandy for the Englishman and beer as he had requested for Franz.

"But that's why I wanted to see you, dear boy. You see, I was once married to Nell, a dear girl, but restless; it didn't take. I soon realised that her emotions were already committed elsewhere: to Eli Czinner as it transpired. Only, she thought him dead, when we married. It was a long time ago, in the war."

When he talked of the war his voice lightened. Some of the cynicism he wore like obsolete armour fell away from him. If Franz had read Ivan Murison's autobiography, he would have found that the war chapters sang. There was a tune there he had lost since. Yet his success, springing from the miseries of ravaged Europe, had coarsened him. Ever since, the pity he had then experienced had been directed inwards. He had spoken of the war as "setting him on the road to fame", and it had indeed made him for a few years a best-selling author. But when, in the middle Fifties, the vogue for war books had vanished, there had been nothing to put in its place. In the Savile Club he began to find that people drifted away from his corner of the bar. He spent long afternoons at the Gargoyle or the Colony Room. A flirtation with television came to nothing, there was something antipathetic about the image he offered on the screen. He had retired to Italy to write novels. A couple were published, without success. Then he had covered the Eichmann trial for an American magazine, with only a flicker of the real flair he had once exhibited. But it had been sufficient to persuade a Sunday newspaper, whose editor remembered *The German Catastrophe* and *Twilight of the False Gods*, to recruit him for his present assignment on the Kestner case.

Franz hadn't known that Becky's mother had been married twice. Did Becky herself know?

"It will be interesting to meet Nell's daughter. You spoke so movingly about her, dear boy. When is she arriving?"

What made him think she was coming?

"I'm waiting to hear from her," Franz said. "Why did you ask me that question this morning?"

"I wanted to hear your answer. Simple, isn't it?"

"You must have known I couldn't… and who is this person who has told you so much about me?"

"Charlie? Carlo Bastini. I am sure you remember the little Bastini. He speaks of you so … warmly. I call him Charlie." He looked at Franz over the rim of his brandy glass. Franz's cheeks warmed; it might be too dark to see the blush.

"Small world," Ivan Murison said.

"I haven't seen him in years."

"A dear boy. Very sensitive. He remembers you so well. Why, he even carries your photograph. He has several of them, you know."

His fat fingers delved into his breast pocket and brought out a tattered brown envelope. He extracted two prints and pushed them across the table towards Franz. He stubbed out his little cigar and lit another, looking over the flame at Franz, who leaned forward and picked up the photographs.

"It's a pity the light's not better. They're only snapshots, of course."

The top one showed Franz sitting on a wall or parapet. He was wearing only a pair of shorts. One leg was drawn up, the knee nestling under his chin, the other hung loose. He was smiling. It had been taken, Franz recalled, on the terrace of the *hacienda* Bastini's stepfather rented a dozen miles out of the city. He had gone there, once, for the weekend. It was a weekend that often returned to him at night. Shortly afterwards, Bastini and his family had left Argentina.

"It's charming, isn't it?" Ivan Murison said. "Very pretty and quite innocent. Touching that Charlie's kept it. Look at the other, dear boy. These are only copies, of course."

It showed Franz lying back on a low chair beside a swimming pool. His legs stretched, long, towards the camera. He might have been naked – there was what could have been a pair of wet trunks discarded to the left of the chair – but you couldn't tell because another figure, with his back to the camera, was kneeling in front of the chair, his body between Franz's legs, his head lowered. He wasn't recognisable, but the shape was a boy's and the mass of soft dark wavy hair was Bastini's. One of Franz's hands stroked the hair or was buried in it, the other lay or perhaps pressed on the boy's shoulder.

"As I say, they're copies. We have the negatives. Charlie's stepfather took it, with a telescopic lens, I suppose. He liked doing that sort of thing. Of course, you know he was the first man to seduce Charlie, if seduce is the right word, which I suspect it isn't. Charlie claims it was because of him he married his mother, but then Charlie likes to preen himself, as you will remember. You know, I'm almost jealous. This snap" – he retrieved it from Franz and gazed at it – "makes me feel young again, it's so Greek, don't you know."

He took his cigar from his mouth and smiled, "You know, I really think you should have some brandy." He called to the waiter. "Leave the bottle with us, will you," he said.

"What do you want?"

"You know, Charlie was thrilled when he found out about your father. He said he could just imagine you in SS uniform. Of course, you were cadets together, weren't you?"

"What do you want?"

Ivan took the bottle from the waiter and passed him his American Express card.

"Co-operation, dear boy. I'm not sure what form it will take, but I intend to write the book about this case."

And he began to ask Franz all sorts of questions about his early life, his relations with his father, his memories of Rudi in Argentina, any expression of political, moral or philosophical opinions. It was thoroughly and professionally done. To his horror, Franz found himself answering, and taking trouble over his answers, as the brandy sank in the bottle, and confused memories disturbed his imagination.

He didn't remember getting to bed. He woke – as he recorded in his journal, along with an account of this meeting and of his day at Ashkelon – with the sensation of Bastini's rather damp mouth nuzzling his cheek. It must have been the last wisp of a dream as it slid into misty oblivion. He lay there for a long time with that past invading him, tried, in a surge of conscience, to banish it by summoning up the disgusting picture of Bastini and Ivan Murison together, as (it was clear) they must often have been. But conscious effort of the imagination did not work; it was displaced at once by Bastini's hands fumbling at the snake-belt and buttons of his flannel shorts. He leaped from his bed, naked, and took a shower, seeking with the rush of cold water to dispel shame. But shame returned, when, after coffee, he sat at the writing-table with his journal before him.

"If Father feels no guilt," he wrote, "is it because the past is truly dead for him, because he feels himself to be an entirely different person, and so is able to make no connection between the man he is now and the man who ordered these atrocities? If so, that is a failure of imagination. It must be. And yet isn't it only by stifling the disturbing imagination which memory breeds that we make it possible for ourselves to advance from one stage of life to another?"

Rachel was making dumplings for goulash. She took pleasure in binding the flour with egg and suet, and forming them into neat balls. She ran her finger round the bowl, and licked it; it was an action recovered from childhood. As she worked she listened to the wireless. Someone was telling a story, a folk-tale, about a rich man who gave all his money to the poor (who can always be found to accept it), and retired to the desert to live in a community of hermits and worship God. One day, the story-teller said, the man was sent to town to sell two old donkeys. The donkeys were past working, but the hermits still hoped to get a good price for them. He stood in the marketplace, and soon a man looking for donkeys approached him, and asked if these were worth buying. "If they were worth buying do you think we'd be selling them?" the man replied. Then another prospective customer came up and asked why the beasts had hollow backs and ragged tails. "Because they're very old," the man said, "and we have to twist their tails to make them move." So this customer went away and the word got round and no other buyers came near. In the evening he took the donkeys home, and his companion who had been trying to sell them with him told the other hermits about his unhelpful answers. Then they all asked him why he had answered buyers in this fashion. "Do you suppose," he replied, "that I left home and gave away all my cattle, and sheep and goats, and even my camels, to make myself a liar for the sake of two wretched old donkeys?"

The man who was telling the story laughed, and said life was like that. He said it was extraordinary how people cut off their nose to spite their face and then protested how handsome their nose still was, calling on others to admire the way it grew.

This explanation puzzled Rachel. She didn't think that was the point of the story at all. She wasn't sure what the point really was, but nevertheless it seemed in an obscure way significant to her. Then it struck her that it was really rather like life in Israel, for an American like herself at least. Perhaps she had given away camels in order to tell lies about two old donkeys?

Rachel finished making the dumplings and put them in the fridge. She had invited Franz to bring Becky there for supper, and then hesitated, wondering if he mightn't prefer to spend the first evening of her time in Israel alone with her. But he had seemed almost relieved – yes, there was no almost about it, he was relieved – to hear her invitation. Maybe that wasn't surprising.

She listened to Luke's typewriter in the next room. That meant he thought a chapter in the novel had reached the stage when he could lay it out for others to read. It was a step forward when she heard the machine going, even a step towards the USA. There was no chance that Luke would accept an invitation there until he had got his novel done. She had been afraid that his obsession with Franz and the Kestner case would make it impossible for him to continue the novel. But it didn't seem to have worked like that. On the contrary, Franz had acted as some sort of agent who had released the flow. Rachel began to sing, then broke off, in case the machine stopped.

If the man had told lies about the donkeys, in what way would he have been worse off?

She put the question at supper. They had eaten the goulash and dumplings, which were spicy and very good, going well with the red wine from Sharon which Luke had chosen. Conversation had been slow, not just on account of the excellence of the food, but because each of the four was conscious of areas of talk that seemed to them forbidden territory. Consequently all welcomed Rachel's question because it lifted the conversation away from minefields of the immediate and personal, and into the abstract and general.

"Of course, he should have told the necessary lie," Luke said. "He had been sent out to sell the donkeys and had accepted that commission. Well, he was wrong to do so if he was going to chicken out on the deal."

Rachel knew that Luke was talking to provoke. He didn't really believe that the end justified the means, though he sometimes pretended he did. Maybe in some contrary moods, it wasn't just a pretence. But now he was twisting their tails as if they had been donkeys themselves.

"That's all very well," Franz said. "But you know, his question was a good one. What was the point of giving up all that if it wasn't to live in some better relation with truth?"

"If Luke's right," Becky said, "maybe he should have refused to take the donkeys to town."

"Sure, OK," Luke switched sides, "but if he had said, no deal, someone else would have done it, and told the lie. So the man would have been guilty by omission. He would have been an accomplice in guilt, like everybody who stands by and sees injustice being done."

"Like the Levite in the story of the Good Samaritan," Franz said.

"OK, OK, that's enough Christian one-upmanship."

"But," Becky said, "what could he have done?" She looked pale, and tired from her flight, and beautiful as an autumn morning. "I suppose he could have argued with his companions that they had no right to offer the donkeys for sale."

"Then he'd have got clobbered," Rachel said.

"So?" Luke said. "You must suffer to be virtuous. That's the whole point of religion, all religions, I guess."

"There is a German saying," Franz said. "At least I think it's a German saying, Mamma always used to quote it with a shake of her head as something her own grandmother used to repeat: 'You need a long spoon to take meat with the devil.' "

"That's a proverb in every language, I guess," Rachel said.

"Yeah, and the man who made the spoons went bust," Luke said.

"Why was that?"

"No demand."

"Why, do you mean people no longer want to sup with the Devil?"

"Not so. I mean they don't choose to stay on such distant terms."

Everyone laughed. Luke poured more wine. The sound of a woman singing in a neighbouring apartment carried through the night; she was crooning in an American accent, a song that had been popular before the war. Then they found they were out of cigarettes, and Luke and Franz went down to the corner shop to fetch some. Luke would have gone alone, but Franz insisted on accompanying him. He was halfway down the stairs when it occurred to him that, after that newspaper article, Luke might prefer not to be seen with him, in his own quarter of the city. But it was too late to turn back, and he knew that if he told Luke what he had been thinking, he would receive a proud and indignant denial.

"Franz has been telling me how kind you have both been," Becky said.

"Oh no… it's nothing."

"Do you think he minds me coming?"

"I'm sure he doesn't."

"I think he does, probably. It makes things more complicated for him, and they were complicated enough already. But I couldn't not."

Later, when they were alone, Rachel said to Luke, "She's crazily in love with him. Like I used to be with you when we were first married." So, she didn't add, she's afraid of him, and for him.

But, before then, when they were still all together, smoking and drinking wine, and starting conversations which stopped all at once, not because they were embarrassed with each other, but because the talk threatened to lead them into deserts where none of the four wished, or dared, to travel; when they were all the same acquiring a sense of being a quartet, making the music of their own generation as an act of liberation from history; then Becky said, out of the blue, "My father used to tell me folk-tales when I was a little girl."

"Fucking folk-tales," Luke said.

"They were the only Jewish things he did for me, I mean, that's not grammar, doesn't make sense, they represented the only sort of Jewishness he offered to me. You don't know my father, Luke. He's awfully down on other Jews. That's why he didn't come to Israel after the war, he used to say, too many bloody Jews. He's really anti-Semitic, I tell him, for a Jew."

"Ought to meet Rachel," Luke said, putting his arm round his wife, hugging her, and then giving her a kiss on the cheek. "They'd be great buddies."

"Of course I don't remember most of them, and those I do usually puzzled me." Becky crinkled her brows to prove the puzzlement lasted. "There was one about a Jew who worked for a Christian prince. He got across the prince, I don't know how, and was sentenced to death. So he said, 'Your Excellency, let's make a bargain. You give me a year in which to teach your dog to talk, and if I don't succeed, kill me at the year's end.' Well, this appealed to the prince, nobody knows why, maybe he just wanted a talking dog, and so he agreed. So the Jew went home, and all his friends said, 'Crazy guy, have you gone quite mad? How can you teach a dog to talk?' 'So, maybe I can't,' the Jew said, 'but a year is a long time. Much can happen. Perhaps the prince will die, perhaps the lessons will kill the dog. Or, who knows? – perhaps the dog learns to speak after all.'"

She told the story in the accents of a Jewish comedian, and then blushed, because that was how she had been accustomed to tell it, it was how her father had told it to her, and it didn't seem right here, in Israel, where the Jews had no need to make a comedy of themselves or apologise for being.

Luke said, "Well yes, but the dog didn't, did he? Still, I see why your poppa told that story."

"Oh do you," she said, "oh, I hadn't thought of that. I suppose you're right. I thought he just found it funny."

"Fucking folk-tales," Luke said again.

"Mind you," Becky said, "I do think it's funny."

*   *   *   *

"They are nice, aren't they?" Franz said. "I told you they were."

They were walking home, arm in arm, in a mood that was both lazy and lively with anticipation. A breeze blew from the sea, soft as love's fingers playing over the cheek. That morning each had been nervous of the night; now they stopped and kissed under a high wall, with the scent of lemons around and the sound of Chopin coming from an apartment block across the street. There was even a moon.

"Yes," she said, "I like them. Rachel's on edge though, isn't she?"

"Everyone's on edge, here. It's a place where you feel things may happen at any moment. Not like Argentina."

"But things happen there."

She didn't add: look what happened to me.

"They're incredible, even so," he said. "In Argentina, any action is a sort of protest against despair."

They strolled on, alone, in the night street, with Chopin fading into silence. She had been suspicious of Luke and Rachel; she couldn't understand how they had come, as it were, to adopt Franz, to take him under their covering wing. It didn't make sense in the circumstances. Then she saw them all together, at the supper table, saw the look in their eyes, and she knew that there would always be someone willing to do this for Franz, that it was perfectly natural. It was one reason why she loved him herself, if it was also a reason she resented.

"I was afraid you wouldn't want to," he said. His left arm lay under her neck, tickled by her hair, and he stroked her left arm and her breast, just above the nipple. "It really frightened me."

"Why did you think that?"

"Because of what you said that day. That's Jewish flesh."

"Oh that."

"I'm no closer to understanding him," he said. "Every time I visit him in that neat antiseptic visiting room, with the two soldiers watching over us, a chill enters the air, though in fact the room is overheated."

She had never been able to imagine what he hoped to achieve by coming here. She found the whole thing odd. When she first met Franz, and loved him almost at once, he had seemed indifferent to his father. Oh yes, he respected him, in his old-fashioned way, was perhaps somewhat in awe of him – which was gauche and youthful and lovable – but didn't give her the impression of anything more. She had been able to envision a married life in which Franz's father represented little more than the dullest sort of dutiful Christmas present, and perhaps lunch twice a year. Why should he matter more now that he stood revealed as a monster? Was Franz simply reacting, again in an awkward and immature fashion, to the glamour of notoriety? Or did he feel that he had an essential part in a terrible drama that was being enacted? But the truth was: the drama was a damp squib. She could see its ending so clearly. For them it was merely a matter of holding on, six months, nine months, until it was over and they could resume their life. And yet she had made that remark – "that's Jewish flesh" – there was no getting away from that.

He hadn't dared ask her why she had come. And now that they had made love, and it was all right, they had found each other again, perhaps he would be even more frightened to put that question. Which she didn't know that she could answer: except to say, I came to make love to you, for fear that if I didn't we would never be able to do so again.

"I didn't know that your mother had been married before."

"Why should you? It's not something she talks about. I don't suppose it's the sort of thing people do talk about. I only found out myself by accident."

"Well, her first husband's here. He's a journalist or something. He made himself known to me the other night. I didn't like him."

"Why are you telling me this?"

"Because I think he'll make trouble if he can."

"What sort of trouble?"

"I don't know. Maybe nobody can make worse trouble than there is."

"I don't know," she said. "There's something else I have to tell you."

"What's that?"

"It's my father, this time. He intends to come to give evidence."

She screwed round to kiss his mouth. Their legs intertwined. They pressed against each other, bone against bone.

"It can't make any difference," he said.

THREE

Preparations for the trial advanced. Witnesses arrived from the United States, Europe, even Australia. Depositions were taken and scrutinised. Franz found himself engaged in long conferences with Saul, who declared himself anxious about Rudi's indifference. Franz realised that professional zeal now dominated Saul; he was a man of law for the moment, not a Jew. Franz was amazed by his ability to put personal feelings aside, to appear to live the part he was playing.

Though Rudi had been held in Tel Aviv, the trial would take place in Jerusalem. Security reasons had been given as the explanation for keeping him in Tel Aviv, out of the divided city. The authorities feared the possibility of a rescue, effected with Arab assistance. It was not a fanciful notion: to lose Rudi Kestner would be a propaganda setback for the Israeli government. But the symbolic importance of putting Hitlerism again on trial in the sacred city of Jerusalem, in the very heart of world Jewry, now overrode the security considerations. The fears seemed exaggerated in any case: the efficiency of Israel was such that Franz was sure there was no real chance that they would lose their prisoner. And he couldn't anyway contemplate how his father would live if he were freed. It certainly wouldn't be in what anyone might understand as freedom.

But had Rudi ever known freedom?

Rudi's own interest in the trial did not rise above the technicalities of his defence. He was ready to discuss those as if the trial were a chess game. But whenever Franz tried to bring up the subject of what he thought of as the moral significance of the trial, Rudi's mouth shut close, he tapped out a cigarette for himself, he blew smoke in his son's face.

Franz, chilled by the atmosphere of these conversations, attempted to get his father to speak of his childhood. He had been incurious about this. Curiosity had never been either encouraged or discouraged. It had just been assumed that there was nothing of that sort to talk about. He hadn't even known, until that lunch with Becky and her parents at the

Engineers' Club – a lunch that now seemed to have belonged to another, now buried, civilisation – that his grandfather had been a postal official, and a Saxon.

"Did your father fight in the First War?" he asked Rudi. "No, he was too old. Already too old."

"I didn't know that."

"Besides, he disapproved. He was an old social democrat, though he concealed his views on account of his official post, and he disapproved of his party's acquiescence in the war. It did him little good. He died in the influenza of 1919. My mother wanted me to become a priest, did you know that?"

"No, I know nothing of your family ... our family."

Rudi smiled, "Josef Goebbels used to say his mother had the same ambition for him. Perhaps we were both spoiled priests. I often thought that in Argentina."

Hadn't the SS, Franz thought, seen itself as a *corps d'élite*, like the Jesuits, or more precisely, the Teutonic Knights? Wasn't it perhaps a parody of a religious order, founded on hate and not love?

Luke had said, the other night as they walked through the inky violet of the still hours, "Do you know what the Germans themselves called the camps, the extermination camps? *Der Arschloch der Welt* – The arsehole of the world."

Franz looked across the table at his father, whose fingers, despite the heavy cigarette smoking, were kept free of nicotine stains by use of a pumice stone.

Rudi said, "I hated my mother's weakness, and so I hated her Church. Its doctrines of self-abasement stank in my nostrils. Now I see it is more complicated than I supposed. We thought we had come in our generation to supersede Christianity, to sweep away what we thought of as a faith fit only for slaves and women. But it has since occurred to me that we realised its most lurid fantasies. We made what it had only imagined. Hell. But even that claim is excessive. Hadn't the Inquisition in Spain prefigured our endeavours? Isn't that hatred for the other, for all those outside the tribe, built into the human psyche? Wasn't our chief offence that we compelled others to confront that reality? You know what Freud said, my son: 'Endlich muss mann beginnen lieben, um nicht krank zu werden'? Man must constantly strive to love, so that he doesn't become sick. Are you surprised to hear me quote a Jew, Franz? Well, perhaps it is because I have come to accept the truth of his words, and so to feel the necessity of 'beginnen zu lieben'. Does that amaze you so much?"

Rudi said, "You must understand, my son, that, though I shall fight to the last for my life, because that is the duty of man, and I may add in passing that it was their failure to do this, their acquiescence in our plans, that so disgusted me with the Jews, though, as I say, I shall do this, like a bull in the arena, or a bear tied to the stake, I nevertheless accept my fate. I shall not be testifying on behalf of anything or anyone but my own being. Like Luther, I shall say, Here I stand, Rudi Kestner, as I have made myself. Now that I am in your power, you may make of me what you please. That will not alter. And there is an irony, which is inconceivable to anyone who has not felt the lightness of freedom from the immense and relentless exigencies of abstraction, that I have been brought here to the cradle of what Nietzsche called 'die ungeheuer-lichste aller menschlichen Verirrungen' – the most monstrous of all human errors: monotheism. For if the Jews were our victims, they were also, I insist, the begetters of the error into which we fell: the denial of multiplicity..."

Rudi said: "When I was at the same time master and servant of a bureaucracy of admirable complexity, I was a simple man. Now that I am nothing, I find myself growing daily more complicated."

"Are you, were you, can you still be, proud?"

"Proud of playing God? Who can be? Then again, who can fail to be?"

Rudi said, "No one could have betrayed the Jews if they had not first betrayed themselves. They prated of the truths of self-abnegation, of the lonely spirit in the desert. And they lived a truth of exploitation, thrusting Saxon peasants ever deeper into remorseless debt."

Franz had always known his father as a force. But that force had been contained, like a river that had been embanked and could no longer flood a city. Now it was in spate, the walls had broken, and the torrent tumbled through the civil streets bearing its cargo of fractured nature, broken statues, dead dogs, corpses of sheep, cattle and the occasional child. When the floodwater ebbed away, creeping back into the river's channel, a residue of mud and filth made the houses noisome.

Franz wondered if his father was indeed going mad. "You can't imagine the incoherence of his talk," he said to Becky. She suggested that perhaps he was doing the exact opposite, going sane, and floundering in the attempt like an inexpert swimmer: which wasn't, in the circumstances, surprising. Franz pretended to agree, or at least to be ready to be convinced, or comforted; nevertheless he wrote in his journal:

> Becky doesn't hear his voice. It rings in my ears from one session to the next. It comes between me and sleep at night. When we have made love, and Becky lies naked in my arms, and I ought to be invaded by tenderness, even by that melancholy which is the sequel to lovemaking and which is also (I am sure) evidence of the intensity of that love and of one's fears for its permanence, even then I hear instead that flat, droning monotone regurgitating bits of reading and memories of experience of the utmost horror, which nevertheless I am certain he does not feel, does not allow in any true sense to touch him. It is always as if he is watching something which doesn't concern him, which perhaps – and this is surely still more horrible – never concerned him at any deeper level of his being – if indeed he has such a level. That's what I scream to myself, silently, in the night, as the girl I love murmurs in my arms.
>
> And I write this now, and read it over, and am horrified by myself. Aren't I perhaps guilty of the same fault? This is my father who is in terror or torment. He must be, though he doesn't show it. This is my father who has never been anything but just and kind to me, even when severely kind, who has never (I am certain of this at least) had anything but the best intentions towards me, and who has kept my own best interests at heart: and I analyse him in this manner. Can that be right? Can it be avoided? Am I to blame? If so, of what am I culpable? I never asked … but that's pathetic.
>
> I am pathetic. If it wasn't for Becky, I would … no, I don't suppose I would have either the courage or, to be honest, the lack of curiosity, to kill myself.
>
> I write, "if it wasn't for Becky" and that is true. I need her more, and more sharply and urgently, than I could ever have imagined myself needing anybody. But, but, but, last night, I dreamed twice, or one dream split in confusion, I don't know. I was again in that hut at the Academy with José-Maria and Luis. It smelled of rotten earth and the dirty sacks on which the naked body of Bastini crumpled. Only this time, I joined

in the beating, whipping him till the blood ran and the sperm spouted. There was joy in his degradation, music sounded about us. And then – I don't know what there was between, whether I had woken and then drifted again beyond the margins of sleep, or whether the camera cut to the next scene, but I was walking up a staircase with Alexis. It was a grand staircase thickly carpeted, with marble surrounds. She was dressed all in black, a dingy cap like a railway porter's perched on her head. We mounted the stairs entwined. I felt her fingers on my buttock, slipped down within my waistband. I looked at her breasts which her silk shirt was unbuttoned sufficiently to disclose. She wore a black leather jacket. It was shabby and there was a right-angled tear on the right thigh of her jeans. Everyone watched us as we mounted the stairs. Everyone, I knew, envied me. Then we were in a room. It was a big room and half-dark and there was no furniture there. Cobwebs dangled over the window and from the chandelier. I turned to kiss her, but she slipped away. She raised herself on her toes, and kissed me on the left cheek. It was no more than a brush of her lips, a promise, a sigh, an expression of regret. It was very cold in the room and there was no bed and then I was alone. I stretched out my hands as if reaching for the shore where she had stood, and they were grey with spiders' webs. And then I woke. I reached out for Becky and she was not there. My eyes grew accustomed to the dim light, and she was sitting by the window gazing out on this city which could be hers and never mine. "I was thinking of Jerusalem," she said, and for a moment did not stir when I begged her to return to our bed.

"You were dreaming," she said, "twitching like a dog hunting rabbits in his sleep. Was I in your dream?"

"Yes," I lied. "No," I said, "I don't know. It's vanished."

Ivan Murison has invited us to lunch today. I would have refused but Becky has a natural curiosity to meet her mother's first husband. When I see him, I am afraid that I will again see Bastini weeping on the dirty sacks...

They were both nervous as they prepared for their meeting with Ivan Murison. Becky felt she was somehow betraying her father – perhaps her mother too – in accepting his invitation. It was as if she was eager to spy on their past, on a part of their lives which did not belong to her, to enter a forbidden chamber.

Yet the mood slipped away in the consciousness of her happiness. She couldn't account for that either. She was afraid that things were going to happen, things over which they neither of them possessed any control, which could scatter their happiness, which would blow the structure of love they had made for themselves utterly apart. Perhaps that itself was reason for happiness now. They were like lovers in wartime who may any night find everything destroyed by the bombers that occupy the darkness.

That was true. It would have been easy to advance simpler explanations for her happiness. She had been afraid of coming here. She had been afraid she would find Franz no longer loved her. The intimation of his feeling for Alexis had woken that fear. The knowledge of her father's part in the drama they were experiencing had fanned it. And that drama was all the more terrible because they hadn't been engaged as performers. It was rather as if they had been invited to make up the audience in a theatre, been sent complimentary tickets, and then discovered that what was happening on the stage involved them: as if, for instance, Macbeth's murderers had slunk into the auditorium seeking out fresh victims. That was how the Jews themselves must have felt in pre-war Germany: they hadn't hired out to be players, but had been conscripted. Perhaps that is the meaning, and the horror, of history: that it spills off the stage. If only it could be left to those who enjoy the game.

They took a taxi to the restaurant which Ivan Murison had chosen, which had tables on a terrace within view of the sea. He was waiting for them there, with a bottle of champagne in an ice bucket by his side, and a glass between his fingers. He rose to meet them, and because the table was on a higher level, one step above them, appeared huge and dominating. His cream suit was crumpled and stained, but he exuded a sense of superiority, as if the state of his suit was a mark of his sublime indifference, as if only trivial people needed to take trouble with their appearance. Becky was glad she hadn't put on any lipstick, which she rarely did, but had thought of doing on this occasion.

He had already ordered for them: lobster, and she knew he hoped that one of them would protest a dislike for lobster. He seized the bottle by the neck and poured the wine, and when he passed a glass to Becky, placed his free hand under her chin, lifting it up so that he might scrutinise her.

The gesture was insolent. She resented it, but could not, without equal insolence, repudiate him; and was incapable of that. He held her chin there a long moment, like a man considering whether to buy a horse.

"I see a resemblance," he said. "How is your mother? Does she still love Czinner? Or has that marriage bored her in its turn?"

Becky flushed.

"Father's blind," she said, and then wished she hadn't; she had no desire to offer him to this man as an object of pity.

Ivan Murison smiled, as if her answer satisfied him. Then he talked of coincidence: how strange it was that his friend Charlie should have been at school with Franz.

"And to think," Ivan Murison said, "that Rudi Kestner, whose traces I tried to follow through Germany eighteen years ago, should present himself in such an intimately connected fashion to me now. Well, it just goes to show. I always regarded him as one of my failures: he seemed to have vanished so completely. I never believed, as some said, that he died in the last days in Berlin. Oh no, not old Rudi. But how he got away, who helped him – for he must have had help – these remained mysteries."

His voice sank on the last word, like that of an actor in an old-fashioned melodrama. Then he began to talk as he forked lobster thermidor into his mouth. He talked first of his experiences in Germany, of how he had been one of the first reporters into Belsen and Buchenwald, of how the horrors he saw there had filled him with a loathing of the whole German people. Yet, in his speech, the loathing and repulsion spread further; they seeped into everything he said, soaked up so that it was like a newspaper spread on the floor where a bitch has squatted to urinate. He had never been an idealist; Franz got the sense of a man who had always taken a narrow view of experience, whose response to everything had been, "What's in it for me?" Well, he had got something out of the concentration camps: a book and a reputation. The camps had, in a sense that was almost as horrible as anything which had happened there, made him. Now he dwelled on what he had seen with a relish that suggested it meant no more to him than photographs too often thumbed over, photographs from which the original horror had been drained away, leaving instead even a certain enjoyment. They couldn't know how he had really felt. Perhaps it had never been possible to establish that. But now, as Ivan Murison rolled the details around, and dug his fork into the lobster, piercing a thick gobbet of sea-flesh, as he dwelled on the terror of the last camp prostitutes with rags of their tawdry glamour still clinging to them as they ran here and there, desperate because they didn't know whether they would be aligned with the victims or their torturers, it seemed that a transference had taken place. By brooding on horrors, Ivan Murison had changed sides; contemplation of pain and terror had made him an addict. His imagination could now be excited only by what had once made him tremble.

Becky pushed her chair back, so hard that it fell over, clapped her napkin to her mouth, and fled.

"I'm afraid I've upset her, old boy," Ivan Murison said. He sipped his champagne and his eyes searched for Franz's over the rim of the glass; found them and held them.

"But people should know these things. I've made it my life's work, dear boy, to force the face of the public into them."

"What do you want with us?" Franz said.

Ivan Murison called for the waiter and ordered brandy. "Bring the bottle," he said again.

He sat, red-faced, sweating, and smiling until it came, then poured himself a big balloon. He swirled the liquid round in the glass, and drank. Down in one, then poured another measure. "Charlie told me you were an innocent," he said. "Charlie's not innocent, dear boy. He knows the sink the world is. Very well, you're impatient now to get away from me, to see what has happened to Nell's daughter, you wonder if she's all right. You little fool. Nobody's all right. Don't you know that?"

He put the glass down, and lit a cigar. He blew the first smoke straight at Franz. "I want an exclusive with Czinner when he arrives, and I want the details of your father's escape from Germany. Names and dates. Just that. Two simple requests. Nothing to it, old boy, for one in your position. Don't let me down now."

"I can't fix that… I don't see how."

"Oh, I think you can and do, darling. That photograph I showed you might excite Nell's daughter differently from the way it does us, mightn't it now? One other thing. Steer clear of Luke Abramowitz. He's a Zionist. That means he's using you for his own purposes."

* * * *

At the Mandelbaum Gate, Luke said, "We can go no further. We cannot enter the Old City, not even Rachel, though she has an American passport. You can of course, Franz. I doubt if it will be possible for Becky. In any case, not today. You require permission, first from our District Commissioner, then from the Jordanian authorities, who have never been known to grant permission to a Jew. So, you see, Franz, even in our own Holy Land, in the Holy City of Jerusalem, the way is barred to the Jew."

He laughed. They withdrew, retracing their steps towards the Tomb of David. They mounted to the roof, from where they could gaze into the Old City. They could see the crenellated wall, the upper part of Zion's gate, the Temple area with the huge dome of Omar's mosque scintillating in the sunlight, and a corner of the Wailing Wall.

"Jerusalem the Golden," Luke laughed again. "Also Jerusalem the Forbidden. Perhaps that is just as well. Do you know what I've been thinking? As long as we are denied Jerusalem, our exile is not over. We still have something to hope for."

"Luke," Rachel said, "you're talking the most God-awful nonsense, darling. Keep it for evening classes. I'm hungry. I'm so hungry I could eat a camel."

They had come to Jerusalem that morning. They all had their own reasons for seeking escape: Luke from the sterility of his novel, which he had begun to hate, Rachel from their apartment that in the last days had come to represent a denial of every picture she had ever had of her life, Franz from the fears which Ivan Murison had aroused, Becky from … she wasn't sure what. She just knew, looking around her, that her need was the most urgent of all. Her father would be arriving in two days; she wasn't ready to meet him.

They lunched at an Armenian restaurant below the tomb. Each time she found herself at a restaurant table now, Becky was more ill at ease. Their position was false, pretending to be tourists. The waiter had led them to a table on the terrace. There was a drop below to a chaos of red-tiled roofs, terraces, abundant flowers. She took her camera, and, hoping none of the others saw, dropped it over the wall. Rachel's eyes were on her.

Becky said, "I just couldn't stand it any more."

"What do you mean?"

"This game we're playing."

The waiter brought *meze*, little pastries stuffed with aubergine, rice balls, cucumber and salted lemon, tiny fried fish like whitebait, radishes, yoghourt, and pastries with minced meat. He placed a carafe of wine on the table with a lordly flourish.

"But that was a good camera," Rachel said. "It was a Leica, I saw." She laid down her napkin, got to her feet, and left them.

"I'm sorry, I seem to have upset her," said Becky.

"Not to worry," Luke said. "Eat. We all need food."

She saw Franz looking at her, worried. The sun had bleached his hair a paler gold, there were lines formed by fatigue and anxiety on his face. He doesn't need a neurotic like me, she thought. Maybe he needs someone like Alexis after all.

Luke was talking. She didn't listen. He was always talking and while it was good listening, it was too much. He talked about ideas, which didn't help. It wasn't ideas they needed. It was a means of getting through the next weeks without breaking. The prospective trial excited Luke. It excited all of them. And yet Luke didn't need excitement, as an Argentinian might. He wasn't suffering from *cafard*. She picked up a pastry and nibbled it.

A car backfired in the street below. For a moment there was a stiffening of postures on the terrace. Only the two Protestant clergymen, eating a large meal in the corner – there were already a couple of empty wine bottles on their table – paid no attention. They belonged, Becky supposed, to a culture where the sound of a backfire was always and only a backfire, world without end, amen.

"We had lunch," Franz said, "with a disgusting man the day before yesterday. An English journalist called Ivan Murison. He made his reputation with his accounts of the death camps, but I mentioned him to my father yesterday morning, and he said that in Germany in the middle Thirties Herr Murison was well known for his sympathetic attitude towards the Nazis. What do you make of that?"

"The Holocaust was the greatest crime in history," Luke said.

"Worse than Hiroshima?" Becky said, crumbling her pastry.

"Yes. Much worse than Hiroshima. I'll explain why later, if you like. So it was the greatest crime, but you cannot understand it if you don't realise that Hitler held out the offer not only of revenge."

"Revenge for what?"

"What you like. Let us say for the humiliation of existence. Not only revenge, but hope. A clean sweep. A new purified beginning. You cannot understand it unless you are prepared to accept how attractive Nazism was in its early days, if you can't appreciate the appeal it made to the best in men like your father, Franz, as well as to the worst… If I had been a German, and not a Jew, I would, no, I might well, have been a Nazi in 1928. Or even later. Think of what had happened. Defeat, betrayal, total social disintegration. And as for the Holocaust, I am inclined to blame the collapse of the currency. It cost men their sense of reality. Large numbers became playthings. Besides, it is easier to kill a million men than ten. The ordinary person couldn't even bring himself to kill a single calf, but the slaughterhouse worker kills hundreds and goes home to a good supper."

"I don't understand you, Luke."

"I don't understand myself, Becky. There are days, and this seems to be one of them, when I seem to understand nothing. But it's on such days that one may receive sudden shafts of light."

"Yes, Luke," Franz said. "Ever since it started, I've been asking myself: would I have gone the same route as my father? And I can't arrive at a negative answer."

"But I told you, Franz, we are all Eichmann's children and we have our own Jews in Israel, whom we call Arabs. I say these things often. Do you wonder that I have enemies who write pieces in the papers which they hope will destroy me?"

Rachel approached the table. She laid Becky's camera down without a word, and resumed her seat. She was a little out of breath, but also pale and when she tried to lift her glass her hand shook.

"What is it, darling?"

"I saw a man shot. He was only a boy. A young Arab, wearing shorts. He was shot in the stomach and the blood ran out at the leg of his shorts. The man who did it ran away. The police are there now, waving clubs to keep people back."

But, around them, lunch went on. A party of tourists arrived and occupied the next table. There were three, father, mother and daughter, all tall, blond, and heavy: Swedes perhaps. They talked in a rapid tack-tack that Becky could not identify. Each laid a camera in a heavy leather case on the table; you could draw a little triangle joining them round the bowl of flowers in the middle. The cameras were equidistant; the triangle would be regularly equilateral.

"Did you see the murderer? I suppose it was murder."

"Yes, but he could have been anyone or anything, a thin man in jeans and a white shirt."

"They won't catch him. It's a rabbit warren below."

The Swedes ordered their meal, with many questions. Why shouldn't they? What concern was it of theirs, even if they knew of the shooting; and probably they didn't. But it wasn't what they had come to see. Their own lives were – that was certain – orderly. Nobody was shot in a street in Stockholm, not even perhaps for personal reasons. So? That was no reason to feel that these Swedes were somehow inadequate, because they escaped, evaded, were unacquainted with, the violence that is itself the product of inadequacy. Becky wished Rachel hadn't gone to fetch her camera. She really wanted to be rid of it.

"Maybe they won't want to catch him," Rachel said.

"Why?" This from Franz. He was crumbling a pastry on his plate. Then, having asked his question, he licked his fingers, and wiped them with his napkin.

"Oh, because . . . well, in the first place it depends who the boy was, whether he was significant, and of what sort of significance."

"Please," it was the male Swede leaning over, "do I understand you? There has been a shooting? But why? Is it an atrocity?"

"We don't know," Luke said. "Maybe it's only a street killing. My wife saw it."

"Indeed?" The Swede looked at him. "Excuse me, please, I think you are Luke Abramowitz. I read your novel. Very good."

"Which one?"

"Ah, you have written more than one. I did not know. It was called *Messenger from Gilboa*. Very good."

"Ah," Luke said. "I would rather you had read the other one, *Husband*. It's better, isn't it, Rachel? Oh sorry, this is my wife, and our friends, Franz Schmidt and Becky."

It was tactful the way he omitted her surname.

The Swede reciprocated. Wife and daughter as she had supposed. Name of Johansson, ordinary as Schmidt.

"Are you a journalist, Mr Johansson?"

"No, why do you ask that? I am a theologian."

"He is a professor of theology," the daughter said. "He has this ridiculous idea that it is boasting to tell people that. I say," – she beamed on them – "we are not living in the nineteenth century now, and nobody thinks anything of professors of theology. So it is not boasting. It is only accurate."

"My daughter is a freethinker. She does not understand that Protestant theology is freethinking itself nowadays…"

He smiled at her. The girl was big and doughy, and had a rough laugh and horse's teeth, but Becky could see that her father adored her, perhaps with a special tenderness simply because she was awkward. Was that why God had chosen the Jews? For their cussedness?

The professor wanted to talk of Luke's novel. He dilated on it at some length. It interested him partly, he said, because it offered a new slant on what was familiar. They were fortunate in Sweden of course; they had never felt under any kind of racial threat. But Luke seemed to be suggesting that when peoples experience such a threat it is never altogether unfounded. Was that what he really thought now? Now? Didn't that make things difficult for him, as a prominent Israeli figure, with this Kestner trial coming on for example? Because, if Luke really believed that, then it followed, didn't it, that the Nazi persecution of the Jews was not entirely, not entirely, unjustified?

The professor was prolix. His lectures were not likely to enthuse his students. But there was something sharp and probing in his determination to investigate his point; you didn't expect a big heavy fellow like that to behave like a terrier at a rabbit-hole.

Luke said, "Feelings can be justified, when actions can't."

"Yes, that is a good distinction. And I sense something else underlying your thought, something with which I find myself in agreement: that the Holocaust itself has had what is now called a side-benefit. The moral relativism which Freudians made fashionable is now impossible for us. Who can now deny the reality of evil?"

He smiled on them.

"That doesn't sound like freethinking to me," Rachel said.

Franz crumbled another pastry. "I don't understand," he said. "If you take that line, aren't you suggesting that somehow God permitted it?"

"Of course God permitted it," Johansson approved, "he grants us free will."

"And so in some measure is responsible for it, as if it was all part of his plan?"

"My dear boy," Johannson leaned across and laid his hand on Franz's shoulder. "It is now you who are old-fashioned. God does not have a plan, in the sense that our good Social-Democratic govern-ment may have a plan. God does not seek to regulate the human economy." He laughed. "Oh no. God has given us Life and Freedom and the Hope of Glory. But we have to struggle to attain it, which we do first by coming to an acceptance of reality, and that necessarily includes evil."

"Sounds to me," Rachel said, "as if it's all a piece of theatre to your God."

"But sublime theatre!"

"You mean he settles back in the stalls and watches the play? With a box of chocolates on his knee perhaps?"

"Ah, but the struggle is played out in each individual soul. Even this Kestner's perhaps, even now."

The waiter brought them coffee; another, food to the Swedes' table. Professor Johansson took a card from his wallet, wrote the name of his hotel on it, passed it to Luke.

"Please get in touch," he said. "It would give me pleasure to have an opportunity to discuss such matters with you further. Your novel made me think. That is always good."

Then he turned away and picked up his knife and fork.

The electricity failed within the restaurant; it might even have been Argentina. But only for a moment. There was a flicker of light, brief darkness, and normal power was resumed. They drank their coffee, paid the bill. Becky picked up her camera. "Thank you," she said to Rachel. "It was silly of me. I don't know what got into me."

Outside, there was now no sign of the shooting.

"It was just there," Rachel said.

"They've cleared it up nicely," Luke said.

Heavy clouds had gathered while they were at lunch. The air was dense. There was a darkness over the Old City.

Franz said, "I meant to tell you, Luke, I was warned against you yesterday."

"Oh yes?"

"By that English journalist. He said you were a Zionist, who would use me. He didn't say how."

"You didn't believe him?"

"No."

"That's right. Just remember, kid. The war nowadays is between gen-erations. It's turned horizontal. So the four of us *contra mundum*. OK?"

Rachel said, "The boy who was shot, he was even younger than us. He was an Arab, I think. Did I tell you I thought he was an Arab?"

"Sure, but you don't know. Maybe it was love, not politics. People still kill for love as well as hate." Luke put his arm round her.

Franz and Becky dropped a few paces behind. "Let's go back to the hotel," Becky said. "I want you."

FOUR

Rudi said, "When I was a young man, I made my way to Berlin. Why? For the most old-fashioned reason. I thought I might escape in the city. I was desperately poor. You must understand. This was 1922, I was sixteen. I lodged in a poor working-class quarter. It disgusted me. These people, I said to myself, are animals. They have no aspirations except to fill their bellies – and they are not even good at that. My landlord was a Jew. Every Saturday night he went round the rooms where his lodgers lay drunk if they had been paid that day, and shook all the money he could find out of their trouser pockets. He did that though it was his Sabbath. The lodgers were too stupid to realise what he did, and in any case most of them were so drunk that they did not know how much money they had spent or how much they should have left. Then, on the second or third day of the week, or even earlier on the Sunday, when they needed money for tram fares if they were working, he would offer to lend it to them. It was their own money he was lending, and if they did not pay him back, with 50 per cent interest, then they were out on the street.

"I saw that happen to many of them.

"I had one friend. He was called Karl. Sometimes he was in work as a barman, but often he was not. I didn't know what he did then, and I didn't suspect, though Karl was a strong handsome blond fellow. He was the only one of us who was not undernourished even though he was often out of work. As for me, I had found a job, as a clerk in a factory where they made glue out of bones. The stench was appalling.

"I tell you this, Franz, that you may understand the care I have had for you in your childhood, my determination that you should never suffer as I suffered.

"Well, one day – it was winter and raining – Karl came to me and said, 'Will you help me?' 'To do what?' I said. 'Kill the Jew.' I thought about it, and replied that I didn't approve of violence. Besides, I said, what was the point? Karl explained. The Jew had a wife, a thin bedraggled wretch, bullied and tormented by her husband. I don't know whether she was a Jew or not, I think she was perhaps Hungarian. Karl had seduced her. It wasn't difficult, he said, seduction was too grand a word. 'She was dying for it,' he laughed. She would marry him if her husband was dead, and then the lodging house would be his. He promised me a share in the takings. 'Besides,' he said, 'the man who has not killed is a virgin.' In those days I was a virgin in the normal sense of the word. Sex disgusted me, and continued to do so until I was in a position to have a bath every day and live in a house with a bathroom. 'Have you killed a man?' I said. Karl laughed. He put his hands on his hips and laughed. I can see him now, in that filthy bug-infested hovel, and hear him laughing as if he was a god. 'What do you think?' he said. So I said I would think about it. That Jew would be no loss, I told myself. He was loathsome. But then, to be an accomplice to a murder! So I asked Karl what his plan was, and I saw that it was more likely to be dangerous for me than for him. 'I must keep in the background,' he said, 'on account of my affair with Lola.' That was the wretch's name, Lola, not very suitable. And so I told the Jew what was going on and what was planned.

"I saved that Jew's life. And then I left, because I was afraid of Karl. As for the filthy Jew, he struck his wife so hard that she fell, hitting her head against the kitchen sink, and was killed. That was the result of my benevolent intervention. Somehow or other, I heard later that the Jew was acquitted of manslaughter. They said he bribed the judge. Or perhaps the judge was a Jew. Many were, in those days.

"As for Karl, I came across him, years later. He had become a Communist. He was always scum, I knew that. But for a time I was fascinated by him, and he had almost persuaded me to join him in the murder he desired but did not dare to commit. Later I despised him for not daring."

Neither of the two young soldiers who acted as warders paid any heed to what Rudi was saying, except that once, as he hesitated, the younger of them caught Franz's eye, and lifted his own left eyebrow. A whiff of friendship was carried across the zoom, rising with the cigarette smoke towards the ceiling. The other warder plugged in the electric kettle, and put tea bags into mugs.

Rudi said, "I hated my work. The bone factory stood in a dismal eastern suburb of the city. Suburb is the wrong word; it will give you the wrong impression. It was a place where the city trickled like dirty water into a countryside that had no grace or charm about it. The factory stood between a canal that needed dredging and a railway line. Trucks bearing bones from various abattoirs halted there. There were fat yellow and white maggots clinging to the bones, to which a few shreds of flesh and sinew were still always attached. If you picked up a bone a handful of maggots would fall off. That wasn't the worst of it. Far worse was the stench from the furnaces. It hung over the dismal quarter. Even the beer they served in the two bars at the end of the street tasted of that smell. It was never my job to touch the bones, I was a clerk keeping records, but I would sit at the grimy window overlooking the yard and watch the seagulls that picked at them, always quarrelling. And though I never touched the bones, the smell clung about me. However often I scrubbed myself in the public bath-house it was there. There was a girl who worked in one of the bars who would sell herself to the workers, and when she leant over the table, exposing her breasts, the stench came off her, and I was nauseated. Yet I stuck to the job eighteen months. It was miserably paid, but it was a job and in Berlin in 1923, you didn't abandon a job because of a bad smell.

"The man who owned the factory was a Jew. They said that whenever a new consignment of bones arrived, he picked over them, choosing those that would do for his own soup.

"I think that was true."

Rudi tapped out a cigarette.

"Is all this boring you, Franz? I don't know why it is, but those early years have been running in my mind, disturbing my sleep. It is sometimes as if I can still smell that slut in the bar.

"One night I thought I was going mad. It was winter, I had been working late, and the tram which I took back to the quarter where I now had my lodgings was empty. It was raining, and the few poor lights in that fringe of the city were mere spots, like a bulb shining through a shroud. Then, though the tram had not stopped, the carriage was full of people, and they all had the same face, they all wore damp overcoats with the collars turned up, and all gazed at me. They did not speak, but they directed their eyes at me. Only they had no eyes. The rest of the face was normal, pale wet skin stretched over bones, but the eye sockets were empty."

The older soldier had added water to the tea bags. Now he removed the bags from the mugs and poured in milk. He put one spoonful of sugar in each mug and stirred the tea. He placed their mugs in front of them.

"I speak German, you know," said the soldier. "My mother was from Berlin. She was a poor Jew, so she didn't get out. Maybe she didn't want to. I'm told she loved the city. I don't know. It was an aunt who brought me and my sister out. I shouldn't be saying this, but you can't expect us to forgive. Or forget. Ever. When you speak of your landlord and your employer as filthy Jews, that's as may be. But don't you think they would have been just as filthy whatever their race or religion? I'm sorry, I shouldn't be saying this. I'm not supposed to be taking part in your conversation."

"No, you shouldn't be," his companion said. "All the same, it's a good question, isn't it?"

Franz sipped his tea.

"I think you should answer that, Father. I think it would help if you did."

"So?" Rudi said. "It's not difficult. You are quite right, Moshe. But don't you see, sticking on the label made it easier to hate. If you were swindled by an Arab, my friend, would you say, 'What a swine' or 'Filthy Arab swine'?"

Rudi said, "I was a young man without purpose. For months I was on the verge of losing the last imperative: to survive. I dreamed of killing myself. Believe me, no one knows better the temptation of suicide. I was twenty-three, twenty-four, twenty-five, and still nothing. At night I lay awake and listened to the noises of the lodging house and of the city, and I knew that my life was of no importance to anyone. Not even it seemed, in my blackest moments, to myself.

"And then I was rescued..."

Becky was uneasy when Franz went to visit his father. She knew he had to; it was why he had come there. But she wished he could leave off. He came back depressed and edgy. "I really despise myself," he said. "I've known nothing. Do you believe it's true that the man who hasn't killed is a virgin?"

"No," she replied, "I think it's a stupid saying. I've heard it before, and it's stupid. It's sort of Argentinian."

But that didn't help him. So when he was away she fretted; she was afraid each time that he would come back and look at her and see a Jewess. She told herself none of that meant anything to Franz; then a voice reminded her of touching pitch and the unavoidable consequence of defilement. Once she even thought: "It's not fair that I should have to bear this," and was disgusted. She had never thought of herself as cheap.

She started to hear the telephone ring. She sat letting it ring. It threatened her, alone in her hotel room. It stopped, recommenced almost at once. This time she answered, and was relieved to find it was Rachel.

"Was it you a minute ago?"

"It was. Were you in the bathroom?"

"No. I couldn't bring myself to answer. I don't know why." She went round to Rachel's apartment. Luke was out. Rachel told her she felt nervous too.

"This whole goddam thing makes me jumpy," she said.

She made coffee and pushed a plate of doughnuts at Becky. "Go on," she said, "we need spoiling. Made them myself, American style. Go on."

There was maple syrup in them, and Becky licked the syrup that escaped and trickled down her chin.

It was cold outside and they sat in front of the gas fire. Rachel kicked her shoes off and curled on a cushion on the floor.

"I couldn't stand being alone this morning," she said. "I'm glad you've come. Is Franz with his father?"

Becky nodded. Rachel put her hand out and squeezed Becky's leg just above the knee.

"And that worries you, does it?"

"He comes back, oh I don't know, different. As if he's seen something that … Franz is innocent, you know."

"Sure I know."

"And then he's edgy. We quarrelled yesterday when he came back. It was horrible."

"Sure. He would hate it. It's meat and drink to Luke but Franz would hate it. And when people hate quarrelling they find it hard to make up. Luke and I are different that way. He makes up easily. This case is hell for him too. It's damaging him. Do you know why?"

Becky shook her head. Her hair floated over her eyes, obscuring Rachel's face. The grip on her leg tightened.

"He can't let it go," Rachel said. "He worries. He's on the point of speaking out against it, and to hell with the damage that does him. He knows he's wrong, or that everyone will say he's wrong, and he can't use the argument he has that's driving him on. Do you understand that? It's Franz, you see."

"No," Becky said. "Look, it was maybe a bad idea me coming here today."

Rachel took her hand away. "You're free to go," she said, "but I hope you won't. Listen, it's not like you may think I mean. Luke isn't queer. It hadn't even entered his head. But Franz still means something special to him. Maybe he does to all of us. I think it's because he's plastic."

"What do you mean?"

"We each make of him what we want him to mean. Do you know, maybe I shouldn't tell you this, but he showed me that letter you wrote him about your ... experiences, and if he had wanted me to make love to him then, I would, without question. And I've never been unfaithful to Luke."

Becky pushed her hair back and looked at her. Rachel's face was eager, explaining, American. It was the face of a newer and franker culture than any she had known, a face that suggested that the way to deal with a problem was to talk it out. But Becky had been raised the English way, in secrecy and silence and reticence. Eli had never interfered with that way of Nell's in rearing their daughter. There were things he had been happy to leave in the dark of silence. So now, in conversation, Becky knew she had no words for feelings.

"I was so touched he showed me that letter. It showed he had confidence in me."

Becky liked Rachel. She was sure that Rachel was good, that she wasn't the sort of girl who liked stirring up trouble. But she was intrusive, Becky felt, and then she looked at her again and saw she was also unhappy.

"You really want to get Luke out of here, don't you?"

Rachel, who had seemed to her in charge of things, aggressive to the point of bullying, began to cry. She sat on the cushion and rocked forward and back, and sobbed. Becky slipped out of her chair and put her arms round her.

"Don't," she said.

The sobbing intensified. To Becky it seemed as if her sympathy was making it worse. She disengaged, retiring to the window, turning her back on Rachel's distress. It was too much. Rachel had no right. Tomorrow her mother and father arrived. In a couple of hours Franz would return from listening to his father – he assured her that all he did was listen. In a week the trial would be under way. The frontier was closed until sentence was delivered, judgement executed. She was caught in a vice. She looked out and the street was bare. A dustcart trundled round the corner. It disturbed a pigeon which had been pecking in the gutter. The sobbing subsided. Rachel began to sniff. The pigeon, not seeing her, landed on the windowsill. For a moment they met eye to uncomprehending eye. Then it pecked at the pane. Her dark clothes were serving to turn the glass into a mirror. It hadn't, whatever she had thought, seen her at all. It was another pigeon it saw challenging itself there. She turned away, to free the bird, which, alarmed by the movement, flew off.

"I'm sorry about that. I don't know what got into me."

"That's all right."

"Let's have some more coffee."

Becky took a doughnut. "They're awfully good," she said. Rachel had told Becky what she already knew. She had known that about Franz from the start.

She said, "I wish you hadn't told me that."

"I'm sorry. Oh hell, why do I have to keep apologising for my goddam self?"

They settled again. With a moral effort, Becky got down on the floor, on a level with Rachel.

"It doesn't matter," she said.

"There's one thing I've wanted to ask you. When you were kidnapped, when these men held you, what did you fear most?"

"Oh," Becky said, "no, I can't talk about that, about that time. I don't know why. It, it makes me feel dirty."

Rachel pushed her a cigarette, held the lighter to it. Becky kept her eyes lowered, not to meet Rachel's.

"OK, honey, I understand. I am sorry."

"No," Becky said, "it wasn't that. Not what you're thinking. We were afraid of that but that didn't happen. It's just that it makes me feel dirty. It made me feel diminished. It showed me anything could happen, that was it. As if we were just … pieces. Like debris you know, washed up by the waves. Does that make any sense?"

"Sure it does. Let's get out of here. What do you say to a walk by the sea?"

The bus dropped them at the end of its run. They had left the popular beaches behind, and the path ran along little cliffs for half a mile or so until it dipped down to the shore. It was shingle now and they walked just above the shingle among sea-grasses and reeds. Inland there was scrub. They looked north and east to a wilderness, stretching, it seemed, to the hills. There was a valley in between which they could not see and that was fertile, but this part of the coast was desolate. There were coils of barbed wire between them and the sea, and though they were only a mile beyond the city, they were all alone. It wasn't Rachel's place at all; her short, city legs were not made for walking in this country, and she swore when a thorn pierced her jeans. Seabirds flew around them mewing. They reached a little knoll and Rachel lay down. The scent of lavender mingled with the smell which the breeze carried from the sea.

"Is it tomorrow your folks come?"

"Uh-huh."

Becky chewed a grass stem.

"Nervous?"

"A bit."

"I would be."

"Yes, well, we've decided Franz can't come to the airport."

"Does he get on with your parents?"

"Well, yes."

"Sure, he gets on with everyone, we'd agreed on that, hadn't we."

"Mummy adores him. I don't know about Daddy."

Aeroplanes – three fighters, wing almost to wing – howled out of the sky, above the sea, zoomed low over them lying there and turned towards the mountains. The sound died behind them. Becky sucked at her grass stem. Rachel had put her hands over her ears and lowered her head. She did not move until they were well away.

"It's a reminder," she said, "whenever they come. Luke's a reserve pilot, you know."

"No, I didn't. Does that worry you?"

"No, it doesn't worry me, it scares the hell out of me. Do you think it would be different if women ran the world?"

"Not really," Becky said.

"I do."

Becky threw away the grass stem, which was torn and ragged and had lost its sap.

"Will they hang him?" she said.

Rachel looked at her and waited.

"They hanged Eichmann, didn't they?"

"Sure. You know that, honey."

"I can't believe it," Becky said. "You know, I can't believe it. I've had proof. They wouldn't have taken Gaby and me, if he hadn't been Kestner, and so I know he is, and I don't need a trial to prove that if he's Kestner, he's guilty. Nobody needs a trial to prove that. But I can't believe it. Do you know what I mean?"

"Go on," Rachel said. "Why can't you?"

"Because … I've only met him that once, you know, but he was nice. He was shy and he was anxious to make a good impression, for Franz's sake, and he showed off a little. Franz has always been a bit afraid of him, but do you know? Do you know what I thought? I thought he was sweet. He wasn't a person you could get to know well. I could see that. And I never thought we'd be easy together, but … there it is. Do you know what? He seemed to me like someone who'd been badly hurt. And he loves Franz, he really does. It doesn't make sense."

"We all love Franz, we agreed on that."

"OK, but. But he's his father. It makes a difference, knowing your father loves you. It must."

"Does it?" Rachel said. "I wouldn't know, but I guess it does."

"They will hang him, won't they?"

"I guess they will. Luke says they will, unless…"

"Unless what?"

Rachel rolled over on to her front. She kicked her heels up behind her. Her feet did a little dance in the air.

"Unless what?"

"I don't know whether I should say this. I guess I shouldn't. Still, to hell with it, Luke's opinion is that he hadn't a hope according to the law. There's a chance that politics could help. I told you, Luke doesn't like this trial, he's got to like it less and less. And it's not just Franz and you, not just because of you. It's that he thinks it's time for Israel to look ahead, to show magnanimity. He thinks that could do wonders. So he's agitated, debating with himself, wondering if he shouldn't be the one to take the lead. That newspaper piece didn't help. Still, he's got influence, Luke has. People listen to him. And then he said – and it started as a joke, well not a joke exactly, you know what I mean, that the second barrel could be you and Franz. You could appeal, he said, to the great warm heart of the Jewish people – he put that in quotes, you understand. And then it wasn't a joke, because it made sense."

"I'm sorry," Becky said, "I'm lost … confused. You'll have to spell it out."

"OK then. He thinks you should get married, here, in Israel, in

Jerusalem. Before the trial, or while it's going on. He thinks that would have an enormous effect."

Becky shivered. The sun had gone. Big purple clouds mounted the sky behind the hills. She dusted her hands on her jeans.

"We couldn't," she said.

"But you love each other. You plan to get married."

"Yes, but don't you see? How can I explain it? That would be, it would be like using our marriage, it would, I don't know, make it dirty, as if it was some sort of a stunt."

"Don't cry," Rachel said, "you don't need to cry. It was only an idea, a silly idea of Luke's. He gets them, you know."

She held out her hand. Becky took it, and Rachel pulled her to her feet. For a moment, they stood, holding hands, looking at each other, with the angry sky behind them and a wind scuffing the sand.

"But there is something," Rachel said. "When Franz's father is hanged, how will Franz feel about marrying you then?"

"God knows," Becky said. "Do you think I don't ask myself that, again and again, in the dark when I can't sleep and feel him there, sometimes tense and not sleeping either? And the answer is never the right one, never. And we don't dare talk about it. We don't dare ask each other the question."

Nevertheless … Nell used to tell Becky that life was a matter of nevertheless. "Everything told me I had lost your father," she said, "nevertheless…" The secret was to accept that things were going one way, whether it was the way you wanted or quite the opposite, and yet to cling to the theory of "nevertheless".

Becky sat in the airport lounge, waiting for the flight which had been delayed and was already an hour and a half late, twisting her handkerchief between her hands, lighting cigarettes which she stubbed out before they were half smoked, gazing at the drink she had ordered and could not touch.

Franz hadn't come. They had agreed it was impossible: impolitic. Franz had even consulted Saul Birnbaum, who had for a moment brightened at the notion, scenting mischief and the opportunity of confusion; then he had shaken his head. It wouldn't do. It might prejudice the court against them. He couldn't say how; logically it shouldn't; nevertheless (again).

And Franz not being there at least gave Becky the chance which she had scarcely had since her conversation with Rachel the previous day, to consider Luke's suggestion. She saw the logic of that too. She saw how it might influence opinion. And yet she continued to rebel against it. It would be making what should be a thing in itself a means to an end. It would be making ... A shadow fell on the table.

"Dear girl, a delightful surprise."

She looked up. Ivan Murison was still wearing the shabby cream suit. The liquid in his glass tilted towards her. He bent to kiss her cheek. She submitted. He was sort of family.

He sat down, lit a cigar.

"Where's the boyfriend?"

Becky didn't answer.

"Mind if I sit here too?"

It was a girl, not much older than herself. She spoke with an American accent. She wore a canary-coloured trouser suit and had delicate features. She put her glass on the table. Her fingers were grubby.

"Can I get you a Coke, Miss Czinner?"

Becky shook her head. Ivan Murison was frowning.

"Surprised to see me, Ivan?" the girl said. "But Czinner will speak to the Press, he'll have to. That's why I'm here, you won't get an exclusive."

She leaned towards Becky.

"My name's Minty Hubchik. I'm a freelance, covering the trial for the *Toronto Star*, and *Insight* – that's a Canadian news magazine, maybe you've heard of it. I'd be grateful of the chance to have a long talk with you. Can I ring you at your hotel and fix a date?"

Ivan Murison said, "I warn you, dear girl, she'll turn you inside out."

"Oh fuck off, Ivan."

Becky said, "I don't know. I'm confused."

"It's in your interest..."

"Oh all right, but now..."

The tannoy crackled. The arrival of the flight was announced. Becky lit another cigarette, stuffed her things into her bag, knocking her lighter on to the floor. Minty Hubchik picked it up. She held it out, and when Becky advanced her hand for it, seized her by the wrist.

"OK, baby, I will. I know it's hell, but I promise you, I'm on your side."

"I don't know what side that is."

Ivan Murison laughed. He got up, with a movement like a man heaving himself from a deckchair, and shouldered his way to the bar. He lifted his glass high above his head and shouted for attention.

Minty Hubchik said, "Maybe you don't need me to tell you, but he's bad news."

"No," Becky said, "that's clear to me already."

"'Bout four then? OK?"

"All right, but what's it about?"

Minty Hubchik released her wrist, restored the lighter to her.

"Look," she said, "do the authorities know you're here? They don't? Because your father, believe me, is going to be whisked away, VIP treatment, and you'll miss him. Here, let me take charge of you."

She did so. It was necessary. She talked to the right people, and doors were opened. They were invited behind the barriers and found themselves in a small room with imitation leather banquettes and potted plants and magazines on glass-topped tables. There was a pot of coffee waiting and Minty poured them each a cup. Then, instead of resuming conversation as Becky feared, she sat in the corner, pulled a file from her shoulder-bag and began to read in it. Becky sipped the coffee and waited; it was like being at the dentist's.

The door opened. Airport officials entered first, then a group of hard-looking young men, two of whom wore revolvers in shoulder holsters, and then Kinsky leading Eli. Becky got up and moved towards them. The men with revolvers exchanged a look and for a moment seemed as if they would bar her approach, but Kinsky called out, "Becky, darling ... Eli, here's Becky," and they gave way.

Eli's hand sought hers. They embraced. Their cheeks met. A camera flashed. One of the men with revolvers advanced on Minty Hubchik. She engaged him in argument.

"I'm tired," Eli said, "and I'm having trouble with my back."

Someone thrust a glass of fizzy wine into his hand. He sniffed it and passed it on to Kinsky, who held it, away from his face, his arm stretched out, while he extended his cheek towards Becky.

"Where's Mother?"

"Shh." His other arm settled round her back and hugged her. "Not now, we'll talk about that later."

Someone, who might have been important but didn't dress it, was welcoming Eli to Israel. He started in Hebrew and then someone else tugged at his sleeve and he switched into English. He said it was sad that it was such an occasion which had at last brought the distinguished economist to Israel, a man whose work had done credit to the whole Jewish people.

He went on. There was something about the Nobel Prize, which should have, and hadn't, but might nevertheless… Becky didn't listen. She had never believed in her father's eminence. She wasn't going to start now. He had aged. The expression of discontent and mockery had deepened. He looked like an actor who had put on greasepaint for a farewell benefit performance. Yet when, listening to this, he held out his hand, pushing it towards her like someone fending off unwelcome attentions, she took hold of it. His face registered nothing, but he squeezed back. She supposed he knew it was her hand.

There was more talk, now of the Press. They went through into another room, where a half-ring of chairs had been assembled opposite rows occupied by a few journalists. The dirty cream-coloured suit was over on the right propped against the wall. Unlike all the other journalists, Ivan Murison kept his glass in his hand and disdained – she supposed it was disdain – a notebook.

Introductions were effected. It was explained that Professor Czinner could not talk of matters which were *sub judice*. He would not at this stage answer questions. But he was prepared to make a statement.

Becky glanced at him to see if this had taken him by surprise. Apparently it hadn't. It must have been agreed in advance. He got to his feet, resting his right hand on the arm of the chair as he did so. He spoke in English, in a weak voice which had several of the journalists straining to hear him.

He said how happy he was to be in Israel at last, or how happy he would have been if the occasion had been other than it was. He had come because it was necessary, because certain things could not be forgotten, but must be remembered. The crime committed against the Jewish people was also a crime against humanity. Only God could forgive it. Their business was justice.

He sat down. He had said nothing, but he was sweating. Would he be able to withstand the pressure of giving evidence? He laid his fingers on his breast, as if feeling for his heartbeat.

The man who was acting as chairman said they would now permit photographs.

"One moment. Is it true, Dr Czinner, that you have a personal interest in bringing Kestner to justice?"

"No questions, Mr Murison. I said no questions."

"Is it true you knew Kestner before the war, had extensive dealings with him during the war, and personal ones more recently?"

"Mr Murison, I must protest. The conditions of this Press Conference..."

"Were such as to make it no conference, merely a farce. Very well, no more questions."

And Ivan Murison brought his glass to his lips, gazing at Becky over the rim.

They were in the car driving away from the airport. There was a man from the Ministry of Justice with them. He was called Aaron. Minty Hubchik had managed to string along, and was sitting in one of the tip-up seats opposite Becky. Eli sat between Becky and Kinsky. He rested his head on the back of the seat. As they drove along the man from the Ministry pointed out places of interest and historical significance.

"There, Professor," he said, "is the Benei-Atarot settlement. As you will surely know, this was established in 1902 by Germans and named after the Kaiser: Wilhelm... I believe a great-uncle of yours was among the pioneer settlers. Yes? ... This village is Yehud. It is mentioned in the Bible as belonging to the tribe of Dan, I forget to which tribe... Ah but, we are now passing through the Plain of Ono. You will remember that when Nehemiah returned from the captivity in Babylon, his enemies sought to lure him out of Jerusalem into the plain, and he, realising their intentions, sent a message, 'I am doing a great work, so that I cannot come down. Why should the work cease?' You remember that, Professor? You must often have thought that way yourself. 'I am doing a great work, so that I cannot come down – why should the work cease?' "

"It's a long time since I read the Bible," Eli said, not moving his head.

"What was the great work?" Kinsky said. "I don't think I ever heard of this Nehemiah."

The man from the Ministry, who had a plump, serious expression, frowned.

"He was rebuilding the walls of Jerusalem."

"Ach so?" Kinsky said, and giggled. Becky bit her lip. She felt Minty Hubchik's foot move against hers, and looked out of the window. There wasn't much to see in the Plain of Ono; lorries were loading oranges into a warehouse.

Eli said, "That journalist can't have been Ivan Murison?"

"Yes, it was."

"Astonishing. I knew him in Berlin before the war. A shit then, and I would guess a shit now. He was married to your mother for a time,

Becky, but you know that of course. I hope you haven't been seeing much of him."

"If you see Ivan Murison, you see too much of him," Minty Hubchik said.

The man from the Ministry left them at the hotel. He asked if they would like a sightseeing tour in the afternoon. Eli said that, in the circumstances, he thought not. Minty Hubchik told Becky she would wait for her in the bar.

"I guess your father will want to rest before long."

"You shouldn't be here," Eli said when they were in the room. "It's no place for you, I can't think why your mother wouldn't see that."

"Where is Mummy? Why isn't she with you? What's happening?"

Eli said, "All hotel rooms everywhere are the same. It's remarkable, and depressing. Your mother thought I shouldn't come. So she hasn't accompanied me. That's all there is to it. Now that I'm here, I fear she may be right, especially if we have to suffer more idiots like that one they assigned us this morning. Still, it is necessary. Your mother tells me you are living with the young Kestner."

"Yes, I'm living with Franz, Daddy. I don't think of him as the young Kestner."

"That must stop. It's unseemly. It's obscene in the circumstances. You are mad to think it possible. You must come here. Kinsky, will you get the Ministry to find her a room."

Becky looked at Kinsky. He shook his head. He was occupying himself unpacking suitcases and he looked at her over the lid of a suitcase and put his finger to his lips.

"I'm tired," Eli said. "I'm going to sleep. Sightseeing! What a gift to a blind man! I've been having trouble with my heart. I need to rest it. Kinsky, find my pills, will you. And a glass of water. I suppose there is bottled water."

He went through to the other room. They heard him shuffling about. Kinsky found the pills and took a bottle of water from a cabinet and followed him through. Becky sat on the settee, which creaked when she moved. She closed her eyes. The lashes fluttered and a nerve jumped in her left temple. It was quiet outside. The city was suspended for the lunch hour.

"That's him settled. I think he'll sleep. I could do with a drink. Let's see what they have supplied us with."

She heard a cork pop.

"Kinsky, why are you here? And why isn't Mummy? Is she all right?"

"Here, darling, drink this. I've a letter for you from Nell. And why am I here? Because, ducky, he insists on coming and he can't be by himself. So, old Kinsky has to turn to. That's all. How's Franz?"

"I don't know."

"But you are with him?"

"Yes, but I don't know how he is. I don't know how he'll ever be again. He says he's all right. Oh Kinsky, I am glad to see you."

"All part of the service, darling. Look, here's Nell's letter."

"I won't read it now. I'll read it when I'm alone."

"Suits me, darling. Don't worry, and don't cry."

"I can't help it, Kinsky. I try to be brave but it doesn't work."

FIVE

Rudi said, "In 1927 I lost my job as a clerk when the bone factory went into liquidation. I became a salesman. For two years I struggled to sell ladies' cosmetics, powder-puffs, scent and lipstick. I suffered insults from the shopkeepers on whom I called. My job took me all over Germany, and everywhere I went, one thing was clear. All the political parties had betrayed and abandoned Germany, except one. It was in Frankfurt I first heard Hitler speak. That was the moment of rescue: the sweetness of his voice which rested in the memory like the taste of liquid honey in the mouth. And at the same time: the challenge. 'Others,' he cried, 'have set themselves to deny us life. It is our duty to seize it. If they oppose us, we shall break them, destroy them utterly, they are anathema.' Do you not understand, Franz, how these words echoed in my dismayed and wounded heart? He spoke to me, directly to me, in an audience of thousands. And every man who listened felt the same. That was his genius. He made each of us feel his own unique identity, and simultaneous membership of a wider and nobler community. He spoke to those who had been isolated and who in their isolation had ceased to believe even in the possibility of their own existence. Unless you understand that, you understand nothing.

"I joined the Party. Oh, moment of blessed release and fulfilment! I had become someone. And, as a reward, my abilities were recognised. For the first time in my life I delighted in study. I abandoned my humiliating work. I found other employment which left me time to study. I passed exams by correspondence course. And all the time I was assiduous in my work for the Party. In January 1933, I joined the SS. This was, as I well knew, a rare privilege."

He moved his pudgy hands about the table. He looked beyond Franz at the blank wall, and spoke as if he read words written there which were invisible to all but himself. Moshe and Yakov, the two guards – "Guards also," as Franz later remarked, "of a seemliness which neither took notes of these conversations nor recorded them on tape" – said nothing, smiled at Franz, made tea, passed cigarettes. They listened. Occasionally. Moshe shook his head, Yakov (the younger of the pair) frowned. He was trying to imagine that life was not what he had found it to be. And the same problem perplexed Franz. The more his father revealed himself, the farther he receded into a cloudy distance.

But now Rudi said, "Once, during the war, in Prague, after dinner in a palace that had once belonged to a Count of the Holy Roman Empire, I escorted Reinhard Heydrich, the master of life and death, to the house where he was staying. We mounted a wide and darkened staircase, climbing in long slow turns, till we came to a drawing room brilliantly lit by chandeliers. He leaned over a table, pouring us brandy, when, as … as if twitched by an invisible thread, he turned and caught sight of his reflection, his double, the blond god with features transposed, in a gilt-framed mirror that ran the whole height of the wall, so that the double seemed, by some trick of the light, to loom over him. Without warning he whipped his revolver from its holster, and fired twice, from the hip, shattering the glass. For a moment it was as if the body of the double flew apart in all directions. Then, without a word, he handed me brandy, and we drank. Three hours later, he lay on a sofa. Tanks lumbered through the empty streets. He tilted the bottle to his lips, and drank the last drops, some of which, escaping his mouth, trickled down his chin towards the unbuttoned collar of his tunic, which rose up the side of his face as he rested among the cushions. He said: 'Has it ever occurred to you, my friend, that it was sheer madness on the Fuehrer's part to have invented this Jewish problem? Which nevertheless it is our duty and historical task to solve. Or, perhaps, help them to solve for themselves?' I didn't then know what he meant. Later, when he had been murdered, I pondered these words in my heart."

"Father," Franz said, "why do you torture yourself with these memories? Isn't it enough to have lived the past when it was happening?"

Rudi said, "I have often wondered whether it was Heydrich's knowledge of his own Jewish blood which forced him to make himself the ideal figure of the SS officer."

He smiled.

"What else is there for me to do, Franz? I have become a man who must live without illusions. There is no promised land for me, you know. I understand Czinner is arriving today. I should like to see him. Would that be possible?"

"No," Yakov said, "I am certain, Rudi, that would not be possible."

Rudi smiled.

"But you see," he said, "I am persuaded that Czinner is the only man in Israel who can understand me."

"Is it so important to be understood, Father?"

Rudi said, "I was trusted in the SS from the start. I, who had never been trusted in my life before, enjoyed the confidence of my commanders. As proof, I was among the select band ordered to arrest Ernst Roehm in what became known as the Night of the Long Knives. Knives! We used guns of course. He had derided the Fuehrer as 'an artist', 'a dreamer'. We showed him what dreams are made of. The boy in bed with him screamed at the sight of us, but Roehm, despite the guns aimed at him, got out of bed, waddled across the room, thrust his fat little legs into his breeches and said, 'So it's come to this, has it.' He threw some clothes to the boy. 'You'd better get dressed, Günter. The party's over.' "

"Father," Franz said again, "why do you torture yourself with these memories?"

Rudi said, "Just so, the party's over. We shot him later that day in the Stadelheim Prison in Munich. But that is not a crime with which I am ever likely to be charged. Besides, the Fuehrer had announced that Roehm was a traitor, and I was only obeying orders.

"Czinner would understand," he said. "He was an intimate of Schacht then, and they were greatly relieved by news of Roehm's execution."

Yakov switched on the electric fan. It dissipated the cigarette smoke. He made more mugs of tea. Franz said he must go. He had an appointment with Birnbaum.

"Saul could arrange for me to see Czinner. Ask him to do so."

"Father, it is impossible. Besides, what would be the use of it? What can you have to say to each other?"

"Czinner would understand me," Rudi said.

Becky was meeting Minty Hubchik in the bar. She took Nell's letter, postponing still the moment of reading it. As she left the apartment, Kinsky said, "You will tell Franz that I would like to see him?"

"Of course. But, Kinsky, is my father right? Are we wrong to be together?"

"He is quite right and absolutely wrong. It is in his word unseemly, but I don't see how you could do anything else, darling."

"Thank you, Kinsky, that's a help."

"No, it's only the truth. How can it be a help?"

The hotel bar was dark and international. There was nothing of Israel in it. Minty Hubchik was waiting for her. She was sitting in a corner with a file on the table in front of her beside her glass, which was empty but for an olive on a cocktail stick. She wore big-framed spectacles that made her features look small and juvenile. She smiled at Becky as if they were old friends.

"I don't know why I've come here," Becky said. "I don't want to talk to any journalists."

"All right," Minty Hubchik said, "don't think of me as a journalist, just think of me as another girl."

She ordered drinks – a Coke for Becky and another Martini for herself. Then she called back the waiter.

"Make it a Gibson," she said, "I can't stand these lousy olives." She smiled at Becky.

"It's crazy," she said, "I still get a kick out of being a girl on my own in a place like this and knowing I have the right to be and do what I like. It's like I haven't gotten used to being adult and free."

Then she began to talk about herself, about a childhood in Toronto which had seemed to promise only security and prosperity. She could see a round of social events, fund-raising coffee mornings, sherry at gallery openings, stretching before her, a good marriage and well-scrubbed obedient children. Her father was a surgeon, he could buy anything he wanted. Her mother smiled when she thought anyone was watching her daughter. They were proud of their only child.

"It was the best cotton wool they wrapped me in."

She took the onion from her cocktail glass and sucked it.

She was something new to Becky, who was dazzled by her trim confidence. Sure, she said, her parents were Jewish, but it didn't signify. She was Canadian herself. What did she mean by that? Canada has certainly its tight little, right little, conventional side, but for Minty that wasn't important. She laid down the cocktail stick, sipped her Gibson, lit her Peter Stuyvesant. She was going places, that's what it meant, and going easy because there was no harness holding her. Life was what you made of it; Canada had afforded her that gift.

"I guess it's different in Argentina," Minty said. "You want to cut loose. Life's become horizontal, hadn't you noticed?"

"No," Becky said, "and I don't know what you mean."

"Maybe you have to be Canadian," Minty said. "I mean you can move, you don't have to listen to what's going on in the mine-workings of the past."

"But you're interested, or you wouldn't be here, doing this job."

"Sure, but it's academic in one sense. I'm interested in what happens from here, not in what went on then. I'm more interested in you, Becky, than in your dad and his memories and guilts. I'm more interested in you than in Franz's father, I'm human. How are you going to make out, kid?"

And then Becky, who hadn't meant to, unfolded her doubts, her love, her fear, her suspicions. She talked as if they had met on a train journey and would never see each other again, as if they were blessed with anonymity.

"Look," Minty said, "Look, baby, this is where it's at…" She was full of phrases of that sort, they tripped off her tongue. She had a little girl's voice, and at first it sounded like silly, slot-machine talk, the ill-digested jargon of some thin philosophy. But she stuck to it, she urged Becky, who could not understand her concern, to begin life now, her life, assumed by her alone without reference or responsibility to anyone or anything that belonged to an older generation. "It's all part of what I mean by horizontal," she said.

"The past fucks you up," she went on. Her own parents had gotten free of it, that was one thing she had to be grateful to them for. Sure, they were Jewish, but they weren't obsessed by it. They were Jewish the way their neighbours were Scots or Irish. It meant something, but not much. Minty was a propagandist for the Now. "You can get free," she said. "All you gotta do is be yourself. Nobody else is gonna be you, that's for sure. Nobody else can live your life. All this dead shit, forget it."

What sort of voice was hers? (She ordered another Gibson.) Was she a new breed of serpent, denying good and evil? Or was it, as she suggested, that humanity had a duty to get beyond those concepts? She was an unlikely emissary; even Becky saw that, even then. And yet, horizontality, living life on the plane of the present … Becky looked at the small-featured face that was pale even in the shadows of the bar, and found the offer it held attractive.

"What do you really want?" Becky said.

She looked away from Minty's answering smile, and then Kinsky entered the bar.

He came towards them with that walk of his like someone moving on ground that shifted under his feet. He was wearing a white suit now, and it was too youthful for him, stressing that he was no longer a dandy but instead only a man who had once laid legitimate claim to that description. He sat down and the waiter approached and Kinsky looked quickly at him, and then away, and ordered whisky for himself and whatever the girls wanted.

"Am I interrupting?" he said. "This isn't an interview, I hope?"

"No," Minty said, "it's all off the record, I'm here as a friend."

"Have you known … ?" He paused.

"No," Minty said, "not long, but well enough."

Becky nodded, "It's all right, Kinsky."

She didn't explain Kinsky to the other girl, who had anyway seen him at the airport and probably gathered what she needed to know.

"We've had telephone calls," he said. "I hoped you would still be here."

"Telephone calls?"

"Yes, from Franz among others. Your father insisted on speaking to him."

"Oh God! What did he say?"

"What he said to you."

"And … ?"

"And at first Franz protested, I think, because Eli grew angry. Then there was a change. 'I'm glad you see reason,' Eli said. 'You have behaved like children, irresponsible children. You might have done incalculable damage.' "

"Who to?" Minty said.

Kinsky smiled, "Perhaps Eli would ask whether damage is ever, can ever be, restricted to particulars. His own experience, his own guilt might drive him to reject such a notion. I don't know, my dear, I am only an ageing *antiquaire* who never had any talent for general discussion and who is lost when the conversation moves away from the few things I cherish. Anyway, there was a long silence, or Franz may have been speaking, I don't know. But in the end it seems that Franz promised he would send your things round. So I said, no, don't do that, I'll come and fetch them."

"And where do I come in?" Becky said. "Don't I have a say?"

"Well, my dear, Franz and Eli are agreed."

"Bloody hell," Minty said.

"In any case I'm coming with you," said Becky.

"Me too," Minty said.

Kinsky sighed, drank his whisky, assented. Perhaps he had been expecting, even hoping for, this response. After all, he was on her side, wasn't he?

The evening was spread out peacefully as they left the hotel, and looked for a taxi. It was the wrong hour of the day. They turned towards the sea front. A red gash of light was thrown by the setting sun down to the distant water and upwards until it was lost in the heavens that turned first violet then shades of ever-darkening grey. Heavy clouds massed landward. They walked between the two worlds in silence. At the third junction, they left the sea and the colours behind them. Becky thrust her hand into her jacket pocket and touched her mother's letter. She bit her lip. Minty took hold of her elbow and squeezed.

Franz's hair was wet and tousled. He kissed Becky, allowed Kinsky to brush his cheek with his lips, and looked over his shoulder at Minty.

"You shouldn't have come," he said, holding Becky again. He was near tears. Had he been crying already?

Becky kept hold of him.

"How were things today?"

"How they always are, only worse."

He looked at Minty.

"Don't mind me," she said. "I'm off duty. It's off the record."

"I've seen you before," he said. "I don't know where."

"Sure, at that Press Conference you gave. Minty Hubchik."

She held out her hand.

"I don't understand," he said, taking it.

"It's all right," she said again, "it's off the record. I've been giving Becky moral support, that's all. She needs it, you know."

There were suitcases on the bed.

"Your father telephoned," Franz said. "He was very firm. He told me our being together, now, was scandalous. He said he'd spoken to you."

Becky wanted to lay her finger on his upper lip and arrest its quiver. He wasn't in a state to be by himself.

"I think you should go," he said. "I think you should leave Israel, wait for me somewhere, London perhaps."

"No," she said. She shook her head. "No. Don't you see? It's surrendering to them, to the past. I won't."

She went through to the bathroom, sat down and drew her mother's letter from her jacket pocket …

Darling: I am letting you down by not coming to be with you. I am sorry, more sorry than I can say. But I can't be with you because I can no longer be with your father. All this has ended our marriage. In my opinion he has gone mad. He sees this business of Franz's father as a means of expiating the guilt he has always felt and never admitted. He doesn't admit it even now, but to get rid of it, and make himself acceptable, as he believes, to the Jewish people, he is ready – no he is more than ready, he is charging like a mad bull at the possibility – to break everything. I have argued with him till I am hoarse: "The past is the past, Becky and Franz are the future, why do you choose the past?" He won't listen. He is as deaf to reason as an Old Testament prophet. I think he sees himself as an Old Testament prophet. When he speaks to me, I hear hatred in his voice, as if he blames me for his failure over so many years to make his peace with his people. As if I wasn't ready in the years after the war to move to Israel with him, and as if he wasn't the one who said, "Certainly not, too many bloody Jews."

Darling: I'm leaving him. I'm going back to England. Kinsky has promised to take care of him, I don't know why; he says he has been looking all his life for someone to take care of; you know how he jokes.

So I am returning to England. I shall go to stay first of all with my cousin Sheila. But I can't stay there long, Sheila and I used to get on, but now of course we don't know each other at all. Besides I shall have to find a job of some kind, I've no money. I don't know what. It's too early to think about that. Matron in a boarding-school perhaps, I do know schools after all. But I'm rambling.

It's you I'm worried about, not myself. I don't know if this terrible time will break your love for Franz and his for you. I pray it won't. I really mean that, I pray. I went to the Cathedral the other day, and knelt and prayed till my knees were sore. Words I hadn't said for years flooded back into my mind. "Lighten our darkness we beseech thee, O Lord," I said, "and visit this habitation."

Becky, be guided by your feelings, not by what people say.

Your father is very angry that you are with Franz. There are moments when I think it is just the jealousy that fathers feel, that he hates Franz as fathers often hate the young men with whom their daughters – especially an only daughter – may fall in love. But I know it is more than that. He is horrified, he shudders to think of that man's son touching his daughter. It is irrational and hateful, yet I understand this.

He is also afraid there will be a scandal. Sometimes I sympathise because I am afraid of how such a scandal will hurt you. Hurt you both. But when I argue that there would be no scandal if you were left alone to allow your love to grow and perhaps be strengthened by these terrible events, and that this would be possible if he remained here in Buenos Aires, and left it to others – and there are hundreds of them – to give evidence in the trial, he shuts his face against me. It is like arguing with a Communist: all you hear is *nyet*. It is like praying to a stone idol.

And so he insists. And I say to him, "If you go to Israel, to give evidence, don't expect to find me here when you return." "Very well," he says, "I shall remain there. I shall make my home in Israel, and lay my bones in the Holy Land." Those were his words; he has gone mad to speak like that.

Darling: I don't know what you will do. I don't even know what you should do. Because I would not wish to have you hurt, visibly and perhaps irremediably hurt, I would urge you to join me in England until the trial is over. Then I would hope that Franz will come to us, and you can get married.

I can even see the church. It is fifteenth-century Decorated, a victim of Victorian restorers, but in a country churchyard with yew trees and flat tombstones.

Talk about it with Franz. I do not think you can help each other in Israel with this going on.

Remember: I love you. M.

There was a post-script.

It is decided, and he is definitely going. So I have asked Kinsky to deliver this to you. Silly: you will know all that by the time you have read even the beginning of my letter.

But I am reluctant to let it go. It is as if you are being torn from me, and yet as long as I write I still feel the touch of your fingertips.

Give my love to Franz, tell him how much I admire his courage.

She folded the letter, returned to the bedroom. It was in darkness. For a moment it seemed as if all had deserted her, in a wilderness of rock with no shelter. Horns sounded from the street. The traffic was caught in a jam, exhausting patience. Then Franz spoke from the bed, "Are you all right?"

The inadequacy of the words emphasised his seriousness. He could find no better ones because his imaginative and inventive powers were stunned. She heard despair in his tone. He had shut out Kinsky and Minty Hubchik, turned off the light, stretched himself face down on the bed, and asked this question which contained no note of enquiry. The answer, he knew, couldn't be other than negative.

The width of the room hung between them. She couldn't cross the desert of carpet that intervened between her and the bed. On the contrary, for a moment she was tempted to retire again into the bathroom, lock the door behind her. But she did not move. She stood there in silence for a long time, perhaps three minutes, perhaps five. Franz's shape came into focus. He was lying on his front, his head turned to one side, the face towards the wall. His cheek was pressed into the pillow. Shouts from the street entered the room. Still she did not move. The telephone rang. Neither lifted a hand to answer. They had made the room empty of all but themselves. Silence resumed, and still she stood there.

"Why don't you go?"

Muffled words, to which she made no reply. Her weapon was pathos; it was all she had left. She was the Lily Maid, Iphigenia dressed for sacrifice, Andromeda chained to her rock. She felt this, despised her weapon, yet employed it. In response, Franz swung himself off the bed, advanced into the middle of the room, poured himself a glass of brandy, and stood with his back to the open street.

"We'd better talk." His tone was judicial, "Your father's right. I've been off my head. I've been as mad as my father."

"Mummy thinks my father's mad as well." She held out the letter. "You'd better read this."

Her pose broken, she sank into a chair. For a moment she feared he would refuse to read the letter, but, with a sigh, he laid down his brandy glass, and complied.

"Well," he said, "that settles it. It's the solution. I'm very grateful to her."

"What do you mean?"

"That you must join her, it's the solution."

"Don't you want me here?"

"Becky…"

She had thought her presence helped him. She was revolted by the eagerness with which he seemed to welcome her departure. When he said – as she had known he would – "It's for your own sake," she accused him of lying. "Like your father," she said.

"You want rid of me," she said, and more in that vein. She wept, as she had resolved she wouldn't.

He protested, swore he loved her, couldn't expose her to the horrors that were in store, accused himself of selfishness in the past.

"You want rid of me," she repeated. It was the sole line that he could disprove only by action; and then, as if coming to the end of a long tunnel and seeing an unsuspected garden laid out before her, she said: "I'll leave, if you will come with me."

"You know I can't."

"Why not? You can do nothing for your father, any more than I can for mine. Let them fight it out. Let their generation deal with its own affairs. What have we to do with any of it? I bet, if you put it to your father even, he would agree with me."

"No," Franz said, "he still has things to tell me."

"You can't make me go. Nobody can make me go." He turned and was going to kiss her.

"No," she said, "if you don't want me here, you can't kiss me. Don't even touch me."

"Jewish flesh," he said.

"That's not the reason. None of that matters."

"You're not being reasonable. Can't you see it's for …"

"Of course I'm not. I'm afraid. I'm afraid if I go and you stay here, that's the end of it. It's you who don't see what they're doing to us, what's happening to us."

She looked up.

"Let's go and see Luke," she said. "Let's talk to Luke about it."

The taxi driver was talkative. That helped; it kept them from each other. Yet they held hands, or rather Franz had laid his hand on Becky's, and she didn't resist or try to move hers. They scudded through the streets and the driver talked of America where he had grown up. He would have been a rich man if he had stayed there, but what the hell – Israel was a duty.

"Every Jew feels it in the end," he said. "Look at this Kestner trial. There's this economist, blind they say, who's come to testify. I'm told he fought the idea of Israel, tried to escape it, but we've got him in the end. You can't escape the destiny of the Jewish people. We have made ourselves out of suffering and strife."

He sucked on a cheroot and spoke out of the corner of his mouth, throwing remarks at them over his right shoulder, as he lurked at traffic-lights which he broke on the first show of amber.

"Know what I'd do with this Kestner? I'd put a bullet in him. Like that. Save the state the expense of a trial. I mean, what's the point? Everybody knows the truth. We don't need it all repeated."

"But isn't that just what people want?" Franz said.

"What the hell."

Luke opened the door to them. He wore blue running shorts and a yellow sweatshirt, and he smelled of sweat and embrocation.

"So how goes it? I've been exercising. On the mat."

He opened a bottle of wine, explained that Rachel had gone down to the grocery store, would be back in a minute. He was full of fizz and bounce. He kissed Becky.

"Didn't your folks get here today? Of course they did. I heard it on the news. Your father's arrival has made quite a noise." Rachel returned. She cried out on seeing them, put carrier bags on the kitchen table, re-trieved an aubergine which fell to the floor and rolled under a chair. She kissed them, still holding the aubergine in her right hand. She rubbed it against her cheek.

"I like the feel," she said. "Has Luke told you?"

"Hell no, they just got here. I don't shout my wares straightaway. I let our guests play their tunes first, before I blow my trumpet." He took hold of Becky's hand and swung it up and down in the manner of children impatient to start on a dance. "But it looks like the tunes are sad. Something's up. What's wrong?"

213

"Let's have your trumpet first."

Luke dropped her hand. The trumpet worried him. He had done something which pleased him, but which, he feared, they mightn't like.

"He's committed himself," Rachel said. "Against the trial."

"Look," he said, "I don't know. It could still be stopped. Maybe you'd better read it. Dammit, it concerns you."

He went through to his study. Rachel began to put vegetables into dishes and a basket.

"You're pleased?" Becky asked.

"Sure."

Franz put down his wine glass and helped Rachel. He hadn't met Becky's eyes since they entered the apartment.

"So, what's wrong?" Luke said. He held a couple of sheets of paper. "You've quarrelled. Well, OK, you know you've had me worried the way you never quarrel. It's healthy to quarrel. We quarrel all the time, don't we, Rache? It's creative."

Becky sat down. She couldn't trust her legs. Voices, raised in anger, came from the apartment across the courtyard.

"Just listen to them," Luke said. "They're called Shegin and they have five kids under the age of eight. We should hear the crockery fly any minute."

"They want to send me away," Becky said.

"It's not that at all," Franz said. "Why do you distort things? It isn't like that, or if, yes, it is, then it's for her own good."

"I'm here, you know. Sitting here. Don't speak of me as if I wasn't. You can do plenty of that when you've got rid of me."

Franz began to explain. He told them of Eli's anger. His voice trembled. She heard its fatigue. Maybe her presence did add to the strain he was under. Why "under"? Yet, if he let her, she could give him support. It was why she had come. If he rejected that support, how could they ever be what she wanted them to be? He was denying her, agreeing with her father. The light picked out the down on his cheek which shimmered golden. His face was thinner. The cheekbones stood out in a way that people called Slav. It didn't make sense sending her away. What was she expected to do if she went?

"Can I stay here? With you, Rachel?" she said. It hadn't been in her mind to ask. That wasn't why she had come here. It was only seeing Franz looking so tired and drawn that gave her the idea.

"My father says it's indecent me living with Franz. So can you put me up? Please."

She kept her eyes fixed on the table, on a ring burned by a hot plate or coffee pot, and they looked at each other, all three, over her head.

"I can't go to England and watch it on television."

Rachel hugged her.

"Sure."

Luke held up the sheaf of papers.

"I don't see why that should make any difference," Rachel said.

"Maybe not. I hope not." He lit a cigarette, and grinned. "I'm a fool. I'd forgotten you don't know Hebrew. I'll have to translate as I go along."

He pushed the bottle towards them. Rachel set a dish of nuts and another of pastries which she'd bought at the market on the table, and he began to read an English version of his article. Sometimes he paused, searching for a word or the best way to turn a phrase, so that his delivery was slow and a bit awkward. When he was lost for a word, he would glance up and smile. A couple of times Rachel put her hand on Becky's knee and squeezed. Franz kept his eyes on the table. He held his wine glass in both hands, but drank nothing.

> There is not a citizen of Israel who has not learned that it may be necessary to die for Israel, and we are ready to do so. Most of us know also that we may be required to kill for our country and on behalf of our people and future generations. Our way to Israel has been rough. It has been cruel and difficult. We have journeyed through the valley of humiliation, we have crossed desolate mountains, we have endured dry seasons, parched in the wilderness, without shelter. Our country has been formed through suffering and our people shaped in adversity. There is not a single family in Israel which does not mourn its murdered members, which does not recall its martyrs in sorrow, grief, pride and anger.
>
> We have been taught by experience, and we know we must be vigilant in defence, not merely of our homes, but of our very lives. We have learned to strike first and to repay blood with blood. We have earned respect.
>
> It is natural in our condition of perpetual crisis, conscious as we are of the stark existential realities that confront us every

day, if we have come to neglect tender emotions. There will be a time for them later, we think, when we are at last secure. We would wish for instance to do justice to our Palestinian neighbours, to the Arabs within our State, for we recognise and honour justice. We would wish to be generous and to live in peace, for we know that generosity is the glory of man, and peace what he most desires.

But that, we say, must wait...

He looked up, smiled.

"I quote Auden here," he said. "Maybe you know it in the original, Becky?"

She made a small negative motion of the head. She couldn't see where this article was taking them. But Rachel had said "yes", hadn't she? She clung to that. She couldn't be shifted unless she chose.

"It's from 'Spain'," he said. "You know, the bit about tomorrow the bicycle rides, the young poets exploding like bombs, but today the conscious acceptance of guilt in the necessary murder. I can't quote it right in reverse. But I've always thought it good."

He resumed:

But that tomorrow, which we long for, is always postponed. There are new dangers, new emergencies, and we live not with tomorrow but with today, and always too with yesterday, which we employ in a manner that is almost shameful in its pride in suffering, to justify ourselves, to account for and excuse that postponement and also indeed whatever brutalities we may feel called upon to perform today.

And now, with a zest which I find unholy, we are about to enact another drama for today, a drama which is in truth, no more, or little more, than yet another performance of a ritual that commenced as consolation but is in danger of becoming a macabre form of celebration instead. I refer of course to the approaching trial of Rudi Kestner.

Now of this I shall say only that it will tell us nothing new. Of Kestner I shall add only that it is impossible for anyone to pay even lip service in this instance to the principle that a man must be presumed innocent until proved guilty. There is no doubt of Kestner's guilt, of his willing, even eager, participation in the most horrible of crimes...

"I am sorry if that pains you, Franz."

"Carry on."

It is precisely because there can be no doubt, no rational doubt of this, that the time has come to cry "halt!" The moment has indeed arrived when we must ask what this endless repetition of these matters – this grand theatrical recital of offence and horror, which is what we mean by a trial for war crimes – to ask what it is doing to us. To us ourselves, rather than to the decayed villains who perpetrated the atrocities that we recount.

Isn't it the case that we have come to delight in them? To take a hideous pleasure in presenting the story of the Holocaust yet again to the world – certainly, a world, I admit, which is inclined to forgetfulness? But hasn't it become for us a form of self-gratification? Aren't we claiming, when we remind the world of what we Jews have suffered, when we rub the faces of the Germans yet again in their atrocious guilt, that our suffering has rendered us who survived it, and who are its heirs, strangely privileged beings? Aren't we asserting, or at the very least appearing to assert, that on account of the crimes committed against us, all must now be permitted us? Doesn't this terrible memory allow us, in a narrow immediate political sense, to forget those whom we have dispossessed and indeed subjugated here in Israel?

And there is another consideration, still more grave. By dwelling on the insult to humanity which the Jewish people suffered, isn't it apparent that we are enabled in our turn to deny or devalue human values? We talk of justice, but the word in our hearts is revenge. Many will say this is justified, but man entertains revenge at his peril. Indulgence in its joys lures him towards another delightful engine of self-destruction: the will to power.

What can we set against this? We may timidly advance what are usually called "human values". The term is inadequate and false, for who can deny that the lust for revenge and the will to power are themselves human values? This indeed can only be denied by those who would elevate humanity to a status it has done little to deserve. Nevertheless, in using this expression, "human values", we imply a recognition of what we judge to be good. It tells us what we aspire to be. And the emotions to which we apply this term are: tenderness, generosity, sympathy, friendship and love.

He coughed, sipped his wine, and began to read again.

Let me tell you a story. It is a very simple and common one. Perhaps I don't even need to recount it. The title may be sufficient: Romeo and Juliet. A boy and a girl, the son and daughter of two families locked in vendetta.

"Hey, Luke," Rachel said. "You can't use that. You just can't."

"Why not?"

"Why not? Hell, can't you see? It's corny. Kansas in August also ran."

Becky said, "I see where this is going."

"You don't like it?"

"I liked everything before it. The last bit said what I really believe, really and truly."

"But you don't like this?"

She looked at Franz. His face was in shadow. He had moved back into the shadow. He was withdrawing from her, and as he did so beauty was deserting him. He looked pinched and starved, like one of those boys who used to enter the buffet of the main railway station in Buenos Aires, moving on automatic pilot, their eyes roving the room in search of something which they never found. They used to puzzle her as she waited there for the train that would take her back to school.

"No," she said. "I don't. I'm sorry, Luke. It's kind of you."

"It's corny," Rachel said again.

Franz got to his feet, into darker shadow. He stood very still in his expensive Scotch navy cashmere jersey and his cheap cotton trousers. He pressed his hands on the back of the chair. The veins stood out.

"It's no good. It's none of it any good." He passed the back of his hand over his forehead. "You mean well. I know that. But they're going to hang him. There's no question. It's just a matter of getting through the days till it's done. He knows that himself. It's why he's gone back into the past."

* * * *

When Franz stumbled out of Luke's apartment, he had no idea where he was heading. He began to walk, making speeches in his mind. He used angry words, which he could not have brought himself to say aloud. He walked faster, then he began to run, to stop the words. It was quiet in that part of the city. The shops were closed. People were taking their evening meals in their apartments, or watching television, enjoying family life, already perhaps making love. He stopped running and leaned against a lamppost at a street corner, out of breath. His chest heaved. But the run had done him good. He felt that when he had rested a couple of minutes.

He hadn't been able to tell Becky, because of what Eli had sprung on them, but his visit to his father that morning had been a disaster. At first Rudi had seemed as usual. But then he had begun to talk. In the last few days his talk had become less and less controlled. It was becoming daily harder for Franz to recognise in the figure on the other side of the table the taciturn, austere father he had known. This morning the words had been a torrent. And they meant nothing, that was the terrible thing. They were a babble. Sitting there for maybe quarter of an hour, even twenty minutes, Franz had been compelled to let them flow over and around him. They tumbled forth, like a river in spate, carrying all sorts of debris, filth, spume, the irrelevancies of a life that – it was clear – Rudi had, overnight as it were, despaired of. Self-pity, recriminations, rage, protestations had bobbed around him. He was divided between disgust and pity. Then all at once the torrent stopped. For a moment Rudi lifted his gaze from the table where it had been fixed. There was a game which Franz had seen played in a low cantina to which Luis sometimes took him; they drew a chalk line on the floor and placed a cockerel on it, pressing his beak down against the mark. And the creature was powerless to lift its head, although in reality nothing held it there, except the conviction, he assumed, that it was tied to the mark. As Rudi broke now, it seemed to Franz that he had been exactly like that bird. It was horrible.

But then Rudi had raised his eyes and looked beyond Franz, at the blank wall over his shoulder. His face crumpled. Whatever he saw there was too much for him. Tears trickled down his cheeks. He uttered a sound between a strangled cry and a sob. The young soldiers guarding him looked at Franz, sharing his horror; and then Yakov drew a shawl around him, almost like a mother comforting a child.

Franz looked at his own face in the mirror behind the bar which he couldn't remember entering. He searched in it for symptoms of the same disintegration. He was holding a glass in his hand. Brandy. He ordered another, then another.

It hadn't been like that at all. He was imagining things. It had been a normal morning. Yes, Rudi had talked freely, but not in that manner. He had talked of Heydrich, hadn't he? Or was that the previous day? And anyway Franz knew nothing, or almost nothing, of Heydrich. He drank his third brandy and pushed the glass across the zinc counter. The bar-man hesitated. Then he sighed, and, saying nothing, tilted the bottle. He named a price. Franz dropped some notes on the bar, and took the glass over to a little table in the corner.

Perhaps he was going mad. It would be a sort of solution. Had he dreamed what he had heard that morning, or was it conceivably some sort of precognition? He held out his hand. It was steady. It had no right to be steady. Or had the brandy created that right?

He had run away again. That was the worst of it. And Becky? She couldn't really believe that he didn't want her, when he had proved his need. All the same, her father was right. There was something shocking in their being together – if you were anyone else, that is.

Luis used to say that men and women needed each other in different ways. It was one of his favourite remarks. But Luis, as an Argentine, saw the relationship as a war. There was the macho boast: *la tuve en el culo* – I've had her in the arse." That was their way. That expressed male au-thority. Woman was dishonoured even in the moment of the man's tri-umph. Franz couldn't think of it like that. Yet the temptation was there. He could feel it. It was a way of saying, "Nothing is good, and yet I assert myself." Most girls rejected it. Those who didn't, who instead submitted, achieved their own victory, even in the moment of degradation. He laid his knuckles against the swelling over his right thigh.

Wasn't that also what his father could have said of the Jews: *los tuve en el culo?*

SIX

Eli had been almost silent since they left Buenos Aires. He had spoken to Kinsky only to give orders, which Kinsky had carried out without resentment. It was why he had come. He was making his own act of atonement. It was absurd. He had been a victim himself. Yet the insistence on German communal guilt hung so heavy around him that he felt as if he too had been associated in the crimes for which Rudi Kestner now stood as symbol. And there was a sense, Kinsky knew, in which he had indeed shared in that guilt. He had made more than his own share of anti-Semitic remarks. No one from his background, in his Vienna, could have done otherwise. It was as if he and his friends had encouraged the whole terrible business to buy indulgence for themselves. Well, it hadn't worked. Standing naked, having just emerged from the bath, he fingered the still legible tattoo of his concentration camp number. He slipped on a silk dressing gown and went through to the sitting room of the suite where Eli sat facing the window gazing, blind as Samson, over the Promised Land where he had at last arrived after so much resistance.

"I wish I knew the Bible," Kinsky said. "My ignorance of the Old Testament is complete."

"I always thought of myself as a German. I've told you that often enough, Kinsky. What a charade I made for myself."

"But you were a German," Kinsky said. "I should say you still are."

"No," Eli said. "I am a naked man, neither Jew nor German."

"Aren't we all, my dear?"

Eli drummed a little tune with his fingers.

"I almost envy Kestner," he said.

Kinsky mixed them both a whisky and soda. Eli's face had changed. It had taken on a look he had never seen. He had often seen him angry or obstinate; never until now implacable. More than thirty years ago, in Berlin, they had stood together before a painting in an exhibition. It was a landscape by Max Ernst, a ravaged wilderness with trees like broken crosses, and, in the background, the figure of a man turned half away from them and lurching into … what? The night? Oblivion? Nothing? And Eli had turned to him and said, "Yes, it disturbs me, but I would still call it cheap. It's life-denying, you know, and that is always a pose." That had been their first meeting. Kinsky had laughed. Everyone else in the gallery had frowned on them. It was too much to say they had been friends from that moment. Or was it? Hadn't their friendship been founded in fact on their agreement that to indulge in despair was a species of emotional masturbation? But if Kinsky now said, "Do you remember the Max Ernst?" Eli would deny it.

Eli said, "Yea, though I take the wings of the morning and fly to the uttermost part of the sea, yet art Thou there also."

"Kestner must feel like that about you."

There was a knock at the door.

"Answer it, Kinsky. Send whoever it is away, unless it is Becky."

It was Franz. He was not quite steady, and he looked lost, and touched his lower lip with his tongue before he spoke.

"I must see him, Kinsky. I must speak to him."

"Wait here."

He went back to the chair by the window and spoke to Eli, who shook his head. Kinsky continued to urge him. "It's necessary for all our sakes," he said.

"Send him away."

Kinsky whispered to Franz.

"Go down to the hotel bar. I'll join you there as soon as I can." He closed the door.

"You ought to have seen him."

"Never say 'ought' to me, Kinsky. Nobody tells me what I ought to do. You should know that."

It was half an hour before Kinsky entered the bar. He was afraid Franz might not have waited, but he was still there, at a corner table, with an empty glass before him. He stared straight in front of him, as if he was gazing at nothing and seeing too much.

"I only wanted to tell him he had won," he said. "It's only Becky who doesn't yet concede his victory. She won't go home. She's staying with friends, Jewish friends. Kinsky, what's happening to us?"

"What's happening is that you've been taking too much strain. Maybe you should go to bed, my dear."

"That's the worst time," Franz said.

Kinsky sat down, and laid his hands on the boy's arm. The waiter hovered over him. He ordered whisky for himself and "whatever my friend's been having for him".

"Did it feel like this in the war?" Franz said. "In the last weeks perhaps?"

"You forget. I was, as it were, out of action. The last weeks were for me a time of mingled terror and hope."

"Hope? There's none of that now."

Later they walked out from the hotel and towards the sea.

"So we move to Jerusalem tomorrow," Kinsky said. "Remember, my dear, Israel is an impossibility made actual. Or that's how it seems to me."

They leaned on the rail, listening to the sea lap against the wall below them.

"I wanted to get drunk," Franz said. "I couldn't manage it. Why couldn't I, Kinsky? Will you to try to persuade Becky to go to her mother?"

"No," Kinsky said. "Becky must choose her own course. She's not a child to be told what to do and what not to do. Eli doesn't realise that. I had thought you did."

He laid his arm around the boy's shoulder.

"Remember, it will end," he said.

"That's a lie. It's not true. We're here now precisely because things don't end."

"But they do. Tomorrow we go to Jerusalem. That's the beginning of the end, my dear, I promise you. Don't be too hard on Eli. He is suffering too. Coming to Israel has brought him face to face with the guilt from which he has been fleeing for more than thirty years. Do you know why he is blind? Sometimes I think it is so that he does not have to look at the faces of his fellow-Jews and see the reproach in their eyes. For him, this trial is a sort of purification. He will accept any sacrifice to achieve that."

"Will he sacrifice Becky's happiness?"

"Oh yes, he will willingly sacrifice that."

Becky arrived at the courthouse with Luke and Rachel. They had been compelled to park several blocks away. There was a blue sky, gentle breeze and light, dancing air. Sour saliva filled her mouth. She took hold of Luke's arm, then released it: there was a photographer lurking. They encountered Franz at the entrance to the courthouse, under an inscription she could not read. He was waiting for them and he was pale and looked too young to be there.

"According to you, we can't even sit together," she said. "No," she said, "you'd better not kiss me. Photographers."

"I won't be used," she said to Rachel as they mounted the steps.

"Franz didn't mean it that way. You know he didn't."

She had dressed in a grey suit, bought in a department store in Buenos Aires, at her mother's insistence. It was a dull anonymous thing that didn't prevent her knowing she was beautiful that morning. She wasn't always that; some days she thought herself ugly, mostly plain, which she never was, but couldn't see. She held her head up and her back straight. They all had to submit to a body search before entering the building, even Luke, even though the guards had recognised him and one of them had slapped him on the shoulder as an old comrade. The public gallery was small. Only ticket-holders were admitted. Luke left them, waving his press pass. He entered by a different door and by the time they had been admitted he was in his seat. Minty Hubchik was to his left. She waved and smiled to Becky, and then said something to Luke, who gave her that open smile of his that made the world seem a franker, more generous place. An usher of some sort escorted Franz to a seat reserved for him just behind a glass box which dominated the centre of the court and which resembled a telephone booth. It was empty and Franz was put behind it and just to the left within touching range. He was isolated there. Everyone else in that part of the room was still standing, mostly in attitudes which suggested that all this was nothing out of the ordinary; none of them was within ten feet of Franz. He lowered his head. It looked as though he was praying.

But it was the glass box that held her attention. She hadn't expected it, though she had seen the television pictures of Eichmann in his transparent bullet-proof cage, connected to the rest of the world only by the earphones clamped to his head and relaying the simultaneous translation of the narrative of his atrocities.

"To catch a fox, and put him in a box, and never let him go."

That was silly, that nursery rhyme: the point of the box was to isolate the prisoner, to remove him from humankind, to consecrate him to death.

He was led in. They had permitted him to wear the dark glasses which a thousand press photographs had made familiar. Perhaps they had done so because people wouldn't have recognised him without them. He was surrounded by soldiers carrying guns; at the ready, though it was absurd to suppose that anyone could attempt a rescue there. And who, anyway, would want to? Surely it had been agreed that he was to die. It only awaited public confirmation. The thought that the aimless and incompetent people who had kidnapped her and Gaby could somehow interfere was ridiculous.

Kestner paused before Franz, and inclined his head; only a couple of inches. Then he was in his box. A grey-faced man who was some sort of court attendant brought him a cup and saucer.

"Do you see that?" Becky whispered to Rachel.

"Sure, they can always astonish you. They astonish me after five years living here."

Then he was hidden from sight by his lawyers joining the guards and standing round the box. The big man, who was Saul Birnbaum – she recognised him from Franz's descriptions – crossed over and spoke to Franz. He squeezed his shoulder. It was a physical place, Israel, given to body contacts.

There was a late arrival in the press box. It was Ivan Murison in his dirty cream-coloured suit. He caught Becky's eye and waved to her. Then he made a gesture like a prize fighter, clasping his hands over his head and waving them, and then took his seat. She was aware of the other occupants of the press gallery being disturbed by the manner in which he settled himself. He took out a big, red, white-spotted handkerchief and ran it round the back of his neck, and dabbed his temples with it.

The court rose for the judge. So that was why Franz's father had been permitted to keep his dark glasses. Without them, he and the judge might have been brothers.

There were earphones attached to each seat. You pressed a button and got translation in the language you had selected. But she didn't put them on. They had discussed it, and Luke had assured her that the first day would be taken up with legal argument. She preferred to watch. She knew from Franz that Saul Birnbaum would challenge the right of the court to try the accused, the grounds being that his arrest had been illegal, an offence against international law. But, Franz had said, "There's no chance that it will succeed. Apart from any other considerations — and there are plenty of them — I talked about it with my stepfather. He is adamant that the Argentinian Government isn't going to protest about the violation of its territory, or whatever it is that has been violated. It's just a ploy of Saul's. he concedes, even to me, that it will be futile."

Then why's he doing it?"

So, instead of listening, she watched. She was at an angle to Franz's father, so that his face was in half-profile from the rear. He cupped his chin in the palm of his hand and leaned his elbow on the shelf in front of him. He wore his earphones, but after a few minutes, removed them and sat back and crossed his arms. Saul Birnbaum was speaking, and it was as if Kestner had satisfied himself that the argument was proceeding along agreed lines, and so required none of his attention. Perhaps his eyes were closed behind the dark glasses.

The air in the room was already sultry. Saul Birnbaum's forehead sparkled with beads of sweat. He moved his shoulders as he spoke. The tone was level. Becky had been led to expect histrionics, but he might have been debating an insurance case.

The previous evening, after Franz had left them, they had all three sat up drinking wine. At first they talked about Luke's article.

"All right, I'll tear it up," he said.

"No," Becky said, "publish it. Only please leave out all the bit about Franz and me. It's bad enough as it is. I don't think he's ever going to want to marry me anyway after this. It's turning everything sour."

Luke opened another bottle of wine.

"Does the word *herem* mean anything to you?"

"No. Should it?"

"I don't know. Probably not. You've never really thought of yourself as a Jew, have you?"

"I haven't been encouraged to. So what does it mean? Why's it important?"

"It's only just occurred to me," Luke said. "*Herem* was a form of ritual slaying. The Greek word is *anadema*, and it corresponds, I believe, to the Latin *consecratio*. In time of war – I'm referring, you understand, to Old Testament times – an enemy and all his possessions were dedicated to Jahweh. They became *herem*, a consecrated thing, removed from ordinary use. It was forbidden to spare any of them because to do so meant that you had withheld what was due to Jahweh, who would then revenge himself by taking life for life. Do you see, do you follow? The Romans explained their rite of *consecratio* and the slaughter that went with it by saying it represented the devotion of the enemy to the gods of the dead. But the Jewish practice was older and different, since it was to God himself that the enemy was devoted. I remember reading that it was originally a form of magical rite. The walls of Jericho fell down of their own accord because the city had been devoted to *herem*. It was a sort of curse, you see: what the Christian church later styled 'anathema', which is of course the Greek again. Later, in the time of the kings, the execution of criminals was performed under the guise of *herem*. But earlier it was perhaps a sort of taboo. Perhaps some member of the tribe had violated customs and so offended the deity; very well, let him be removed. He had become unclean. It's a sort of *herem* we are about to enact now. Looked at like that, I may be wrong, and it may indeed be necessary. Psychologically necessary."

"OK," Rachel said, "but am I right in thinking it was a German custom too?"

"I think it may be universal. Only, on account of the apocalyptic nature of Judaism, and the accompanying morality, it has a peculiar urgency with us, which even millennia later we can't escape."

"What I'm getting at," Rachel said, "is that the Jews were maybe *herem* to the Germans."

"Sure they were," Luke said.

"Wasn't King Saul punished," Becky asked, "for sparing the people of some conquered tribe?"

"He was indeed. And do you think our leaders have forgotten that?"

Birnbaum was speaking. He paused, made an abrupt remark. Rudi Kestner turned his head towards him and nodded. He smiled. Then he removed his headphones and dabbed a handkerchief at his temples. The smile stayed fixed. Becky leaned forward. She saw Luke in the press gallery make a note. She was aware that Minty Hubchik was trying to catch her eye. Ivan Murison withdrew a small flask from his breast pocket, and gulped. A guard frowned and gestured as if it had occurred to him that he should perhaps confiscate the flask; perhaps drinking in court was an act of contempt. A formal offence? It seemed probable.

Birnbaum shuffled his papers. He paused for a long time, as if he had lost his place. But perhaps it was calculated, for when he resumed, he spoke with fluency. Twice he stabbed his finger through the air in the direction of the judge, who was himself writing industriously.

"If Father defends himself," Franz had said, "he will speak in defence of the bureaucratic institution to which he belonged. He will tell how everything – identification, transportation, selection for work duties or for immediate extermination – proceeded according to prescribed form, which was adhered to with the utmost scrupulosity."

"That sounds more horrible than anything," she had said.

"But his only defence can be to deny personal responsibility, or at least to limit it, by throwing everything on to the machine. You're right, it's horrible. He toys with that defence. He sees it as some sort of game."

But wasn't it precisely sport of a similar nature which was now being enacted before her? After all, there was nobody in court, least of all Franz's father himself, who had any doubt concerning the outcome.

"Of course, in other moods," Franz said, "he glories in doing his duty. I think he baffles Saul. And Saul is very clever."

The judge rose. They would adjourn for lunch.

It was the evening of the seventh day of the trial. Franz lay on his bed. He had refused Saul's invitation to supper. He was exhausted.

The nightmares had begun after the third day, which had been the first on which survivors of the death camps had given evidence. Some of them were more than survivors. They had made good. Their dress and their well-fed condition made that clear. Yet, as they spoke, as they pointed towards his father (though there were two who could not bring themselves to look directly at him, even when they were asked by the judge to identify the man in the cage as Kestner, whom they were accusing of atrocities which would have been unspeakable if they had not nevertheless contrived to speak them), even as they relayed their catalogue of horror, the years fell away from them; they grew simultaneously younger and immeasurably old. They resumed their former personalities: you saw the Jewish student, the young mother whose children had been torn from her arms, the bank clerk who looked like Kafka. These figures stood in the witness box, having taken possession of the lecturer in statistics from an Australian university, the plump satiny matron of a nursing home in Indianapolis, the financier whose story was utterly convincing but whom you would not have trusted with an investment. (He had indeed, as Saul extracted from him in what was no more than a perfunctory effort to undermine his credibility, served a four-year prison sentence in Belgium for fraudulent conversion, and somehow this admission of human frailty made his willingness to enter a court of law again, this time to testify to what he knew to be the truth, seem more impressive.)

It was, however, a woman who made the nightmares.

She entered the witness box with a toss of shoulder-length hair, dyed blonde, and she held her head at an angle that recalled certain American film stars of the 1940s. She looked straight at his father. It was impossible to see movement behind the dark glasses, but he sat down, as he was permitted to do on account of a medical report presented on the first day by Saul Birnbaum, and lowered his head to examine his notes. He didn't then alter his position throughout her evidence.

She was born in 1926 and her name was Trudi, birthplace Danzig, where she grew up. She had not been aware that her grandmother was Jewish, perhaps because her father was a Polish cavalry officer. He had been captured by the Russians in 1939. She supposed he was dead. Then she and her mother had gone to stay with her father's parents on their small estate some fifty miles from Warsaw. They were good people. That grandmother was German. Her grandfather bred horses. He was very proud of them, and even in the war managed to mount her on a pony. It was a chestnut mare. They all thought they were safe because her grandmother was German. They didn't think of the other grandmother at all. Anyway, nobody talked about it.

Then, in 1942, two days before her sixteenth birthday, German soldiers arrived and arrested her mother and herself. When her grandfather protested, they struck him and he fell down. He was a tall man, a handsome man, and he lay there and didn't get up. She never saw him again. She and her mother were taken to a station and loaded into a cattle truck. Their journey was so terrible. It was cold and everything was so dirty and squalid. Her mother wept. She kept saying that this couldn't be happening to them, there must be some mistake.

The train stopped somewhere, in a grey country of barbed wire and empty fields. In the distance were some trees and perhaps a river, she didn't know. They were in a siding. Some of the women were forced out of the trucks and driven to a long hut. There were German officers there. They selected half-a-dozen, including her mother and herself, and they were pushed into a lorry. They sat there and the train moved off and disappeared into the yellow grey of the mist.

They waited in the lorry a long time. It was very cold, and several of the women were in tears. Trudi was the youngest, but she didn't cry. It might be better to be in the lorry, she thought, than in the train on the way to a rumoured destination which they all feared.

They were taken to some army barracks. There were a lot of officers with shiny boots. A woman in nurse's uniform took charge of them. Yes, she probably was a nurse. They were told to strip and get into a bath, all six of them together. Then they were given other clothes, dresses that sparkled when they moved and silk stockings and high-heeled shoes. When her mother saw the clothes she began to scream, but another woman told her there was no sense in that, and that they must make the best of what was about to happen. Trudi's dress was blue, like her eyes. It stopped short of her knees. She supposed she looked pretty in it. She was young, wasn't she, and they hadn't endured real hardship yet.

They were taken to supper with the officers. No, Kestner wasn't one of them, that came later. They were given wine and then each officer chose a girl or woman and took her for his. They were raped. Maybe it wasn't always rape. Maybe some of them submitted. What else was there to do? Her mother felt shame, she knew that, but she didn't. "If you must know," she said, lifting her head and throwing off twenty years or more, "I thought I was probably lucky. Besides, my one was a nice-looking boy. I could have fancied him in other circumstances. He was very young, and I could see that he had to nerve himself to do it. In fact he was shy. He let me undress myself and watched me. He kept saying, 'You're so pretty, so lovely.' He hesitated to take his clothes off. In fact, I had to help him. Why did I do that? If you must know, I was excited. I suppose it was some sort of nervous reaction. After that we got on all right, and I thought I was probably lucky."

Kestner arrived a few days later, probably on some tour of inspection. He saw her, wanted her, and took her. The lieutenant didn't dare to protest.

She was with Kestner for six months, even though he had told her the first evening that she was too old for his tastes. "But we'll see," he said, "you've got a very nice bottom." Sometimes he beat her, sometimes he was kind.

She looked across the court at the man in the cage who remained with his gaze fixed on his papers as if indifferent to what she was saying.

"You don't want to hear about our lovemaking," she said, "if that's the right word. He was a bit kinky, a bit perverted. It felt wrong to me then, though I know now his tastes were not so very unusual. No, he never showed emotion. When he beat me, which he did with a leather strap on my bottom, he did it without passion. All the same I remember thinking, 'Perhaps he loves me to beat me like this.' He called it beating the Jew out, and said if he took me to Berlin he could easily pass me off as an Aryan. No, I don't think he ever intended to take me there; it was just a way of talking. He talked a lot some nights, often about what he called necessity. I think he meant feeling he was right to do what he was doing."

He got rid of her. One day another girl with red curly hair was there. She said she was fourteen. Make the best of it, Trudi said. Some soldiers took her away. She never saw Kestner again, not until now. She was taken to a camp. She supposed he wanted her dead. That would have been sensible, wouldn't it? But she had learned how to survive. So she did. She wasn't proud of it. On the other hand she wasn't ashamed either, even though she had had a hard time after the Liberation. Some of the other women in the camp had attacked her and beaten her and stripped her and might have killed her if an American soldier, a Negro, hadn't come to her rescue. She couldn't blame them, she might have done the same in their place. The Negro was a lieutenant. She became his lover. Then she was put on trial for collaboration, or rather threatened with it, but he saved her again. He had got tired of her eventually. "After what I've been through, people do get tired of me," she said. "There comes a time when a man looks at me and doesn't see me but only what I have been." Now she was the manageress of a restaurant in Johannesburg, South Africa. She supposed she was lucky. She had one regret. The doctors told her she couldn't have children. Not after what Kestner had done to her.

And again she looked at Kestner and this time he raised his head and turned it towards her and held it there a long time with his eyes hidden behind his dark glasses and his mouth shut as tight as a well-fitting lid.

But she came to Franz in the night, thrown down on a pile of dirty sacks, like Bastini, her young rounded thighs quivering and streaked with blood. Then a heavy gate clanged and steel-tipped boots marched towards him down a corridor that was long and dark. He heard another gate thrown open and hands stretched towards him, and he was in his father's cage with Becky and Alexis and Bastini on the bench looking at him with cold eyes, while Ivan Murison, in his dirty cream-coloured suit, relayed the charges brought against him, chief among which was being in every way his father's son. And the three judges disputed among themselves the right of punishment.

So now he lay on the bed, with his eyes heavy and his limbs trembling, and was afraid to sleep.

* * * *

The telephone rang.

"Ivan here, old boy. I'm still waiting…"

"There's nothing I can do to help you."

"Then help yourself. These photographs … burning a hole in my wallet."

Franz put down the receiver. He waited a moment, then called Saul Birnbaum.

"It can't do any good," Saul said.

"No," Franz said. "But I need to, for my sake."

"All right, I'll see what I can do."

Half an hour later he rang back.

"Amazingly, the answer is 'yes'. I don't pretend to understand it. I suggested my office, but that won't do, so you go to her hotel and take the lift to the third floor, room number 345. OK. I'll be interested to hear…"

She was the sort of woman who can make a hotel room feel like home. He couldn't tell why – it wasn't as if she had filled it with personal belongings. Perhaps it was simply that she filled it with herself.

"I don't know why I've agreed to this," she said. "I must be mad. Most people would say I am. So you're really his son? You don't look like him, that's one thing. Maybe you look like your mother. He had a photograph of your mother beside his bed, I didn't say that in court, what was the point? But I don't remember now what she looked like."

"She looks a little like you," he said. "I think when you were both young, you maybe looked even more like each other."

"Could be. Drink?"

She gestured towards a bottle of Johnnie Walker.

"Come on," she said, "I'm having one. I've already had several, but I'm having another. I don't think I can go through this sober. It's a wonder to me how I managed in court."

"How did they find you?" he said. "How did they track you down? Or did you volunteer? Did you come forward of your own accord?"

"No," she said. "I wouldn't have done that. I wouldn't have been interested. No, I was contacted."

She laughed and pushed a glass towards him. She rattled the ice in her own. Something warm and affirmative was communicated to him. At the same time he was a little afraid of her.

"You're the only person in this case who seems secure," he said.

"And I've no right to be? But I have. I've come through. So you're his son." She smiled. "And you're standing by him. I like that. Are you fond of him, has he been a good father?"

Franz made a vague, hopeless gesture, like a ruined man summoning up philosophy.

"I don't know. Like others, I suppose. We've never been close. I've lived with my mother. They're divorced, you know."

She sat down on the sofa and patted the cushion to her left.

"Come on," she said, then when he had obeyed, turned the upper half of her body round, laid her right arm behind his neck, and kissed him full on the mouth.

"There," she said, "I've wanted to do that ever since you came in."

She crossed to the table and fed herself some more whisky. She hummed a little tune.

"I'm like Piaf," she said, "*je ne regrette rien.*"

"Not even…"

"Not even. There's nothing gained by regrets. All right, so your dad was what people call a monster then. Take it from me, there are precious few who aren't that when they are let loose. Do you know what the war did? It gave an awful lot of people the chance to live out their fantasies, that's what it did."

"But they're going to hang him."

"Sure they are. Revenge is the resident fantasy here, I guess."

"They call it justice."

"I bet they do."

She sat on the window-seat and tugged her legs up under her. It was a young girl's gesture, and for a moment, with the light behind her, Franz saw the girl his father had abused.

"I don't understand you," he said.

"That's good. Who wants to be understood? People complain when they're not, they squawk louder if they think they are. Take it from me, as one who knows. Listen, my mother was killed by the Nazis. You know what happened to me. My father was killed by the Russians, nobody knows how. My Polish grandmother was strung up by her peasants, and she thought they adored her. You want me to hate everybody?"

"But you've a right to hate my father surely?"

"D'you know," she said, "I'm hungry. Maybe if I was to ring down they would send us up some chicken sandwiches. I bet you haven't eaten in days. Maybe you should have a steak."

She picked up the telephone and gave the order.

"If you don't hate him, why are you here then, giving evidence?"

"I wondered when you'd get round to asking that. I was pressured. That's right, I was pressured. There was an English journalist I had a little fling with in Jo'burg. I told him about your dad then. I don't know why. It's not something I often … but he knew I'd been in the camps and, hell, it doesn't matter why, I told him. Then when this came up he rang me. Told me it was my duty. I told him what he could do with my duty. 'The poor sod will hang without my help,' I said. Sorry, dear, for the expression, but I'm quoting. 'Oh,' he said, 'but I think you'll make an impression.' 'Fuck the impression,' I said. 'I've been after Kestner for years,' he said, 'and I think you should tell your story. And I think you will,' he said, 'or else.' "

"Or else … Was this journalist called Murison, Ivan Murison?"

"That's the bugger. You know him?"

"We've met, and I can guess, he blackmailed you. I don't know how but he blackmailed you."

"Yes, you've met him," she said. "That's our Ivan."

Franz smiled. It felt unused.

"I wouldn't have thought you were the blackmailable type."

"Too right I'm not. But I live in Jo'burg and my boyfriend is black. Ivan had found that out. He's got some photographs, I don't know how. Wouldn't matter to me, but Mike, that's my boyfriend, is a lawyer and deeply committed. Could be hell for him, from both sides. Prison because it's against the law for a black to fuck a white woman, and God knows what from his own side. So I said to Ivan, right, you louse, I'll sing for you."

But Franz was puzzled. It seemed to him that it would have been more in character (and in Ivan Murison's interest) if he had kept Trudi in reserve, and sprung her as his own personal scoop, either in the newspapers or in his book.

"No," she said. "He knew I was the one witness who might make your dad feel really bad. He couldn't pass up on that. Ivan likes to see folks squirm."

The food arrived. She was right. He was hungry, and the steak was just what he needed, even if by Argentinian standards, it didn't amount to much.

"It's you I'm worried about," she said. "I am glad you came, though. Have you got a girl of your own?"

So he told her about Becky, told her the whole story, and she listened to it like someone who needed stories, who thrived on them, and the way she listened did more than anything she had said to make him understand how she had come through, emerging with neither guilt nor resentment from an unimaginable ordeal.

Later she nuzzled his cheek and murmured, "It doesn't worry you what I did with your father?"

He shook his head and pushed his face against her breasts. She stroked his hair.

"At least I won't beat you."

"Doesn't matter. Mike does, you know. Some men need to. That's all."

In the morning she drank hot chocolate with cream on top, and ate a pastry.

"I've never had to worry about my figure," she said. "I'm a big girl, but I don't get fat." She applied lipstick. "It wasn't all hell, you know, even then. Sometimes he liked me to talk of my home and what it had been like before the war. Sometimes we even pretended we would be together afterwards, in a chalet in the mountains. And he played music to me, Brahms mostly. I got to quite like Brahms, I never hear that sort of music now. If you like, tell him I remember the Brahms."

"That's all," she said. "I'm flying out as soon as I can. I don't want to see Ivan and I don't trust Mike out of my sight a moment longer than necessary. Hope you and your girl make out all right. You're a nice boy. But you've been lucky till now, haven't you?"

Becky listened to the murmur of conversation that came through the wall of her bedroom. The apartment was not well made. She could catch the occasional sentence. They were discussing the trial, as she had feared they would, which is why she had asked Rachel if she minded if she excused herself.

Rachel had apologised: "It was fixed weeks ago," she said. "It's Luke's publisher and they're bringing an American who wants to take over his books in the States."

"That's all right," Becky had said, she understood. But was it all right with Rachel, she didn't want her to feel she was using her.

"Oh honey," Rachel said and gave her a hug.

So Becky lay on her bed and listened. Sometimes there was silence, and that was the hardest. She had got so she found silence tough. Which was new; until now, she had needed it often.

There was a half-written letter on the desk. It was to her mother, but when she reached the point where she knew she had to talk about herself and Franz she hadn't been able to go on. The first part was all about her father, and how she understood why her mother had left him. "I never felt further away from him in all my life. But it's not me that has moved. It's him. I think it's the same with you and Eli, isn't it?"

But she knew it wasn't. And what she had written about herself wasn't true either. They had all three moved.

So now she thought about Franz. That was hard too. She was angry because he had given in to her father. He had colluded with him. They had tried to decide for her. There couldn't be a marriage where one partner decided for the other. Not the sort of marriage she wanted. And that was new. She had never thought that before.

Anger didn't drive out the wanting. She knew that every time she saw him in court, where she watched the back of his head, and his neck and the way he turned half round, exposing the long fragile line of his jaw. His blondness shone in the court. Every sentence stabbed him, made him question everything he had ever thought about himself. She knew that. But he kept his distance. At the time when she needed for both their sakes to comfort him, he withdrew.

She couldn't offer love, because if love was rebuffed now, it was re-buffed for ever. He had to come back to her. There he would be, in his hotel room, in the other city now, perhaps lying on a bed just like her now, and longing for her as she longed for him. She had only to go through the apartment and pick up the telephone. But she couldn't, and not only because of the people in the other room. She had to wait. Waiting, silence and the distance between them had become her weap-ons. But it was wrong to think of weapons in this connection.

She remembered the Swedish professor of theology who had asked with something approaching excitement if that shooting in Jerusalem was an atrocity. If he was still in Israel, he would be made aware now of no end of atrocities. They tumbled over each other, spewed out of every mouth.

When Franz's father met her in the Engineers' Club and looked her over, had he imagined stripping her and beating her as he had stripped and beaten that woman who had given evidence today? Would she have been rejected as too thin, too angular – she lifted her leg off the bed and held it aloft in the air. Or had he put aside all that, after the war, in his new life? Was a new life possible? Surely, essentials remained.

Nobody brought up in Argentina could dissociate pain from pleasure.

There was a knock, a gentle knock, on the door, and her name was called. She didn't reply. The knock was repeated, a little louder.

"Are you asleep, Becky?" Luke said.

She slid off the bed, in sudden shame as if she had been taken in self-abuse. She was trembling, as she opened the door a crack.

"Won't you come through?" he said. "I know you and Rachel decided, but maybe the company would do you good."

"I'm half-naked," she said.

"So? Put some clothes on. Or come as you are."

"Give me five minutes."

When they had gone, Rachel upbraided Luke. It had been too bad of him, dragging the poor girl through to show her off, as if she had been some sort of freak. When she said that, Luke caught Becky's eye and they both giggled.

"Aw, have some more wine, Rache. Nobody thought of her as a freak or treated her that way. Did you feel a freak, Becky?"

She shook her head, still giggling.

"Honestly, I don't understand the pair of you."

"No," Becky said, "They were nice. I was silly in the first place, that's all."

And she had handled it well. She knew that. Even when Luke's prospective American publisher, a fat balding man called Ed, had suggested that, hey, there would be a book in her story, she didn't respond badly.

"Well, Luke'll have to write it. I couldn't. Nor could Franz. Maybe you should sign Luke up."

Since that was precisely what Rachel hoped Ed would do, admittedly for a quite different book, it wasn't a bad answer. "What about it, Luke?" Ed said.

"Luke's gotten himself into enough shit over this shitty trial already," his Israeli publisher, a bright-eyed, keen-faced girl called Miriam, said. "I don't know how long it's going to take to live down that article, Luke baby, but," she threw her arms up in mock hopelessness. "You know what the schmuck did, Ed? He called for forgiveness. In Israel."

"So?"

"Forgiveness is a Christian concept, that's so?"

"What's the Jewish equivalent?" Becky said.

"Atonement. You ought to know that, being a Jew yourself."

"Not on my mother's side. It's the mother's side that counts… isn't it?"

"Your father gives evidence tomorrow, they tell me."

"Yes."

"Should be interesting," Ed said.

"Yes."

"He's quite a guy, isn't he?"

"Maybe you should sign him up, Ed," Luke said.

"Maybe I should. Maybe I will. But I was offered a book already today. By a British author. Seems he's got a London publisher, but no New York one signed up. There'll be a lot of books, maybe I have to move fast."

"This author. He's not called Ivan Murison by any chance?"

"That's right. You know him? Used to have some kind of reputation, I gather."

"Used to," Luke said. "Don't touch it, Ed. It'll stink."

"But the whole trial stinks," Ed said. "So why shouldn't I publish a book that stinks?"

Now they sat round the table, drinking wine and smoking, and none of them wanting to go to bed.

"Do you believe in evil, Luke?"

It was silly to ask him that. He was so obviously good himself. Franz and she had agreed on that. But how did you define good? Was it simply that life seemed more significant, more positive, whenever Luke was about, or indeed, whenever you thought of him? Franz had said it was more than that, that there was something which emanated from him: benevolence was a weak, dead word. So it was more than benevolence. On the other hand he frequently exasperated Rachel. Becky had seen that. He was doing it now as he played with a cigarette before answering. And, though Luke was intelligent – as intelligent as anyone she had met except her father – it wasn't that which impressed her; and in an odd way the feeling you got from him was the same feeling you got from association with a healthy animal. So, she asked Luke, was evil, if it existed, only something negative?

"Oh yes, it's negative," Luke said. "You've read *Macbeth*, I suppose? Don't you get the impression as Macbeth stumbles into the dark that everything is departing from him, that his world is narrowing?"

"But this catalogue we have been listening to, which is so terrible it makes you feel sick at the stomach, and dirty as if you couldn't remember when you were last clean, both at the same time, it is all indescribably horrible, and yet I can't escape the impression that even for the witnesses who tell these awful stories, it seems like a bad dream."

"It was the realisation of a nightmare," Luke said. "Even the Germans knew that, even while they were making it happen. They called the camps 'The Arsehole of the World', did you know that?"

"Do you know something?" Rachel said, "I want to get drunk."

"We all want to get drunk. We've had too much of the nightmare of reality. For almost two thousand years the Christians set themselves to imagine the geography of Hell. Then when they no longer believed in Hell, or in Heaven, or atonement or redemption, or anything, except good manners and culture, they were able to make Hell real in the Third Reich. If they had still believed in Hell they couldn't have done so."

"What about the Spanish Inquisition? What about the witch-hunts?"

"They were different. They were perpetrated for the sake of a faith that still believed in all these things which the Nazis rejected. The terrible thing about the Nazis is that they believed in nothing beyond themselves."

"Drink some more wine, Becky. Open another bottle, Luke. I am going to get drunk, there's nothing else for it…"

Becky frowned.

"If we were drunk," Rachel said, "none of this would matter. The only good thing I know about the Holocaust is that some of the soldiers and guards had to be drunk to be able to do what they had to do. The drunkards among them retained some moral feelings."

"I don't think Franz's father was ever drunk."

"No," Luke said, "I think he was an idolater."

The telephone rang. Luke rose to answer it. She heard him speak a denial, then another. It was, she was sure, a good denial; no cocks would crow.

"Very well," he said, "but no. Don't call again, please."

He opened the new bottle, as Rachel had asked, and filled the three glasses, and resumed his seat. He sat frowning. The refrigerator in the kitchen beyond began to hum. A large moth battered itself against the light-shade. Silence of the dark night rose from the street below. Then from an apartment across the courtyard, someone laughed. It was a sharp laugh, like a fox's bark, and there was no mirth in it. It was a laugh directed at misfortune.

"We were talking of evil," Luke said. "That was small evil, undistinguished evil. That English journalist we were talking of, Ivan Murison. He wanted to speak to you, Becky. You don't mind that I said no, that I spoke for you, you don't mind, do you?"

He put his hand on hers, and let it lie there, pressing gently. "No," she said, "this time I don't mind. He gives me the creeps."

"He's a shit," Rachel said, "that's all. He's a shit in spades, redoubled. I've seen him look at you in court."

"He wanted to come here. I wouldn't have it … he said he'd something for you. I said he could give it at a better time."

Even his name disturbed her. It sucked something out of the room; a moment of peace, enchantment, was destroyed. "He gives me the creeps."

Perhaps because he sensed the effect of Ivan's name, Luke now put some music on the gramophone. Becky didn't recognise it. Then a trumpet floated, melancholy, away from the band. It left the beat, the rhythm behind, and moved into a world of its own making. It was like evening by a great river in autumn, when the dying sun has no power to warm, but only casts lurid streaks on the still water, while mists gather. It was music that was maybe played in a nightclub but spoke of a world which the player, confined in the smoky dark, had lost long ago.

"Bix…" Luke said. "Bix Beiderbecke. There's no one like him. Do you know what his secret was?" he said, as the music died and he rose to turn the flip side of the record. "He knew that the music he played so beautifully was foreign to him, that it wasn't in his blood, that however beautifully he played it, he was outside it. He could only clutch at the magic which always receded from him. That's why he is for me the most poetic and most truthful of jazzmen. Of course, he's the most truthful because he is the most poetic. It's an image of the Ideal that he makes. Rachel's asleep."

He smiled.

"Always the same. She wants to get drunk, poor girl, and always she passes out first. It's a mark of virtue perhaps. Who knows? Do you want to get drunk?"

"No, no."

"Me neither."

He put the cork back in the bottle, screwing it well in so that the wine would still be drinkable the next evening.

"Not with your dad giving evidence tomorrow."

"I hate the thought of it."

"It'll pass. Hold on to that, kid. All this will pass. You and Franz. You can still be all right. You can still make it."

"I don't know, Luke. Jewish flesh."

"Like I've said, we're all Eichmann's children. We're the heirs of the hell he made. Rache says I say that too often. Maybe I do. Am I a bore, Becky? Am I boring you?"

"No," she said. "No."

"Honest?"

"Honest. I don't think you could."

He picked up the glasses and took them through to the kitchen and rinsed them under the tap. She followed him, emptying ashtrays.

"You know, Becky, I could fall in love with you. Easy."

"I think maybe I could fall in love with you too, Luke."

"Better not, eh?"

"Better not."

He took her arm and led her to the window that looked over the street. He pointed to a group of lights faint in the distance.

"That's not a farm. They're watch-towers, keeping us safe. I often think of them when I lie in bed, those boys out there, in the frost, on the edge of the desert."

He kissed her cheek.

"There'll be other light there in an hour. Dawn. Rosy-fingered and all that. Time for bed. I'd better get Rache through. Poor girl, she wants to get drunk and she passes out. But it's better this way."

"Yes," she said, "much better. Thank you, Luke. For everything."

I could finish my letter to Mother now, she thought, but better not. Sleep first, sleep.

SEVEN

Guided by attendants, Eli stumbled on his way to the witness box. He corrected himself quickly, shaking off the hand which would have supported him. He lifted his chin, throwing back the mane of white hair (not cut since his arrival in Israel). He wore a dark pinstriped suit, which Becky could not remember having seen. It had a waistcoat, and the thin gold chain of a pocket watch flashed as he mounted the steps. She wondered if others were struck by the incongruity of a blind man providing himself with a timepiece which he could not read. He had resurrected, though she did not realise this, a pre-war persona. He was dressed as he would have dressed to go to work in the Reichsbank. His collar was as stiff as Hjalmar Schacht's used to be.

He would give his evidence, it was announced, in the form of a statement on which he could subsequently be cross-examined. Becky glanced at Saul Birnbaum to see if he would protest; but he kept his seat.

Eli began to speak. He spoke in German, apologising for the inadequacy of his Hebrew.

"But in any case," he said, "I wish the accused to be able to understand what I say without the possibly distorting medium of simultaneous translation, though I would also pay tribute to the excellence of the translators' work.

"You will forgive me if the first part of what I say, which is also the reason for the unorthodox approach – in which context allow me to add that I am grateful for the understanding which the defence lawyers have extended towards me – if this introduction takes the form of a personal memoir, an essay in autobiography. I may claim a certain right to this indulgence since it was on account of my action, my recognition of the man posing as a German-Argentinian engineer calling himself Rudolf Schmidt, as Kestner, that this trial has been made possible. You will come to understand what anguish that recognition cost me, and you will in this way understand the overriding importance of this trial."

(But had there been anguish? Hadn't there been, as her mother thought, a proud and steely joy in what he did?)

"I was born a German. I was also of course a Jew. We were three generations from the ghetto, perhaps four. I was born in 1904. We had travelled from Vienna to Frankfurt to Hamburg, where my grandfather was director of a bank and a steamship company. He was a great figure in the city. Our house might be called a mansion, and the drawing rooms were full of flowers that grew only in hothouses. When the Kaiser visited Hamburg and was given a dinner by the Chamber of Commerce, my grandfather was selected to second the address. He had, I believe, little admiration for that bombastic and inadequate figure, but an immense veneration for everything that he represented. His speech was widely admired; even twenty years later old men remembered it and spoke to me of the effect it had made on them.

"In 1914 my father was recalled to the colours. He served on the Western Front, and was awarded the Iron Cross. In 1917 he was gassed. His health never recovered.

"After the war he no longer went to the synagogue. I never asked him why. Religious practices dwindled in our household; my mother, a beauty, was more interested in fashion. We had preserved our fortune, by good management, but my father was embittered. Like many, he believed that Germany had been betrayed. I grew up aware of the enemy within, whom my poor father identified with the Bolsheviks, and even the Social Democrats. He admired Rathenau, later adhered to the German Conservative Party. Franz von Papen visited us. There was much talk of reconstruction and the need to stabilise the currency.

"I grew up deeply conscious of the iniquities of the Treaty of Versailles. The clauses concerning reparations seemed monstrous; they were, I was told and I believed, a crime against the German people. Except that I actually understood economics and finance, my views on such matters did not differ greatly from Adolf Hitler's.

"But, when the Nazi Party started to grow, we had no time for it. We despised Hitler and his gang as ignorant opportunists."

He looked up and smiled, directing his blind eyes at the cage where Kestner sat, very straight, his mouth a little open and his tongue wetting his lower lip.

"I may say that I have never altered that opinion, at any time.

"We were, however, assured, by von Papen and others, that the Nazis were necessary; that they diverted support from the non-German or international parties, and because they were nationalists, of the most fervid sort, they could be employed by their betters in the service of the nation.

"This seems naive now, but I have observed often how the received wisdom of one generation seems simple folly to its successors.

"I grew up scorning conventional economics, hating the irresponsibility of those who had permitted the great inflation which condemned millions of Germans to degradation and poverty. But I must say that I knew nothing of this at first hand. Our family affairs were well arranged. The hothouse flowers were replaced before they wilted.

"So, ignorant of the passions and the hatreds surging and seething below the agreeable surface of my personal life, and below the less agreeable surface of national life, I was confident of my own abilities and of my place in the world. Only in one respect was I idealistic: I wanted to serve Germany. For I must stress, that with our familial attachment to Judaism so diluted, I identified myself absolutely and unquestioningly with Germany. Only a few of you listening to me now will be able to comprehend that patriotic intensity.

"Even now, I sigh when I recollect the sweetness of that lost bourgeois way of life.

"Hitler came to power. I was only a little disconcerted. My Conservative friends assured me that he would be given only so much rope. Besides, they said, if he offends, the Generals will deal with him. I had a great faith in the integrity and sagacity of the German Officer Corps.

"Besides, I was engrossed in a great work. Why, I might have asked myself, should the work cease? I had been chosen by Hjalmar Schacht, on the strength of personal recommendation and the effect made by my dissertation on the relations between the availability of credit and economic activity, to assist him in the financial and economic reconstruction of Germany. If I had paused to question the work we were doing, I should have stilled my conscience by arguing that as the Nazis were the product of a sickness caused by the slump, so they could be eradicated or at least emasculated by renewed prosperity.

"Later, in many conversations, as war approached, I justified my position by arguing that the best way to cheat the revolution was to lead it.

"Both arguments, I came to see, were sophisms. But I had to endure much before I arrived at that opinion.

"When did I begin to know that I was still a Jew, and was perceived as a Jew?"

He paused, sipped water, dabbed his temple with a white handkerchief. The question was not directed at the court. He seemed oblivious of his audience. At times his voice had dropped to a murmur, so that even Becky had to strain to catch his words.

"Was it one day in Berlin in, I think, 1934? The street was blocked. Yet another parade, I sighed, for there were already too many of them, and they bored me. Bored me. There were days when I was consumed with boredom. Only my work saved me, only my work seemed real. But these were middle-aged men, in civilian clothes, with an air of the utmost respectability. Each of them wore a medal or a row of medals pinned to the breast pocket. They carried banners proclaiming that the Kaiser had praised them.

" 'Who are they?' a woman next to me said.

" 'Can't you read?' her companion replied. 'Bloody Yids, pretending they were soldiers in the war.'

" 'But weren't they?' she said. 'Look at all these medals.'

" 'Course they weren't,' he said. 'Bought them for a song off soldiers down on their luck, put out of work by their fellow Yids, that's how they got them.'

"I might have despaired at that moment of everything I was struggling to accomplish.

" 'So why are they marching?' the woman said.

" 'Like to make a fuss, don't they. Bloody Yids.'

" 'They are marching,' another man said, 'because Our Leader has just cancelled their war pensions.'

"I asked myself, if my father had still been alive, would he have been marching with them? Or would he have still pretended, like me, that we Jews had no need to worry?

"It must have been that day, or soon after, that I realised my Jewishness, for I got into conversation with the man who had supplied the information about the pensions. I can't think how I didn't know him already. He was Wilfrid Israel."

The name meant nothing to Becky.

"You will all know him," Eli said, "as the bravest and most selfless defender of … our … people. You will know how he negotiated ransoms and escapes, resettlements and funds. No single man did more to save European Jewry.

"We fell into conversation, a conversation that developed into argument, argument that continued in friendly and fruitful style right up to the moment of his final departure from Germany. Though morally and spiritually I recognised him as my superior, we had, intellectually, much in common. We both believed in an older Germany, enduring tenaciously, under the vile scum of the Nazi movement, a Germany which was open to reason and to what I can only call spiritual Enlightenment, the Germany indeed that was the heir of that great movement of the European spirit which we are accustomed to call by its German name, the *Aufklärung*, the Germany that inherited values from Goethe and Heine, Schiller, Brahms and, yes, Wagner too, whom the Nazis perverted for their own cause. It was Wilfrid who put me in touch with men like Adam von Trott and Bonhoeffer, and one who was to become my greatest friend, Albrecht von Pfühlnitz, all men who were to form the German resistance to Hitler, who were doomed to die at his hands, and with whom I am proud to have been associated. And who is to say that we did not triumph, for has not the Germany we dreamed of been reborn?

"It was Wilfrid too who said to me, often: 'Never forget, Eli, that it is the German people, not only the Jews, who have been the first victims of the Nazi oppression…' "

"He urged me to emigrate. I refused. It is strange that he who believed in so much should have left Germany, while I who believed in nothing should have remained. I insisted on the all-powerful influence of fact, and yet saw only those facts I chose to see. At the Reichsbank I worked to produce figures which proved how rearmament was damaging the German economy, how it was impossible that Germany could again sustain a long war. I worked under the direction of Schacht, and when he was dismissed in January 1939, I should have known we had failed, that war was certain… Yet even after his dismissal my technical ability kept me safe. I was still, it seemed, needed.

"I was not myself dismissed for another eighteen months, and even then I remained at freedom for another year before I was arrested and sent to a concentration camp. I shall not speak of my experiences there. There are others more entitled to testify, and some of them have already done so in this court.

"I now turn to the prisoner, Kestner, and to my relations with him. These were never close. When I first became aware of him, as a political officer in the SS, he was a nonentity. His position was nothing in comparison with my own. I regarded him only as a squalid nuisance.

"I met him once only, before the war. Though I steered clear of involvement in matters of refugees, it so happened that one day in the early summer of 1939 I received a message from Wilfrid Israel, asking me to act as an intermediary on his behalf. He was arranging to buy free-dom for a group of Jewish academics. The financial arrangements were complicated. He thought I would perhaps be the best person to handle them. To my shame, I resisted, I tried to avoid the dangerous honour. But Wilfrid was very persuasive, and in the end I consented.

"Following my instructions I drove east from Berlin. It was a beautiful day, and the cornfields were turning yellow. I regarded them with a sort of misery, for I knew that each day of ripening brought war closer. Hitler would move when the harvest had been gathered. And yet, though I was conscious of this, and the pain and despair those fields of ripening grain portended, I was also, I remember, curiously at peace with myself.

"I had not been told the name of the man I was to meet at a little inn in a remote Prussian village, which had been selected for some reason never explained to me. But I recognised him as Kestner, who had been pointed out to me as what he was by my friend Albrecht von Pfühlnitz in a Berlin restaurant. So I was surprised when he announced himself by some other name, which I now forget. It was stupid since he was wear-ing his uniform, and I would have had means of checking if I chose. He must have known that; perhaps the alias amused him. I got the impres-sion that the business on which we were engaged amused him.

"There was something pathetic about him. I had not expected that this proud and brutal Nazi I had prepared myself to encounter should wear such an aura of pathos. I may say here, though it will shock many, that I had never been able to bring myself to dislike Hitler. I hated him of course, and loathed everything for which he stood. I feared his power over men's minds. But I could not bring myself to dislike him. He always reminded me of a neglected dog, left outside in the rain and howling to be admitted. Kestner gave me the same feeling. He was a man who seemed to me injured by experience. Remove the uniform and he would be nothing."

Becky could not stop herself from looking at Franz's father, who, how-ever, remained impassive, as if indeed what Eli had to say concerned some other person. He sat back detached from what was happening around him, and then, aware perhaps that so many eyes had turned to see how he reacted to this assessment, to this attempt to strip even pride from him, the left corner of his mouth drew itself into a narrow smile. Her eyes sought Franz, on whom her father's words seemed to have a greater effect. He had crumpled. Until now it seemed to her he had supported himself by the reflection that whatever his father had been, he had also been someone who commanded respect. And yet, Eli wasn't speaking the full truth: for the uniform had been removed, and the man was not nothing. That was the point she couldn't grasp. How had he transformed himself, so that the man she had met in the Engineers' Club had seemed in every way the equal of her father? And how indeed had he brought himself to undergo that meeting, remembering as he must of his previous encounter with Eli?

"He offered me wine. I accepted. Not only because it would have been poor tactics, perhaps even compromising my mission, to have declined, but also because refusal would have seemed to throw him back into that darkness from which it was clear he had with such difficulty struggled. But, in that judgement, I was both right and wrong. For he had indeed struggled to emerge from darkness, that was true, only to find himself not in the light of reason, but in a still denser night. And perhaps it was not darkness from which he had emerged, but only the shadows, a grey world where nothing connected, where there was loneliness and the scuttle of rats' feet on crumbling walls."

Eli had forgotten where he was. He was speaking not to the judge, nor to the court or the world's press, but out of some secret world of sympathy, and the words stumbled forth as if each one was a new discovery even to himself. And now the man in the cage was listening. The ironic smile was dislodged. If she could see his eyes, would they reveal that he and his accuser were bound together in a private theatre of embarrassment, that each had recognised the other? She remembered that when he had urged Franz to try to arrange for him to see her father again, even here in Israel, he had insisted that "Czinner would understand." It was too clear he did. He must have been so lonely in himself since.

"So I accepted the wine, and we talked, of banalities, pleasantly. I remember that, because I was astonished that this creature could engage in civilised nothings. I hadn't expected it, my experience was limited. We talked of our families, as strangers will. We even exchanged confidences. I admitted I was in love with an English girl. 'You should join her,' he said. 'I respect you, Dr Czinner, but for your own sake I must tell you that you will be foolish if you remain in Germany.' We even laughed about that. He told me he was a Saxon. 'They call us stupid Saxons,' he said, 'but we're persistent. We're like an old dog that has got hold of a mangy bone and won't let it go.' "

The man in the cage nodded his head. The smile returned to the corner of his mouth.

"And then we proceeded to our business. It was arranged with a certain sympathy. And courtesy. He understood the complicated financial arrangements very well. When we parted, he said: 'This is not the first time I have saved a Jew's life. Let that be remembered in my favour when we have lost the war that is coming.' 'Do you really believe that?' I said. 'That war is coming? It's inevitable, I should have thought.' 'No,' I said, 'that Germany will lose it.' I was astonished and repeated my question, even wondering if his remark was some sort of trick – our way of life had made us so suspicious. 'But yes,' he said, 'you must have made the same assessment yourself.' 'Then why?' 'Why am I a Nazi? Why do I wear this uniform? My dear Dr Czinner,' he said, 'I used to be a miserable clerk. Later I sold cosmetics from door to door. You can have no conception in your solid world, how insubstantial mine was.'

"I did not think he meant me to understand that he was only an opportunist. I did not think that at all.

"That was our only meeting in Germany. He cheated me, by the way. The men whose release I thought I had negotiated were not released. The money I had arranged to be paid in advance was not returned. It was a squalid trick.

"Over the following years I heard much of Kestner. People spoke of him with awe as of something inhuman. Never with hatred, but always I think with a certain revulsion. He became a man of power, great power. I wonder if he ever believed in it. I have never met someone who seemed emptier."

He sipped his glass of water.

"I have little more to say. A few months ago, in Argentina, where I have lived for many years, my only child, my daughter, announced that she was going to marry a German boy."

Franz's head turned. For the first time since the first day of the trial he met Becky's eyes. They looked at each other, frozen in immobility.

"He seemed agreeable, or so my wife reported. We arranged to meet his father. I am, as you will realise, blind. In compensation my other senses may have developed an unusual acuity. I was aware very early in our meeting that I had heard this man's voice before. It was not until he made that same remark about being a Saxon, which I have reported to the court, that I realised who he was. It was with difficulty that I held my peace. I told myself I could not be sure, it might be a coincidence, though I knew it was not, and I was sure. I telephoned the next day and lured him into repeating the remark. I had no doubt, I took the necessary steps to bring my positive identification of him as Kestner before the relevant authorities... The rest you know.

"I have only this to add. For a long time, all my life it seems, I have struggled to avoid ... to avoid ... commitment. I set myself up as a judge of right and wrong, even as a judge over Israel ... I was guilty of the sin of pride, guilty a thousand times over. Not even what I endured in the camps dented my pride. Now, at the cost of much pain to myself and my family, I was given the chance to make atonement. Do not think I have not suffered in doing so. But I lay that suffering on the altar of Israel ... Let justice be done."

He sat down, wiped his eyes. There was a long moment of silence.

The judge rose, announced an adjournment. Dr Czinner's examination would be postponed. He was interrupted. Eli pitched forward, his hands folded over his breast. Someone cried for a doctor. Kinsky rushed forward also. Becky stood up. She drew a cardigan about her.

"Get me out of here, Rachel. Please."

EIGHT

Becky spent part of the evening at the hospital: Eli had suffered a heart attack. The doctors called it mild. He would certainly recover. There was no cause for concern. One of them laughed and said they were not going to lose such a distinguished patient so soon after his "return" to Israel.

She telephoned Nell in England, hoping that she would get on a plane the next day. But Nell made no such suggestion, and Becky found she couldn't ask her to come.

"I can't forgive your father for trying to break you and Franz up," Nell said. "Anyway, you say he'll recover. He'll be happy now in Israel."

Becky took a bus back to Tel Aviv. Luke was out, at the office of his newspaper. Rachel asked her if she wanted food, but she was too tired to eat.

"We're all worn out," Rachel said. "Except Luke. He thrives on this, you know."

Becky was no longer welcome. She sensed that, though she couldn't account for the shift. Rachel could have no idea of how she and Luke had talked the previous night; and even if she had, how could it matter? Her marriage was safe, as long as she wanted it. Rachel was depressed. It was like that day when they had gone to the beach, and cowered in the sand-dunes under the fighter planes. Eli's evidence had once again emphasised the monstrous weight of Israel. If he, after so many years, was drawn back by its magnetism, what hope could Rachel retain that Luke might ever break free? And so perhaps the sight of Becky distressed her, for she saw how Eli was prepared to sacrifice his daughter to the jealous God, as Abraham had led Isaac to the altar on the summit of Mount Moriah. "Thou shalt have no other Gods before me"; and this mighty "Me" was Israel itself.

Rachel stubbed out her cigarette. She looked at the kitchen table, with its dirty cups and saucers, packets of cereal and crumbs of toast. She pushed back her hair, and said she was going to bed.

"I'm not going to sit up for Luke," she said. "You can, if you like. But he'll be hours."

Becky sat there, with the window open to the night air and the murmur of the courtyard. Then she went through to the other room and stood by the window listening to the night. She rang Franz's hotel. No answer from his room. The note of the telephone sounded forlorn. Then she was surrounded by the loneliness of silence.

She leafed through a stand of gramophone records, though she did not play one for fear of waking Rachel. But there was music you could hear in your head. Here was Gluck's *Orfeo*, which her father detested. "Che farò senza Euridice?" "Get on with your life," Eli would snap.

But Orpheus had gone back, gone under, into the shadows to fetch his dead love, refusing to submit to death. The potency of the myth could be explained of course in psychological terms: truth was inward, in the heart of darkness. That was where it had to be sought. Or again: no man is an island. (When you were very tired, you thought in the words of others.) The bell tolls, but we cannot surrender love to death. Was she Orpheus or Eurydice? Did it matter? In the end they had lost each other. Orpheus had looked back at the wrong moment. The condition imposed on him, that he should not do so, was fraudulent, for his quest had been retrospective from the first.

An early cock crew, though there was no light in the sky. It was calling the morning into being from one of the yards behind the little houses beyond this street of apartments. There was no sound of traffic. Only the impatient bird. She leaned forward, with her elbows on the windowsill, listening.

In the morning she told Rachel she was not going to the trial any more. It would be always there, but she was not going any more.

Rachel said, "So I won't either. I only went for your sake. I've hated it from the start."

But if they didn't go, how to get through the day? And tomorrow, and the next day?

"You want me to move out, don't you?"

"Yes," Rachel said. "I don't know why, but I do. It's nothing personal."

Kinsky was at the hospital when she arrived to see Eli.

"Don't go," she said, "wait for me, Kinsky. Please. I must talk to you."

"Why should I go?" Kinsky said. "I have nothing to go for, believe me, my dear."

Eli would not speak. She took hold of his hand. She called him

"Father", dwelling on the word as if it would extract a reply. But even if he spoke he would not answer the question that anyway she was too proud to ask.

"Does he speak to you, Kinsky?"

"Yes, yes."

"Then why not to me?"

"I don't know. Perhaps he feels you are judging him. Perhaps he is afraid of what you would reply. I don't know. When he speaks to me, he likes to talk of Berlin before the war."

"Tell me about the trial. I can't go to it any more. But I would still like to be told."

"It's going. After Eli's evidence, Kestner seems no longer interested. He pays no attention. It is as if none of it concerns him, not now."

"Kinsky," she said. "I must see Franz. I can't continue without seeing him."

"Very well," he said, "I shall arrange it. I don't see…" He spread out his hands, smiled, kissed her and led her to the bus stop.

"I'm moving into a hotel," she said. "I don't know which yet. I'll let you know."

She booked into the YMCA on King David Street. A young clerk with thick curly hair smiled as he examined her passport.

"A name honoured in Israel," he said.

She explained that she would bring her luggage in later. First, she wanted to sleep. Very well: would she pay now please?

The little cell was cool when she awoke. The sun had moved round. It was late afternoon. From the vestibule she telephoned Rachel. Luke answered.

"I don't know why you're doing this," he said. "Have you and Rachel quarrelled? She won't say anything either. I'll bring your luggage in myself."

"No," she said, "can you put it on a bus maybe?"

"Don't be silly. I'll be there by eight o'clock. Becky, I want to see you. All right?"

"All right."

She had four hours to kill. There was an inscription on the wall by the telephone booth: "These buildings are the fulfilment of the inspired vision of James Newbigin Jarvie of Montclair, New Jersey." It was a big claim, perhaps natural if you came from Clear Mountain. There was a map on the floor of the vestibule. She asked the clerk – a different one, this time – about it.

"Sixth-century Jerusalem," he said. "A famous map. This is a reproduction."

"Yes," she said, "I thought it might be."

But it gave her an idea. She purchased a map and guidebook from him.

Following its directions, she climbed Mount Zion again to David's Tomb, to gaze over the forbidden Old City. If you turned to the south, you could see what must be Bethlehem. A sign directed her to the Chamber of the Martyrs. She hesitated and entered. People stood, with heads bowed, in reverence before the tablets covered with names. A few names stood for millions. It was on account of them that Franz's father was held in the prison near the Damascus Gate, scarcely a mile away, and was carried every day to the law court on King George Avenue. But this silent chamber and these silent people were what it came down to; she was out of place.

Again she looked over the Old City. Jerusalem was divided, like her heart. She turned away from the mountain, down the hill, into the valley. She stopped at a café and ordered tea. She read again in the guidebook.

This valley with its mean cottages, its tin-roofed shacks, its yards where chickens pecked around the base of fruit-trees, where women in headscarves sat in the doorways peeling vegetables and calling out to their children or their neighbours, where at a little petrol station across the road, two men in singlets and cotton trousers that sagged from their waists were arguing, not fiercely but in the grumbling manner of an argument that has gone on for days, weeks, months, and can never end; this valley, she read, was Hinnom. "Because in ancient times it was a valley of depravity and sin the name Gel-Hinnom or Gehenna was given to the place for the wicked in the world to come to." Well, that was Franz's father. Perhaps they should bring him here: "Therefore, behold the day cometh, saith the Lord, that it shall no more be called Topheth" (which was its other name, it seemed) "nor the Valley of the son of Hinnom, but the valley of slaughter, for they shall bury in Topheth till there be no more place. And the carcasses of people shall be meat for the fowls of the heaven and for the beasts of the earth, and none shall frighten them away."

She took the slice of lemon from her glass of tea and sucked it. That was the prophet Jeremiah, according to her guidebook. She knew nothing of him. Her scriptures were stories, read to her by Nell from the Children's Bible, or cursorily examined in school. She had wept with Ruth, been dazzled by Joseph, pitied King Saul who was cheated by the disagreeable Samuel and cast out because he showed mercy. "Ye daughters of Israel, weep over Saul, who clothed you in scarlet with other delights." Well, she had wept, whether she was properly a daughter of Israel or not, though she was ambivalent towards David, the author of the lament, at least until the moment when he too wept over his son Absalom. And who was the king who had said, "My father chastised you with whips, but I shall chastise you with scorpions'? Franz's father had been a scorpion. This Gehenna, this Topheth was, she saw, the place for idols or idol-worship and child sacrifices: the Auschwitz of the ancient world. Didn't that suggest that history was merely a cycle of atrocities, that, with each turn of the wheel ... she remembered what Ramón, her old dancing-partner who was now an officer, had said, when she met him by chance two days before she had left for Israel: "I am leaving the army. I'm going to breed horses. Last week I was compelled to watch a man being tortured. They ripped out his fingernails."

A car stopped in front of the café. It was a taxi. A white shape leaned over towards the driver, then backed out of the car, turned, and she saw Ivan Murison. He was not alone. A curly-haired boy, in jeans and a short-sleeved blue shirt, emerged from the other side of the car. Murison stopped on seeing her.

"How clever of you to have found my favourite café in all Jerusalem," he said.

Her eye took in, as for the first time, the battered iron tables, the chairs that sat unevenly on the rough beaten earth, the bead curtain lacking three strands that hung over the door, the chickens pecking around the dusty oleanders, the withered fig tree. Ivan Murison took hold of the boy's arm, his fingers pressing hard on the *café-au-lait* flesh just above the elbow.

"This is Yusuf," he said. "Yusuf, the beautiful Miss Czinner." The boy smiled, showing very white teeth. He looked about fifteen.

"Yusuf works here, which is why I have chosen it as my place of relaxation. We've had a nice little outing." He let the boy go. "Be a lamb," he said, and the boy, understanding, slipped into the café.

"And to think I've been trying so hard to find you, my dear. Mind if I take a pew? Remember I'm one of the family. That's why it hurts that you've been avoiding me. Has someone said something nasty about me?"

"I didn't think we'd anything to talk about."

"Oh, but we do. But that will keep. What brings you to this part of town?"

She explained that she had merely been following her guidebook. She had had no particular intention…

The boy returned with brandy, a Coca-Cola for himself, and another glass of tea for her. He sat down between them, pulled up his shirt and stroked his flat satin-smooth stomach. When another customer arrived, he got up and served him, and then returned to his chair.

"Yusuf's a Christian Arab," Ivan Murison said during one of his absences. "Charming, don't you think?"

He talked of the trial. His manner was almost sympathetic. He spoke admiringly of Eli, and said how difficult it must have been for him. And Franz: how brave he was, how he admired that. "Not being a brave man myself," he laughed. He told her he was sorry Nell hadn't come. It would have been so nice to see her again. "We separated on friendly terms, you know." He talked of Israel and of his love for the country, "Though I wish they treated their Arabs better."

He exerted himself to please her. But he failed. The light died away. The street lamps came on, spots of yellow in a purple haze. Away in the distance, in the mountains, they could hear the rumble of thunder. Or perhaps it was gunfire. Ivan Murison talked of the significance of Gehenna. "Israel has always been apocalyptic," he said. "I prefer Yusuf's attitude to life. He takes things as they come. He lives in Gehenna and still knows how to laugh. Don't you think laughter is what we need, my dear?"

"Oh," she said, "laughter. I think I've forgotten."

Ivan poured himself another brandy and lit one of his little cigars. There was a tremor in his hands. He mopped his brow with a red, white-spotted handkerchief.

"You don't like me much," he said, "do you? I'm used to it, you know. Nobody does. Oh, in the right mood, I still amuse people, but they don't like me. I have to buy what affection I can get."

She was repelled by his self-pity.

"You could be my daughter," he said.

"I don't think so."

"Oh I'm not suggesting you may be. Besides, I have a daughter, by my second marriage. She's at some redbrick university, I forget which. She hasn't much time for me either, you know. And so I've pursued success. Without success, I'm a hack. This book I'm commissioned to write on the trial, it'll be no good. Oh, it sounded great when I outlined it, and for a few months I was excited to be back on the old trail. But it's gone. *Où sont les neiges d'antan* … 'The moving finger writes and having writ, moves on,' " he waved a cigar-clutching pudgy hand. "I'm talking rot, you think. Wait till you're my age. You don't like me. You think I was trying to blackmail Franz. So I was. Pointless. What do I care about Kestner or Czinner? Oh, I'll hack out a narrative, and I'll be paid and it will sit in a few bookshops, and then be remaindered. But I could write once. Ask your mother."

"What went wrong?"

"Writing's character, you know," he said, and smiled. "I was fond of your mother. And admired her. I was hurt when I thought she had seen through me. I still carry her photograph. Silly, isn't it?"

He drew an envelope from a stained wallet and extracted some photographs and pushed them across the table in her direction. Nell had been caught laughing, in a way Becky remembered from childhood, but not often recently. Her hair flopped over one eye; she looked a bit like Lauren Bacall. Then there was one in which she was leaning against a bar. She wore a suit cut to resemble uniform and held a cigarette dangling in her right hand. She was challenging the world to surprise her.

Becky stopped short.

"Why do you have these photographs of Franz? Where did you get them?"

"I didn't mean to show you those," Ivan said. "I thought they were in a different envelope."

She looked at them again, and then at him.

"Yes, you did," she said. "You thought they would upset me. Where did you get them?"

"No," he said. He set his glass on the table, steadied its rocking, and planted his finger on the back of the other boy in the photograph.

"That's Charlie," he said. "Carlo Bastini. He was at school with Franz. He's a friend of mine and he gave me the photographs to help me identify Franz."

"I don't believe you," she said. "You thought you could use them. You thought they could hurt me."

"Have it your way." He drank some more brandy. His eyes flickered towards Yusuf who was now with a group of boys of his own age at another table where voices were raised in argument.

"They're talking politics," he said. "Politics and resentment. They're all full of resentment. I can't blame them, you know. All right," he said. "Charlie didn't want to give me the photographs. I insisted. I thought they might come in useful."

"Well, they haven't, have they? I understand them, Mr Murison. But you've missed one thing. When I first fell for Franz, I was warned by kind friends that he was queer. Maybe he used to be, but he isn't now. So I don't care, you see. They mean nothing to me."

She tore the two prints in half. Ivan Murison made no move to prevent her. Then she quartered them, and dropped them in the ashtray. She leaned forward and held her lighter under the corner of one of the pieces.

When the flame died down, Ivan said, "I did a piece on old Willie Maugham once. He's gaga now, you know. They shouldn't let him give interviews. He said to me, 'My tragedy is that I pretended all my life that I was three-quarters normal and only a quarter queer, whereas it was the other way about.' I made the same mistake myself for twenty years. Then I said, to hell with it."

He looked at the other table. Yusuf had swung his chair back, stretching his legs out and clasping his hands on the top of his head, his fingers lost among the curls. He turned and gave Ivan a radiant smile.

"I'm thinking of buying Yusuf. We're waiting for his father to complete the deal. Does that shock you?"

"What sort of life can you offer him?"

"Better than he'll have here. He'll always be a white blackbird, you know – an Arab in a Jewish State, a Christian among Moslems … a poor boy among … Don't think too harshly of me."

She was half an hour late, but Luke was waiting for her. He was talking in Hebrew to the clerk. When he saw Becky, he waved, kissed her, and waited till the clerk finished a long sentence.

"Miss Czinner," the clerk said, "I have a message for you."

It was from Kinsky. It said that he would be with Franz at the King David Hotel from nine o'clock.

"Well, that's just down the street," Luke said. "We could talk for a bit first, then I'll walk you there. Where have you been? What have you been doing?"

She told him. "The strange thing is," she said, "I don't think too harshly of him. I even felt sorry for him. If he was planning something nasty, he's given it up."

"And this business of the boy, it doesn't shock you?"

"Shock, no. Disgust, yes. When I think of it. Can you stop it, Luke?"

"What about the boy? How does he feel?"

"Oh, happy, at the moment. But ... later?"

"Yes, there's always later, isn't there. You're right. I told you I could fall in love with you, Becky. You're not only beautiful, you have the right instincts. You're moral. It's what we need, a renewed sense of what's moral. David – that's the boy at the desk – and I have been talking about just that. He's a philosophy student. He says he's an existentialist. We agreed it's a perilous position. Here we are, on our own, and we have to construct for ourselves a means of ethical recognition."

"Will you do something?"

"Yes," he said, "there are people I can speak to. I think we can arrange to ease Mr Murison out of the country, on his own. I'll also undertake to talk to the boy myself, like – what's the expression – a Dutch uncle. Why Dutch? Perhaps I shall take an Arab friend along. I have them, you know."

"Oh Luke, I don't know what to say. He's an unhappy man. I almost liked him some of the time we were talking."

"But he shouldn't repair his unhappiness at the expense of the boy, should he?"

"No. Do you suppose that's what Franz's father was doing? Repairing his unhappiness at the expense of others? Oh, I know it's absurd to ask."

"Absurd?" Luke smiled. "David and I were speaking about absurdity. We can't judge the reasons why people do what they do. We can only judge the actions themselves. As for liking Ivan Murison, you told me you liked Franz's father the time you met?"

"Yes."

"Well, there you are. Perhaps people are at their best with you, Becky. We are none of us a single entity, you know. The self one perceives oneself is never known to others. I'm not the same Luke for Rachel as I am for my mother... Do you still want to marry Franz?"

What if she said "no"? She looked at his strong hands, at his broken nose, at the brown eyes which did not move away from her gaze.

"Yes," she said. "More than ever. I was doubtful when I came here. I had a dream in which I confused him with his father, or they blended into each other, I don't know how. But I do: I'm already wedded to Franz in my mind, in my heart, in my body… Luke, what are you doing to me? I can't explain myself, I've never spoken to anyone like this before."

"Very well, good," Luke said. "Your friend Minty came looking for you. I didn't let on I was meeting you. I left her talking with Rache. There were getting on fine. Can I say something? I told you I could fall in love with you. Well, I'm on the brink. Just remember, I'm here if you need me. What time are you meeting Franz? Right, can I give you some advice? Do as he asks, go to England, stay with your mother till this is over. Sure, Franz needs you, but I've a feeling he needs you not to see what he's going to go through in the next months. It's cathartic for him. When he emerges from the ordeal – and it is an ordeal – then he'll have made himself ready for you. So go to England. Don't worry. I'll look after him for you. Now give me a kiss."

Franz was alone, in the corner of the bar. She stood, unseen, and watched him. There was nobody else. Luke was a mirage, a false dream. Franz was wearing a white shirt. The sleeves were rolled up just above the elbows. He sat very still, his gaze fixed on the table, where there stood a glass of beer which he had not touched. There was a mirror behind him, and his shadowy hair was dark, the gold dulled. He showed no impatience and did not move his eyes. When they made love she was one with him, but now she was conscious of his otherness. Ivan Murison had held the boy Yusuf's arm as if he would draw him into himself. A fan whirred overhead.

She turned and, crossing the lobby, approached the desk. Could they book her on a flight to London? The next day? Yes, she had an open return ticket. She waited while they telephoned the airport. She looked into the bar, but Franz was now out of her line of vision. "Yes," the clerk said, "an afternoon flight, leaving at 16.30, would that be suitable?" "Yes," she said. "Thank you, it has to be afternoon because I must go to the hospital in the morning." When she gave her name, Czinner, the clerk stiffened. "Would you be Dr Czinner's daughter?" he asked. "We all admire him so greatly." He was wondering about what the newspapers called her doomed romance. "Thank you," she said.

In the flower shop to the right of the reception counter, she bought a single red rose. She entered the bar. The clerk was watching her back. She laid the rose in front of Franz.

"I'm sorry I'm late," she said, and sounded as if she was out of breath.

"There's one condition," she said later. "You've got to sleep with me tonight. I'll cancel my reservation if you say 'no'."

In the morning he waited for her outside the hospital.

"Will your father mind," she had said, "you not being there today?"

"Will he notice?" Franz said.

"I'm sure he'll notice."

She said goodbye to Eli.

"I'll be out in two weeks," he said. "I'll see the end of the trial. They've excused me cross-examination. It's not necessary. Saul Birnbaum admits that. He's a good lawyer. His aunt married a cousin of ours, a long time ago. No, they're not alive; they were among the slaughtered. Young Kestner isn't going with you, is he? Good. It wouldn't have worked, Becky."

"It will."

"Well, we'll see. I may be in London in the autumn. I've been asked to lecture. I've become a celebrity again, for the third time."

He didn't send any message to Nell.

"He's cut her out," she said to Franz. "Right out. Just like that. You won't cut me out, will you? Never?"

"Never."

She telephoned Rachel from the airport, to say thanks and goodbye.

"Minty wants a word."

"Is she there again?"

"I think maybe she'll move into your room. Here she is."

"Hi, kid, just remember what I said. Don't let them fuck you up. Remember, life's horizontal."

"Give my love to Luke, ask Rachel to give my love to Luke, and thanks again."

"I hate airports," Franz said. "They're so anonymous. Odd, isn't it, when there's nothing I would like more than to be just that."

"Will you be all right?"

"It's better this way," he said.

"When you see Luke, ask him about the boy Yusuf, he'll understand. Franz, I love you. Always."

"Always," he said, "for ever and ever, amen. We're going to be all right, remember that. Last night..."

"... was wonderful."

"Better than that. It ..."

"... sealed things."

"That's your flight being called. Oh Becky."

"Franz. We're lucky, in spite of everything."

They embraced. Then he held her face, a hand on each cheek, and kissed her again with lingering lips. He drew his index finger along the line of her jaw.

Beyond the barrier, at the corner of the stair, she turned and he was standing there, hands stretched towards her as if reaching for her on a distant shore.

The aeroplane lifted, pointing its nose to the heavens. The sea danced beneath them as they left Israel behind. She started to cry. The man in the next seat passed her a handkerchief.

"So, you have left your lover," he said. "That is always sad. But re-member, without parting there can be no beautiful reunion. Hey, think of that. Is that not a beautiful thought, beautifully expressed? You have a good cry, daughter. You don't mind that I call you 'daughter'? You are in love? Yes? That's good. Without love, life is *bubkes*. You know what that means, daughter?"

"No," she said. She dabbed her eyes and passed him back his handkerchief.

"It means a big nothing. That is what *bubkes* means. Yes, without love, life is a big nothing."

NINE

When the trial was over and his father had been sentenced to death and they were waiting for the appeal, Franz's way of life fell into a routine.

He rose early and walked up the hill to the Tomb of David from where he could gaze over Jerusalem. Then he had a cup of coffee and a bagel in a little bar, and returned to the hotel. He studied Hebrew for an hour, and then read philosophy. Sometimes he explored the city for an hour before lunch; some days he swam in the pool at the YMCA. He had got himself a visa that enabled him to pass beyond the Mandelbaum Gate into the Old City denied to Israelis. He read the newspapers over lunch: the *Jerusalem Post*, which was written in English, and the *Yediot Hayom* which, despite its Hebrew title, was a German-language daily, and usually a selection of the foreign press. He spent the first part of the afternoon in a café, studying the newspapers over glasses of mint tea. At four o'clock he went to the prison for his half-hour with his father. Though they knew him well and were friendly, he was still searched every day. Some of the guards made jokes about it.

"We don't forget Goering," one said.

"What do you mean?" Franz asked.

"The Reichsmarshall – poisoned himself, didn't he?"

But mostly the guards treated him very gently. He played chess with his father, and Rudi told him what he had been reading. He no longer spoke of the past, and he did not believe in his appeal: it was a device which would allow him to play so many more games of chess and work his way through Dostoyevsky's novels, which he had never read before. "We were stupid to despise the Russians," he said. "Dostoyevsky ... it is as if my own mind is revealed to me."

When he had kissed his father goodbye (getting a whiff of the aftershave lotion which was delivered to Rudi in tiny sachets every day), Franz went to the American Express office to collect his mail. Becky wrote to him every evening, but the post was irregular and some days there were no letters, others two or three. She always told him how she missed him and longed for him. She was taking a secretarial course with a view to getting a job in London. She and Nell were very short of money. Franz had no worries in that respect; his stepfather was making him a generous allowance. The General was pleased to have him out of Argentina, but he had no need to be anxious; it was unthinkable that Franz should return there. His stepfather told him that the murderers of the policeman, Lieutenant Vilar, had not been found. "It has been thought better to dismiss it as the consequence of his perversion."

The evenings were the worst time. Melancholy and loneliness hung over Jerusalem as daylight withdrew; the mountains closed in on the city.

There was Kinsky, but Eli was demanding and Kinsky was seldom free. Besides, he was diminished; he had no purpose there except to care for Eli, and that was a penance. With the loss of his independence, his old vivacity was dulled. He had dwindled into a sort of nursemaid and, conscious of what was happening to him, was querulous whenever they spent the evening together.

Sometimes Franz took the bus to Tel Aviv and had supper with Luke and Rachel. In the first weeks Minty Hubchik was there. Then she left, on another assignment, and after that Rachel was often bad-tempered; she drank her wine too quickly and sniped at Luke. When she talked of America now, it was in the past subjunctive, "If we had gone."

It was better when Luke came into Jerusalem and they had dinner in a little Viennese restaurant in Agrippas Street. Then they talked as they no longer could when Rachel was present. It saddened Franz that they couldn't talk that way when she was there. The trial, as she had feared, had bound Luke tighter to Israel. But they did not speak of the trial. They talked of literature and history and marriage and the philosophy Franz was reading. He had gone right back to Plato. "Don't think I see my father as Socrates waiting for death, however," he said.

"So we are all dreamers," Luke said. "No life is ever fulfilled. When I write a novel the book that is published is a shadow of the book that was there to be written."

"And love?" Franz said.

"Sure, the person we love is always someone we have made for ourselves."

One evening he took Franz to the café in Gehenna where Becky had met Ivan Murison. He felt responsibility for the boy Yusuf.

"After all, I denied him the Côte d'Azur, or wherever," he said. "Not the Cities of the Plain, I guess he'll find those wherever he is. But he's a nice kid. Besides, as Einstein said, the test of Israel is the manner in which we treat our Arabs."

"When you say 'our' Arabs, isn't that itself a sign that you regard them as inferior?"

"I wish it wasn't, but it is."

The boy Yusuf was resentful. Luke persisted. Perhaps he had chosen Yusuf as his own personal Arab; if he did well by him, then Israel could come to some form of accommodation with the Arabs in general. That wasn't absurd, or rather the principle behind it wasn't absurd. Everything begins at the personal level; as long as you keep things personal, individual, you can't fall into the abstractions which allow you to judge people by the label you have attached to them. The boy sat at the table with them, chewing melon-seeds. They drank beer. There was no one else in the dusty garden of the little café.

When Luke went for a pee, Yusuf spat out a melon-seed, and smiled for the first time.

"You like boys?" he said. "You like me? I do what you want."

He unzipped his jeans.

"Look," he said, "nice."

Franz shook his head.

"OK. Is all right. You give me a cigarette."

"Sure."

"My friend Ivan tells me about your father. Good man, OK. He has right idea about bloody Jews. Yes, sure has. I think they hang him, yes?"

"Yes."

All the same he found himself returning there, two or three evenings a week. He sat in the warm twilight and watched the moon rise over the mountains of Judah. Sometimes he talked with other Arab boys, Yusuf's friends. They all spoke English of a sort. They made him think of Argentina: they spoke of great things which they would do, tomorrow, if only … and they spread their hands. They quarrelled with each other and went home arm in arm. They sipped Coca-Cola and cursed the United States. Sometimes one of them would have a car, not his, or only for the night, and half a dozen would pile into it, and roar into the darkness. The air of that unfinished improvised place hummed with the murmur of their discontent, as they spat melon-seeds at chickens and claimed hits.

265

One evening he arrived to find Yusuf with a bruised eye and swollen lips.

"Bloody Jews beat me up. Go home, fucking Arab queer. Is my home, I say. So they beat me up. Bloody Jews."

He grinned and touched his lower lip with his tongue.

"Bloody sore. So I'm queer, I say. Should be OK for you, I don't make no Arab babies, yes? So they beat me up. Crazy."

Franz had resumed his journal:

> I'm tempted to introduce Yusuf to Kinsky. Mightn't it be the answer for both? And I wonder if Luke was right to drive Ivan Murison away. Mightn't it have been better for Yusuf to have gone with him? What future is there for him here?
>
> Hatred is felt as liberation. When you hate, everything is permitted to you, and you become an avenging God. It doesn't matter what the object of your hatred is: Jews, Arabs, queers, women, the poor, the rich, blacks. As soon as you admit your hatred you are filled with what I think must be exultation. The object of your hatred becomes automatically your inferior, your enemy, your prey.
>
> I should have known this in Argentina, but I've had to come here, and listen to my father speaking as he would never have spoken if he had not been brought here, to endure his trial, to understand this.
>
> But something more horrible: when Yusuf described what had happened to him, he frightened me. It was like my dream of Bastini.
>
> And then I saw that this liberation is entirely illusory. It's a cheat. When you surrender yourself to it, you do not become free, for how can a prisoner be that?
>
> I tried to write some of this to Becky, but I couldn't. I love her, I need her, I cannot imagine life without her, and yet I can't speak to her about things that matter. And something else: the more I know my need for her, the more I want to escape. Ivan Murison recognised this, I think Luke suspects it. I even found myself wondering if Luke took me to the café in the hope that I would, or as an experiment? Because the thing is, as he confessed to me, or almost confessed, he too is in a

different way in love with Becky. But he also loves Rachel, who adores him and is yet going away from him.

So love itself is a prison. And in a curious way it's quite separate from sexual desire, which presents itself as not only a temptation, but also as a means of evading the responsibility of love. The contemporary dream: sexual fulfilment without emotional attachment. Which is crazy, because there isn't fulfilment, ever, without feeling for something more than the shape of a body, the touch of skin, the pressure of lips. But I know the temptation: Alexis, and now.

I'm a little drunk. When I got back to my room I opened a bottle of whisky and it's sinking ... like ... like ... I'm lost.

My stepfather once said to me: "Remember, in Argentina everything is very simple and the simplest things are impossible."

Love is very simple and ...

Another drink.

I went to the café today from Saul's office. He called me to give me news of the appeal which has been rejected. He will tell my father tomorrow morning.

So they have set a date.

And I write this stuff about sex.

I went to a church this morning. I entered the confessional. When the priest spoke, I found that words had deserted me. I stepped out of the box and knelt and tried to pray. Then I felt a hand on my shoulder. It was the priest.

He said, "If you can't confess, my son, perhaps you would like to talk."

It crossed my mind that I was trying to talk to God, but ... I think I dialled the wrong number.

The priest knew who I was. That frightened me. I had thought I would be anonymous there. So I told him I was afraid, and then I asked him if he would be prepared to go to speak to my father.

"He nearly became a priest himself," I said.

"Oh yes, I guessed that," he said.

TEN

My dear Franz, my dear child, my son:

It was good of you to send that priest to me; but also foolish. We talked, we argued. In the end he denied me. He could not believe my protestations.

And do I believe them myself? I wish I knew.

Is it because I believed too much that I believe too little now? Or is it that even my former, and so impassioned belief, was an act of self-deception, in which I assumed conviction to persuade myself that I was capable of such attachment?

So: this will be the last letter I write to you, the last letter I write, and we shall not see each other again. Tomorrow, at 8.30, I shall be no more. Curious to have been provided with this certainty.

I am grateful to you, and I am grateful also to have been granted this opportunity which, had things gone otherwise, would not have come to me, of knowing you truly, and of achieving a closeness denied to me in any other relation. It has been good also, my son, to have had the reassurance of your devotion.

And so, by the time you read this, I am dead. But these are not yet the words of a dead man.

It is a moment when I should sum up my life, as I failed to do in that trial, which nevertheless was not the parody of a trial I once feared.

But what can I add to the hours of talk we have had?

Only this: that I repeat my wish that I should have been granted a conversation with Professor Czinner.

You remember his testimony, which I did not question. It was impressive, I think, but it was also misleading.

There was one error, or an error of implication. It was not my fault that the Jews whose release we negotiated did not escape. Matters were taken out of my hands. I always regretted that, for I have ever tried to be a man of my word. As for his complaint that the money he had paid was not returned, that is only in a sense true. In fact, I arranged for a credit to be transmitted to the Jewish Agency in Zurich. What happened sub-sequently to that money, I do not know, but the responsibility for its disappearance rests with the Jewish Agency, not with me.

Czinner chose his words carefully. Let me remind you of what he said. "I met him once only, before the war," and "that was our only meeting in Germany." A supreme example of *suggestio falsi*. His intention was to suggest that the occasion when I advised him to leave Germany was our only encounter.

But we did meet again, in Poland, in the autumn of 1944. Czinner, having failed to make use of the great latitude which had been extended towards him, on account of his previous services to the Reich, was by then in Auschwitz. I discovered this, and, on the occasion of a routine visit to the camp, asked him to be brought before me. I dismissed my attendants and we talked in private.

Naturally I cannot repeat the whole substance of our talk, but I re-member he asked me if I understood the full evil of what we were doing. And I answered him, as he must have expected, with Nietzsche. "Do you not remember," I said, "that 'evil is man's best strength ... Man must become better and more evil ... The greatest evil is necessary for the su-perior man's best ... I rejoice over great sins as my great consolation.' "

Czinner was silent for a moment. He was in good physical condition, but he grew pale at my words, and I rejoiced, for I knew that I had spo-ken what in his own heart he believed.

"Yes," he said at last, "is there nothing you would not betray?"

"Dr Czinner," I replied, "there is nothing either of us would refuse to betray if it seemed necessary."

"One cannot betray oneself," he said.

"That exception was understood," I said. "It is why you are where you are, and why I am here before you today. Why do we pretend that we are free agents? Necessity is the law of life. The expression 'crime' comes from a world that has been superseded. There are only positive and negative acts... You would not hesitate, Dr Czinner, to advocate the closure of a factory in the name of economic necessity, though hundreds were thrown into misery as a result... What else am I doing?"

Franz, I told you Czinner would understand me. He has always under-stood me. He looked at me as I said this with a profound respect. I knew then that like me he had always striven for a higher goal, and would permit nothing small or tender or scrupulous to defeat him. The goal of life is self-realisation: to find out and perform the utmost of which we are capable.

When Czinner informed on me, he broke a thousand small things on behalf of a greater.

Be strong, Franz.

It is ironic to reflect that it was my succumbing to my affection for you, my wish to do what seemed most desirable to you, that has brought me here. I am not suggesting you are culpable. The fault was in me, as Czinner would tell you.

And yet I cannot regret that fault, that betrayal, in the name of affection, of my constant purpose in life.

It is only by deeds that a man defines himself; words lead him into a maze of uncertainty.

Franz: I have no more to say. You will please express my thanks to Dr Birnbaum. Your mother will not wish to receive a message from me. For her, I died long ago.

As for you, if you choose to marry Fräulein Czinner, whom I thought a charming girl, you do so with my best and warmest wishes. Yet you will have to overcome terrible obstacles.

You should continue to call yourself Schmidt, though pride and natural affection might prompt you to resume the name of Kestner.

All my actions were justified by the law of the SS which commanded us to spare neither our own nor the blood of others if the life of the nation demands it. Nevertheless it is too late, and also absurd now, to die with the words "Heil Hitler" on my lips. If you wish to give a statement to the press you may say that I admire the development of Israel as a National Socialist state.

It seems absurd to die like this, but then life has often seemed absurd to me. Only recognition of necessity keeps absurdity at bay.

And so I say "Farewell"; may you be more fortunate than your loving father.

PART THREE

AFTERWARDS

ONE

Becky was for a long time a name on Christmas cards, and then, the cards stopped, or I couldn't be bothered to look at them. I forgot about her. Then she was a girl standing beside an old-fashioned bicycle with a basket in front of the handlebars, and the basket full of red and yellow roses. That was outside my stepmother's cottage, and she was wearing denim shorts and a cream-coloured cotton jersey. She was warm from bicycling, her face dewy, and she smiled and said, "You must be Gareth." I was just back from Vienna, and she looked so English.

I was twenty-five and training to be a historian. My subject was the Rosicrucians, with particular reference to the influence of Rosicrucian ideas on the court of the Hapsburg Emperor Rudolf II. It is not a subject of general interest, but it had kept me occupied in Vienna, with trips to Prague for two years, with time off for beer drinking and Austrian girls who were as emotionally undemanding as I found them willing.

My mother (who was Welsh and had landed me with my Christian name, not that it matters) was killed by a flying-bomb in 1944. My father, a regular Army officer, but nevertheless only a major at the end of the war, then married Sheila Macmaster, who is the cousin of Becky's mother Nell. Then Dad went off his head, after they had produced two children. He was shunted into a bin with no prospect of recovery. So I couldn't blame Sheila when she took a lover, an Australian painter called Doug. They had two more children – Sheila liked breeding. I always got on well with her, but this explains why my home life was fairly non-existent, though I still used her place when I was in the UK. But we didn't correspond, bar the odd postcard. I just dropped in and kipped when I felt like it, if there was an unoccupied bed, which wasn't always. I had an income from a farm on the Welsh Border, which used to be my granddad's, and which was let to an uncle.

So I didn't click when Becky told me her name, having forgotten the Christmas cards. But looking at her cheered me up. She was a nice change from my Viennese girls who mostly ran to fat and smelled of onions or chocolate. Straightaway I found myself considering questions of time and geography – the eternal when and where of seduction – especially after Sheila told me that on account of other people having got in first I would have to doss down on the sofa in the living room which converts into a bed. Though I would have had no objection to that as a location, I didn't expect this girl to share my broadmindedness. It would have to be outdoors first, I thought. There was a spot near the river I had found convenient in the past.

It's not exaggerating to say that that first evening I thought about little but how to get Becky into bed with me. I stress this because nothing in the previous manuscript can have conveyed to you just how sexy she was.

I never find descriptions of girls much good, and in the detective novels by which I make my living nowadays, I usually leave them out, though I've known my editor insert them, perhaps for her own pleasure. So what can I say of the way Becky looked? She had long legs, and I can't tell you how many girls I have fancied seeing them seated and then gone off because they stood up and revealed their legs were short. There was a touch of rust in her hair, her eyes were grey and her mouth what is called generous. Her face was not quite symmetrical, and as she sat sideways to me at the supper-table, showing her left profile, her nose was on the short side as if the tip had been broken off. Her breasts were small. In the half-light, sideways on, she looked like a boy, but I didn't find that a turn-off, though I've never seen the point of boys myself, unlike many of my friends at King's. It did occur to me though that she was the sort of girl queers might fancy. So do I, however, I said to myself. She hardly spoke that evening, and I didn't mind that either. I've never been able to stand chattering girls. It's not often anyway that a woman says anything worth listening to. They've better uses for their tongues than talking, as an Austrian friend of mine, a barman, once said.

One thing did puzzle me. Doug, whose attitude to women is that they're fuckable and paintable objects, treated her with a gentleness I'd never seen in him before, or since, come to that. But I don't mind being puzzled.

The mystery was revealed the next morning when Sheila took me aside, which was never easy in that house.

"You know this Kestner trial," she said.

"Well, I haven't been following it. These things bore me." Which was true, incidentally. I generally speak the truth, except in certain matters.

"But you know who Kestner is?"

"I'm not actually buried in the sixteenth century. Sheila. It's just that I find it more interesting."

"Weird. Anyway, the point is that Becky is engaged to Kestner's son. They're in love."

"That's usual, I understand, when there's the question of an engagement," I said, doing my impersonation of Max Freyer, who used to be my tutor at King's.

"So, hands off, Gareth."

"For Christ's sake, Sheila," I said.

"I'm serious. There's something else you should know." And then she told me about Czinner and how he had been responsible for Kestner's arrest.

"It strikes me," I said, "that it would have been simpler for everyone if he had hired a gun to shoot the bastard. That shouldn't have been too difficult in South America."

"Well, that's how it is," she said.

"So, what happens now?"

"Well, Nell, as I say, has left Eli, and Becky is waiting for Franz."

"You mean she's waiting till they hang his dad?"

"Yes."

"Christ," I said, "I have led a sheltered life."

"Yes, you have. So, remember, hands off."

"Sheila told me all about you," I said.

It had taken me two days to get her by herself, but here we were down by the river as I'd planned. The scene was a sort of cliché South of England landscape: meadow-grass, willows, elms. It was a hot day and she was lying there on her side with her chin in her hand, and her elbow arching her body at an angle that made the striped cotton jersey she was wearing ride up to expose a few inches of flesh above her jeans.

"I thought she might have," she said.

I stretched over and laid my hand on her crotch which, on account of her small breasts, I thought might be her surest erogenous zone.

"You've had it tough," I said.

"Oh I don't know," she said, and removed my hand. She nibbled a grass stem.

"You must be gone on this Franz," I said.

"It hurts waiting."

"Well, we'll have to see what we can do about that, won't we?"

So, two days later, I drove her over to Cambridge, which was about an hour's drive from Sheila's cottage. I showed her round the colleges, not forgetting to point out E. M. Forster as he doddered across the lawn in a dirty mackintosh. She hadn't heard of him, which was a point in her favour. Another point. She said the right things, which were blessedly few. She looked very decorative lying back in the punt as I poled her up to Grantchester. She trailed her fingers in the water as girls nearly always do, but when I moored under some willows, she sat up and said, "No."

Instead she asked me why I was a historian. "Are you really going to be a don?"

"I expect so."

"You don't strike me as …"

"If you mean that I'm not a eunuch, I take that as a compliment. But not all dons are eunuchs."

"No," she said, "it wasn't that. It's just that I can't understand someone like you burying himself in the past."

This sounded more hopeful, so I set out my philosophy of life at some length. We were having supper in the Bath Hotel by now and eating mixed grills and drinking pints of Pimm's No. 3.

"Now it's your turn," I said. "Tell me about yourself. How you've got into this mess."

She shook her head.

"I'm at a disadvantage," I said. "I've never been in love."

"Maybe you're lucky."

Two brush-offs would usually be enough to make me say, oh hell, plenty of other fish in the sea. I had no desire to be entangled with a girl, and I was pretty sure that any girl who played hard to get was the entangling type. But I felt different this time. My curiosity was aroused. I even drove back into Cambridge the next day and read up the account of the Kestner trial in back numbers of *The Times*. I've a strong enough stomach but it sickened me. Not being interested in the Nazis, I hadn't then come across Hannah Arendt's phrase "the banality of evil", but I came to the same conclusion, though I'd have put it less pretentiously. It disgusted me that none of them ever seemed to have asked himself any questions about why he was doing this. Actually, I mean, that Kestner hadn't. He talked as if organising the arrest, transportation and extermination of millions of people was a perfectly natural activity. If you go back to the sixteenth century, I thought, at least the Inquisition believed they were saving heretics' souls and, more important, saving other people from the contamination of heresy. They may have been crazy (I think they were) but you could see there was some purpose to it, even by their standards a sublime purpose. But Kestner had no such justification. It was extraordinary that he had never felt the need of one.

I had arranged to collect Becky's mother at the station, she having been up in London for a job interview, which we didn't talk about beyond her saying that things could have been worse.

"It's not bad to be in England," she said, as we drove through the early evening, with the wheat turning yellow. "I always missed the countryside."

That seemed to me a cue to stop at the next village pub. There were tables outside and roses climbing up the wall. A couple of Jaguars in the car park. Nell said she would have a half of bitter.

"People talk of German beer. Give me good old English bitter," I said, coming back with a pint for myself as well as her half. "I've been reading the Kestner trial," I said. "You met him, didn't you? What was he like?"

"I've no idea."

"What do you mean?"

"I mean that the man I met was civil, even friendly, a little nervous, but I've still no idea what Kestner was like."

"You're not suggesting some sort of mistaken identity."

"Good God, no. No, what I'm suggesting, I suppose, is that the whole idea of identity is more fragile than we usually think. That doesn't make much sense, does it? But how well do we know anyone? How well do we know ourselves?"

"Becky seems to think she knows the young Kestner."

"He's a nice boy. I wasn't sure at first, but I got to like him more and more. That's why I can't forgive my husband. You read his evidence? It wasn't necessary, he could have left it to others."

"Sheila says you knew Germany before the war."

"That's right. I loved it. I still do. Despite everything. But I was back there with UNRRA during the Occupation, in '45–6. I saw hundreds of the survivors. Well, Eli was one of them. None of it made sense."

She smiled at me over the rim of her tankard.

"I bet you've had lots of Austrian girls."

"I haven't done badly."

"Do you ever ask them what their fathers did?"

TWO

I never got Becky into bed that year. It even became a joke between us, my attempts, that is. I was back in Vienna when the news of Kestner's execution came through and I remember wondering whether she and Franz would really get together and make a go of it. I've never been much of a correspondent, and so I didn't hear that he had arrived in England. Then I got an invitation to their wedding. Becky had pinned a postcard to it. It showed Humphrey Bogart, Ingrid Bergman and Paul Henreid standing outside Rick's Café Americain; "As time goes by," she'd scribbled. I puzzled over that message a long time. I wasn't sure if it meant that she wanted me to accept her invitation, as she hadn't accepted my numerous ones. It's always disturbing when you don't see the joke.

I didn't go of course. A couple of weeks after the date of the wedding, I got a parcel containing a little box with some wedding-cake in it. It hadn't occurred to me that people still sent out wedding-cake.

Then she sent me a postcard from Switzerland where they were on honeymoon. "Having a wonderful time. Wish you were here."

I began to wonder if she was already regretting it, but concluded this was probably another joke. I wrote on a card: "Sure I remember. You wore blue. The Germans wore grey," but I had no address to send it to.

Then I heard nothing of them for two years.

The marriage started out OK. There must have been a risk it wouldn't, even without the special circumstances in which they found themselves. They had been separated for some time.

They had both invested enormous emotional capital in the thing. That it happened at all testified to the strength of their love. It wouldn't have been surprising if cookies had crumbled from the start. But as I say, I don't think they did.

They settled in London. Franz still had an allowance from his step-father. He joked about being a remittance man. He abandoned his engineering studies. I don't know what he worked at for the first few months, but I think he had a succession of odd jobs. He must have had some difficulty with his papers. Even in the easy-going Sixties I think he would have found it hard to get a work permit. Becky was all right of course with her British passport.

But London was easy living then. Franz began to write, worked on the fringe of the film world. Becky did some modelling, but she wasn't the baby girl beloved of the Sixties, and had no great success. Still, either through modelling or through some connection of Franz's, she was offered a part in a film. She couldn't act, and she moved awkwardly: on the stage she would merely have been inept. But the movie camera liked her. They made out.

Eli came to London a couple of times, delivering celebrity lectures at the London School of Economics. When he came, Becky had lunch with him and attended his lectures. But that was all. He had no contact with Nell, who was working, as she had predicted, as a matron in a boys' preparatory school in Hertfordshire. Then, sometime in 1967, Eli had another heart attack, on an El Al flight from Tel Aviv to New York. It was just before the Six Day War. The obituary I read made no mention, or only glancing mention, of his part in the Kestner case. That surprised me.

I had completed my thesis and taught for a year at the University of Madison, Wisconsin, an experience which completed my disillusion with academic life. It being all I knew, however, I stuck to it for a bit, getting a job at Queen Mary College, London.

It would be wrong to suggest I had been carrying a torch for Becky those two or three years. I'm not that sort of guy. My sex life had been perfectly satisfactory in the interim. There was a girl claiming Red Indian blood at Madison, but she's nothing to do with the story, and I merely mention her to confirm that I wasn't pining for Becky.

All the same I thought of her now and then, and when I got back to London seeing her again was one of the bonuses I promised myself.

It was still some months before I rang her up.

"Gareth," she said. There was a note of exaggeration in her voice, a sort of floating tremble, and I wondered if she was drunk. "We're having a party on Saturday night. Why don't you come? It'll be fun to see you again."

"We're living in Brook Green," she said. "It's the outer limit of anywhere. Or so they say."

The music was party-loud and pop. I didn't recognise it, but it wasn't right for them. I was sure of that, though all I knew of Franz was what Becky and Nell had told me. I pushed my way through long hair falling over Indian cotton shoulders; joss sticks smoked in empty bottles. It was a film director's idea of a down-market Bohemian party. I had been there five minutes or more before I located Becky. She was dancing opposite a small slim young man with curling black ringlets and a lemur's face. She wore a cream-coloured tunic that rested on her buttocks over very short pink shorts. They gyrated for some time and then the lemur took her by the elbow and led her over to a table where there were bottles and glasses. I advanced and joined them there.

"Gareth," her voice floated, and this time she was drunk. But it was a nice drunk, wopsy drunk, and she put her arms round my neck and kissed me on the lips.

"Charlie," she said to the lemur, "this is terribly terribly imp. Gareth's my dearest cousin and we haven't seen each other for years and years and years. Mind if we …"

She put her arm round me and was about to lead me away when she stopped and said, "But you haven't a drink, darling. No, don't drink that. We'll go through to the kitchen and find some lovely Scotch."

I didn't meet Franz at that party. I saw him, several times. He looked older than I expected and he had lost the pretty boy look of the photographs I had been shown. He was moving as if he didn't belong there. From time to time he danced, with different girls, scarcely moving and no expression on his face. I wondered if he was stoned.

"Franz stoned? You must be joking. He's bored, that's all. He thinks this sort of party's terribly terribly un-him. But it's me. I think it's fab. Don't you think it's fab, Gareth darling?"

She was trying awfully hard, I thought.

Later, when we had drunk a lot of whisky, she said, "Let's get out, let's slip away."

"It's your party," I said.

"I always slip away from my own parties. It's the only thing to make them tolerable."

We went to a Chinese restaurant, but it was closed. In the taxi she threw herself into my arms, and kissed me and didn't stop kissing me. Then she cried. When we got to my apartment, she fell through the doorway. I picked her up and put her in my bed. I ran my hand the length of her long beautiful legs and laid a quilt over her, and slept on the sofa. It took me a long time to get to sleep, and the light was creeping grey through the gap in the curtain before I did so. There was no sound from the bedroom. I had left the door ajar in case there was.

She sat up in bed with the quilt pulled round her and the mug of black coffee laced with brandy held in both hands. She pushed her lips out to it, and looked about fifteen.

"Why me?" I said.

"I passed out," she said. "Tiresome for you."

"It was OK. Why me?"

"You looked so out of place at my party, Gareth."

"Are you saying you felt sorry for me?"

"No, for myself, I guess. Silly, isn't it?"

She took to coming to my flat once, sometimes twice, a week. She came in the late afternoon when she had finished filming. The first two occasions we didn't make love, though that was why she had come. I like sex on my own terms and I was afraid of being used, though I have never liked to use the word "afraid' in connection with myself. Instead we talked: about her childhood, about her father's strangeness – "He was pleased, you know, to be blind; it put him at an advantage. Of course he hated it also, but one part of him, an important part, was pleased. I never trusted him. He liked to humiliate me." We talked about Nell and about my time in the United States. "The two girls I've liked most were North Americans," she said, "but maybe I saw them differently." We didn't talk about Franz. Once she started and stopped and said could we go out to the pub.

I thought after that second visit that she might not come again, but the next time she said, in the middle of a conversation about Vienna, "Will you make love to me?"

Then in bed, she said, "We still make love, you know, and it's wonderful."

"Thanks," I said, "Thanks a bunch."

But she came back, and now because I knew that for the moment at least she was what I wanted, I accepted her unspoken terms. There's a coarse side to me which has never shrunk from discussing my sex life, but I find I can't write about making love to Becky then. She sought reassurance through passion. That's all I can say about it. She wasn't a happy lover. "Make love, not war," they printed on T-shirts then, as if they were always alternatives.

One day she asked me what I thought about what was happening in Paris. I told her I didn't know what was happening in Paris. The news bored me. It was the students, she said, they were rising up against de Gaulle. It was a revolution. "Not another," I said, "haven't they learned? What do they want this time?"

"Franz has gone," she said. "To join them. I've never seen him so excited. Do you mind if we turn the telly on?"

"He must be mad," I said.

It was on his return from Paris that I met him at last. Becky asked me to come round.

"Is that a good idea?"

"Yes."

He was sitting in the kitchen in a denim suit. He was reading a pamphlet and held a biro in his hand with which to mark passages. He finished underlining something, and leaped up.

"It's ridiculous we haven't met."

He emphasised the "ridiculous". He began, almost straightaway, to ask me about my students. Were they politically active? A few were, I said; most were sensible chaps and girls who wanted a degree and saw it as a necessary step towards a good job and the semi in Kingston-upon-Thames, I added. Then he talked of the French students he had met: their wonderful vitality, their generosity and unselfishness, their commitment to a better world. He was overwhelmed by the manner in which they had received him into their ranks. Did they know who you were? I refrained from asking. He had had long discussions with Rudi Dutschke himself. It had been an enlightenment. He realised how his own time at University had amounted to nothing, just nothing. He had been politically unaware. He didn't even know that the fault line lay between generations. Though it was of course possible to cross it; it had been extraordinary when Sartre had spoken out for the students, most of whom – he had to confess – hadn't read a word the great man had written. But that didn't matter. He was a name.

He went on in this manner a long time. His English was very natural sounding; only the occasional intonation, the excessive weight accorded to particular words, suggested his foreign upbringing.

He said, "I was brought up in a society erected on a basis of injustice, and it never occurred to me."

He was very lean, the skin was stretched tight on his cheekbones, and he moved his hands a lot as he talked. Then he gave a sudden smile, and I saw his charm: "But I'm monopolising the conversation. I'm sorry. It's just that I've never felt anything like this before. This exhilaration."

Becky cooked fettucine, which we ate with butter and garlic, and we drank a litre of red wine. Franz relaxed. Every now and then, however, he reverted to the subject of Paris.

"I wish you'd been there," he said, "both of you. It was a liberation. It liberated the spirit."

"It failed, didn't it?" I said.

"No," he said, "it didn't fail. Objectively it was a triumph. We achieved a breakthrough, a fundamental reorientation of feeling. We brought a new world into being. Things will never be the same again."

Later he walked with me to the Tube station. At the corner of the street he took hold of my arm.

"Don't feel embarrassed with me because you have been sleeping with Becky," he said. "Besides, I don't have the Argentinian cult of honour. That's quite out of date."

"I didn't realise you knew," I said.

"Oh yes," he said. "I understand Becky very well, you know. It's because I love her. And so I realise that at the moment you can give her something that I can't. She needs you. Don't think I'm not jealous. Of course I am. I would like to be able to be everything to her, but, since I'm not, well then. She's very fond of you, you know, and she admires you. She admires what she calls your very English common sense. So it's true that you can give her something I can't. And since I love her, I accept that."

But what I gave her was a child. It was deliberate on her part. She stopped taking the pill without telling me or (I think) Franz. Either of us could have been the father. We took no blood tests to determine paternity, but Becky was sure it was me. The baby was called Jessica, Hebrew apparently for "Yahweh is watching". That was Becky's decision and explanation.

"It's a sort of talisman," she said. "I think that's what a name should be. Do you know what Rebecca means? 'Noose'. Perhaps that's what I am, what I will be to Franz."

"That's silly. I didn't know you felt so Jewish."

"Nor did I, till I was feeding her. Then I came all over Jewish momma."

Jewishness is inherited through the female line, and Nell of course wasn't Jewish. So there was a break in the line. But the choice of name disturbed nobody. Not many people think of Jessica as a Jewish name, despite *The Merchant of Venice*. Franz adored her. He would sit for a long time by her carry-cot letting her twist her tiny fingers round his. She was a bond between the three of us.

Then it was the year of Vietnam. Franz denounced American policy. He took part in the famous Grosvenor Square demonstration, and had his head broken by a police truncheon. He was lucky not to be arrested that time. He was now writing regularly for the left-wing press and various underground magazines. When you called at the flat in Brook Green, it was often infested by long-haired chaps in beards and jeans, of great intensity and no humour. Franz listened to them, agreed with them, was one with them, yet remained detached, uninfected. It wasn't that he was playing a part. His sincerity was not in question. It was rather that he moved through life as if it didn't belong to him, as if he was enacting a dream. I liked this. However fierce his opinions might be, he was the gentlest person I had known.

Becky was drinking less. Indeed for six months after Jessica's birth she was on the wagon. She often went down to Nell's cottage in Hertfordshire, especially during the school holidays. I sometimes went with her. We were given separate bedrooms. I believed Nell thought we were just good friends, without irony, though Nell had the habit of irony.

It was a good time, and a strange one. There was no strain between us. *Ménage-à-trois* living suited. Maybe all women need two men, for different sides of their nature.

Becky shook her head.

"Makes you both sound inadequate," she said. "Or me some kind of queen bee, sacred figure. Which is not so."

We went on holiday together, to a fishing village on the south coast of Ireland, where a friend had lent me a cottage. It was soft and damp. We lived on mackerel which we caught ourselves, and crabs and lobsters which the local fishermen delivered to our door. We went for walks along the shore, with Jessica slung in a backpack. We took turns in carrying her. She spoke her first words there, I think; none of them was "Dadda". She would grow up calling Franz and me by our names.

In the evening Becky sent us along to the pub, which was part of the village store, while she prepared supper. She liked doing that, getting rid of us for a bit. Was she preparing for the role of put-upon woman?

We drank Murphy's stout, never more than a couple of pints each. I talked against politics. I told Franz they were crazy, that people became political activists only to conceal from themselves the deficiencies in their characters. He gave me his sweet smile.

"Maybe, often. Not true of Barbara."

Barbara was a young actress from a famous theatrical family. She belonged to some revolutionary splinter group and loved to make speeches in drab meeting halls and in public places. She looked marvellous on a soap box. Franz had got to know her the winter before, and thought her wonderful. He could laugh at her, but he still thought her wonderful.

"Oh well," I said, "life's an extension of theatre for her. She's just a girl who finds Shaw's parts too small and meanly written."

"No," he said, "she's sincere."

"Actors are always sincere, but good ones can move a cigarette box that's out of place on a table, even during the most impassioned scene. You can't take Barbara seriously."

"I'm not in love with her," he said, "but …"

But …

"It's not expiation on your part, is it?" I said.

"You mean my father? No," he said, "that's over."

"You told me once he found 'meaning' in political involvement."

"On the wrong side."

"Does the side matter?" I said.

"You've read the account of the trial. You remember what Becky's father was like, how he thought he could do deals, could bargain with the rottenness that had enslaved my father. He hid for years from the impossibility of his behaviour. I admired him only when he betrayed my father. Do you understand that?"

"No," I said.

I ran my finger round the inside of my thin, straight-sided glass. It came up covered with foam. I held it up to Franz.

"I find reality and meaning in this," I said. "And in the lobster that Becky is cooking for us."

I licked the creamy foam from my finger.

"No," he said, "it's not true that the senses are the best guide to action. Did you meet my friend Charlie?"

The lemur?"

"That's right. I knew him at school. He was the most improbable member of a military academy. Carlo Bastini. He was a nice boy …" He paused and looked across the little smoky room, gazing beyond the fishermen in their high-necked sweaters and big sea-boots, who sat over their pints. "He's queer, you know. He was the boyfriend of that journalist Ivan Murison, you know who I mean. Ivan was killed last year. In Tangier, by a boy he'd picked up, who robbed him. Or so they thought, the boy wasn't ever identified. Charlie was excited by it. He says he's still in love with me, but he isn't. He just likes the idea, the same way he likes pretty clothes. Charlie's on drugs now, and he goes in for what they call rough trade. I don't think he'll last long."

"So what?" I said. "What does that prove?"

"Only," he said, "that I could have gone that way. Maybe Becky saved me, but I'm not enough to make her happy. The point is, Barbara could never make that sort of mistake. She'll never suffer from lack of commitment. That's why I admire her."

You poor dear confused sod, I thought.

Franz was arrested at a demonstration. It was featured on the television news, which showed him being dragged, limp, by four policemen to a van. He looked like a Saint Sebastian painted by a High Renaissance artist in love with his model. I went to see him in the Scrubs two days later. It had been difficult to get access. Becky was pregnant again, and refused to come. She said it would upset the baby.

The left side of Franz's face was bruised and pulpy. His eye was closed and his mouth swollen and discoloured. It hurt him to speak.

"That didn't happen when you were arrested?" I said. He shook his head.

"You're lucky," I said. "The TV cameras caught the moment of your arrest. They can't have realised there's a record. That ought to be photographed."

"They won't allow it."

"They'll bloody well have to. This isn't Nazi Germany," I said. "I'll speak to your lawyer. Is he any good?"

"It's a her. Barbara fixed it for me."

"Christ," I said, "that's a disaster."

"No," he said. "She's too clever for that. The lawyer's straight down the middle, Cambridge and a Member of Parliament's daughter. Sorry if I'm indistinct. I've lost a couple of teeth. Is Becky all right?"

"Well," Becky said, "he's always wanted to be a martyr. You don't know that side of him, Gareth."

There was talk of deportation.

"I can't stand Argentina," he said. "I'll get on the first plane back to Europe."

"Where to?"

He made a gesture of spinning a globe and stabbed his finger in the air. "Rome," he said. "We once talked of living in Italy."

Becky miscarried. It sounds corny. But that's what happened. When I called on her in the hospital, she turned her face away from me and wept. I watched her body shake with sobs and slipped my hand between the sheets, and pressed her thigh, which was warm and damp.

I walked across the park. Everywhere, that pale October afternoon, there were women with prams and push-chairs. I bought a hot dog from a stall to feed to the ducks. The black-veined leaves of plane trees floated like dead faces in the water. I passed a boy kissing a girl who lay on her back on the wet grass. She hugged him, bent her knee, and the action threw her skirt back, exposing the creamy flesh of her thigh. The siren of a police car howled behind Knightsbridge barracks. An old man passed me, muttering to himself, jerking a string to which a scruffy terrier was attached. I swung left into Shepherd Market and stood for twenty minutes outside the Grapes until opening time.

Barbara's lawyer was good, too good perhaps for Barbara's interests. The charges against Franz were dropped. Then Barbara and the lawyer both urged him to bring an action against the police, or perhaps the warders in the Scrubs, whichever (and I forget now) had been responsible for beating him up. He was eager at first. There were conferences where, I imagine, the pigs were denounced. Then Becky was released from hospital. Her doctor first summoned Franz who asked me to accompany him. The doctor explained that he was reluctant to discharge her. He was worried by her frame of mind. She might even be suicidal. But he needed the bed, and besides, you couldn't keep people in hospital – did we understand? – merely because you suspected that they might do themselves some damage.

So we took Becky back to Brook Green in a taxi, and she sat, white-faced in the kitchen, and drank tea and didn't speak. It wasn't that she refused to speak. She answered questions in a manner that was polite, uninterested and remote, as if they didn't concern her. She sipped tea, and nodded when you spoke to her, and asked her if she was OK; but she vouchsafed nothing. Jessica was in Hertfordshire with Nell, and Becky didn't enquire how she was. Then she said she was tired and would go to bed, and left Franz and me in the kitchen. She left us wondering if it was safe for her to be on her own in the bedroom.

"She hasn't any pills, has she?"

"I don't think so. I don't know."

"All right," I said. "Don't you see, Franz, how unimportant your concerns and Barbara's are, compared to this?"

"Maybe it's part of the same thing. It is to me," he said. "You don't need to knock Barbara. Becky has no cause to be jealous of Barbara."

"Hasn't she?"

"No. Not like that. Barbara's on a different plane."

Perhaps she was; but it was one where Franz aspired to join her. She dazzled him, as she dazzled so many, but it was not, I think, the glamour which attracted him. It was her complete certainty, her self-surrender to a cause which, however mad it seemed to me, presented itself to Franz as a justification, an escape from the torment of the responsibilities he had accepted. I say "self-surrender" even though I also saw her behaviour as evidence of the most monstrous egoism. Contrary to what many think, the two coexist happily. Franz longed to lose himself in her magnetic field, and hoped thereby to find himself.

Becky was different. There was nothing glorious in what she demanded of him. That made it all the harder. Her demands had really by this time come to appear to him acts of selfishness. She was impatient when he denounced the rottenness of society and all social arrangements; she would have liked him to be more efficient at finding a taxi when she wanted one.

So for the next months there was friction. It never became more than that. Each shrank from open argument which might turn bitter. Aware of what she wanted, he allowed himself to be persuaded to drop the proposed action against the warders (I am almost sure it was the prison staff, not the police, who were responsible for his condition). Then he resented the silent pressure she had exerted; and resented his resentment. Her misery in these months hurt him; but it was also a bore. When he came home to find her sitting in the kitchen with an open wine bottle on the table, and Jessica blank-faced before the television screen, he felt her apathy as a reproach. She had committed herself to

him, at first absolutely, and her unhappiness was proof of his own inca-
pacity. There is nothing more bitter to taste than an unhappy marriage
founded in love.

Curiously he didn't blame me. Indeed, quite the opposite. He hoped
to revive the *ménage-à-trois*, for that had allowed him the freedom to
escape into the anonymity of political action. But I was myself helpless
to help. Becky had for the time being gone beyond me. She was concentrated again on Franz, and she could do nothing to please him.

THREE

Franz had avoided deportation, but the idea of moving to Italy stayed with him. He was restless, depressed also by Becky's unhappiness and perhaps disillusioned by public events: the solidity of English public life weighed upon him. There was not, after all, going to be a revolution. Then Barbara went to the United States. Her principles did not prevent her from accepting the lead part in a big Hollywood movie. Though he said nothing against her, he was like a ship which had lost its anchor. Suddenly the comrades appeared to him as a bunch of misfits. This was a rather obvious fact which her glamour had concealed.

So they left for Rome. It was not clear what they would do there. It wasn't necessary that it should be. Change was what they needed. They were like Victorians sent abroad for the sake of their lungs.

Nell opposed their move, or at least tried to persuade them to leave Jessica with her. She didn't trust Becky then; she thought she was in no condition to bring up a daughter. On the contrary, I said; without Jessica things would be very much worse.

As for myself, I was in favour of the move. My affair with Becky was unsatisfactory. I found it diminishing. I spent too much time with her, and left in low spirits. Perhaps – we agreed – it was London that was at fault. This may have been true of her. She had developed a hatred of the 73 bus route, and of the pub below their flat where young men in advertising or sales congregated. She would stand looking out over the soot-speckled green watching the rain form puddles on the tennis court, and Irishmen from lodging houses settle on benches with pint bottles of Guinness and copies of the *Donegal Herald* or *Limerick Gazette*.

They found an apartment in the old Ghetto, in the Via Portico d'Ottavia. Immediately Becky's spirits soared. The rhythm of Roman life suited her.

"Why the Ghetto?" I asked, suspicious.

"Because it's beautiful."

"And not in any way connected with Kestner, and Franz's guilt?"

"Of course not. That's all in the past."

I didn't see them for eighteen months. We exchanged letters, few of which have survived my various moves.

Here is one:

Dear Gareth,

Tame opening I know, but you know how I hate to commit myself, and anyhow you have a new girl, you say.

Let me tell you what I did yesterday. It's been like most of the days, because there is really nothing unusual to write about.

That's good, don't you think?

I got up early, seven o'clock, which is a good change from London days, you'll agree. It's all right, I suppose, for some people to laze in bed, but I'm coming to know myself and I believe it contributes to depression and low spirits in my case.

I went down to the little bar below us for a cappuccino and then bought some peaches, one for Jessica's breakfast, because she's got a thing about peaches just now. So we had breakfast on our little terrace which gets the early morning sun. It's at the back of the building and is really not much more than a balcony. Swifts zoom over us. They nest in the Teatro Marcello at the end of the street.

Then Jessica drew while I worked on a short story. She really draws very interestingly, I think there may be a genuine talent there. The short story will surprise you, but I must do something besides being a mother and I don't think I can stand movies again. Maybe pretending to be other people contributed to my breakdown, and it was a breakdown, I see that now. I write very slowly; it's awkward.

Then we went shopping. That's to say, to the market. I hate shopping but I love the market. It's in Campo de' Fiori, very animated. There's a statue of Giordano Bruno there which is where he was burned apparently. Isn't he something to do with those people you used to be interested in?

I met an English boy we've got to know there. He's called Antony. Like almost everybody he taught English here, but unlike almost everybody, he stayed. He's been in Rome seven years, and never wants to leave. I'm beginning to feel that way myself, but then Jessica's schooling may be a difficulty, though there are English schools, but v expensive, they say. Antony's a journalist now, and a Communist. You hardly ever meet anyone who isn't. He has a Calabrian girlfriend who is v suspicious of me, and glowers whenever we meet. She looks like a young Anna Magnani.

Anyway, she wasn't there today and so Antony gave me lunch. (Well, actually, I paid, but he suggested it.) We ate *spaghetti al pescatore* and drank wine from Marino in the Castelli which is OK. The waiters all adored Jessica. They took her through to the kitchen and then she wandered round the restaurant with a squid in each hand. It's her blonde curls.

We sat outside the restaurant long after they closed and nobody minded. Antony can be very funny. Do you know, I'd forgotten how to laugh. Then he strolled back home with us, and I put Jessica to bed and slept for a little myself. Antony and Franz were drinking beer when I woke up.

Jessica comes to restaurants in the evenings too, and if she wants to fall asleep falls asleep. Nobody minds. We crossed the bridge to Trastevere and met some other friends and all had dinner together. So I was a little drunk when we got home, but, like you say, wopsy drunk, not sad drunk.

Do you know what I'm learning?

I'm learning to be happy.

I'd forgotten how.

Lots of love, B.

And here's another:

Darling Gareth,

Sorry about your girl, but she sounded a bitch.

Nell arrived safely yesterday and said you were well rid of her.

She's in good form. She's already told me: my hair needs washing, my clothes are a disgrace, I look like a slut, my kitchen is insanitary, and Jessica has developed a terrible accent. Pretty good, eh?

We had a lovely surprise last week. Our friend Luke Abramowitz arrived here, out of the blue or at least a Boeing.

He's been in New York. His wife Rachel left him, which is sad or not sad depending on opinion. She couldn't stand Israel. She always wanted to be an all-American girl. Now she's living with another one, or at least a Canadian, a journalist we met covering the trial, called Minty Hubchik. Rachel wrote me a crazy letter saying men were out and only a woman could make a woman happy. I think Minty wanted to make me happy back in Jerusalem. No thanks.

You would like Luke. He has twice the vitality of anyone I know, except you. He has only 50 per cent more than you. He gave me his new novel, it's marvellous. It makes me despair of my own piddling attempt to write. He was fine with Jessica. He hates not having children of his own. Apparently you are also practically a traitor to Israel if you don't breed a new generation of Israelis.

"You'll get married again," I said.

"Well, what about it, Becky?" he said. "You know that's why I've come to Rome."

Franz was with us at the time and he smiled in that way he has as if he's excusing an error of taste. But you know, Luke meant it. And I was tempted. God, I was tempted. It wouldn't be fair to Luke to land him with a neurotic like me, but maybe it's my only hope of not being a neurotic. Only, I couldn't live in Jerusalem or Tel Aviv, where every corner has a memory of misery. So I said, "You give up Israel, I'll give up Franz."

And he laughed and squeezed my hand as if it was a joke, and in his gesture and the warmth of his grip acknowledging that it was no joke at all, that he knew I was deadly serious, but asking him to do something which was beyond him.

"No," I said, "I can't ask you to do that. Love and marriage aren't that important compared to what you mean to Israel, or Israel to you."

"You sound like your father," he said.

"Oh yes, indeed, he came to think that way, didn't he."

It was all light-hearted and flirtatious, we hopped about like canaries in a cage, and Franz sat there pretending to smile.

"Besides," Luke said, "you'd be tired of me in a week, missing Franz. After all, you're bound together, don't think I don't know that."

Franz took the empty wine-flask and went down to the shop to get it refilled. I think he left us alone at this moment, precisely, on purpose, which was kind of him. Or was it?

The truth is: Franz and I are nearly finished. That's sad, isn't it? When we used to mean so much to each other. He was everything to me once. I remember – I've never told any-one this – that time we were kidnapped in Argentina, & Gaby – you know who I mean – was terrified of being raped, & my fear was that if we were Franz would think I was someway contaminated, & wd have nothing more to do with me. He's so sensitive, I kept thinking. Well, that at least was true. Of course Gaby thought that way too, about her fiancé Luis, but that was different, that was crazy Argentinian macho sense of honour. Franz was different.

And then later I was afraid on account of his father & what he meant to Franz: "That's Jewish flesh you're touching…"

I was terrified that wd come between us.

And now we don't make love any more, & I pretend to be asleep, the Jewish flesh still, & listen to him & I don't know whether it's Barbara (whom I can't stand) or boys he's imagin-ing. Charlie Bastini is always dropping in to the apartment again.

Of course the real reason we've gone off each other is that we make each other unhappy in ways that we can't control because we don't begin to understand the causes. If there are causes. Do you think there are reasons for the way we behave, any of us, to each other? I don't think there are, now.

I know what you're thinking: Becky's plastered again. But look at my handwriting, Gareth darling, it's straight and regu-lar & sober. Becky's drinking, but she's not drunk.

I came so close to saying all this to Luke. I really adore him, always have. But it's like with you. You love me, I know that, Luke loves me, but you cd neither of you live with me. I'd drive you crazy. I don't drive Franz crazy, I just drive him back into himself & away from me.

Besides, he's involved in what he calls politics again. Revolutionary nonsense. God, I hate Barbara. Though it's not her fault. Not really.

Kisses,
Becky.

I bought a novel by Luke Abramowitz at Heathrow. It was a short book, only a hundred and fifty pages of big print with wide margins, and I read it on the Rome plane. It was the story of a married man in love with a girl he couldn't have. She was a friend of his daughter's, and she wasn't much like Becky. Actually the daughter resembled Becky more, and there were moments when you wondered if the narrator wasn't using his daughter's friend as a substitute for the incestuous love he felt for this daughter. I liked the way it was written, the descriptions of the weather, and the manner in which emotions were presented and neither analysed nor accounted for. Things happened this way, and then that, the way they do in life. I could see why Becky was in love with Luke. There was a good physical feel to the way he wrote. It was like Hemingway without the bullshit and the self-pity. He had imitated Hemingway's habit of having the narrator address the girl he fancied, in his thoughts at least, as "daughter", and in the context of this story, that was even more un-settling than when Hemingway does it. I liked the way he combined a sense of moral unease with a firm and decent morality.

When I finished the book, I looked out of the plane window and saw the Mediterranean. That looked OK too. I had never been in Italy before.

Franz collected me at the airport. He was thinner than ever, and wore jeans that made him thinner still, and open-toed sandals and a blue cot-ton shirt. There was a sore at the corner of his mouth.

"This isn't the real Rome," he said, twice, as we rode in from the air-port, "you have to wait till we get inside the Aurelian Wall."

But it looked fine to me. I liked the pine trees and cypresses and the dust and the colour of stone and sky.

"Can we stop for a beer?" I said.

The melancholy that was the foundation of his charm had deepened, paradoxically reducing the charm. A balance had been destroyed. He had been a boy who wore an air of perplexity – expensive, soft as a cash-mere cardigan – as if he could not account for the fact that life was not quite as it had been sold to him; now he resented the certainty which had drowned that perplexity. He had the petulance of a man who has been cheated, and can't accept it. Italy was a spoiled Eden, stinking of corruption.

"But it always has been," I said. "Throughout history."

He brushed my suggestion aside. His hand trembled as he lifted his glass of beer. I couldn't take my eyes, or keep them long, from the sore that disfigured his mouth.

"I'm not going to sleep with you. You needn't think I'm going to sleep with you," Becky said.

"No," I said.

Franz had already told me she had a lover. He had been in the middle of explaining how worried he was; how she was drinking too much – "Half an hour after Jessica's in bed, and she's making no sense. I'm not sure how much longer I can stand it." And then he had said, "David encourages her. He drinks like a fish and she wants to keep up."

"Who's David?" though I guessed half the answer.

"You'll meet him. He's always around now. David Williams. His father was Llewellyn Williams, the actor."

"Ah yes," I said, "what they used to like to call a hellraiser."

There was a story of how, playing Hamlet, he had fallen into Ophelia's grave before Laertes and the rest arrived, and been too drunk to clamber out. That had happened on Broadway. Some of his television interviews were even more famously disastrous; there was one with Muggeridge, I think, but I don't recall the details.

"I'm not in love with Dai," Becky said. "I suppose Franz has told you we're having an affair. Well, he's fun and I've been starved of fun. Jessica adores him."

He sat there, smoking and drinking and sweating and laughing. "Us Welsh buggers," he said.

"Ah, but I'm North Wales," I said, "and I've never lived there."

"Me neither. Not since I was a kid. Wet, windy, wicked, and sodden with beer, my dad used to say. All the same, the place had a hold on him. It was always Welsh approval he wanted. Cardiff Arms Park, the *Western Daily News*, Gwennie Roberts next door, and weak Welsh bitter. He used to argue that Shakespeare was Welsh, though he bloody got out, he would say."

Franz slid from the apartment.

"Politics," Becky said, and passed me the flask of white wine. "It's called a fiasco, isn't that a lovely word for a wine bottle?" she said, and ran her hand through David's curls.

"My dad was once asked on the telly what he thought of Welsh

Nationalism. He replied in three words. Two of them were Welsh Nationalism."

"And bugger revolutionary politics too," Becky said. She stroked his cheek which was round and freckled and flushed.

"No," Becky said, "I'm not in love with him, and if I'm having an affair, it's one that is not going to hurt me. I'm never going to be in love with anyone again, I've decided. Dai's fun. He's got vitality. So I drink him up."

It was the next day, or the day after, and we were having a picnic on the Palatine. We had bought food in a *rosticceria* – stuffed tomatoes and salami, olives, bread, cheese; cherries from a fruit shop and a bottle of wine, and *aranciata* for Jessica. It was hot and quiet, the dead hour of the day when the tourist buses were still. We lay against a crumbling wall, and Jessica made daisy chains.

"I like it when he talks about Wales," Becky said. "Don't you ever wish you lived on that farm of yours?"

After a little, Jessica crawled into the shade and fell asleep. We poured more wine and didn't speak. The hum of traffic was distant from us, there among the ilexes and roses.

"I'd rather stay here," I said.

"Oh yes, this is perfect. If it could always be like this."

"So, what's wrong with Franz?"

"He likes it that I'm having an affair with David, just as he did when it was you. Do you know, when Luke was here, I really believe Franz hoped I would go back to Israel with him. That's not normal."

I slipped my hand under her thin cotton skirt, decorated with poppies.

"That counts as an offence against public decency, here," she said.

"There must be a lot of it about."

There were good moments: a day in the Castelli, when we ate strawberries and cream at Nemi, and Franz laughed, playing with Jessica; an evening that began in the little English-language cinema in Trastevere, where we saw a revival of *A Streetcar Named Desire*, and identified Burt Lancaster as one of the audience, and which continued at Sabatini's restaurant in the Piazza, and ended with Franz playing the "St Louis Blues" on his trumpet; a day spent exploring Ostia when I realised that Franz had set himself to learn about the economy of Ancient Rome, and had indeed learned enough to interest a historian ignorant of the period.

Such moments take on an added happiness in recollection. Memory works in such a manner that it is tempting, in certain moods, to suppose that they represent the true sum of that visit to Rome.

But there was too much on the other side. Worst of all was the realisation that, finding them together, one was breaking into a silence, not interrupting a conversation.

Or there was the evening David took me to a *birreria* and moved from jokes and happiness to a dazed perplexity as he talked of them. He was frightened. He had told Becky that he was leaving Italy – he had been offered a job in America – and she had threatened suicide. He hadn't supposed he had done anything to bring that upon himself. Their affair, which he didn't deny – and why should he? – had seemed light-hearted, physical, to him. He said several times that he knew she wasn't in love with him. So why this?

"Is it just talk?" he said. "Or does she mean it?"

What could I say? It was impossible to forget the warning which that doctor had delivered in that London hospital.

Or the afternoon when Franz insisted that I accompany him to a housing estate, one of the many on the periphery of the city into which the poor have been decanted, to rot, forgotten, conveniently out of sight. Those were, more or less, his words.

"There's this sort of thing everywhere," I said.

"It's capitalism," he said. "It's evil."

"But Italy is scarcely a capitalist country."

Yet I couldn't disagree altogether. These barrack-like structures, with waste lands between them, gave off an air of sullen hopelessness. Life was diminished even under that sun and those blue skies. You couldn't even kid yourself that it felt dangerous, though it may have been dangerous, I wouldn't know. It didn't feel dangerous; it felt only dead.

"There's got to be a clean sweep," Franz said. "All this needs to be swept away, exterminated. There's got to be a new start."

"But, Franz," I said, "there are places like this everywhere. You get them the other side of the Curtain – the outskirts of Prague and Budapest and Leipzig. It's not capitalism, it's not Communism, it's not the Church, it's not even bloody Zionism, or whatever bloody Ism you choose, that causes them. It's just the way things are."

His tongue licked the sore at the corner of his mouth.

"You're talking like … oh, I don't know … Eva Peron perhaps," I said. "The revolution of the Shirtless Ones. You can't think a revolution would make things better. You can't be that naive, not in the second half of the twentieth century. We've surely had it up to here with revolutions."

He turned away from me.

"No," he said, "there's got to be a clean sweep."

FOUR

David Williams left for New York. A couple of months later Becky followed him, taking Jessica with her. It wasn't a success. Dai had in those two months found himself an American girlfriend. She was a girl of his own age, which was five years less than Becky's. The difference is not great, but there was more distance than years between them. He was frightened by what Becky had gone through. He wasn't anyway willing to assume the responsibility of a woman who claimed she had left her husband for his sake. I suppose he knew it wasn't true. Away from Rome, he found her demands tiresome. She embarrassed him, and that killed their affair. She was in a bad way emotionally. His girlfriend said Becky should see a shrink; Becky threw a bottle at her head, cutting her brow. But the question of analysis was allowed to drop.

Nell telephoned me. She was worried about Becky's state of mind, she said, and still more anxious about the effect all this might be having on her granddaughter.

"Becky's devoted to Jessica," I said.

"Well, her devotion takes a peculiar form. And what about Franz? He needs her help, clearly, and so she walks out on him. It's so irresponsible. I've lost patience with her. She's no reason to indulge in these games. It's nothing but self-dramatisation."

I thought it was more than that, and said so.

"And Franz is difficult," I said. "There were times when I was in Rome last year when I thought he hated Becky."

"Only because of the way she was behaving. You don't need to tell me about how Franz feels. I've had the poor boy on the telephone by the hour. Sometimes in tears."

She said this, as if it established her daughter's guilt.

"And it's not right for Jessica to be taken away from her father."

*   *   *   *

It was raining the day Becky returned to England. I drove to Heathrow to meet her. I was living in a decayed seaport on the Kent side of the Thames estuary, from which thousands commuted to Charing Cross every day. I had bought a semidetached bungalow in a street built between the wars. The previous occupant had filled the garden with dahlias, now in lugubrious bloom. My neighbours were a couple who owned or managed the local launderette, and a red-faced retired Commander (RN) who now worked as a travel courier. "Only the Japs or the Yanks, mind you," he said. "The Brits are too poor to be properly appreciative." He had put me up for membership of the Conservative Club, a yellow-brick building with a sham classical portico in the High Street, and I sometimes played billiards with him there at lunchtime. When acquaintances expressed surprise that I chose to live in such a town, I told them it was "forever England for me". They thought this was a joke, but it wasn't. Nobody there gave a damn for abstract ideas.

I hadn't been there a month before half-a-dozen people told me that the Naval Commander had done twelve months for GBH, after sticking a kitchen knife into his "good lady" when she accused him of having an affair with the blonde who worked behind the bar at the Four Feathers. "He was dead lucky," they said. "It was worth two years to be rid of that bitch." Nobody thought it odd that he hadn't been asked to resign from the Conservative Club, where he had stood a round of pink gins on the morning of his release.

People are incalculable. Commander Pilkehorne (Ted) approved of Becky from the moment of their meeting. They got each other wrong too. He told me she was "a regular goer"; what he liked about her of course was that she was, despite everything, what he still called "a lady"; and that she didn't evince any disapproval of him. It hadn't occurred to me, until she pointed it out, that below the veneer maintained by the pink gins and pints of bitter, he was wary of such disapproval. Perhaps he always had been, even before prison; they said his wife had nagged him for years, that her jealousy had been pathological and that she had never ceased to reprove him for his failure in life, or what she interpreted as failure. "She married me," he once said, "because she was told I would make Admiral. Of course her own father didn't get that far."

Becky found a new interest thanks to Ted; they studied the *Sporting Life* together. He fell into the habit of calling in for coffee about eleven o'clock every morning, and they would brood over the day's racecard. I don't suppose she'd ever thought of racing before; now they plotted doubles, trebles and accumulators together. They had a lot of fun out of it, though they didn't approach it as light-heated fun, and occasionally picked a winner. Jessica adored Ted Pilkehorne. She liked to sit on his knee and light his cigarette for him. (He smoked Gold Flake, thirty years or more out of fashion.) Ted gave her a kitten, then apologised to me, "Should have asked you first, never know if people like cats or not. Always loved them myself."

Mrs Chartered (the launderette woman) sniffed, "Shouldn't like to leave my daughter alone with Ted Pilkehorne, has a reputation that way."

"Beastly woman," Becky said.

I hadn't expected Becky to take up residence when I drove to Heathrow that morning. She had merely asked me to collect her. Then it was clear that she had no other plans. She was in flight, couldn't bear the notion of landing herself on Nell. It sort of happened therefore that she moved in. We were soon sleeping together again. For Becky it was reassurance. "I've been through almost more than I can take," she said. She tried to laugh about it. Her looks were going, or they were in abeyance.

She was setting out to be a character, in consequence.

It was all right by me, having her there. Besides, I was Jessica's father. So we settled into a sort of ménage. Jessica went to the local primary school and made friends and copied their accents.

"So what?" Becky said, when Nell objected. "That sort of England's finished. Even old Ted knows that."

Of course she had never really known any sort of England herself.

We were a ropey sort of couple, but it was a ropey sort of time, the mid-Seventies, when things were falling apart all round, and our being together seemed some kind of assurance. No more than that. We often bored and irritated each other. Becky hated my snap judgements, though she wasn't short of them herself. There were money problems. I had given up on my academic career, or it had given up on me. In pompous moments I said I could no longer believe in historical truth, but that wasn't the real reason. It was just that it all seemed futile: researching, teaching, everything. None of it made sense, and I couldn't stand my colleagues who pretended that it mattered. I looked around the town where we lived and saw that there was no connection between education and happiness or even decency. I fell in love with the smallness of English lower-middle-class life, with its rejection of the possibility that horizons mattered. I was becoming an urban peasant, reverting to the narrow ways of my Welsh farming forebears. This was some sort of relief to Becky. Indeed it was what made our life good for her.

And it was good, for a time. We were helped of course by the fact that she was still getting an income by way of Franz, though for more than a year there was no other communication from him; just the banker's order paid monthly into her account at the local branch of the NatWest. We had many good moments, in bed and even out of it. I wasn't faithful to her; the way she had landed herself on me, making me responsible, meant that that clause wasn't in the contract. There was a girl in London, a married woman, whom I saw once a week. Becky knew of it and shrugged it off.

"It doesn't matter to me," she said, "what you do."

"No, you're still in love with Franz."

"I never want to see him again."

Both statements were true. She was still in love with the boy she had known in Buenos Aires.

She had no interest in what the man whom that boy had become was doing now. She had written him off. It would be something that she found either absurd or offensive.

Once, we went to London to see Barbara as Rosalind in *As You Like It*.

"She's too old for the part," Becky said. "The whole point about Rosalind is that she has the confidence of a girl of eighteen."

But Barbara made herself that age. I dislike Shakespeare, though the comedies a little less than the so-called tragedies, but I was captivated; she made everything seem possible. "I can see why Franz…" I said.

"Oh quite, she would appeal to anyone who refused to grow up," Becky said.

I didn't add that Franz himself had complained to me in Rome of Becky's disinclination to do just that. What was the point? Nobody agrees with another's definition of what constitutes grown-up life. One of the things Becky liked about Ted Pilkehorne was the manner in which he shied away from any discussion that moved from the particular.

It was for Ted she left me. His sister, a childless widow, had died of cancer, leaving him a little money and a small-holding in Hampshire where she reared turkeys. Ted was going to take over the business and live there.

"But he can't be alone," Becky said. "It scares him. So he's asked me if … and I've said, yes. You don't mind really, Gareth, you'll be glad to be free of me."

"You're crazy," I said. "You on a turkey-farm, Becky? You'll go mad."

"Ted needs me," she said. "You don't. It's nice to be needed."

"You're crazy," I said again. I was surprised to find myself jealous. The silly bitch, I said to myself, after all I've done for her.

"Franz needed you," I said. "That got on your nerves, you couldn't stand the weight of it."

"Oh fuck off, Gareth, leave Franz out of it, will you."

"And what about Jessica?" I said.

"She can go to the village school. She'll love it."

"She's my daughter," I said.

"Is she?"

"You've always said so."

"You didn't show yourself so eager to take responsibility for her when I was with Franz. Anyway you can still see her, I'm not proposing to cut us off from you."

"Franz was different," I said.

"Besides, Ted adores her, you know that. And she him."

"Humbert Humbert," I said.

"God, you're foul. Besides, if you must know, that old cow next door got it all wrong. It's not little girls that's been Ted's problem."

"Oh," I said, "I see."

"He's frightened of being alone, that's why … He'll be all right with me, I've always been a queer's woman."

"I still think you're crazy."

"I know what I'm doing."

In a curious way she was right. Her five years with Ted, before he too got cancer (in his case, of the liver) were good ones. She didn't exactly take to the simple rural life, and they got through a bottle of gin a day between them, with wine and other drinks on top. But Ted was happy, and she was happy to have made him so. Jessica flourished. Ted bought her a pony and drove her to Pony Club rallies and gymkhanas. It was, in a somewhat rackety fashion, English life as one likes to think it is. I used to go and spend weekends with them, often enough in the first years until I got married myself, and Ted would tell me these were the best years of his life and he owed it all to Becky.

"What about Franz?" I asked her.

"He writes me crazy letters. He's still in Rome. Reading between the lines his political group is not far from the violent ones, you know, the Red Brigades. It's mad. I ask myself if it's my fault. Well, sometimes, I ask myself that. He keeps in closer touch with Nell, and he still sends Jessica presents at Christmas and her birthday."

"But do you miss him?"

"Often. But there it is."

"Ah yes," I said, "and things are as they must be."

"Don't be philosophical," she said. "I can't bear it."

FIVE

So far it has been easy, this part, this account of my own personal, if often detached, relationship with Becky and Franz. But now comes the hard part: Franz himself, Franz alone, Franz moving quite beyond me.

In his essay on the Aldo Moro Affair, the Sicilian author Sciascia (one of the few modern writers who seems to me to tell the truth about the way things are) asks this question: "Why does the Moro Affair give the impression of something already written, something inhabiting a sphere of intangible literary perfection, something which can only be faithfully rewritten, and, while being rewritten, be totally altered without altering anything?" "There are many reasons," he adds, "not all of them comprehensible." I like that final phrase, that suggestion that even Latin lucidity stops short on the borders of personality. But he goes on to say, "The impression that everything which occurred in the Moro Affair did so, as it were, in literature, derives mainly from the elusiveness of the facts – when they occurred and even more so in retrospect – a sort of withdrawal of the facts into a dimension of unfailing imaginative or fanciful consequentiality, from which a constant, stubborn ambiguity overflows. Only in fantasy, in dreams is such perfection achieved. Not in real life."

By his own token, borrowing an idea from Borges, I have changed these words by writing them down in a different context. Or rather the words remain the same; it is the significance which has altered.

Because you see that is the way I feel now about Franz: that his life existed to be read.

Of course you could certainly say the same of Jesus Christ or perhaps of any of the saints, in whom I nevertheless decline to believe, except when I read their stories. The life which you read takes on its own authority, and achieves a perfection which its original could not have, or could not have known himself to have.

What puzzles me about Franz is why he sought commitment, when he had its awful lesson before him. But he did, lurching like a drunk man in search of support from one cause to another.

It is easy to say that he made of his life an act of atonement for his father's sins. I suppose that is the way some people naturally think, and it is certainly true that his attachment to causes could always be justified by a sort of idealism. But when that idealism expresses itself in violence, the argument withers. He was, I am sure, a member of that little group called the Proletariato Armato per il Comunismo, which, during the Moro Affair, or a couple of days after, shot and lamed two Italian doctors, one of them belonging to the National Institute for Insurance against Illness.

Then Franz recoiled from politics in the early Eighties. I met him soon afterwards. He was in London and telephoned me, seeking news of Jessica, and finding himself "suddenly" as he put it, reluctant to speak to Becky.

"I don't know why, since I never think of her except with tenderness. Perhaps it is because to speak with her risks opening wounds for both of us, wounds which time has, or should have, healed."

I suggested we should meet.

After some hesitation, he agreed.

"But not for a meal," he said. "I have come to detest that. I no longer feel comfortable if I have to encounter someone across the lunch table and give orders to waiters."

He paused.

"I detest the falsity of the relationships established," he said.

He was leaning against the parapet of the Embankment, waiting for me. He was thinner than ever and the coat which he wore over a grey suit hung loose from his shoulders. His hair was lank and grey. At our last meeting he had still looked younger than his years; now he might have been ten years older than he was. He turned away, stretching his hand towards the dull swell of the river, on which two stationary barges were the only craft.

"And this too has been one of the waste places of the earth," he said. "You read Conrad, don't you, Gareth?"

We walked downstream, towards the distant sea. A cold wind, spitting rain on the water, tossed discarded newspapers and dead leaves around our feet. Traffic rumbled past, making conversation difficult. We walked on for perhaps twenty minutes, a mile to the east. Then Franz turned aside and leaned over the parapet, gazing down on the oily water which now flowed black below us. Office lights on the South Bank shone from tall buildings whose tops were already lost in dark mist.

"Jessica first," he said. "I've failed by her, but I'd like to see her. Will Becky object?"

"Why should she? She is your daughter."

"No, Gareth, she's yours. Let's not pretend."

"Does it matter?" I said.

"You can hardly expect me to say that genetic inheritance is not an important factor."

He smiled for the first time.

"Anyway," I said, "legally she's yours. You speak as if you were going away. For a long time, I mean."

He turned and resumed our walk, at the same steady pace. Seagulls swooped and howled around us. The rain was heavier, settling in for the wet night. It was necessary to lower your head and drive into the wind. I was aware of a hole in my right shoe, leaking badly. It was half-past five.

"I'd like a drink," I said. "Does your anti-restaurant ideology permit pubs?"

"Oh yes. It's not like that, you know."

"Well then, let's look for one, though it'll be full of office-workers, I'm afraid."

We found one, a mean place, which had mysteriously escaped redevelopment, even there, so close to the City. It had a long public bar and men in overalls arrayed on the line of barstools. I got two whiskies, and we retired to a corner, out of range of the dartboard.

"Bars are different," Franz said, "not everyone is pretending to be happy here."

I looked about me.

"No," I said, "no, they're not…"

I lit a cigarette, and waited. I like bars when they have just opened in the evening. There is a rhythm to English life which will be destroyed when we all adapt to the Continental practice of the ever-open pub.

"Do you know," he said, "the temptation that has attacked me, again and again? It is to throw off all my clothes in a public place, and cry out, 'I'm Kestner's son. I'm the son of a mass murderer, Rudi Kestner.' And when I've done it in dreams, an old woman comes up to me and puts a coat round me, and says, 'But you're an ordinary man, an ordinary average miserable specimen of humanity.' Don't you think that's crazy?"

"If you did it now," I said, "chances are that nobody here would know who your father was. And if they did, they'd behave like the old woman."

"Once, in Rome," he said, "I went to bed with a girl, and, after we'd made love, or what passed for love, I told her then. And she replied: 'Yes, darling, that's why you're here.' What do you make of that?"

Without waiting for an answer, he picked up our empty glasses and went to the bar. I heard him ask for doubles.

"I've often thought," he said, "about the part chance plays. Or is it some sort of joke, some joke of a malicious Fate. Think: you know the circumstances in which my father was identified by Becky's. Suppose he had failed to do so, as he might easily have done – remember he was blind. Or suppose he had had his suspicions and said to himself, maybe I'm wrong, or again maybe Becky's happiness is more important than justice. Another man might have said that. Alternatively, suppose my father had found his moment of truth at a Communist meeting rather than a Nazi one – and he might have done so. Suppose any of these things. Does it make sense?"

He sipped his whisky.

"You used to study chaps, didn't you, Gareth, who believed in a magical basis to things, theories of eternal recurrence and so on?"

"Oh yes," I said, "they believed all sorts of things."

"The transmutation of base metal, that was one of them, wasn't it?"

"That too. It was all nonsense."

"No," he said, "not nonsense, it's what happens. It's what life is all about, it's the meaning of life. It's building the other side of the street. I must tell you, I have become a Catholic."

"Well," I said, "there's your answer. Maybe that's what it was all for. Maybe that's how it makes sense."

"You're laughing at me."

"Only up to a point."

Eighteen months previously in Paris, Franz was with an Arab boy whom he had picked up because he looked like a boy he had known in Jerusalem. He had gone back to boys. It was perhaps, he wasn't sure, an expression of despair, self-hatred. And yet it was also because, even today when everything was permitted, it was for him the acceptance of the condition of an outlaw. He didn't expect that to make sense to others, but that was how he felt. Besides, always, in bed with a boy, he remembered his father's account of the Night of the Long Knives, and saw Roehm's boy wipe sleep from terrified eyes and Roehm himself pad across the floor, with the guns trained on him, to fetch his trousers.

He had spent two weeks in Venice with his friend Charlie Bastini, and it had been an orgy. He had come to Paris, satiated, but then there was this boy at the Gare de Lyon, in a pink shirt and torn jeans and eye-shadow, and now they were in a little bar with its posters of boxers and ballet dancers and footballers, and they were drinking Pernod and were both a little lit…

He smiled to remember that bar; it had been such an absurd and ultimate example of its type.

He told me all this without shame and with that smile which I had thought he had lost.

There was an old man in the bar, perhaps sixty. He had a boy with him, of course, a Michelangelo type in T-shirt and jeans with curls falling over his brow. And the man, who was heavily built and bald and soft-faced, kept looking at Franz until at last he rose and approached their table and said, "You're the young Kestner, Franz isn't it?"

He spoke in German.

"Don't deny it," he said, "I used to be a priest…"

And Franz knew who he was, though not his name. He was the German priest who had attended his father in the death cell in Jerusalem, and who had argued theology with him, and then refused him the last sacraments Rudi had, without warning and after hours of contemptuous rejection, requested.

Franz stood up and hit him. He smacked his right fist straight into the small, full-lipped mouth of the man who admitted he had been a priest: that priest. He fell backwards against a table, and Franz hit him again, this time with a left in his stomach. Then the Michelangelo type hit Franz, and the Arab grabbed the type's arm, and there was a general scuffle and confusion. Somebody blew a whistle and the boys were all at once not there. Franz was left with the priest, who was leaning over the table against which he had fallen, and panting for breath. He held out a hand towards Franz.

"Don't go," he said, "there are things I must say to you." He straightened and looked around.

"Or rather, let us both go. There are things which perhaps are better suited to a different ambience."

Franz looked up. I indicated his empty glass. "Another?"

"*Warum nicht?*"

The priest led Franz back to his room in a small shabby hotel, the kind of place where even those who stay for months know they are transients. He took a bottle of brandy from the bottom of the wardrobe and rinsed two glasses. He filled them and pushed one to Franz.

"I'm not surprised you hit me," he said. "I'd have done the same in your place. I should have introduced myself more gently."

"Your mouth's still bleeding."

"It doesn't matter."

He hesitated. He began by saying his name was Ernst, and repeating that he was no longer a priest, "though of course, unless you are unfrocked, you are always a priest, and I have not been unfrocked. But I have been destroyed by doubt, and your father is at the root of my perplexity."

He had been both excited and appalled when assigned to Kestner. It was the greatest challenge he could imagine; yet at the same time, the prospect of spending hours in talk with such a monster (which was how he had thought of him, one moreover who had contributed to the great sin that had brought shame on the whole German nation) was terrible. He had been still more appalled when he found himself liking Kestner, who impressed him by his good manners, intelligence, courage in his predicament, even charm. The intellectual duel too was fascinating, and when he realised that Kestner was indeed contemplating submission and a return to the Church, Ernst's joy knew no bounds. He was exhilarated with an assurance of triumph.

"But was my father serious, truly serious?"

"He was serious, and yet not serious. There was something playful about him, and at the same time obdurate. Ultimately, he would not repent; ultimately he could not accept the enormity of his actions. He saw it was all a mistake, but he did not understand the concept of sin. How could I commit to God's mercy one who could not confess himself a sinner? To the last, he was arrogant. It was a bargain he was trying to conclude with God. And then I saw something else. He was attempting to make a work of art of his life. His reception into Holy Mother Church would make a great curtain. He even said so, with that laugh that always disturbed me. But a life is not a work of art; a life belongs to God, I told him. 'Well, I'm willing to sell mine,' he said. It was not his to sell. 'What you can surrender, you can sell,' he said. And so ... nothing ..."

"Nothing. I refused. And I have never known if I did right. I was correct, there is no question of that. His proposed submission was a lie. That was my judgement, and I have never known if his attitude was a test of my judgement or a comedy which put me in the place of the sinner… And though I have never ceased to trust in the mercy of God, my faith in myself as a priest began to crumble."

"But surely," Franz said, "you separate the priest from the man? Surely the efficacy of the priesthood does not depend on the qualities of the man?"

"Indeed, no," Ernst said. "Nevertheless …"

Franz looked up.

"And that was it. The Michelangelo type returned, and I made myself scarce. But that evening changed me, I don't know how, and so, here I stand, a Catholic. More whisky?"

He paused putting the glasses down. "That's partly why I wanted to see you, and speak to you. I may not come back. No," he gave me a smile that took twenty years from his face, "it's nothing romantic. I'm not that sort of character. It's not a leper-colony or anything like that. It's quite simple and straightforward. I'm joining a team engaged on famine relief. That's all. Besides, it's East Africa, the southern Sudan, not the heart of darkness.

"But I would like you to be my executor. Will you do that for me, Gareth? I'm quite rich, you know, since my mother and stepfather died, and, despite my vicissitudes, I have retained enough sense to play the stock market quite successfully. That surprises you, eh? You see, I'm not exactly the broken man you may have been imagining.

"My will's lodged here, in London, because, despite everything, London is still where I feel things are safe; and most of my money is in this country. I'll send you the details, if you accept. You will accept, won't you? Good. And there are papers, several boxes, diaries, letters, and things relating to my father. It would please me if you would take charge of them, if anything happens to me. It's quite simple. There's a Trust Fund, with income to go 50 per cent to Becky, 40 per cent to Jessica and 10 per cent to Khaled."

"Khaled?"

"Yes, the boy from the Gare de Lyon. I've taken charge of him, seen to it that he gets an education. That's all, now, that's between us. I try to practise chastity. The Trust will be wound up when Becky dies, and then be divided between Jessica and Khaled in the proportion of nine to one. I've put you down as the trustee, with my solicitor. All right…? It's a long time since I've drunk so much whisky."

He sat back. Whatever I'd expected from this meeting, it wasn't this. He smiled again.

"You once said: it's no bloody Ism that's to blame. Do you remember? What do you say to Original Sin?"

"The same," I said.

In a little we left the pub and went out into the darkness of a street where the lighting had failed.

"There's no chance of a taxi here," I said.

"Then we must walk."

"I do practise chastity," he said. "It's not so difficult, you know."

SIX

I think he meant it as a farewell. He didn't seek death, but he expected it, I don't know why. But he did come back, and I went to see him in the Middlesex Hospital, where he was stretched out, thin and bony, and looking as if he had already put off the flesh.

"It's not AIDS," he smiled, "it's some rare blood disease, it really is. Nell comes every day," he said, "it's more than kind. I'm glad Jessica's in California. You'll tell her I was thinking of her. Tell her you're her father, if she doesn't know. I wouldn't like her to imagine she had my father's genes."

"Do you want to see Becky?"

"What's the point?"

All the same I urged her.

"No," she said, "it's finished, it was finished a long time ago. You disgust me, Gareth, you pretend to be tough and you're a bloody awful sentimentalist at heart."

The priest tripped through the funeral service as if to deny the meaning the words were meant to bear. Perhaps he didn't believe in them, in the resurrection of the body or eternal life; perhaps it was all a jaded metaphor to him. Then the drizzle began, and we turned away, a few shapes moving between the yew trees and people not speaking to each other. A young man in a duffel coat came up and said that Barbara had sent him, she wished she could have been there herself; and a man in a mackintosh looked hard at him, and I wondered if, even after all these years, he was Special Branch. It would have amused Franz if it had been true.

Then Nell placed her hand on my arm, demanding as a brown envelope you don't want to open, and I forgot the man in the mack.

"Becky didn't come."

"Well, no, as you see, she didn't think…"

"She should have been here … she's a selfish, cold-hearted bitch, even if she is my daughter."

In her old age Nell has got this habit of saying what she shouldn't, and wouldn't have ten years ago when she still had her judgement and respected conventions. The freedom she has taken in her old age is disconcerting.

"You know that's not true," I said.

"He was worth ten of her. I always adored him."

I steered her towards the gates. I had sent Khaled a telegram. He could have made it from Paris, but he hadn't come either. Franz said he'd forbidden him the hospital, but perhaps that was only a last flicker of pride.

"She should have come," Nell said again. "Poor boy, nothing went right for him."

"I'm not so sure."

"Well, she should have come. I'll never forgive her."

I had tried to persuade Becky the night before, in the basement flat where she now lived, in West Kensington, with its smell of sour milk, cats, Virginia tobacco and loneliness. No, she had said, talking instead of a television serial she watched, and of how Jessica had telephoned from California about a part she had been offered in a play.

She had drunk too much gin, as she always did when we met now, and probably when we didn't. I told her he never stopped loving her, and she said he was "sentimental and guilty, a rotten combination".

"She couldn't make it," I said again.

I ought to have had an umbrella to hold over Nell. The rain dripped off the collar of her dirty mackintosh and made rats' tails of her white hair, which had once been abundant and was now thin.

"Well, there's us anyway," she said, and squeezed my arm, and warmed by her implied praise, and touched by her refusal to surrender as perhaps everyone else had done, I fingered the notes in my breast pocket and said I would buy her lunch in a pub.

"I came by Tube," I said. "Do you have a car?"

She pointed to a shabby Volkswagen, B-registered, parked near the cemetery gates.

She picked up a locket on a chain from the pigeonhole to the right of the steering wheel.

"I meant to throw this into the grave. I bought it in Berlin before the war. No, I didn't. That's stupid, Eli gave it to me. But I meant to leave it with Franz. You can guess why."

She screwed her body round so that she could look out of the back window into the cemetery, but she must have known it was too late. We had already seen them place boards over the coffin, and it wouldn't have been the same thing to place her memento on top of the boards.

"It doesn't matter," she said, "it was sentimental, and if it wasn't, maybe he knows anyway."

The pub had that sickly aroma that English saloon bars have in the first half-hour of morning opening time: of furniture polish and cleaning stuff fighting against the beer and tobacco fumes. The food wasn't ready, and we sat, Nell with a brandy and ginger and me with a large Scotch, waiting until they brought the shepherd's pie to the counter.

"I wish Becky hadn't given up," she said. "I've always thought of you, all three, as my children. Do you give her money?"

"Ted left her a bit," I said. "But I help out now and then. She'll get something from Franz," and I wondered if he had really forgotten Nell in his will, or if he had forgotten to tell me. Maybe he had expected her to be dead before him.

"Don't think I'm blaming you," she said. "Blame doesn't enter into it. If I blame anyone, I blame myself. I should have stopped Eli. I suggested she should come to live with me when Ted died, but she refused. I was so glad really."

The food arrived.

"I've always liked shepherd's pie. Comes of being a schoolmaster's daughter. If you're brought up to eat school dinners, I've always said, you'll never starve through being finicky. You're a bit the same with your writing, aren't you?"

"If you mean I'm a hack, yes."

"No," she said, "I think you've done awfully well. I liked the one about the abbess. I don't know how you think these things up. They're . . ." she paused as if searching for a word, against her habit, "ingenious."

It was not true. The detective novels by which I make my living now are well made and competent and don't insult the reader's intelligence, but they are not ingenious. I have no gift for ingenuity, just as I have a dull imagination.

"You ought to write about Franz," she said. "I would really like you to do that. Tell the whole story. After today, there's nobody to be hurt."

"Becky?"

"It can't hurt her more. It might even heal her."

We left that dangling. There is no remedy for cancer of the spirit.

"I'll think about it," I said.

"I wish you would."

She leaned over and kissed me.

"Poor Franz," she said. "You know when I first saw him, I thought, if only he was English."

The bar filled and emptied, and Nell drank more brandy as she talked about Franz, and Argentina, and the Germany of old newsreels and her first loves. The years fell away, and I could see her as she had been then, and the type of that now all but extinct Englishness she would have wished on Franz. Then, despite the brandy, she said of course she could drive home – "I drive better when I've had a few. I do most things better, so why not driving?" – and I watched the Volkswagen swing wide round the corner and out of sight.

I turned towards the station. Leaves were falling from the plane-trees, and the mist settled in sparkling droplets on my overcoat. Well, I thought, why not? It couldn't be biography, because you couldn't write Franz's life without supposition. If I was going to have to suppose, then I would use what I distrusted – my imagination – and present it as fiction, at least till my own acquaintance with him began. Fiction, I said to myself, might deliver truths of a type denied biography. There would be Franz's papers to draw on: that store of sad confessional and horror I had not yet seen. Why else, I thought, had he left them to me, if it wasn't to ask me somehow to employ these materials to rebut the assertion of a character in his favourite Conrad, that "life doesn't stand much looking into"?

But hadn't a reviewer called the novel in which that line appears "too sordid to be tragic and too repulsive to be pathetic"?

Nevertheless, I thought, I'll do it, and stood a long time on the open suburban platform waiting for the train.

There is that scene in *The Secret Agent*, in which the poor half-wit, Stevie, falls into great distress when a cabman whips his miserable old horse. "Don't," he sobs, "don't…"

Did Conrad know – he must have known – that Nietzsche's permanent mental collapse began in Turin when he behaved like poor Stevie, throwing his arms round the wretched mare, and then sliding to his knees in the gutter?

When I told Becky that evening what I was going to do, she said, "Let the poor bloody fool be."

"No," I said, "we owe him more than that. More than oblivion. He came through, in a way. You could say he died trying to save others."

"Others?" she said. "What about himself?"

"Don't ask the impossible."

She put down the receiver. In the dead buzzing in my ear, her question took on different forms: what about me? what about us? what about humanity?

www.vagabondvoices.co.uk

Allan Massie's *Klaus and Other Stories*

About the book

Allan Massie, the prolific novelist and non-fiction writer, is here revealed as a consummate master of the short story. This should not surprise, given his dense and highly effective style. Some of the short stories come from his early career, and some are the product of a recent return to the genre.

Klaus, the novella that opens and, to some extent, dominates this collection, tells the story of Klaus Mann, son of Thomas, and in spite of the long shadow of so famous a father, an important novelist and political activist in his own right. His struggle against Nazism gave him a focus, but its demise and what he perceived as Germany's inability to change led to depression and an early death.

Massie succeeds in evoking that period of courage and hypocrisy, intellectual fidelity and clever changeability, sacrifice and impunity, personified by the tragic Klaus and the mercurial and indestructible Gustaf Gründgens, his former brother-in-law and ex-lover. Between these two lie not only those broken relationships but also a novel – Klaus's novel Mephisto, a thinly disguised attack on Gründgens that for many years could not be published in West Germany. Massie's subtle prose merely suggests some intriguing aspects of this network of relationships and the self-destructive nature of literary inspiration.

Comments

"Allan Massie is a master storyteller, with a particular gift for evoking the vanishing world of the European man of letters. His poignant novella about Klaus Mann bears comparison with his subject's best work."

Daniel Johnson, editor of *Standpoint*

"The tale of Klaus Mann's final days is, however, tremendously interesting, a warning and an example. Aspiring authors should read it. They'd do worse than study Massie's craftsmanship."

Colin Waters, *Scottish Review of Books*

Price: £10.00   ISBN: 978-0-9560560-6-1   pp. 208

www.vagabondvoices.co.uk

Allan Massie's *Surviving*

About the book

Surviving is set in contemporary Rome. The main characters, Belinda, Kate (an author who specialises in studies of the criminal mind), and Tom Durward (a scriptwriter), attend an English-speaking group of Alcoholics Anonymous. All have pasts to cause embarrassment or shame. Tom sees no future for himself and still gets nervous "come Martini time". Belinda embarks on a love-affair that cannot last. Kate ventures onto more dangerous ground by inviting her latest case-study, a young Londoner acquitted of a racist murder, to stay with her.

Allan Massie dissects this group of ex-pats in order to say something about our inability to know, still less to understand, the actions of our fellow human beings, even when relationships are so intense. It is also, therefore, impossible or at least difficult to make informed moral judgements of others. This is an intelligent book that examines human nature with a deft and light touch.

Comments

"Massie is one of the best Scottish writers of his generation. *Surviving* – sympathetic, unsentimental, atmospheric – is an overdue reminder of how good he is."

Alan Taylor, *The Herald*

"... an impressive novel which poses moral and philosophical questions but works equally well as a compelling thriller."

Joe Farrell, *TLS*

"... an excellent little novel."

Ben Jeffery, *The Guardian*

"The dark brilliance of Massie's style ... *Surviving* may be an instant classic in the alcoholic literary canon."

Patrick Skene Catling, *The Spectator*

"This is Scotland's Stendhal at his best: clipped but sympathetic to his fragile characters in their haunted wood."

Christopher Harvie, *The Sunday Herald*

Price: £10.00   ISBN: 978-0-9560560-2-3   pp. 224